W9-BSK-836

NO LONGER THE PROPERTY OF
BALDWIN PUBLIC LIBRARY

COUNTDOWN to MECCA

ALSO BY MICHAEL SAVAGE

Stop the Coming War

A Time for War

Train Tracks

Abuse of Power

Trickle Down Tyranny

Trickle Up Poverty

Banned in Britain

Psychological Nudity

The Political Zoo

Liberalism Is a Mental Disorder

The Enemy Within

The Savage Nation

MICHAEL SAVAGE

COUNTDOWN
TO
MECCA

ST. MARTIN'S PRESS

NEW YORK

BALDWIN PUBLIC LIBRARY

This is a work of fiction. All of the characters, organizations, and events portrayed in this novel are either products of the author's imagination or are used fictitiously.

COUNTDOWN TO MECCA. Copyright © 2015 by Michael Savage. All rights reserved. Printed in the United States of America. For information, address St. Martin's Press, 175 Fifth Avenue, New York, N.Y. 10010.

www.stmartins.com

Library of Congress Cataloging-in-Publication Data

Savage, Michael, 1942–
    Countdown to Mecca : a thriller / Michael Savage.—First edition.
        p.   cm.
    ISBN 978-1-250-03526-4 (hardcover)
    ISBN 978-1-250-03525-7 (e-book)
    1. Reporters and reporting—Fiction.   2. Terrorism—Prevention—Fiction.
3. Terrorism investigation—Fiction.   4. International relations—Fiction.   I. Title.
    PS3619.A836C68 2015
    813'.6—dc23

                                                                2015007264

St. Martin's Press books may be purchased for educational, business, or promotional use. For information on bulk purchases, please contact the Macmillan Corporate and Premium Sales Department at 1-800-221-7945, extension 5442, or write to specialmarkets@macmillan.com.

First Edition: May 2015

10 9 8 7 6 5 4 3 2 1

Cast of Characters

Jack Hatfield: fearless San Francisco freelance journalist, defrocked former host of the cable TV program *Truth Tellers*

Doc Matson: former soldier, current merc, trusted ally of Jack

Dover Griffith: one-time Department of Naval Intelligence analyst, now FBI agent . . . and Jack's lover

Sammy Michaels: Jack's younger half brother, former Marine, now a professional clown

Sol Minsky: San Francisco–based gangster

Boaz Simonson: Minsky's IT wizard

Ric: Minsky's driver and bodyguard

Carl Forsyth: FBI field director, San Francisco

Pyotr Ansky/Peter Andrews: Russian national, assassin

Thomas Brooks: Three-Star General, U.S. Strategic Command

Montgomery Morton: One-Star General, U.S. Strategic Command

Steven Reynolds: Captain, U.S. military

Andrew Taylor: Colonel, U.S. military

Anastasia Vincent: Russian-born escort

Ritu: Indian-born escort

Miwa: Japanese-born escort

Daniel Jeffreys: Captain, San Francisco Police Department

Helmut Schoenberg: CEO of German multinational company Der Warheit Unternehmen

Bernie Peters: eccentric physicist based in San Francisco

COUNTDOWN to MECCA

Prologue

Saint Petersburg, Russia
Aeroport Pulkovo

Pyotr Ansky's pale eyes were dead as he walked through Terminal Two toward his flight. He saw everyone without empathy or interest. It had been that way since his first assignment years before.

Passing through the last of three security checkpoints, Ansky glanced uncaring at two middle-aged transportation officers, his face like that of any distracted, put-upon, thirty-something traveler. That was his disguise this day. Pulling on his shoes at the end of the security line, Pyotr imagined himself to be what his visa said he was: a computer contractor headed for a programming job in Jordan.

Pyotr made his way through security without incident. Rossiya Airlines was justly proud of its Aviation Security Program, which found no weapons or contraband on him, or in his backpack, during his third and final search prior to boarding.

He smiled as he found his seat at the rear of the cabin. Pyotr allowed himself a sliver of satisfaction as he appeared to stretch before sitting. He was not just an assassin. There were plenty of those on the international market. He was one of a unique breed: a professional chameleon doing a consummate infiltration.

There was no time to savor his successful boarding. Pyotr went to the lavatory where he reviewed the next scene of operations. The 737-500 had a cruising speed, 850 kilometers an hour. Maximum flight altitude was 12,300 meters. Seating capacity was 117. He mentally reviewed the layout, the exits, the cockpit configuration.

He emerged and looked around.

The flight was not full but Pyotr noted every face onboard: intense young businessmen, older businessmen drunk from the airport bar, a family with an eight-year-old, women in burkas accompanied by their husbands or brothers.

Pyotr did that for every single face of the ninety-four people onboard before deciding who the Russian security agent was. Pyotr had no doubt there would *be* a plainclothes undercover operative. This was, after all, a flight to Amman, Jordan. Islamic terrorism had long been considered a major threat to the security of Russia, both before and after the Soviet era.

Four things would mark him. He would have a sport coat to cover his weapon. He would possess a penetrating stare as he analyzed passengers for potential threats. He'd be middle-aged, retired from the military, but with enough bulk to suggest he'd once been athletic. And he would be a man: there was only one woman in the force, and Pyotr already knew she was assigned to flights originating to Moscow and New York.

Ahead, aisle seat. Row sixteen, aisle seat, economy class. Near the exit door. He saw the shadow of a shoulder holster as the agent leaned forward.

The man sat alone. That would make things easier.

Satisfied, Pyotr Ansky fell into his seat but did not relax after takeoff. As the aircraft started over the Black Sea one thousand miles from Pulkovo, the copilot emerged to use the bathroom. Pyotr knew that was coming: the man had used the lavatory when he boarded to put a full bottle of Putinka vodka in the trash. Many Russian pilots, also former military aviators, had a drinking problem. The agents who had taken this flight during the past fortnight reported where the copilot and first class flight attendant kept the key to get back in.

As soon as the cockpit door opened, Pyotr rose and removed his wallet. He grabbed a blanket from the overhead bin, slung it over his shoulder, and slipped the Nalchik Bank ATM card from its pocket. He walked forward nonchalantly as if to be next in line for the lavatory. As he reached the aisle seat where the Russian security agent was sitting Pyotr appeared to stumble. He leaned on the back of the agent's seat, extended his right arm, and sliced the sharpened edge of his credit card deep across the agent's neck, from ear to ear. His body shielded the view of the young woman across the aisle. The wound gurgled as the man drew breath, the air rushing into the wound, not his mouth. Pyotr dropped the credit card and gripped the MP-443 Grach semiautomatic in the dying, gurgling man's holster. Pyotr quickly spread the blanket across the doomed operative, who was busy drowning quietly in his own blood. He moved swiftly now toward the front of the plane.

He held the agent's sidearm low and in front of his leg. It was not so unobtrusive that it couldn't be seen, but he passed smoothly and a gun was the last thing anyone expected to see—especially since Pyotr's face displayed no sense of the power or arrogance that often comes with a gun.

A male flight attendant finally took notice of Pyotr as he neared the cockpit door. The man seemed about to protest when the passenger failed to stop at the lavatory door. He never got the words out. Pyotr pressed the gun into his chest and pulled the trigger, angling down to keep the bullet inside the body. Decompression, now, would not be good for the mission. Pyotr took the key from a chain around the man's neck.

The rest happened quickly. Though muffled, the noise alerted about a dozen people in the front of the plane but it also froze them for the moment Pyotr needed. He unlocked the door, pushed into the cockpit, and locked the panel behind him.

The pilot heard the commotion as the door opened and he began to turn. Pyotr pushed him down, pressed the gun barrel into the crown of his skull, then pulled the trigger. The 9mm bullet went through the man's brain and most of his body before lodging in his coccyx.

Not bothering to move the pilot, Pyotr slipped into the copilot's vacant seat, buckled up, turned off the transponder that broadcast the plane's identity and position, then shifted the course southeast. Someone, probably the copilot, shouted from behind the door, then began pounding. Pyotr ignored it. With the partition's reinforced bolts, no one would be getting in.

Pyotr also ignored the radio, whose questions were becoming more strident. Instead, he appreciated how smoothly he transitioned from flight simulator lessons to airline control. In reality, once he'd reprogrammed the course, the autopilot did ninety percent of the work. The only tricky part would be to get down.

He began his descent into the sunset.

The pounding got louder but Pyotr concentrated on the plane's descent. By then, the airport was starting to announce that if he didn't acknowledge at once the air force would shoot the 737 down.

The threat was certainly real, but Pyotr knew the nearest Russian command was more than forty-five minutes away. Even if they had a plane in the air—they rarely did—his assignment would be completed before any could intercept him.

Checking his position, he adjusted his course slightly so that he was over the center of the 143,000-square-mile sea—far enough from the shore and the oil platforms to avoid being seen. Finally parallel to the Azerbaijan coastline, he steepened his descent by two degrees, lining precisely into the glide slope he had memorized during flight training.

There was a loud crash at the cockpit door. The passengers and crew had decided to use a service cart as a ramrod. A decade and a half before, that tactic had saved America's Capitol Building, as a group of brave Americans stormed the cockpit of Flight 93 over Pennsylvania and managed to take the plane down.

But that was before cockpit doors and bulkheads had been uniformly reinforced. A service cart would no longer cut it.

Pyotr pressed the DITCH button that closed the outflow, extract, and flow control valves, as well as the air and avionics inlets. In theory, a water landing wasn't much different from a runway landing. An American pilot had done it on a river in 2009; in June

2011 a South African aircraft belly-flopped in the Atlantic. In both cases, all aboard survived.

With the exception of himself, Pyotr didn't care who lived or died on this water landing. Like the people he'd seen in the airport, they were inconsequential. Nothing mattered except the mission.

He steered the plane into the wind to slow it down, watching as his airspeed slipped toward one hundred knots. He needed to slow down, but not too slow. If the plane stalled it would nosedive into the water. If it went too fast it would literally shatter on impact.

At fifty meters above the waves, the left wing jerked up suddenly from a rogue current of air spitting off the Caspian. Pyotr resisted the urge to overcorrect as he'd done in the simulator. Coolly, he got the wings parallel to the dark shadow of the water and kept the wings exactly parallel, nose up, tail drooping as if for a normal landing.

There was a jolt followed by a loud, metallic clang as the rear of the plane struck the water. The plane jerked, shuddered, but it did not come apart. His hands remained firm. The plane coursed through the water like a bullet through gelatin, the cabin bucking, twisting, and screeching, but the old Russian bird held. The Caspian waves pounded against the fuselage. He heard the shrieks of passengers still in their seats, the cries of those who fell. They seemed to get louder as the engines shut down. Now, there were only the screams and the slosh of sea water.

The engines fell off as they were designed to do on impact, disappearing into the depths so they wouldn't drag the plane with them. The surface of the sea was just below the windows. Pyotr threw off his seat belt, pulled himself from the seat, unlocked the cockpit door, and emerged gun first. Lit by the emergency lighting system and the shadowy dusk penetrating the windows, the cabin was a disjointed collection of wailing passengers and fallen luggage.

The copilot, who'd been standing when the plane hit the water, was curled on the floor near the first row in business class. Pyotr drove his left foot into the man's side, more to get him out of the way than to guard against a threat. Then he cast an eye toward the back of the cabin, making sure no one was in a position to interfere.

Certain that they were all too distracted to bother him, he stepped into the small crew area directly behind the cockpit. There was a tall cabinet here; he opened it, exposing a set of metal lockers used to transport high-value cargo.

"Why?"

The strident word cut into his mind like a laser. He snapped his head around to see, standing in the aisle, a mother and her baby. Pytor had noted the child in her mother's arms when he first came aboard. There was blood and a deep crack in the infant's thinly haired skull. The baby was limp. The mother was not enraged or vengeful. She just seemed confused, clearly in shock.

Certain she was no threat to him, he just answered her honestly while reaching beneath his shirt for a plastic key that was taped there.

"Because it's easier this way."

He left it at that as he opened a locker and took out a small attaché case. His employers had originally wanted to smuggle this attaché case onto a military plane to avoid just this sort of collateral damage to innocent victims. But he couldn't figure out how to get it there, and then retrieve it, without setting off alarms in every major military office in the world. He remembered the chain of events, the intense investigation, that a Chinese attack on an American military chopper in Afghanistan had wrought the year before. It was safer to attack civilian aircraft. Only the insurance companies cared until they wrote a check. Then this "act of terror" would be forgotten.

He pushed past the woman and went back into the main cabin as passengers began to organize an egress. Flight attendants were trying to organize the removal of seats for flotation. The back of the plane had suffered extensive damage, but the middle and forward sections were entirely intact, and one of the men in the emergency exit rows began struggling with the door over the wing. Blue twilight flooded in as it opened. People in the seats nearby began to shout to others to come and escape.

That was fine with Pyotr. Concerned with survival, they left him alone. He turned and went to the main door, pushing the

handle without arming the slide. The door was heavy and difficult to open; he had to give his full attention to it. This left an
opening for two passengers from the first class cabin who wanted
to follow him out. As he pulled the door back, water flooded in.

One first class passenger came up behind him, yelling, "Out!
Go, go!"

Pyotr shot him in the head, then looked outside as the other
passengers fell back, blood-spattered and wailing. The relatively
calm, black waters were bathed in yellow, gold, and orange, the
sun slipping behind the low hills at the west. But Pyotr only had
eyes for the rigid-hulled raft speeding toward him from the distant shadows.

Everyone who wasn't dead or unconscious were out of their
seats now, struggling to escape the downed plane without getting
near the gunman. The rigid-hulled raft pulled up next to him
without incident. Pyotr swung the attaché case at the nearest man
in a wet suit aboard the craft. That man stumbled with it and
landed seat first in the bottom of the boat.

"Careful!" Pytor shouted in Russian. "It's worth your life. More
than that."

"Sorry, sir," huffed the man, trying to regain his balance.

Pyotr had hopped into the raft. He cut the man some slack because it had been he, disguised as an airline galley supplier, who
had gotten the case onboard. "Get us out of here."

"Yes, sir," said another man at the engine.

They backed from the plane, then turned. Someone yelled from
the aircraft, pleading for help. Other voices joined the cry, like
the Sirens of Greek mythology.

"Stop," Pyotr told the man at the engine.

As the operator throttled back, Pyotr reached for the large,
waterproof bag that sat between him and the man in the bow. He
unzipped it, revealing the case of a Russian rocket-propelled grenade launcher. He removed the launcher and made it ready to fire.

Russian rocket-propelled grenade launchers had become the de
facto man-portable weapon among terrorists and guerillas everywhere; they were rugged and dependable. The most famous
weapon, the RPG-9, dated from the early 1960s. It came in a number of different flavors, including a folding paratrooper model, and

had a range of explosive charges. The weapon in Pyotr Ansky's hands packed even more destructive power, with greater range and accuracy.

Known as the Kryuk, the RPG-30 had been designed to fire an armor-piercing, two-part projectile capable of penetrating a main battle tank. Such a shell would have probably flown entirely through the aircraft before exploding; that would not do. So instead, Pyotr was using a hand-built phosphorous explosive shell. The explosive had been developed in China and recently sold to Syria, which had also acquired a small amount of RPG-30s to fight against its rebels. Anyone examining the destruction would see the connection, and be misled.

Pyotr looked through the night sight, setting the crosshairs on the wing root, aiming for the center fuel tank that sat between the wings under the passenger deck. He glanced over his shoulder, making sure he had a clear path behind him for the escaping gases, then pulled the trigger.

The air itself seemed to sizzle. The explosion that followed was disappointingly quiet and small, more a flare than the spectacular cascade of red and white. But the secondary explosion, as the fuel tanks caught, was far more showy, with brilliant orange flames reaching to an impressive height.

"Circle, to make sure there are no survivors," Pyotr told the man at the controls. He threw the launcher over the side, putting the briefcase into the waterproof container. Then he took out his satellite phone. "Keep the engine noise down," he said as he punched in the number. "I have to tell the general that his parcel has been procured."

"Colonel," said the man who had fallen. "Is that wise?" His expression and the circling motion he made with his hand communicated the sentiment that ears were everywhere.

"Do not worry," he told his subordinate. "No one will think anything of a pleasure boat that happened to witness an explosion."

1

San Francisco, California

Samuel Michaels was dozing on his comfortable, threadbare sofa when he heard a key move in the door of his second floor Montgomery Street studio apartment. As his eyes opened so did the door. A blonde, barefoot, platinum-eyed vision in a low-cut, form-fitting black micro-mini-dress jumped in, panting. His neighbor Anastasia Vincent and his half brother Jack were the only ones who had a key—and this *definitely* wasn't Jack Hatfield. Jack hadn't been here in over a year, which was the last time they spoke. It was to thank him for a jazz CD Sammy had sent as a birthday present and peace offering.

"Sam!" she gulped in her charming Russian accent. "They are after me!"

"Who is?" Sammy asked.

"Very bad men!" she said, shaking. Her eyes, normally alert as those as a Nordic wolf, seemed wary, frightened.

Sammy's Marine training was a little rusty. He hadn't worn a uniform for years, not since he was on one of his motorcycles when a teen driver had hit him, sending him into a year of physical therapy and paving the way for a handsome settlement with the insurance company. Still, as the saying goes, Once a Marine, Always a Marine. Sammy was up and moving past her in an instant. He slammed his apartment door shut behind her, rattling the painting he'd bought at a flea market showing a shipwreck in the Farallon Islands, out in the Bay. Then he locked and bolted the door and turned toward her.

"It's okay," he said. "You're safe now."

Her Arctic eyes locked on his. "Are you sure?"

He wasn't, but he said, "Absolutely. No one would ever expect to find a beautiful girl in my apartment."

She smiled halfheartedly. "You are making a joke."

"I wish. Now, relax and tell me what's going on," Sammy coaxed.

She began to calm. He maneuvered her to the sofa and sat next to her, looking intently into her eyes. It was easy. They were the brightest, lightest blue he had ever seen. But he kept one ear trained on the door, on the steps outside. They were old wooden steps and they creaked. It would be difficult for anyone to sneak up on him.

Anastasia Vincent was a strong, very special girl. Within weeks of her moving here from Moscow he had learned she was a high-class call girl. That was probably how she got into this country, paying her way with favors, but that didn't matter. If there was one thing he'd learned in his thirty-seven years, people did what they had to do. Hell, he was a professional party clown. Not a party animal, but a bona fide clown: big red wig, big red nose, big red slippers, and lots of polka dots in between. Who was he to judge others? Ana had character, wisdom, and she had seen more in her twenty-seven years than most women see in a lifetime. He figured she was on the lam from an angry john, someone he could handle.

"You want a drink? Water? Something stronger?" he asked.

She shook her head. "Thank you, though." Once Ana caught her breath it all came out in a rush. "I met a military officer six months ago at a party hosted by a wealthy armament manufacturer. He introduced himself as General Montgomery Morton. He seemed very taken by me."

Sammy smiled. "That doesn't exactly put General Montgomery Morton in the genius class for pickers."

"You are very sweet," she replied graciously.

Ow. Sammy was used to hearing *that* from women, which is why there weren't many of them trying to get in to see him. They wanted the younger, the studlier, the wealthier. Even in San Francisco, there were still enough straight guys like that to shrink the dating pool for guys like him to zero.

"So you met this general," Sammy said.

"Yes. Soon he was calling me every week and paying very well," she said. "We were always staying in the city's best hotels, ordering room service, expensive champagne." She smiled wryly. "No gifts, though. Nothing that could be traced. But that was all right. His money was good. The last time we met he asked me to bring other women to party with his friends. That was today. He said it was a special occasion."

"A birthday? A promotion? An appointment?"

"He did not tell me," Ana said. "We met at a Tower Suite of the Fairmont Hotel."

She was right about him spending lavishly: a suite like that, high on Nob Hill, cost more each night than he made in a couple of weeks.

Anastasia explained that she had brought along Ritu, a voluptuous girl from India, and Miwa, an ethereal Japanese girl. The oldest man, whom she mentally named "Pallor" for the whiteness of his skin, lit up at the sight of Miwa. The youngest man—whom Anastasia nicknamed "Kid"—immediately put his arm around Ritu's shoulder and drew her toward the bedroom.

"The general took me to the couch," she said. "He seemed to be thinking about something far away. But I had gone there to do a job and—I did."

She said that for the next hour the general was rougher than usual, though it was nothing she couldn't handle.

"Still, I was relieved when it was over," she said. "The two other girls left but I stayed to get ready for my next engagement. I went to dress and fix my makeup in the bathroom and was about to step out when the general's smartphone rang. As he answered he jumped over and slammed the bathroom door but didn't realize there was a towel on the floor. The door did not shut all the way."

Ana decided to wait until he was done. There was a short

silence and then the general uttered a single word. "Good." The next pause was longer, so long that she thought the call was over. But just as she placed her hand on the doorknob she heard him again.

"He said, 'Firebird moves to stage two,'" Ana told Sammy. "It was spoken softly, almost like a prayer."

"Military code?" Sammy wondered.

"That was what I thought," Ana told him.

When the call was finished, she said she shook her hair, opened the door, and froze. The general's eyes were on the rumpled towel, on the open door. And then they were on her.

"His expression was dark and very, very angry," Ana said. "He demanded to know what I had heard. I told him I hadn't heard anything. He just stared at me with those evil eyes. "'What did you hear?' he shrieked, this time rising from the bed and coming toward me. I repeated that I had heard nothing, but he didn't believe me. He lunged for me, like he wanted to grab my hair, but I got around him because he was still tangled in a sheet. I ran toward the door."

"Wow," Sammy marveled. "That's quite an extreme reaction, especially for a high-ranking military officer." He shook his head after considering the matter. "He must be under enormous pressure to go off like that."

"No, he wasn't under pressure once we finished," Ana said innocently.

Sammy stifled a grin; he knew she meant it as a professional observation.

There were tears in the girl's eyes as she recounted how he had shouted for the others to stop her. Pallor and the Kid tried to grab her, but Ana said that she had spent a lifetime escaping—from local bureaucrats who wanted favors when she was sixteen to border dogs when she was eighteen and left the country without permission. The next thing she knew she was out in the hall, running.

"You ran here from the Fairmont?" Sammy asked. He glanced at her legs, following their shapely curve down.

She raised her luminous eyes to the face of a man she had come to like, to trust. She nodded.

"That's nearly a mile, most of it up hill!" Sammy said incredulously.

She nodded. "I have run farther."

"Barefoot?"

She seemed surprised when he said that. She looked at her feet. Her stockings were torn, the bottoms bloody. "Oh. I could not run in those heels and I dared not stop. I just left them in the lobby."

"A regular Cinderella," he said, trying to inject some levity. It didn't seem to work. Her eyes were still full of fear. "Did they follow you?"

"I do not know," she admitted.

Even if they had, Sammy did not think a group of officers would go after her in broad daylight. "Well, it's over now. Relax and we'll see what we can find out about this General Morton and Firebird."

He walked around the kitchen table and moved the clown suit that was stretched out there to dry after he had sprayed it with fabric freshener. He had come back from a gig just an hour before and, as usual, the costume was damp with sweat, along with splashes from excited kids holding cups full of juice. Anyone who thought making balloon animals, doing magic tricks, honking a horn on his belt, and talking in a funny voice was easy should walk a mile in his oversize shoes.

He grabbed his laptop from the table and brought it back to the sofa. He pressed the ON button and looked at Ana.

"I have never seen and heard a man so frantic," she said.

"When men take chances, and those chances bite them in the posterior, they are already a little on edge or guilty or both," Sammy said.

"He never worried about that before," she said.

"Maybe he was afraid you heard someone's name and would blackmail him, threaten to tell a wife or superior."

She shook her head. "I only heard 'Firebird,'" she insisted. "No names."

"Well, we're gonna get through this," he assured her as he tapped in the word 'Firebird.' "Sammy Michaels doesn't know the meaning of the word 'retreat.'"

"You can look that up after 'Firebird,'" she joked.

He grinned. That was actually pretty funny coming from a woman who was afraid for her life.

The first cite on the search engine was from that day, just ninety minutes earlier. He clicked on it as Ana sat and hugged his arm. It felt good.

"I feel safe with you," she said. "I always have."

"Really?"

"Even if it was just talking at the mailbox, you made me feel like I had a neighbor, a home, a friend."

Those weren't exactly the words Sammy had wanted to hear, though it was a start.

"But who is—what did you call her?" Ana asked. "Sindrella?"

He grinned. "Cinderella. A fairy tale character. A poor girl with a fairy godmother, loses her glass slipper at the prince's ball—"

"Ah, *Zalushka*!" she said. "It is a Russian story."

"Of course it is," he said as her cell phone beeped. "The Russians came up with everything."

She didn't seem to have heard him, her expression souring as she retrieved her phone from her purse.

"You expecting any calls?" Sammy asked. She shook her head as she looked at the text message. Sammy started reading the Firebird reference on the computer then heard Ana gasp. "What is it?"

Her breathing sped again as she handed Sammy the phone. **We know where you are. Come back now.**

"How could they know?" she asked.

Sammy felt a chill but remained composed. "With the NSA spying on every American, you ask how the military *knows* something?" he asked. "He probably cloned the GPS signal from your phone the first time he met you."

"He what?"

"Copied your data, just in case you ever tried to blackmail him."

"*Chyort voz'mi!*" she said and rose suddenly.

Sammy didn't know any Russian, but that sounded like something you wouldn't say or hear in polite company.

"Where are you going?" he asked.

"I don't know, but my father taught me that waiting for the

executioner was the worst way to live. It is better to keep one step ahead. I'll have to go."

"You mean—for good?"

"What choice do I have?"

"I don't know, but there has to be one."

"An escort cannot go to the police—"

"No," he said firmly. "But I have another idea."

He took his own cell phone from the end table beside the couch.

"What are you going to do?" she asked.

"I'm calling the one man in this town who can help."

"Who?"

"Someone I thought I'd never call again," he responded hollowly. "My big brother."

2

Before going to the hotel for a press conference, Jack Hatfield walked around the park atop Russian Hill, the prime real estate location in the Gilded City. As he did, he wondered about exclusion. How the uber-liberal city "leaders" excluded all but their sycophants from any and all recognition. Jack had long ago accepted his status as an outcast and wore it as a measure of pride in a corrupt and soulless place. The top families were filled with whores, thieves, drug addicts, alcoholics, and sex maniacs. Of course there was the Petty family, living off the old man's oil fortune while espousing "green" nonsense, cashing in on fraudulent solar contracts. Then there were the two politicians. One whose husband did deals with China that crossed the borderline of treason and the other whose husband and son did land deals that violated zoning codes while appearing on the boards of other "green" groups. Then there was Mr. Berkowitz, one of the chief donors to socialist causes the single largest recipient being the ACLU. His money was made by selling his savings and loan chain to a major bank just before the housing crash of '08. He made billions while the bank that bought his junk mortgages went under. Jack could only ask how a city, let alone a nation, could survive with such abject thieves running the show.

Yet, of the many species of liars Jack Hatfield dealt with, no one topped a CEO. This was not because they were particularly skilled at lying; their techniques were obvious and predictable: deny, deny, deny. Jack's interest was entirely philosophical. He wondered if having renounced their moral compass as they climbed the corporate ladder, they could no longer distinguish between truth and falsehood. He suspected that they believed every word they spoke was the truth.

Not that all CEOs were liars. It was just that he had personally dealt with quite a few: those who had appeared on his cable TV series *Truth Tellers*, and those who had pressured the station to cancel his controversial show because of an hypothetical question: "*If it came down to it, would you rather see a hundred million of us killed, or kill a hundred million Muslims?*" Jack lamented the fact that in the old days—the *very* old days, the time of the Continental Congress—one delegate, he forgot who, seconded the debate on Independence because he felt there wasn't a topic so dangerous you couldn't at least *talk* about it.

Now, if talk wasn't all about political correctness and spin, the mainstream media and CEOs shunned it.

Take the man standing at the podium across the Hyatt Hotel's meeting room, holding forth to a group of eager news stringers and bloggers for a cross section of business websites. As CEO of Der Warheit Unternehmen, Helmut Schoenberg represented a German multinational company with a wide array of products and interests from coal mining to health care, with high tech and textile manufacturing thrown in on the side. It was German in name only; like many internationals, it had long ago located its corporate offices in a tax haven.

Jack wasn't here to talk to Helmut about DWU's pledge to donate several million dollars to a Silicon Valley fund aimed at finding jobs for the homeless. The press already knew that the real purpose of the donation was to burnish Der Warheit Unternehmen's image after a horrendous fire in one of its computer chip factories in Manila where hundreds of poor Filipinos perished. They were lobbing softballs, since DWU was a major advertiser in print and on the web.

Finally, Jack raised his hand. "Jack Hatfield, Hatfield Independent News," he said when the German nodded in his direction.

There were muffled groans among the assemblage. They actually made Jack smile. A reporter who didn't piss people off wasn't doing his job.

"Sir," Jack said, "I was struck by the speech you gave last year, denouncing the work by Der Schlauch on the Iranian-Pakistani pipeline. It was quite courageous. You were criticizing a brother German company."

Schoenberg smiled superciliously. "Any trade at all helps Iran build a bomb."

"Right." Jack looked down at his tablet, which was also recording the press conference. "Yet earlier this year, one of your subsidiaries, Der Große Kreis, shipped two hundred centrifuges to France, supposedly for medical use. But they never got to the institute in Nice. Instead, another company owned by DWU picked them up at a warehouse in Dresden, took them directly to the airport, and flew them to Tehran over a period of ten days."

Jack was quoting almost verbatim from the summary of a CIA document assessing how close Iran was to getting the bomb. Apparently Herr Schoenberg had read the report because he denied the charge, criticized Washington for its program of anti-European propaganda, yet offered no facts to refute it.

Not that he tried very hard. Schoenberg's answer was brief and it was also his last. He thanked the group and left.

Jack called the man's name, was ignored, and rose to plan his next move. That was not a lot to form the basis of a syndicated radio piece. But Jack was not one to be deterred by a man's back, handlers, or hasty departure. European nations were doing more to prop up Iran's sanctioned economy than Russia and China combined. The only reason the United States had turned to diplomacy to deal with Tehran's nuclear ambitions was to get a piece of that, too.

Jack intended to break that story like a brick over the heads of the perpetrators.

None of the other reporters came over to chat with Jack. Even though he had saved San Francisco from destruction, associating with an accused Islamophobe—or gay basher or climate change denier or any of the dozens of other politically charged landmines that crippled free speech in America—was tantamount to professional destruction.

However, one man did come over to talk to the journalist. Someone who was an even bigger pariah.

Standing between Jack Hatfield and the door toward which his quarry was headed was a short, powerfully built, wide-shouldered man. He had thinning, swept-back gray hair, a broken nose, a jutting chin, no neck, and piercing gray eyes. His gray sport coat was bulging under the arm. It was Sol Minsky, one of the West Coast's most notorious and elusive mobsters. He wasn't just Teflon: this guy was porous. Criminal charges sailed through him and hit other people, stooges he had carefully put in place—often without their knowledge.

He approached Jack casually as the reporter headed from the meeting room of the Hyatt Hotel. Jack's manner became just as casual, but he couldn't contain a slight, thin grin of bemused respect. Sol was a strange breed. Of all the big-time criminals he had tracked over the years, Jack had never come across one who was as staunchly patriotic as Sol—and less hypocritical. Sol did not pretend to be anything other than what he was, yet he also worked hard to make sure there was never collateral damage among the general public. He didn't deal in drugs, didn't deal in human trafficking, mostly shilled for corporate clients and their money laundering. That didn't merit a Nobel Peace Prize, but he wasn't as bad as the Vietnamese, the Russians, and other local urban gangs.

"Mr. Jack Hatfield," said Sol. "You just pissed all over one of my biggest clients."

Jack closed the flap on his tablet and stopped to talk to the mobster. "The businessman or the skunk?"

"Ha!" Sol laughed. "I knew you were good, even when you were investigating my operations back in the day."

"That's high praise, coming from you," Jack acknowledged.

"This isn't our first rodeo, Truth Teller," Minsky reminded him. "You know I always respected you."

"Even when I got close to finding out what the cops never could?" If Jack expected the mobster to react negatively, he was disappointed. The blockhouse of a man merely snorted.

"*Especially* when you got close," he said, his grin matching Jack's. "When push comes to shove, you may find we disagree on less than you think."

Minsky's "hail fellow well met" approach put Jack back on his guard. Acquaintances who were this chummy out of the gate bore watching. Jack intended his next words to put Sol in his place.

"So what does Herr Schoenberg run for you?" Jack asked, glancing around to make sure no one was recording them. "Guns?"

"Oh, you're *very* good!" Sol said. He shrugged. "The big *macha* transports them on his planes. Let it not be said that we don't support freedom fighters in Syria, Kurdistan, and elsewhere."

Jack grinned. "No one's listening, but how do you know my recorder was off?"

Sol shrugged. "You got honor. You don't do 'ambush.'"

Jack acknowledged the compliment with a nod. "What about those guys?" He cocked his head toward the hall full of journalists, a few of whom were eyeing Sol as though trying to figure out what he was doing here. "Aren't you worried they'll try to pin your ears back?"

"Those bloggers and hacks? They're here for the free food and ads. Anyway, I could be in Sacramento, buying politicians, before they're done posting anything on their impuissant little minds."

"Impuissant?" Jack marveled. "My, my. A thug with a vocabulary."

"It's called 'an education,'" Sol said. "We're not all no-neck ignoramuses." Minsky was Israeli and Jewish. He spoke fluent Hebrew and Arabic, having grown up in Bethlehem. His father and mother were slaughtered by Arabs in front of his eyes during Sabbath prayers in their little house. Sol was saved at the last minute by a Special Forces squad of IDF. He was taken to the United States to live with an aunt and uncle in Los Angeles, where he grew up. Rather than becoming just another vicious Jewish lawyer, Sol discovered early on he had a knack for something more dramatic. He liked to fight and kill if need be. He was very much the new age version of an ancient Israelite.

Jack chuckled as his phone rang. He was surprised to see the caller ID. He hadn't spoken to Sammy in over a year, since they'd had a falling out over his half brother's fondness for drink and drunk dialing. Still, Sammy was Jack's only family. He answered.

"Hello, Sammy. Is this important or can I call you back?"

"It's important," Sammy said. "Jack, we've got a situation. A general, coming for me and my neighbor."

"Is this on the level?"

"I haven't been drinking, if that's what you're asking," Sammy replied.

"A general coming after you—why?"

Jack glanced apologetically at Sol Minsky whose expression conveyed only curiosity, not irritation.

Sammy explained and Jack listened. A word jumped out at him, a word that wasn't good. A word that sounded like code for something someone should not have heard.

When Sammy was finished, Jack said, "Both of you stay put. I'll be right there."

"Jeez, thanks, Jack. Thanks a lot."

"No sweat." Jack hung up, glanced after the retreating industrialist, then told Sol he had to leave.

3

Jack had walked to the Hyatt. He intended to get a cab.

"You're coming with me," Sol told Jack.

The men started toward the street. "I don't know what this is about," Jack said. "I'm not sure I need heavy artillery. Not your kind."

"You're not sure you don't," Sol said. "Don't worry—this is on the house. The ride, anyway."

There was no time to argue. Sol's car was parked right out front with a goon. The mobster whispered something to the bodyguard then dismissed him with a jerk of his thumb and got behind the wheel. Jack climbed into the passenger's side of the mobster's factory armored S-600.

"Want me to punch directors into the GPS?" Jack asked.

"GPS?" he scoffed. "This is my town, too, Jack. Just tell me where we're going."

Jack did and Sol peeled from the front of the hotel. He shot into traffic like a shark going after a seal.

"What're you getting into?" Sol asked as they zipped through the late afternoon traffic. Jack filled him in on what he knew. "Sounds interesting," Sol said neutrally.

"Yeah," Jack agreed as he used his cell phone to look up the general Sammy had named. "Or it could all be nothing. My brother isn't the best judge of character. This girl could be on drugs or just crazy or lying." *Though that would be a hell of a strange lie to make up*, Jack thought.

"I've heard people spill their guts when they're on drugs," Sol said. "Their narratives lack cohesion."

"Everyone lacks cohesion these days, including CEOs," Jack shot back.

"You know why?" Sol asked, nodding toward the windshield. "See there? You got a trolley driver, a postal carrier, a police officer. You know what they all have in common?"

"Uniforms?"

"Unions."

"Meaning?"

"There's a buffer between them and personal responsibility," Sol said. "You know why I do what I do?"

"Power."

"Not me. It's the risk I like. Every day's a gamble. When I succeed, I make money. Those around me make money. But if I screw up, I'm a dead man. Those guys in the unions screw up? They got strength in numbers. Even when someone makes a mistake and people die because of that mistake—like an air traffic controller who takes a personal call when he should be watching planes— he's got an organization that insulates him, pads the fall. I got none of that. I am rewarded for what I do or I have to answer for it. You, too. You've got personal responsibility." He wove around a car that was going too slowly. "What we're doing *now* is about personal responsibility, about duty to family, about doing what's right. That used to be the American way. It was done during World War II when the government worked with the Italian gangsters to find who was sabotaging ships docked on the East River. And let me tell you something else, Jack. In twenty years, you're going to see the recruitment of white Aryan nation types by whites in gated communities to protect themselves from the armies of Obama's spawn."

"No argument there," Jack said with an angry shake of his head. "He and Clinton let the Muslim interests overrun this country. Not the religious, not the faithful, but the hateful. They failed to filter out the ones who have nothing but hate and murder behind their obsequious smiles and disingenuous eyes."

Sol snorted. "Who's got the big vocabulary, now?"

Jack snorted in return. "Words are like *cojones*," he growled. "I got 'em when I need 'em. Hell, I'll bet those functionaries have got a better health plan than you do."

"My health plan's got six chambers," Sol chuckled. "Hey, if I worried about my health, would I be in the business I'm in?"

Jack couldn't dispute that, either. "Did I miss the connection to the working girl?" he asked.

Sol laughed. "Nah. I go off like that sometimes. So, the girl. I've met a lot more hookers than you—least I hope so. If they talk about themselves they're lying, from the fake name to their sob story. If they're talking about other hookers, rivals, they're lying, too. If they talk about pimps or madams, they're also lying. But if they're talking about anyone or anything else, you can take it to the bank."

The big Mercedes was speeding and weaving toward Montgomery Street when a black SUV sped by as if Sol's car didn't exist. It only slowed when it got to the Filbert Steps in the shadow of Coit Tower. The SUV's pitch-black exterior and blacked-out windows set off alarms in Jack's head. One look at Sol and the reporter could see the mobster's buzzers had been tripped as well.

"Ford Explorer Limited," Sol said. "Even the silver trim and wheel rims have been darkened."

The pair peered after the Ford, which parked a half block ahead of them. They watched as three men emerged. All wore dark slacks, dark zip-up jackets, dark caps, and dark sunglasses.

"They're definitely packing," Sol said.

"By the hang of their jackets I'm guessing suppressed Glocks." He stared grimly at the SUV. "We can't get near them. They'll know they're made and try to deep-six us, too." Jack was still holding his cell phone. "Get to the Filbert Steps. If we move fast, we may be able to cut them off at the pass."

Sol was already on that page as he sped around the edges of Pioneer Park, heading toward the base of the famous stairwell starting at Sansome Street, a locale in the Humphrey Bogart film

Dark Passage. Jack thumbed the LAST CALL button. Sammy picked up on the first ring.

"You got company," Jack said evenly.

"I heard. I figured it was them."

"You got a firearm?"

"I've got a seltzer bottle, Jack'"

"Then get out, now."

"We're in the middle of the second floor. I could drop out the window but if she breaks a leg—"

"No," Jack said. "Just keep quiet. Keep alert. Keep the phone on. And follow my instructions."

While Jack told him what to do he studied a Google Earth map of the area. He zoomed in. He zoomed to the quaint three-story apartment building with its second floor bay windows and stucco roof tiles. It was nestled between two larger buildings on either side, so it was likely that one killer would go up the front stairs while the two others fanned out on either side of the building. The second man would probably cover the back exit and the third would watch any other egress. No doubt a fourth man was still in the SUV, behind the wheel.

By then Sol had already parked at the base of the famous tourist destination. Its concrete and metal stairway rose above them, nestled in the brown hills, green grass, moss, and trees of Telegraph Hill.

As Jack jumped out, he fervently wished he had access to the gun collection back at the boat where he lived. What he wouldn't have done for his Colt Combat Commander .45 or SIG-Sauer .380 right now. As if reading his mind, Sol reached across the seat and tapped the glove compartment release. Inside were two narrow, polished pine-wood boxes. Sol opened one and removed a SIG-Sauer Mosquito automatic with a custom suppressor. He nodded toward the other box. Jack grabbed it. Inside was a suppressed Ruger MK II, its silencer already installed in the barrel.

"Right tool for the right job," Sol grunted.

The mobster hurried from the car. He was loving this. The return of youthful pursuits bolstered by the wisdom of experience— what wasn't there to love? The two hurried up the steps, going as fast as their legs would allow.

"These are twenty-two caliber," Sol wheezed. "We gotta get close."

"These are probably ex-military boys," Jack said. "They may not act like the soldiers in your world—"

"Team players," he said. "Lone wolfs trump 'em every time."

The men saved their breath as they ran up the Filbert Steps. They pushed hard, and not just for Sammy: there was no way either of them wouldn't keep pace with the other. They passed the art deco classic Malloch Building then surged up the final, moss-covered, stone stairs leading to Montgomery Street, Coit Tower glowing above them.

The sight of Sammy's apartment house galvanized them. Jack motioned Sol to slow and, guns hidden against their sides, they shuffled to the building's front door as if they were occupants. They studiously ignored the SUV still parked at the curb. Sol quickly ran his fingertips over the door's lock, then raised his eyebrows at the skill of their quarry's entry. Any casual onlooker wouldn't know that the front door of the building had been jimmied. Jack saw Sol's right hand tighten almost imperceptibly on his gun. Jack didn't use the key Sammy had given him when he was in rehab. He just went in the front door with Sol close behind.

They made it to the second floor without trouble and stepped into the empty hallway. The bulb was out, the doorways dark. They listened. The door to Sammy's apartment was opened a sliver; probably jimmied as well. There were hushed voices inside. Male voices.

Sol kept a lookout while Jack tapped his cell phone's keyboard, sending Sammy a text: **Open door**. Seconds later the door across from them eased open. Jack and Sol pushed quickly inside, closing the door behind them as swiftly and quietly as possible.

"Thanks to God!" Anastasia blurted in relief.

Jack snapped a forefinger to his lips. Sammy went one better: he clapped a hand over the escort's mouth. He looked at Sol curiously.

Introductions could wait. Jack had to get them out of the building and now there was only one way out. He motioned them all toward the window. He would go first, covering their exit, then

Sammy, who'd catch Anastasia, with Sol covering the retreat. It was sloppy and risky, but there was no other option.

Jack never got the chance to see if the plan would work. They heard footsteps at the door. The men must have heard Anastasia's cry, her Russian accent, and were coming to investigate. Sol slipped to the left side of the doorjamb. Jack gave Sammy the Ruger and crouched at the door, ready to tackle whoever came in first. Sammy stood straight, framed in the window, the Ruger straight out in front of his face. Its sights aligned with his right eye. Every Marine must be able to deliver accurate fire on targets of up to five hundred meters, so whatever he fired at in that small space, he hit. Jack hoped he would be targeting the enemy's heads rather than their chests. That was another difference between the military and the mob.

The wait seemed endless. And then the door flew in, splintering as gunfire chewed around the knob.

Sammy stepped forward and fired first. The .22 caliber bullets plowed into the killer's bulletproof vest, saving his life but thrusting him back from Ana's doorway. The next two bullets ripped out pieces of jacket sleeves—cripple the arms and you cripple the killer—and sent the other two killers spinning back.

"Out!" Sammy bawled. "Out, out, out!"

"No!" Sol boomed above him. "Their driver will pick us off!"

"Down!" Jack yelled above the din, as the enemy regrouped in the hallway, raised their Glocks, and returned fire. Sammy grabbed Anastasia and threw her down, behind him. Sol dove for the bathroom as the studio apartment was sprayed with 9mm shards. Jack stayed where he was. He wanted one of those Glocks.

Through the tearing and shattering of bullets into objects, Jack heard one of the killers bark, "Flash in the hole!"

One of them was prepping a stun grenade. Jack eyeballed him with the intention of grabbing his arm when he came near but the covering gunfire kept him back. He saw the grenade loft into the room like a tossed spray-paint can.

Jack prepared for death. Flash grenades are classified as nonlethal explosives, but they are designed to activate all the photoreceptor cells in the eyes, making sight impossible for a full five seconds. Jack knew that by the time he and the others could see again, the hit men would have pumped bullets into each of their brains.

For some reason he thought that he would see his life go by in the flash of the detonation, and, anticipating it, was satisfied by what he knew he would see. He would miss his dog Eddie; he even felt a brief yearning for his former wife Rachel. But overall, he was pleased. Whatever peace he needed to make with his half brother—well, that would have to wait for the afterlife.

Jack didn't know what happened next. Flash grenades are designed to deafen as well as blind, their loud concussions disturbing inner ear fluid to throw off a victim's balance. Later, all Jack remembered was everyone moving, as one, into a closet that seemed to go on and on. When the trio of killers charged into the studio apartment moments later, it was empty.

From around the back corner of the apartment building, Jack, Sol, Sammy, and Anastasia watched the SUV pull away from the curve and disappear. Anastasia's hands rested in the crooks of the Hatfield brothers' arms. Sol's right hand rested on her shoulder. Although a flash grenade's initial explosion is disorienting, recovery time is short, as long as the victim doesn't have an assassin's bullet in their brain.

"What just h-happened?" Sammy stammered.

Each man looked at each other in confusion. Then all of them looked at the blonde. Panting, Anastasia Vincent gazed back at them, her eyes still glowing.

"It is as my grandfather taught me when I was very little, back in Russia," she told them proudly. "Always have an escape route."

"And that was—"

"A domestics' entrance, built decades ago," she said breathlessly. "That is the reason I used all my savings to rent this apartment. I knew something like this might happen someday."

"How could you know that?" Minsky wondered aloud. The haunted look on Ana's face told him more than her words did.

"The men I entertain made it a possibility," she said. "And where I come from—sadly, it is commonplace."

The four ran back down the Filbert Steps as fast as their legs would allow. Ana was still barefoot. Jack took the gun from Sammy and brought up the rear.

"But how did you find it?" Sol asked. He was obviously impressed by the girl's street smarts.

"I noticed it when I looked at the place," she said. "There was a wooden panel on the back wall of the hall closet. Servants' stairs! Behind the panel were long, narrow, steps. Once I saw it, I had to live there."

Sadly, she couldn't live there any longer. And there were still nearly four hundred steep, wooden stairs between her and escape. Thankfully the houses that nestled alongside the stairs were all but enclosed by thick foliage, so it was unlikely that anyone would see or hear them.

While he tried to anticipate what the killers would do next, Jack marveled at his half brother's new friend. He was especially eager to understand how her gold-framed corneas could possibly withstand a flash grenade. There was more to this gal than Sammy knew. But there was no time for that now. He knew from the hit squad's methods that they were on an organized mission. He also knew that every other resident of the apartment building were stabbing 911 buttons within seconds of the flash bomb's detonation. They should be hearing sirens in the distance any second.

"Jack, about this 'Firebird' thing," his half brother said, half-winded.

"I'm listening."

"There was a Russian plane crash," Sammy said. "A hacker was onboard. I saw it online. He reported that someone skyjacked and downed the plane before starting to kill everyone who tried to escape. His last message was something about a raft and a bazooka!"

Jack tried to figure out why an American general would be involved with a downed Russian aircraft. Morton was the real deal: en route, Jack had used his illegal password to access U.S. military records and read the man's dossier. He lived in San Mateo, where many of the state's wealthiest families resided. Like many good officers who had been stationed at the Presidio, he had fallen in love with the city and decided to stay. He had a spotless record with no mention of black ops. Which made sense: they wouldn't be black ops if they were mentioned.

Yet there was something sloppy, makeshift about the way the

hit on Anastasia had played out. But then the Filbert Steps were jolting his brain and he had a higher priority: find safety first.

"All right," he announced, still going down the steps and through gardens full of purple, pink, and red rhododendrons as fast as possible. "There's no way this hit squad doesn't come after us again. Sol, how long do you think we have?"

"Depends," Sol replied, older yet less out-of-breath than the others. He probably had the time and vanity to work out. "Are they scared of their boss? They got any self-respect? They got instincts for self-preservation? Are those instincts good? I've had guys who came back from a contract, look me straight in the eye, and tell me they failed. I've had guys who would drive off a bridge rather than admit they screwed up."

"Which do you think these guys are?" Jack asked.

"A third kind," Sol said. "The kind whose horse gets tired so they light a fire under his belly to get him back on his feet. They'll keep coming. They gotta stop us for what she heard." He pointed ahead at Ana.

"Right," Jack nodded.

"Hey, I got plenty of muscle, Jack," Sol went on. "I can have people on this with a phone call."

"Thanks. Keep 'em in the batter's box."

Jack was concerned about a firefight; he had been in several while he was with the 2nd Marine Division in Baghdad as a reporter. Firefights were surreal, chaotic, life-changing horrors, and he could imagine the effects that would have on Sammy and Anastasia. And that was only if they survived.

It was dusk, a time when light was dull and visibility was hazy. That worked in their favor. Sammy was ahead of them, protectively close to Ana. Both he and Jack were watching the streets. They heard sirens in the distance. Jack thought back to Sammy's father constantly berating his kid, beating any sense of worth from his poor young body. Even when he became a Marine, he wasn't an officer, he wasn't a medal winner. Getting his father's approval was a fool's errand: he would never be good enough. When Sammy fell into the bottle, Jack tried to help. But Sammy didn't want it, especially after the accident. He wanted to hide, not in a military unit but behind a bottle and a clown's makeup. Jack just gave up. He had his own problems, then.

"I'm thinking you're going to have a few other fronts to fight on," Sol opined.

"I know," Jack said.

"What do you mean?" Sammy asked.

"Right now someone is busy finding out who you are, who your relatives are—"

"Meaning my boat might not be a good permanent place to stash Sammy and Anastasia," Jack said. He lived on the *Sea Wrighter* in the Sausalito Marina. Its only protection was Eddie, a poodle.

"Then where do we go?" Sammy asked. "A hotel?"

"Right now, let's just worry about putting some distance between us and here," Jack said. "Keep an eye out for a black Ford Explorer Limited."

They started to cross the street to where Sol was parked when Anastasia's words froze him in midstep. "Like that one?"

Several things happened at once. Jack's head snapped to where the woman had been pointing. The Ford Explorer roared forward like a lion charging. And Anastasia Vincent shot off down Sansome Street like a frightened gazelle.

Sol had fallen back. The hit squad might not have seen him, might not know he was with the group. He peeled off and crossed the street.

Sammy was taken more by surprise than Jack, whose recent experiences made him physically prepared for pretty much anything. Sammy froze. Jack took his arm.

"Come on," he said.

"Ana—"

"We'll get her," Jack assured him. "Come on."

Jack glanced back. Sol's Benz came to life. He fell back to meet it as it sped toward them.

The Ford squealed to a sudden halt. Whoever these guys were, they were definitely instructed not to attract the attention of the police or they would have smashed into Sol's car without a second thought. No matter how well the Mercedes was made, a tricked-out Explorer would make quite a dent. Jack pulled

the back door open. He did not doubt the Mercedes had bulletproof glass. He was equally sure the attackers wouldn't realize that.

Jack jumped in first and pulled his half brother behind him.
Sol stayed idling at the curb, his gun on the passenger's seat. Both
men were ready for what came next; they didn't care if they at-
tracted the police. As the SUV's doors opened, Jack lowered his
street-side window and leaned out. Other traffic stopped and
pedestrians scattered as his silenced automatic started chewing
up the Explorer, keeping the killers inside. Jack hadn't counted
on the rear door opening, however, and an assassin rolled out and
took off after Anastasia.

Sammy grabbed Sol's gun from the passenger seat and jumped
out as Jack swore. "Once a Marine . . ." was fine, but now he knew
that Sammy was also in love.

Jack laid down covering fire.

Take him down, Jack thought as he kept up the covering fire
on the SUV's passenger door. But Sammy didn't fire. He was too
busy closing the gap between himself and the pursuer.

Anastasia was as good a runner as she was a witness. She was
nearly to Levi Plaza, the small industrial park that bridged Sansome with the Embarcadero. But her pursuer was in far better
shape than Sammy. He was forced to stop, aim, and—

Nothing happened.

"Yeah, I shot my load," Sol said.

"He's outta my range!" Jack snapped, about to get out.

"I know. Stay put," Sol said.

Gunning the armored Benz, he reached under the dashboard
and pulled out a Kel-Tec semiautomatic pistol. It looked like a
sawed-off AK-47 and acted just like one, too. Anyone who saw
the four-pound, nineteen-inch-long weapon with the thirty-
round magazine knew they were in for trouble. He handed it to
Jack.

"It's Ric's," Sol said. "The bodyguard. He followed us on his
phone tracker. I told him to leave it for me then go prepare the
safe house."

Smart, Jack thought. It wouldn't have done to make the hand-
off at the hotel. And—of course he'd have a safe house.

Jack leaned through the window as the Mercedes shot past the Explorer. The Kel-Tec's first two shots took out the Explorer's front two tires. The SUV's doors flapped open in response but the occupants weren't fast enough. Jack turned and shredded the front of the vehicle like it was cardboard.

Jack braced himself, shoulder against the window frame, and aimed carefully at the man chasing Anastasia as she raced across the Embarcadero. The killer was slowing, pointing his own weapon in a direct line with the woman's back. Sammy was straining to reach him in time.

Jack fired. He missed. More pedestrians fled. Sammy bellowed in impotent rage as the assassin steadied his firing arm, got the fleeing woman in his sights. Jack would have one more shot, had to make it a good one—

He held his fire. Jack and Sammy both heard the F Trolley car before they saw it. The orange carriage seemed to come from nowhere as it jerked around the corner like a springing alligator, urgently clanging its bell as the conductor saw the killer standing at the edge of the tracks. The men froze at the sensory overload. The car clipped the man from shoulder to hand, sending him staggering back, the gun flying. The trolley screeched to a halt several yards beyond where the man dropped.

Sol's car was careening forward. Jack looked down at the fallen killer as they sped past him. He was crawling on his back, holding his shattered arm, trying to keep the trolley conductor and few passengers away from him.

Jack considered taking him but the guys from the Explorer were after them, on foot. They would be more intent on getting him away than in chasing Anastasia.

They caught up to Sammy. Sol slowed as Jack pulled him in. Then the mobster growled, eyes intent on the road, hands steady on the wheel. He homed in on Anastasia, who was still racing, staggering, her feet raw. To those around her, she was just another panicked pedestrian.

"Ana!" Sammy boomed out the window.

She looked back. As soon as she saw it was Sammy, she switched direction like a cheetah and dove into the door that Sol popped on the passenger's side. Sammy leaned over the headrest and helped her in. Then Sol's foot slammed on the accelerator and they were off.

Jack tried to check the rearview mirrors, but they were set for the driver's point of view. He craned around to see if he could spot the men or the Ford Explorer. He squinted into the sharp headlights behind them. Neither were in sight.

Sol half-turned to Jack. "I'll need about a half hour. You got a place we can sit?"

"My boat, the *Sea Wrighter*," Jack said and started to give him directions.

"Don't need 'em," Sol said.

"Why? You know where I live?"

"No. As soon as I can, you're taking the wheel. I lost my Bluetooth back there. I need to make a call."

"Roger that," Jack said.

"And what are we going to do after we get to your boat?" Sammy asked.

"Regroup," Jack answered vaguely. "Sol has a plan."

Sammy didn't press for details. For the first time since leaving the hotel, the young woman smiled.

"Ana, while I still have my hands free, give me your phone," Jack said.

She did as he instructed. He swiped it against his, then took out the SIM card and smashed it.

"Why did you do that?" she asked.

"If they can text you, they can find you," Sammy pointed out.

She nodded with understanding then cradled herself in Sammy's arm. The man sat back, enjoying the moment of triumph, remembering what it felt like to be a man, savoring the presence of family who were there to help him and not hurt him.

It was worth being shot at to be Sammy right now.

4

West Point, New York

"Stop navel-gazing, Captain," General Montgomery Morton snapped as he and Captain Steven Reynolds marched across the empty field of West Point's skeet range. It was quiet on campus. The students and faculty were on vacation. But as high-ranking alumni and military officers, they still had the run of the place. "The sooner we get this over with, the better."

In normal times, Captain Reynolds—the man Anastasia Vincent had dubbed "Pallor"—wouldn't be anywhere near his alma mater. But these were not normal times.

What he and the others were trying to do had been described as "ambitious" by some members of the team, "crazy" by others. Whether it succeeded depended on how well they all completed their assignments. Reynolds had taken great personal pride in his end of the mission: securing the orthorhombic element they needed, getting it on a passenger aircraft rather than a military transport, smuggling it out of Russia, ditching the aircraft on the Caspian Sea, and conveying it by motorized raft to the Azerbaijani shore.

The plan was flawless. Had something gone wrong with the execution?

"At least it's a beautiful day for a hanging," Colonel Andrew "Bull's-eye" Taylor—the man Anastasia thought of as "Kid"—smirked. As usual, his attitude grated on Morton's nerves. He was the spoiled scion of a wealthy family sliding through life with a smug grin on his face.

"Shut up, Bull's-eye," Morton snapped. "You know your wisecracks don't fly with the General."

"The way he sounded, I'll be surprised if anything will be flying with the General anymore," Taylor said to Morton. "Don't you know when you've been summoned to an execution?"

Silence settled on the three men, unremarkable in their tweed shooting clothes. They made their way onto the United States Military Academy's outdoor rifle range, arriving at the ordered time.

General Thomas Brooks, also in a tweed jacket, was standing at the outdoor rifle table lined with Browning, Caesar Guerini, and Winchester shotguns. A solid, square, man with the swept-back gray hair and a lined, wind-burnished face, he looked at the three with flinty eyes. Bull's-eye felt the man's power, even when he didn't want to. Here was a soldier who became a three-star general by doing incredibly brave acts that verged on insanity—insanity that could just as easily be focused on his subordinates.

"I know what you're thinking," he told them in his gravelly voice. "'Is this wise, General? Should we be seen together?'" Brooks hefted his Remington 1100 and rested it on his shoulder as if on a parade ground. "Well, RHIP." They all knew what that meant: Rank Has Its Privileges. "How do you keep people from noticing a group of West Point graduates? You put them in a place where people are accustomed to seeing them."

Bull's-eye felt even more anxious now. There was no one around.

"You ordered us here, General," Morton said. "We're here. What's this about?"

"What is this about?" Brooks said softly, ominously. "Firebird is fine, if that's what concerns you."

That was both good news and bad news. At once, the other three men knew what this was about.

"'I will cast terror into the hearts of those who disbelieve,'" Brooks quoted, as if Morton hadn't spoken. "'Therefore strike off their heads and strike off every fingertip of them.' Who said that?"

He looked into the face of each man. Reynolds seemed to look back at him but, in fact, his gaze wavered between the general's eyebrows and eyelashes. Bull's-eye looked around, like a soldier on point. Only Morton stared back defiantly, his lips tight.

"The Quran, sir," Morton replied sharply. "Verse 8:12. Just one of the more than one hundred verses that call Muslims to war with what they call 'nonbelievers.'"

"And who do they call 'nonbelievers'?" Brooks asked.

"Anyone who isn't Muslim," Reynolds interrupted. "Quran 5:51 states that Muslims are not to take Jews and the Christians for friends. Allah describes them as 'unjust people.'"

"The Quran invokes 'kill the infidel' a hundred and twenty times," Brooks said quietly, almost to himself. He gazed at the empty sky. "What kind of sane nation permits these people to practice such open hatred?"

"Sir," Morton said. "I thought we were here to discuss Firebird—"

General Thomas Brooks, U.S. Strategic Command, lowered his Remington shotgun and fired a warning blast of scattershot at Reynolds's foot. Reynolds's shins caught a few ricocheting pellets.

Morton and Bull's-eye stiffened. Reynolds fell to one knee, but by sheer force of will he did not scream. After a moment, as the shock fled and pain struck he hissed, then grit his teeth, then slammed both fists into the ground.

Brooks didn't even look at him. Instead he locked eyes with Morton.

"We are planning to detonate a super-weapon in Mecca and you spend weeks—*weeks!*—screwing around with whores?"

Thoughts shot through Morton's head like spears. "That was my fault, not—"

"How do you know I'm finished?" Brooks seethed.

Morton's lips clapped shut. It had been on the news: the pursuit, the shoot-out. But the incident had been scrubbed. There was nothing to tie it to them. The assassins had gone to ground, medical attention was very private, provided by a doctor who asked no questions. General Brooks was never to know.

"You were very thorough covering your tracks," Brooks said. He stepped forward. "Am I unfamiliar with men under stress? FDR had eyes on Ike to make sure he didn't crack before D-Day. Didn't you think I'd have someone watching *you* all once we pulled the trigger on this?"

Morton drew air through his nostrils.

"Thom, we took precautions," he pleaded honestly. "I couldn't discuss Firebird with my family. None of us could."

"I do not tolerate weakness. Or indulgence. Or *incompetence*! You're still needed," Brooks stressed, then looked toward Bull's-eye. "As are you." He looked sadly at Reynolds, who stared back with bloodshot eyes. "Your part of the task was complete. And done well, or you would be dead now rather than crippled." He looked back at Morton. "No more mistakes. Secure the mission *and* its personnel."

Then he turned heel and walked away without another word.

As he left, the other men exhaled audibly, no one louder than Reynolds who bent to examine his wound.

They were committed and they were loyal. Morton would rectify his double mistake—consorting with escorts, then not making sure their threat was not contained. He would rectify it with a vengeance.

5

San Francisco, California

Jack was now at the wheel, his eyes on the road—and everywhere else, alert for a possible ambush. The police didn't seem to mind that they were speeding; the patrol cars were all racing in the opposite direction, where at least two dozen 911 calls had told them to go. In the passenger's seat, Sol was giving hushed orders on the phone. Jack was on his own hands-free device, waiting. Moments later, the woman Jack had called and given short, precise instructions came back on.

"Done," she said.

"Thanks, Dover," Jack said. "Talk to you later." Jack thought about her ultra-thin, athletic body and felt a slight heat run through his head. She was built like a greyhound he thought and cut himself off as he remembered some of their intimacies. It had taken him most of his adult life and many women for him to understand what turned him over and on. He only lusted after her.

Jack took one hand off the wheel to press END CALL. He handed Sol the phone. Sol looked at the information and entered it in his own phone.

"Is that 'gal' as in 'Gal Friday' or—" Sol grinned as he worked the keypad.

"Her name's Dover Griffith and she's a friend," Jack said.

"Is that all we get?" Sammy teased.

Jack did not respond. His brother was trying to be brotherly. Jack didn't want that from him; not now. There was still too much bad history between them to just let it go.

"I can give you more," Sol said. "She's a high-ranking FBI agent, former Department of Naval Intelligence analyst. She's spent some time with Mr. Hatfield here and his mercenary special ops buddy Doc Matson."

Jack looked at him critically. "How do you do it?"

"What? Get intel on people who may be sniffing around my operation."

"No, I mean, sleep with one eye open so you can watch everyone who comes and goes from this town."

Sol shrugged. "I like it. I like the fact that my computer hacker can get through anything the FBI or SFPD or anyone else throws up. Life is a game, Jack. If you take it more seriously than that, you're dead."

"I like that," Ana said.

"Thank you, wolf eyes."

"No," Ana said. "I like that Jack was letting her know he's all right."

Sol was still watching Jack. "I don't think Mr. Hatfield here is that sentimental," he said. "The firefight at the apartment and in the street set off alarms all over the city. Someone had to run interference. Dover is it. What's she doing, filing eyewitness reports that have us going in the opposite direction?"

Jack frowned. "You give me a pain."

"And you love it," Sol said.

They were both right. Dover was also searching the files for any reference to "Firebird," but Jack did not bother sharing that.

Sammy was scowling. "After what you've done for this town, Jack, I would've thought they'd given you a direct line to the commissioner by now."

"Some may give me grudging, private respect, but most think I'm some sort of right-wing vigilante just because I tell the truth.

How many bombs have to go off before they accept that all Islam is inherently radical?"

"I know how you feel," Sol said. "People judge me, too."

Jack glared at him. "That's because you're a lawless smuggler of contraband."

"See?" Sol said. "I'm also a man whose word is gold and who will risk his life for people he doesn't know. Isn't that how you want people to see you?"

All Jack could say was, "Touché."

A moment later he slid into the parking slot designated for his forty-ton, fifty-nine-foot long Grand Banks Yacht. Jack felt relieved at the sight of it, swaying gently in the moonlight that was dappling gems on Richardson Bay. Inside, Eddie was probably wondering what was taking his master so long. The poor poodle probably needed a good ear scratching, walk, and doggy treat or two though the sound and smell of strangers might send him hiding in the portside cabinet in Jack's stateroom.

Jack's tired legs were pulling him from the car when he heard Anastasia inhale sharply. He turned to see the woman's lupine eyes peering beyond him, pointing at the yacht. All three men, now out of the car and positioned around her at the edge of the quay, looked toward the harbor.

"There's someone inside that boat," Anastasia stated, lowering her arm. "I saw a shadow."

Jack looked ahead. The boat was dark but the ambient light of the quay kept it from being black. If someone were onboard, they might be visible against the vessel's muddy silhouette.

"Wait here," Sammy said, snatching the Kel-Tec from the seat and starting forward.

"Wait!" Jack said.

But it was too late. Sammy sprinted ahead. Whether it was an inflated sense of Marine chivalry or personal recrimination for having needed the help of his brother and a mobster, he was already halfway to the yacht. Jack set off after him. By the time he reached the *Sea Wrighter*, Sammy had already sprinted onboard. Jack jumped from the slip onto his boat and burst into the entryway salon just in time to see Sammy Hatfield aiming the Kel-Tec at the grizzled face of a tall, lanky, white-haired man.

Sammy was looking anything but triumphant, however. In fact he looked like he had just about stepped on a rattlesnake. That long-limbed, grizzled, snowy-haired man was pressing an eleven-inch, .45 caliber, Ruger Vaquero single-action revolver right between Sammy's eyes.

"Well, I guess we're all in the same boat, now," drawled Doc Matson.

Jack motioned the others over and made the hasty introductions before he acknowledged Eddie, who had been sitting patiently on his haunches, his little tail sweeping the hardwood floor. Finally, Jack scooped to pick him up.

"I'm pleased to meet you, Doc," Sol said. "I understand you're a crack mercenary—"

"Who tries to work within the law," Jack added, rising.

Doc smirked. "Laws change from land to land. You're *the* Sol Minsky?"

"I am."

"Do you have a way into North Korea by sea?"

"Jesus," Jack said, shaking his head.

"What?" Doc shot back. "May have my next job lined up."

"Your next job is already here," Jack said.

"So Dover said when she asked me to meet you," Doc replied.

"That was, what, five minutes ago!" Sammy interjected. "What did you do, parachute in?"

That made Ana laugh, which made Sammy beam.

"I live nearby," he said and left it at that.

"Cautious," Sol said. "Even among friends."

"Aren't you?"

"Occasionally," Sol replied drily.

They all heard a car pull up outside. Jack dropped Eddie, who scurried under an armchair as if he were trained for trouble, while Jack sidled toward the still-open doorway. Four nondescript men in dark suits were easing from a dark blue minivan and heading for the Mercedes. Sol shouldered past Jack.

"Donnie, get rid of that thing," Sol said, softly but firmly. "If anyone tries to stop you, especially in a Ford Explorer, break bones and take names."

The crew on the boat watched as the men got into Sol's car

and drove off. Jack knew it was destined for a chop shop. He was impressed by their new wheels: despite its almost imperceptibly tinted one-way windows, the minivan wouldn't look out of place at a kids' soccer game.

Jack had heard the mobster giving instructions on the phone while he waited for Dover to make some important calls. They were headed to a mob safe house.

Doc, who had surmised most of the plan, just nodded and said appreciatively, "Sol, someday we gotta compare operations."

While Jack locked the door that Doc had unlocked, the others headed for the minivan. Sammy helped Ana into the back. Doc and Jack, with Eddie in his arms, took the middle seat while Sol jumped in alongside the driver.

Jack noticed the bespectacled wheelman glance into the rearview mirror. "I'm Ric. What kind of food you gonna want for him?"

"He loves provolone mixed with kibble and carrots. But in a pinch, he'll eat any meat or cheese. Just make sure the meat's got no spices even pepper on it."

The driver nodded, filing the information away, then put the vehicle in gear and moved slowly into traffic.

The safe house was nestled behind a halfway house for addicts and prostitutes, tucked between the Mission District and Lower Haight. Jack looked at Sol with a question in his eyes. The mob boss nodded.

"Yeah," he said, "we finance it. Got similar places dotted throughout the state. It serves a variety of uses."

"I know this place," Ana said. "It's for girls who did not choose this life. You are so kind."

Sol just grinned.

Ric hit a button attached to his sun visor as he turned onto Guerrero Street, and the others watched as a small gate opened in front of a fenced alley.

"Dolores Park west," Sol said as if leading a tour. "Food shops south, theaters north, galleries east, take-out and delivery joints all over."

Ric pulled into the alley, hitting the visor button again to close the gate behind them.

"I'd like to see your pursuers infiltrate this part of town without getting nailed," Doc observed.

"You got it," Sol winked.

Ric jumped out and the others followed, each taking in the dank, quiet area in their own way. The driver pressed a button on his phone and a metal door near the back of the structure clicked open. He led them up a stairway to another metal door on the second floor. Another press, another click, and they were inside.

Jack was surprised to find it to be a simple, but comfortable, loft apartment with sleeping accommodations for eight, a nice kitchen, two large bathrooms, and an entertainment area with a large flat-screen TV, videogame consoles, and four computers on a semicircular desk. Doc noted that the monitor screens each showed a different approach to the building.

"It's the tallest structure in the neighborhood," Sol reported as Eddie hopped from Jack's arms and happily skittered away to explore. "No one approaches without us seeing them." He motioned at the windows on each of the walls, displaying nice views of the city. "One-way glass. We can see out. They can't see in."

At the sound of voices, two beautiful women came from the one bathroom, each wearing T-shirts, jeans, and sandals. Ana gasped to see it was Miwa and Ritu, the two young women she had brought to see Morton, Pallor, and Kid. The three hugged each other and chattered with a mix of relief and concern.

"How—?" Ana asked tearfully.

"Remember when I touched your phone to mine before destroying the SIM card?" Jack said.

"SIM?" the woman asked.

"Subscriber identity module. I got their addresses and gave them to Sol. Since these guys were working so hard to get rid of her, there was no way they weren't going to go after your friends."

Ana threw her arms around Jack. Sammy looked unhappy. Jack felt uncomfortable. He eased her back.

"So what's next?" Sammy said confrontationally.

"For now, you're going to look after the ladies while we—" he crooked his thumbs toward Sol and Doc, "—get ahead of this thing."

"Like hell!" Sammy started, but Doc cut him off.

"Cool your jets," Doc said. His words were gentle but there was menace in the delivery. "I know some things that none of you do."

"Oh?" Jack and Sol said simultaneously—Jack with curiosity, Sol with envy.

"The Russians have hired me over the years to help them whenever they have a problem tracking missing Soviet uranium and nuclear components," Doc said. "Dover asked me about something you asked her, Jack, and it fits with a call I got this morning. A call about a missing weapon of mass destruction, what they call 'F.O.' After a ballet by native son Igor Stravinsky." The leathery old veteran turned his head toward Jack. "Firebird Ordnance."

Ana actually gasped. Sammy looked fearful. Jack was too busy thinking to react.

"How're you gonna get ahead of that?" Sol asked.

"I'll tell you how," Jack said to Sol—to all of them—in a voice that radiated certainty and growing confidence. "By doing what I do best."

"And what is that?" Ana blurted.

He looked at the young woman. "By telling the truth to those who think they have the power."

6

General Thomas Brooks sat behind the big desk he had earned, beneath the large window he had earned, and glanced at the remnants of a military career he had also earned. Awards, citations, and trophies were everywhere. But they might as well be part of the wreckage of the passenger plane they'd brought down. He actually felt bitterness toward the accolades and perks: he was being put out to pasture and all his achievements couldn't save him. Ever since General Douglas MacArthur had made his retirement speech before the UN all those years ago they had called it "The Big 'Fade Away.'" And he was being groomed for that by the brass.

No matter, he thought. That was why Firebird had been set in motion. This achievement was for him, for America, not for the brass.

The plan Brooks had been working on for nearly five years was finally nearing completion. It meant that within the foreseeable future, the world would no longer face the greatest threat since Hitler and Hirohito had threatened to divide the globe in half between them.

It meant, too, that the United States would soon be involved in a war that it did not want, but that Brooks knew it must wage to have any hope of surviving. A war better fought now, while the odds were overwhelmingly in its favor, than in ten years, when they might not be.

A war, also, where millions would die, Americans included, people Brooks knew and respected included. Even he might die. But what greater honor was there for a military man than to die with his boots on? He would die a patriot, keeping America in the spotlight of world history. Brooks did not want to die, but he definitely did not want to die like his hero, General George Patton, who had met his fate after the war in a meaningless car accident.

Despite what he had been forced to do to Steven Reynolds's foot, Brooks was content with how the main event had gone off . . . and where things were going.

He checked his watch. It was time for an update. He grabbed the high security phone and called Morton.

The lower-ranking general answered on the first ring. "Yes, sir!"

"Report."

"The men in question have arrived in Yalta, as agreed," Morton informed him.

"The courier?"

"En route with the package."

The package was the remaining cash for the job. "All right," the general said. "And my visit to the labs?"

"Everything has been arranged," he reported.

"I'll be especially interested in a walk-through on the current projects."

"Of course." Morton's voice regained some of its usual professionalism.

"I've also given some thought to next week," Brooks went on. "I'd like to visit the installation in Mt. Keren, and go on to Riyadh and say good-bye to the monitoring unit there."

"Mt. Keren? In Israel?"

"Correct. I assume you can handle that."

"Yes, of course, sir."

"I expect everything to be in place when I get to San Francisco," Brooks told him.

"Yes, sir."

Brooks ended the call. However much they planned, there were

always complications, contingencies to deal with, something new
waiting in ambush. As long as they weren't stupid, sloppy mistakes like the whores, he didn't mind a challenge. He was content in the knowledge that he would triumph, that he would carry
the flag to Bethlehem, then Mecca.

It was the only way.

7

Every cop in the squad room knew the two visitors were Feds the moment they set eyes on them. The man may have been six feet tall and built like a linebacker, while the woman could have been a catalog model, but their suits, expressions, and attitude said FBI.

"Field Director Carl Forsyth," the man told Captain Daniel Jeffreys, the detective in charge, while displaying his credentials. He nodded toward the woman. "Special Agent Dover Griffith."

"Where is he?" Dover asked without further delay.

"Interrogation one," said Jeffreys, already leading the Feds in the right direction.

"Where did you find him?" Dover asked.

"We didn't," Jeffreys admitted. "He just walked in and said he had a story we should hear."

"He turned himself in?" Forsyth said incredulously.

The detective smirked. "Like a spy running in from the cold," he said as they reached the room.

"This is priority one," Forsyth went on with steel in his low voice. "Top secret."

"Naturally," Jeffreys said, opening the door.

Forsyth entered followed by Dover and Jeffreys. Jack turned his head and smiled at the sight of the two federal agents.

"Carl," he said pleasantly, but his voice warmed further as he greeted the other agent. "Dover. It's good to see you."

"Likewise."

The two had been lovers in a working relationship turned steamy under the heat of saving San Francisco from weapons of mass destruction.

Forsyth ignored the pleasantries as Jeffreys closed the door of the windowless room.

"Why didn't you just come directly to my office?" the field director scowled.

"You don't get a home court advantage," Jack said casually.

Forsyth grunted. The two had been at cross-purposes in the past. It wasn't worth a debate. The Fed stopped in his tracks as his gaze settled on a modern, compact, cutting-edge microphone and a small powerful digital video camera resting on the room's one table.

"I thought I said no recordings," he barked at the detective.

Jeffreys parked his rump on the edge of the table. "They're not ours," he explained, motioning toward Jack.

Forsyth looked at Jack in surprise. "Explain."

"I'm doing a news report," he said.

"About?"

"Secret weapons of mass destruction in the Middle East."

Forsyth and Dover stared at him. Then at each other. Then back at Jack.

"You care to elaborate?" Forsyth said.

"Sure," Jack said. "First, tell me what you have about me?"

"You? What is this, one of your games?" Forsyth asked.

"No," Jack replied evenly. "I'm a reporter. I'm asking questions."

Dover cut through the testosterone. "We have surveillance video of you, your brother, an unidentified woman, and—" She looked at the detective for assistance.

"A person of interest," Jeffreys suggested. "We don't have his face or a license number. We're still working on that."

"He's a pro," Jack winked at Forsyth. "Careful, secretive."

Unsatisfied but moving on, Dover said, "We have video from all over Telegraph Hill, the Filbert Steps, and Levi Plaza. We have bullets—about two dozen so far, and eyewitnesses who were too busy ducking to see much."

"I assume, then, you also have video of the professional hit squad we were defending ourselves against."

"We haven't done an analysis yet," Forsyth said impatiently. "We were hoping you could save us some time."

"Sure." Jack calmly looked at the camera lens, then into the eyes of each man in the room, as if he had been waiting for the question. "I believe something very big and very bad is going on."

"Here?" Detective Jeffreys asked.

"In your city for starters," Jack said.

Jeffreys looked at Jack with more respect than Forsyth was giving him. The police captain had been at the Golden Gate Bridge years ago. He had been in Chinatown for the cleanup last year. He had even watched *Truth Tellers* during his ascension through the ranks. He wasn't sure whether to nod encouragingly or ask for an autograph.

"Carl," Jack said, "I know you need more than my say-so to launch a big operation. So here's what you have to do. Get positive identifications of the men who attacked us, and as much evidence as possible that the operation we stumbled on— 'Firebird'—could be the code name for a mass-destruction materials project that brought down a Russian passenger plane."

"Your shoot-out was related to the crash in the Black Sea?" Forsyth said dubiously.

"Terrorism has gone global, or haven't you noticed?"

"What else aren't you telling us?" Dover asked.

He grinned at her. She knew him well. "We have sources saying that smuggled, enriched uranium may have been taken from that downed plane. Do you have any sources that suggest likewise?"

"Who are these sources?" Forsyth asked.

"Not now," Jack said.

Forsyth was about to call for corroboration, remembered the camera, did not bother retrieving his phone from his jacket pocket.

"Suit yourself," Jack said, aware that Forsyth was also a political animal who kept his cards facedown. "But I've already got people working on this. You don't help me, I don't help you."

"You'd rather have weapons of mass destruction at large?" Dover said.

"Ask your boss," Jack replied. "He's the guy who's not sharing."

There was a thick, sudden silence.

"We'll see what we can dig up on the hit squad, Mr. Hatfield," Jeffreys said, standing, and putting his hand out.

"Thanks. You have my contact information."

The men shook hands. Forsyth just glared at Jack.

"I will tell you one thing," Jack said to the FBI director. "The person of interest? He's bankrolling my investigation. And I'll stack his resources against yours any day."

8

Life at the safe house fell into a pattern. The next day, Ric was up early, keeping watch over their section of the building; Ana, her girls, and Sammy all slept late. Late morning, while Miwa and Ritu showered, Sammy and Ana started preparing breakfast, which they all ate together. Normally effervescent, the escorts were noticeably subdued. But even they didn't miss the thoughtful, even longing glances their boss and the party clown exchanged while sharing their domestic chores.

On Sol's instructions, Ric approached their breakfast table on the first day, after having walked Eddie and cleaned up after him in the enclosed yard of the safe house. It wouldn't do for any of them to be seen outside.

"Hey," Ric said to the Asians while holding Eddie and scratching behind the poodle's ear, "I know you're supposed to be our guests and all, but we were wondering if you wouldn't mind talking to the residents here? The lost girls."

Miwa and Ritu looked up at the bespectacled, burly man. He thought he noticed interest in their eyes.

"The caregivers we hired have training," he continued eagerly, "but there's nothin' like advice from people who *live* the life, you know what I mean?"

"You assume they would try to talk them out of it?" Ana asked.

"Well—sure," Ric said. "I mean, look what happened today. Who wants to get shot at?"

"Don't you? Isn't that *your* job?"

"Yes, but that's part of the job *description*," he said.

"Both of these ladies are working their way through college," Ana said. "They chose this life. Perhaps we can talk to the girls about having a greater goal than filling a crack pipe."

"That's it, that's what I'm talking about," Ric said.

"I could contribute something to career week," Sammy said, feeling left out. "I could teach them how to do magic tricks and make balloon animals."

"Actually, your brother phoned with a job for both you and Ana," Ric said.

Miwa and Ritu agreed to Ric's plan and he teamed them with the appropriate staff members. When that was done, he motioned Sammy and Ana to a table with a pair of laptops.

"We got our tech guy setting up a digital rogues gallery of possible hit men to see if you recognize them," Ric said. "It will help to see if they're from our talent pool or the military."

"You people have a tech guy?" Sammy marveled.

"I'm good, he's better," Ric said. "What do you think, we're living in the Stone Age?" Ric gestured for Sammy to take one chair. "Meanwhile, we've got a dossier of high-ranking military men who live in the area for Ana. If we can pin those boys down, that may help lead us to the gunmen."

He gestured toward another chair and the two got to work.

9

Sol and Doc had left the safe house before the others woke to buy video equipment and take Jack to the police station. When he was finished there they drove to his personal "safe house," an apartment he kept secret from everyone. During the run of his TV show he had used it when he wanted privacy or secrecy or both. Upon arriving, Sol drove around the block twice. None of them saw anyone watching from a car, from the street, or from a doorway. No one was following them. Parking in the vast three-story basement garage of the building, Jack took them to his apartment building through the elevator. They went up a flight of stairs and walked swiftly to the elevator. Punching the button, Jack stepped back to look at the street through the long, narrow glass window in the hallway, but got barely a glimpse before the elevator arrived. Inside, he slipped his key into the panel. The car started up almost immediately, taking them to the twentieth floor of the twenty-two-story building in the heart of downtown San Francisco.

Sol took a moment to admire the place, which was filled with mementoes from Jack's life, including his hobby: repairing watches. Vintage timepieces were everywhere.

Jack pointed to a large clock on top of a freestanding wardrobe.

It was made of brass and shaped like a ship's wheel. "In case you're wondering, that's where I hid the surveillance camera."

Sol appreciated the unsentimental repurposing of the antique.

The trio crowded around Jack's desk, where his editing equipment was set up. He clicked on the video he had been working on before Firebird had crashed into his life. The piece cited the case of several companies that had ended contracts with Iran. They watched a sequence showing stock footage of Der Warheit Unternehmen's varied interests before zeroing in on how the firm was continuing to help Iran. Jack had made an interesting graphic that showed just how the company's money flowed while his recorded voice chronicled the company's attempts to mitigate the publicity damage, culminating in the CEO's visit to San Francisco. That set up the final sequence, which would have been Herr Helmut running from Jack's questions.

"Boy, you really have it in for them," Sol said.

"Yes, but that's small potatoes," Jack said. "They're not quite like the radical Islamists who want to drag this country back two hundred years then stick a saber in its gut. No, the big story here may be the CIA. There's a possibility that Der Warheit Unternehmen is unwittingly being used by the West to sabotage the Iran program. Our tech guys have done this before, most famously with the Iranian centrifuges that suddenly went haywire."

"You still got your contact on the inside?" Doc asked.

Jack nodded. "I knew we'd never let potentially dangerous equipment just sail into a hostile nation unless we had a reason for it being there."

"Like bugs planted to send us information or malware to make it all go bad after billions of enemy dollars have been invested," Sol said.

"Right," Jack said. "So I called Kevin Dangerfield. He's a former deputy director, now retired. I explained the situation and, knowing that Kevin would never give away classified information, I asked for a simple yea or nay on whether my suspicions were solid."

"Let me guess," Doc drawled. "Yea."

Jack nodded. "Only this time there's something even stranger going on," Jack said grimly, turning back to the editing program's monitor. "I found my way to a series of stories on the Pakistan bomb program, which had also received at least some clandestine help from Western companies. There were a few video documentaries on that program, which is why we're here. We need to play out this thread to see if it links up with Firebird somewhere."

"Where's the potential crossover?" Doc asked.

"Pulkovo," Jack said. "The airport is pictured as a transit point in the video. That's also where that downed Russian plane took off."

"Thin," Doc said.

"Which is why I want to see if it fattens up," Jack said.

"Run the video," Sol told him, intrigued.

For the next forty-six minutes the three watched intently. Although he didn't understand the words, Jack knew that documentary making was an art, not a science; the images, their sequence, and the way they played off the narrative were as important as the journalism itself. Jack again found himself silently setting his own narrative to the images, even as he analyzed why the piece worked. One of the big reasons was the minimum of talking heads. The experts were always interviewed doing something, and the camera wandered around the environment they were in—focusing more than once on baby pictures, he noted.

When the documentary ended, Jack turned to the others. "Anything jump out?"

Sol grimaced. "The airport is a transit point, security porous as hell it seems. Also, one of the guys depicted is Schoenberg's brother Marius."

"His job?" Doc asked.

"Useless playboy," Sol said. "But he could be a courier. No one takes him seriously."

Jack felt a pang as he thought about his own brother.

"Other than that the documentary's standard stuff," Sol said. "It's all, 'We need advanced weapons technology because the West will conquer us if we don't have it.'"

"You got that from just their expressions?" Doc asked.

"I know a few words of Arabic," Sol replied. "You got to, in my line of work."

"Can you press Schoenberg to open up a little more about his operation?" Jack asked.

"I can make him an offer he can't 'refuse.' " He spoke the word so it meant "trash," not "denial."

Jack laughed and Sol clapped Doc on the shoulder. "The American headquarters of Schoenberg's company has got plenty of shredded refuse," he explained. "Somebody trustworthy has to haul it."

Doc shook his head at the tentacles Sol had in seemingly every strata of society. Then he turned to Jack. "So what do we do, hold tight?"

Jack laughed again, standing up beside his old partner in battle. "Hardly," he said, grabbing up the carrying case with his recording equipment. "We're going to do an interview."

"With?"

Jack replied, "Professor Peters."

Forty minutes later the two were trudging up a hillside overlooking the shoreline of the Point Reyes National Seashore preserve.

"Professor Bernie Peters is a bona fide genius," Jack told Doc, somewhat breathless.

"I know that name," grumbled Doc, "I just can't place it."

"Former childhood prodigy, finished his dissertation at eighteen, worked in the nuclear weapons industry for more than forty years."

Peters lived in a small, rustic, log cabin tucked into a corner of the preserve, but he wasn't there when Jack and Doc arrived in the minivan. Jack acted as if it were business as usual.

"He wasn't here the last time I visited, either," he told Doc. "That was well over a year ago, when I'd personally driven out to bring him to my show. But I had been warned by his girlfriend. He likes to wander."

Doc shook out his legs as he took in the pastoral comfort of the house and the natural splendor of the surroundings. "Nice place."

"Supposedly, the house is leased to him for one dollar a year by the government in recognition of his many years of service,"

Jack explained as he started down the path around the side of the dwelling. "But I strongly suspect it's a padded handcuff."

Doc followed without complaint, his boots having navigated much rougher terrain in their time. "'The Man' wants to keep an eye on him, huh?"

Jack nodded. Doc dodged a branch that swung back when Jack lost his grip.

"Glad to see you've still got your reflexes, old man," Jack teased.

"The day I move a little too slow is the day I end up under a pile of rocks," Doc said. "Hey, did this fella have something to do with the B53?"

"Nice get," Jack said. "Peters made his bones on the team that adapted the W53 Titan II warhead from the B53 air-to-ground bomb. The two-stage thermonuclear weapon tipped American ICBMs well into the 1980s, ranking it as one of the most seminal and long-lasting nuclear designs ever. Peters had worked on all the important nuclear weapons projects, known and unknown, deployed and not deployed, until the mid-1990s. At that point he was assigned to a number of teams developing speculative designs."

"What does 'speculative designs' mean?"

"Bernie wouldn't say when I asked him," Jack confessed, "but from a few hints I guessed they involved miniaturizing atomic weapons. And when he'd mastered that, he was assigned the task of designing wide-array explosives, bombs that could spread weaponized bacteria and viruses without frying them."

"How the hell is that done?" Doc asked. He'd been to many of the globe's hottest hotspots over the years but that was a new one on him.

"With NEDAs," Jack said. "Non-explosive demolition agents. Just add water to the chemical powder. The mix experiences super-rapid expansion and creates a puffball effect to disburse toxins. The atmosphere does the rest."

"Jesus," Doc replied. "Imagine what these minds could do if they tried to help people instead of killing them."

"Yeah, well, no government contracts for that, is there?"

"Not unless you've got a flop of a green earth system like Solyndra had," Doc snickered.

"Anyway, after that our boy was put to work evaluating other countries' programs, specifically those in the Middle East. He had announced that Libya's program was a bluff well before it was proven to be. Conversely, he had correctly blown the whistle on Iran before even the CIA knew what was up there. Though he's also a little loony."

"How so?"

"Believes in UFOs. He writes long papers about mind travel. He likes to roam the wild peninsula, communing with the deer and the trees." Jack stopped and pointed.

The subject of their conversation was sitting on a rock formation marked by a red furry algae. Doc took his first look at Professor Peters. He was tall, angular, and lithe with a hooked nose, a widow's peak of steely hair, and gray eyes that glittered like isotopes. He also wore sandals, monk's pants, and an open kimono.

"Good day, Professor," said Jack.

"Trentepholia," was the first thing he said as the two approached. He pointed at the rock. "Spores of this algae caused blood rain in Kerala."

"Do you remember me? Jack Hatfield."

"Of course," said Peters, his tone a little annoyed. "You're Mister Truth, though you don't believe in flying saucers." He looked Doc up and down.

Doc put out his hand. "Doc Matson, a coworker of Jack's."

Bernie took it and gave it a solid squeeze. He regarded Jack a long moment. "So, you saved the city—twice. But they got to you, like they got to me."

"They didn't 'get' to me. They took me off the air for trying to warn them that Islam and democracy, by definition, don't mix. Anyway, that happened before I got canned. Professor, listen," Jack said. "I need some information about Iran's bomb program. I'm working—"

Peters reached forward quickly and clapped his hand over Jack's mouth.

"Not here," he said, withdrawing his hand. "Follow me and keep your mouth shut. Remember, you're being watched and recorded at all times."

Jack and Doc followed Peters down a trail to a spot where the surf pounded the waves with a roar as loud as a freight train. Jack did not think Peters was being observed or listened to—the government was not that efficient—but there was no point arguing with the man. After a few minutes of walking toward the water, where Doc scanned the area for any sign of surveillance, Peters stopped and faced them.

"An array of companies has helped Iran, though this wasn't always good for Iran—the Stuxnet virus, or worm, in its Western-supplied centrifuges being the most obvious example."

As Peters continued, Jack was impressed to find how wide a range of items might help a WMD program, from tiny nano-switches to a gas used in runway lights. Even when the original manufacturers of a product had not intended to cooperate with Iran, there were plenty of middlemen willing to step in.

"It is a complete failure of morality," Peters went on, "but morality is not to be expected in the modern age with the collapse of traditional religious doctrine and the family unit."

"Amen to that," Doc said from behind his camera.

Jack remembered the line from Revelation 16:16: "And they assembled them at the place that in Hebrew is called Armageddon." The place did not matter as much as the idea: a confluence of events, people, and matériel would define the new Armageddon.

"But here is the key to this situation," Peters said. "What does Iran need most?"

"Bomb-grade uranium," Jack said.

"Correct. And what was inside a cask that was stolen from the demobilization center in Belarus?"

"A cask was what?" Jack asked.

"This happened just the other day," Peters said. "Men in suits came to ask me questions about the nature of the stores there, what they were capable of."

Jack frowned. The scientist's paranoia was no longer quite so quaint.

"What did you tell them?" Jack asked.

"I said there was enriched uranium along with an assortment of weaponized agents."

"Such as?" Jack pressed.

"Such as, I don't know exactly," Peters replied. "There were rumors of sarin, hydrogen cyanide, smallpox, Ebola. But rumors are like flies—plentiful in the right environment. What we can assume is that none of it's as healthy as mother's milk, eh?"

Jack's mouth twisted.

"Okay, assuming that's true, why would Iran steal it?" Jack asked.

Peters waved his forefinger in the air. "Exactly! It makes no sense! Plutonium, maybe. The Iranian bomb program is proceeding nicely with its own uranium, so they have no need for any more."

"Is there anything else the ayatollahs are looking for?" Jack asked.

Peters shook his head. "They're having enough trouble with nuclear weapons. They haven't the manpower or technical know-how to open another front."

"So who can be ruled in?"

"The entire world!" declared the scientist. "Outside of those already with a bomb, of course."

"We don't have time to check the world," Jack stressed, coming clean about what had happened to him in the last thirty-six hours.

Peters listened carefully then gave Jack a list of different companies that specialized in dual-use technologies that could be easily converted.

When Peters was finished, Jack and Doc walked Peters back to his cabin. But before they could say good-bye, Peters put his forefinger to his lips, and mimed someone listening.

Jack put his hand on the professor's shoulder reassuringly. "It's okay, Bernie. No one's there."

"How do you know?"

"First, if they were, I'd probably be dead. There are some boys who want me real bad. Second," Jack grinned. "Doc is still with us. If anyone were out there, he'd be off killing *them*."

10

The clouds looked like smoke from distant cannon.

Ever since General Brooks's first battle, the traditional romance of clouds had lost their luster. Never again would he lie on a hillside, beside a beautiful girl, and play a game of "that cloud looks like a charging horse" or "that cloud looks like a ballerina." Now, his memory was clouded with explosions, with smoke rising from land pockmarked with craters from shells and land mines. And the only people he remembered lying there were fallen, dying, or dead comrades.

They were cruising at thirty thousand feet at several hundred miles an hour, but except for the hush of the jet engines, Brooks wouldn't have known they were moving at all. At that moment, the clouds seemed emotionally remote, shallow, like silent, unthreatening antiaircraft bursts. Like Ebenezer Scrooge led by ghosts, his mind drifted to another part of his past. In his youth at West Point, Thomas Brooks had earned the nickname "Hardcase" thanks to his hard-nosed attitude toward the other cadets. His potential as an ambitious, pragmatic, cold-blooded leader was recognized from his earliest days as a plebe, and he'd lived up to it in the army at large.

The envy of others had always hampered his advancement. At West Point, it had kept him from the coveted position of first captain, the ultimate cadet honor. In the army it had kept him from a fourth star and command of CENTCOM, the joint service command that oversaw American activities in the Middle East. Jealousy had sidetracked him into a lesser command path, in effect fast-tracking him toward retirement. He had been made to understand that lieutenant general—three stars—would be as high as he would go, and that he should prepare for separation.

Brooks snorted, sounding, even to his own ears, like the crack of an antiaircraft shell. *Retirement, indeed*. So be it. If they didn't want him to do what he could, he would have to do what he should.

His reverie was interrupted by a quiet throat-clearing behind him. Brooks pivoted in the plush leather swivel chair to see a gracious attendant coming down the aisle of the Gulfstream 650. She was quite handsome in the tailored, skirted suit that served as the uniform for this private airline.

"Mr. Suckliff was hoping you could spare a moment to chat, General," she said, indicating the telephone in front of him.

"Of course," said Brooks, reaching for the handset. Given that he was in Suckliff's jet, it was the least he could do. He nodded in polite dismissal to the attendant, who graciously turned and left. "John, how are you? Thanks for the jet."

"Tommy, anytime," said Suckliff, his voice crisp over the encrypted satellite connection. "I'm only sorry I couldn't have been in New Jersey to hear your speech. I'm told it was a humdinger."

"Thank you, John. I hope it opened some eyes, and minds."

"I'm sure it did," Suckliff assured him.

"You're a true patriot, John," Brooks assured him in return. "Wait until you hear the one I'm planning to deliver at the Lab."

Suckliff clucked in disappointment. "Can't make it to that one, either, I'm afraid. Perhaps someone will post it online."

"You can bet someone will," Brooks said. "The left to crucify me, the right to crucify them. How is Istanbul?"

"I visited the Hagia Sophia yesterday, saw how the Muslims desecrated the murals of Christ and the Virgin. Disgusting. People should have a look at that. Maybe we wouldn't hear so much propaganda about Islam as a religion of peace."

"Are you kidding?" Brooks said. "The average guy wouldn't believe it. They've been brainwashed into hating the religion of their own fathers. Maybe you should buy it."

"Not for sale," chuckled Suckliff. "Not yet, anyway. Or I would."

Maybe it will be, sooner than you think, Brooks thought. While he liked Suckliff and had depended on him for many things, he didn't trust money men. They had a mean way of keeping score, and could demand humiliating and untimely favors at the worst of times. This particular billionaire had made his fortune by perfecting a fracking technique for the oil industry. He had spent a lot of time dealing with the Islamic world, and knew exactly the danger they posed; he was a true believer. But even true believers could suddenly become traitors when their wealth was threatened, and Brooks's plans would certainly do that. In the short term, though, they shared a vision and made nice to one another.

"This has been a war of attrition, a war spanning millennium," said Suckliff. "I guess we can wait a little longer."

"Exactly," Brooks lied. He glanced at his watch; he'd be touching down in Oakland soon. "Unfortunately, I have a few things I have to do before we land."

"Not a problem, General. I understand you're a busy man."

"As are you. We'll get together soon."

"Roger that," said the billionaire, doing his fawning best to sound like a twenty-three-year-old first lieutenant. It was sickening. To Suckliff, this was all something of a game.

Brooks clicked off the satellite line and glanced toward the rear of the plane, where his security detail was sitting. Brooks had brought only two bodyguards, half what he normally had. He had several reasons for traveling light; while he trusted the hand-picked men with him, he couldn't trust even them with everything. That was why he had used operatives outside his normal channels to obtain the necessary materials. Using Americans, even those under his command, would have been far too troubling. His operation had already taken far too many heroic lives. More would come, he knew, but he wanted only those that were absolutely necessary—not one corpse more. He knew, from experience, that once innocent blood was spilled, it was hard to stem it.

He found his forefinger was pressing the CALL button like a knife. The handsome female attendant was beside his chair in seconds.

"Yes, General?"

"Please ask my event coordinator to join me," he instructed congenially. "The blond gentleman in the business suit, Peter Andrews."

He watched her walk away with appreciation. He sat back, tried to find something more than his lost youth in the clouds.

"Yes, General?" came a smooth, soft, lightly accented voice to his right. Brooks glanced over as a curtain of understated dark blue pinstripe moved past his eyes, and then Peter Andrews, aka Pyotr Ansky, sat in the luxurious swivel chair opposite him. With the suit, olive shirt, and maroon tie, he looked entirely at home in the private jet.

"We are landing soon in the Bay area," the general reminded him in flat, hushed tones.

"Yes," Pyotr said. "We will tie up the loose ends there."

Brooks regarded the man as he would study a map of treacherous terrain to be conquered. If a shark could walk, talk, and wear a suit, it would probably look like his "event coordinator." He had been called from the field and collected for this assignment.

"You've had a chance to review the footage. What are my options?"

Pyotr frowned and shrugged slightly. "The girl was in a panic, but the men—they were not as scared as mere neighbors should have been."

"I know that," Brooks said. "I asked what we're going to do."

"I will not know that until I am on the ground," the mercenary replied. "Meanwhile, what of our good Herr? He is in the news too much."

"Yes, his narcissism is annoying," Brooks said. "But we need him going forward and he's insisting on being paid in person."

"And in cash?" Pyotr stated.

"Of course, which could be quite a problem," Brooks admitted, thinking back to the televised press conference. "A reporter tried to talk to him about some technology transfers. He shut the man down but that doesn't mean he'll give up, whoever he is."

"Excuse me, gentlemen." The two looked around to see the attendant standing demurely beside them. "Please fasten your seat belts. We are starting our descent."

Pyotr nodded, grinning inside. He had actually started his descent years before, when he had tried to extort Brooks during the collapse of the Soviet Union. The general was made of tougher stuff than most of his lustful, greedy peers, but he also knew a good dog when he saw it. Their relationship had started with some small, off-the-record favors, then grew into a solid collaboration that rescued Pyotr from a life of pointless crime and senseless addictions. Brooks was the hand on the gun. Pyotr was the bullet.

He stood smoothly. "I will see who I can find, and what I can find out, about the girl and her rescuers," he told the general as the attendant retreated.

Brooks looked up at him. "Is everything arranged for my inspection tour in Riyadh? There are a few people I want to say good-bye to as my command winds down. I only have a few days, after all."

Pyotr smiled indulgently down at his commanding officer. "The Saudi Arabian coordination is proceeding smoothly."

Brooks nodded. "Thank you."

Brooks watched Pyotr head for his seat with far less enthusiasm than he had for the attendant. The event coordinator was a very dangerous, yet loyal and surprisingly talented, associate. He had a gift for languages and logical thinking, but he also had a hair trigger. Brooks had no doubt that when Peter Andrews said that the Saudi Arabian visit would proceed smoothly, it would, indeed, proceed smoothly.

All of this, the entire operation, went back to the decision to relieve the general of his position a full three months earlier than scheduled. It had forced Brooks to push up the timetable on the Mecca project accordingly. It was chaos, now, a mad rush after years of planning. Still, with Pyotr by his side, it would all go as planned.

Yes, Brooks absolutely wanted to be in Riyadh when it happened. Actually, much closer, if possible.

A plane ride over Mecca when the bomb went off, a bomb filled with weaponized Ebola, would be glorious.

11

San Francisco, California

"I've gotta admit, Jack, you did this right."

Doc was leaning between the two front seats as Sol drove them to Spumante's for lunch.

"What, the interview?" Jack asked.

"No—conceived this thing on the fly. Used your hard-won skills in media journalism and video production to take on their attack head-on."

"Well—thanks," Jack said. It wasn't false modesty talking; it was the only way he knew how to do things, using his gut. "Problem is, the story still has the biggest pieces missing. Namely, how, where, who, and why?"

"Hey, at least we know the 'what,'" Sol said. "From what you told me, someone's trying to piece together a weapon of mass destruction."

"That's our worst-case scenario assumption," Jack agreed. "So the questions remain: how could they do it? If they did, where would they use it? If Iran wasn't responsible, then who was? If Ana's pals Morton, Pallor, and Kid are involved, why?"

"One step at a time, Jack old boy," Doc said. "This presumes a nuclear bomb."

Jack was holding the video equipment and turned Doc's clandestine recording on. "Figuring eighty-five percent enrichment," Peters's voice came from amid the roar of crashing waves, "which is the standard, you'd need roughly fifty kilos—a little more than a hundred pounds—to easily reach critical mass. The more highly enriched, the less you need. Using a neutron reflector can make the amount you need even smaller. Now, if you remember your high school chemistry you may be able to figure out the exact number—"

Jack paused the digital recording, thinking furiously. The professor's words rang a bell, but what possible bell could they have rung? Nuclear physics and NEDAs were far from his own area of expertise, although he had learned more than he ever wanted to know during his previous confrontation with terrorists.

Suddenly he remembered. He took out his cell phone and went to the website for the Bulletin of the Atomic Scientists, quickly found the name he was looking for. Ray Paxton was a regular contributor and Jack was certain he had communicated with him before.

"Sol—I'll be skipping lunch. Mind dropping me off at my apartment?"

"You need a meal," Sol cautioned.

"What I need is my Rolodex card file," Jack protested.

Sol shot him a look. "You still have a Rolodex file?"

"A gift from my father," Jack said. "I'm not getting rid of it."

"Must be tough to get blank cards."

"I bought them in bulk five years ago," Jack said.

"Oh, so occasionally you *do* plan ahead," Doc teased.

Sol chuckled as he detoured to Jack's building and dropped him off. Doc said he needed carbs and was going with Sol. They said they'd pick him up when they were done.

Upstairs, Jack riffled through the old-fashioned, typed, and hand-written file cards of people he had met over the years. He found the man's number in San Francisco. Now, if only he was still there.

Jack lucked out.

"Jack Hatfield, you old Scotch guzzler!" came the man's hearty greeting. It came back to Jack why he had trouble remembering Ray's name. The two had gone out on the town the night of Paxton's appearance on *Truth Tellers*. Between them they had finished a bottle and a half of Glenlivet 18. "How the hell have you been?"

Jack told him.

"So you were at that mess in Levi Plaza," Paxton marveled.

"I *was* the mess in Levi Plaza," Jack said. "Listen, Ray—I've got something for you."

Jack relayed the information about the missing canister. When he was finished he asked, "Got anything that might help me?"

Paxton thought hard but not very long. "Tell you the truth, Jack, there is a rumor going around certain circles that a hundred kilos of HRU was missing from that facility. Other rumors say it was something else, a bio-agent. Since it's checked every other day, it's said that they have a good idea on when it was taken, but not much else."

"So it's still in the wind?"

"Far as I know, but I don't know much and I don't know anyone else who does."

Jack wasn't just listening to the man's words, he was listening to his tone. He didn't seem like a man who was disturbed or concealing something.

"No worries, Ray. Thanks for your help."

"Anytime Jack," Paxton said with bemusement.

Jack smiled as he disconnected the call, acknowledging that the waters they were all swimming in now were deep and murky. And when the waters got this rough, there was only one man to call.

Kevin Dangerfield answered on the first ring. "Hello?"

"Jack Hatfield, Kevin."

"Jack Hatfield. Again? That means you're in trouble or the world is. Which one?"

"Probably both," Jack said. "There was a theft of uranium or a biological pathogen in Russia about a week ago. I'm trying to find out who took it." Jack waited about five seconds. "Kevin?"

"Now come on Jack, you know I can't confirm or deny. I can't even comment on what may or may not be stored there."

"Let me help," Jack prompted. "Material was taken out of Kazakhstan two years ago with U.S. help. Army, I believe." The following silence told Jack he'd nailed it. "Where do you think it went? More to the point, where do you *fear* it went?"

"Jack." Dangerfield drew a deep breath. "You know I like you—"

"And I like you, too, Kevin. It would be a shame if our friendship or maybe a city disappeared in a flash of light."

"Stop jumping to conclusions, Jack."

"I'm assuming this much," Jack pressed on. "Iran already has weapons-grade uranium, so I'm guessing someone else would want it—if that's what we're dealing with. Who and how would it be transported? Come on, help me help you. At least tell me what I'm looking for!"

"Jack—stop. You know I can't answer."

Jack did stop, knowing Dangerfield never said anything unnecessarily. He had to stop asking him questions Kevin couldn't answer and start asking questions he could.

"I wonder," Jack said. "How would it be transported? Radioactive material is—well, dangerous. But there are ways of making it safer to transport."

"Just for the purpose of—oh, conversation—radioactive material and even biological agents are not all that dangerous." Dangerfield said it blithely, as if they were just two old buddies shooting the breeze.

"What do you mean it's not that dangerous?"

"Raw material doesn't make a bomb," he explained. "So just possessing the stuff doesn't hurt you if it's properly sealed, and it doesn't help you in that form."

Jack waited, but Dangerfield left it at that. "Kev, I could use a nudge in *some* direction."

"Jack, you'll need to talk to someone else."

"I already have."

"Who?"

"A scientist. With connections."

"Obviously not the guy you need," Dangerfield said.

Jack cursed inwardly. Outwardly, he asked, "Any suggestions?"

"Gotta go, Jack. Thanks for calling."

The line clicked off abruptly. Jack's shoulders slumped. Frustrated, he flicked on his CD player. A CD from the Blue Note: Collector's Edition was in the tray. Jazz in general calmed him; this set in particular, with Art Blakey, Horace Silver, Dexter Gordon, Donald Byrd, John Coltrane, and others, worked miracles. Fittingly, it was Sammy who had given him the album as a birthday present over a year before

"You okay?"

Jack jerked in his chair and nearly bleated in surprise, which elicited a laugh from Dover Griffith. She stood in front of the apartment's front door, which she had already closed, holding a bag of take-out food.

"Sorry to scare you," she said, stifling a further chuckle. "Chalk it up to the stealth training the Bureau is giving us now." She headed toward the kitchen table, accompanied by Coltrane's mellow sax, giving Jack time to take in her jeans, running shoes, T-shirt, and denim jacket. Always a jacket. Had to put the gun and holster under something. " 'Hi' would be nice," she suggested.

"Sorry," he said with a mix of embarrassment and pleasure. "I didn't hear you come in. My head is somewhere else."

"Evidently," she said, removing containers from her shoulder bag and placing them on the table. "I took a chance that you'd be here. Used my key but I don't think you would have heard it if I had kicked the door down." She looked up at him with warmth as he neared. "Do you even know what time it is?"

Jack glanced at the digital clock on the stove. It was almost five P.M. As usual, time flew when he was working.

"I saw Doc at Spumante's, hoping you'd be there, too," she told him as she finished putting out the food. "He said you had donned your monk's habit, so I figured you'd need something to eat when you finally broke your vow of silence."

He smiled, rose, and gave her a hug. She hugged him back, tightly. He was distracted by the aroma of Bruno's exceptional cooking.

"Wow," she said as he leaned over her shoulder. "Makes a girl feel wanted."

"I've got Italian *and* you," he said. "My life is perfect."

"Is it?" she asked, nodding toward his desk and the laptop.

"There are some shortcomings in the professional side of things," he admitted.

"Join the dead-end club."

Jack took a seat at the kitchen table and opened the container closest to him.

"Carl thought ID'ing those guys in Levi Plaza would be easy," Dover said as she got utensils and napkins and pulling up a chair beside him.

"Nothing in the database?" he asked around a mouthful of egg-plant parmesan, no cheese, a Hatfield special, now on Bruno's menu.

"Not us, nor TSA, nor Interpol, nor even the Mukhabarat el-Khabeya." She took her own bite of creamy potato gnocchi.

Jack recognized the name of Egypt's Military Intelligence Service. "That could mean the hit squad hasn't done something like this before," he mused, chewing.

"The fact that one of 'em got clipped by a trolley is evidence of that," Dover said. She regarded him carefully. "You're really worried."

"Yeah." Jack took a moment, grateful for the food and her pres-ence and the chance to decompress. "The last two times I was go-ing after the bad guys. This time they're also coming after me and those around me."

They both fell silent for a few moments. The only sound was their chewing. When Dover spoke again, her head was down and her tone was hushed.

"I want to do something," she said. "I came here to pool our resources off-the-record. I want to help you find that 'someone else' I overheard Kevin Dangerfield refer to."

Jack put down his fork, went over, and kissed Dover full on the mouth.

"You know something?" he asked when they broke.

"What?" she smiled.

He smiled back. "That's the best-tasting gnocchi I've ever had."

While they were locked together in the primal entanglement Jack sought to stare straight in her eyes. He didn't look away.

Dover was different. Slim to the point of skinny, her slender muscularity turned on neurons he didn't know still existed in him. With her like this it wasn't solely the sexual contact and release that kept him hooked. It was her being itself that drew him in. As their writhing entanglement reached its point of frenzy Jack's brain heard Horace Silver's horn reaching for the impossible note. Just as Silver had maxed his lungs in "The Natives Are Restless Tonight," seeking that impossible note Jack felt something almost snap as he sought the perfect bond with Dover. She pulled at him with her athletic strength "Jack, Jack . . ." and a small tear. Jack thought, *It doesn't matter if you hit that note. All that matters is reaching with all your talents.*

12

"Captain?"

Dan Jeffreys looked up from his computer screen to see Officer Victoria Burnett in her "work" clothes: a low-cut, skintight minidress, visible garter belts, black stockings showing off a swash of thigh flesh, and black high heel boots. As if the visual evidence wasn't enough to clue him in, he already knew she was working the vice squad's latest sweep.

"Yes?"

"Glad you're still here," said the brunette.

He gave her a "where else?" look. In addition to the usual mix of crisis and red tape, there had been a shoot-out in his city that climaxed with a trolley accident. That meant attorneys and union officials, a flood of e-mails, interview requests, and jurisdictional battles with the FBI. No way he was going home until he got a better handle on all that. Besides, Burnett was obviously vamping—in her case figuratively and literally—and had probably argued with herself for some time before appearing in his office doorway. The least he could do was hear her out. And rest his eyes on something worth resting them.

"What can I do for you, Officer Burnett?"

"You said you wanted to know about any unusual street scuttlebutt, right?"

"Right."

"Word is that some Russian guys are looking for some very specific escorts."

That snapped his attention away from the garters. "Oh?"

"An Asian, an Indian, and some Nordic type with 'ice eyes.'"

He stood. "You sure these guys are Russian?"

The officer nodded.

"How many?"

Burnett frowned. "Not sure. The details keep changing—sunglasses, regular glasses, hoodies, hats, even different mustaches, but the template remains the same: youngish, about six feet, slimly muscled, blond."

"So it could be one guy or a dozen."

She nodded.

"Good work," Jeffreys said. "Last contact?"

"About an hour ago."

Jeffreys looked directly into Burnett's brown eyes. "Is your shift over?"

Burnett shook her head. "Just taking a quick break."

"Okay. See if you can track him down and keep in constant touch. If he's anything like the ones who tried to deep-six 'ice eyes' at Levi Plaza, he should be considered armed and extremely dangerous."

Burnett nodded, turned.

"Hey," he said. "You haven't got room for Kevlar under that getup. Don't be a hero: call if you think you see him."

She winked, back in character, before closing the door.

13

"That's him."

As Ana spoke, Ric looked over and Sammy looked up. Her ice eyes, however, were still locked on the images on the computer screen before them. Miwa and Ritu heard her, too, and came over from the sofa where they had been flipping through magazines. Personal cell phone use was not permitted, in case they were being monitored. Eddie, who had been sleeping between them, remained there.

"Yes," said Miwa. "That is him."

Ric studied the face of the Asian girl before turning back to the computer screen. They had been at this all day while Ana's escorts had been down in the public safe house, occasionally advising, but mostly listening to the life stories of the occupants of the halfway house. Ritu, the more sensitive of the pair, had needed some coffee breaks to have a cry, while Miwa had become noticeably more contemplative. Earlier in the day, Ric overheard the girls talking how horrible it was to be a hooker by necessity, not by choice.

Sort of like being forced into a life of crime instead of choosing it, he thought, reflecting on his own life. Ric had been a ball collector at a golf club where Sol was a member. The gangster saw him swing a club in anger one day and offered him a new line of work—using the same club. Ric rose quickly through the ranks, becoming the mobster's trusted driver.

They were now all looking at Sammy's screen where the image from a San Francisco online newspaper's society page showed One-Star General Montgomery Morton, his wife, Cynthia, and their two lovely children—Thomas, five, and Brook, seven—at San Francisco's Flower & Garden Show, held annually at the San Mateo Event Center.

"Nice going," Ric exclaimed, clapping Sammy on the shoulder.

"Thanks," Sammy said, grinning with pride.

One of the reasons they had been going at this all day was that the U.S. military had become extremely cautious and particularly secretive since September 11, 2001. Finding personal information on army officers outside specifically chosen public relations representatives or high-ranking political appointees had become increasingly difficult. It had been Sammy's idea to scour horticultural sources simply from Ana's mentioning that Morton had smiled at a vase in the suite after Ric had her recount her experiences in as much detail as she could remember. She could, it turned out, remember a lot.

"So we've got a name and we have a face," Ana said. "What now?"

"We also know his immediate family," Miwa said.

"You're both right," Ric said. "But none of that is important at the moment. Let me tell you what happens when the cops nail a wise guy. The first thing they do is look into 'known associates.'"

"What does that mean?" Ritu asked.

"It means we start looking out who his pals are," Sammy said, his fingers already moving across the keyboard. "For instance, who served in the special forces, who's been mustered out, who lives or recently arrived in San Francisco."

With that lead, more information came quickly. One of the first things they found was Morton's name in the West Point yearbook. Once they knew he had graduated from that august academy, they trolled the yearbook pages, seeking out any clubs he frequented.

"There!" Ritu suddenly cried, pointing. "There!" They all looked to where she was pointing. It was a picture of the archery team, where Morton had been an advisor.

"Whoa!" Miwa said.

"What?" Sammy asked.

"There," Miwa said, wagging her finger. "The gold medal winner. Isn't that the 'Kid'?"

They all looked closer. "It could very well be," Ana concluded.

"Okay," Ric enthused. "Looks like we're on the right track." He checked the names in the caption. "Andrew Taylor," he read. "Let's see where his name leads us."

Within minutes, Sammy leaned back, his eyes widening. "Sweet mother of Mary," he breathed.

There, on his screen, was a video of Captain Steven Reynolds in a hospital bed, flanked by his sniffling wife, Mary, and his best friend, Colonel Andrew Taylor, apologizing for a shooting accident that occurred at their alma mater just a few hours before.

"This was an unfortunate accident for which I'm totally responsible," he was saying on a raw local news feed. "There is no reason to pursue an inquiry any further and I apologize for whatever inconvenience or discomfort anyone may have suffered as a result of my personal, actions."

"That's Pallor!" Miwa cried.

"Another of our clients," Ana clarified.

"You sure?" Ric double-checked.

Miwa nodded. "He's paler than before, if that's possible, and a little gaunt, but yes, I'm sure. That's Pallor."

Both Sammy and Ric looked to Ana for corroboration. They had all come to depend on her for the final word regarding the girls and the men who were both hunters and quarry. She nodded.

"It's funny, though," Ritu noted.

"What is?" Sammy asked.

"He sounds like a robot."

Sammy returned to the computer keys to find any other information on the shooting. Ric watched his progress.

"It's not on any of the local websites, buried," Sammy said.

"Most of them are joking it up, using it to slam recreational shooters," Ric said disgustedly. "Like when Vice President Dick

Cheney accidentally shot that campaign donor during a quail hunt in 2006."

"Yeah," Sammy said. "You gotta love these guys who use the First Amendment to trash the Second."

"But that's not really the story here," Ric said.

"What do you mean?" Ana asked.

Sammy, who knew about military justice, piped up. "What your friend here is doing is shutting down any investigation into the accident. Why would he do that?"

"Why, indeed?" Ric replied, his eyes still on the screen. "Let's see if we can find out about what else Morton, Pallor, and the Kid liked to do together."

Ric pulled up a chair and relieved Sammy at the keyboard. Miwa and Ritu wandered back to the sofa. Ana headed to the kitchen to make more coffee.

From the suddenly eager looks on the faces of Ric and Sammy, it was going to be a long night. Sammy needed a break and joined Ana.

14

Livermore, California

By all rights, The Lawrence Livermore National Laboratory should have shone like a beacon of knowledge and learning in the morning sun. In reality, it stretched like a scab on the dewy, misty ground.

Doc looked at it doubtfully as he drove another vehicle Sol had supplied: a 2014, tuxedo black, Ford Escape SUV, with tinted windows, fog lamps, a two-liter EcoBoost engine, four-wheel drive, a voice-activated direction, phone, and entertainment system, and everything else short of machine guns and ejector seats.

"I liked the name," Sol had told them before turning over the keys. " 'Escape.' Fitting, eh?"

The whistles and bells aside, the powerful engine and roomy interior had served them well during the forty-five-mile drive from San Francisco.

"This is where you're going to find out what's what?" Doc asked Jack dubiously as his eyes peered through the smoky windows, scouring the seemingly worn, squat buildings.

"Don't let the unassuming exterior fool you," Jack informed him. "In those many walls is the most extensive in-depth knowledge of nuclear and atomic weaponry in the world. It was created in 1952 as an offshoot of the UC Radiation Lab and as competition for Los Alamos."

Doc sniffed. "Looks like they haven't changed the wallpaper since '52, either. But we may not be looking for nuclear material. How's this help us in that case?"

"Gossip," Jack replied. "Apart from lawyers, no one likes telling tales more than scientists, especially when one of their hated rivals screws up."

"You never go wrong trusting the worst in people, do you?"

"The day I do, I can retire happy," Jack replied. "It'll mean humankind is saved."

"You've got a job for life," Doc laughed.

Jack grinned, still looking for the right building. They passed the Center for Accelerator Mass Spectrometry, the Center for Micro- and Nanotechnology, the High Explosives Applications Facility, the Jupiter Laser Facility, and the Joint Genome Institute before Doc spoke up.

"So where do we park for The Lawrence Livermore National Laboratory's Discovery Center?"

Jack was about to answer when the vehicle's installed computer system beat him to it. "The Discovery Center is located off Greenville Road on Eastgate Drive," said a calm female voice from the dashboard. "There is parking on site. Would you like me to give you directions?"

"No," the two men said at the same time. As much as burgeoning technology interested them, they were both a bit old-fashioned when it came to talking cars. Or women telling them how to drive.

"I'll find it myself, thank you," Doc growled.

"You don't have to apologize to the dashboard, Doc," Jack jibed as he opened the door.

"Shut up," Doc replied pleasantly as he stepped out, stretching. "Who are you seeing again?"

"Mel Connors, the media relations director. We've had a somewhat jousting relationship during my *Truth Tellers* years, but he once admitted I kept him honest about possible government excess in his programs. He said he'd point me in the right direction."

By then Doc had found the Discovery Center and they joined a surprisingly large group milling around the lobby.

"All these people going to see your friend?" Doc wondered as he studied the myriad group of everyone from suit-and-tie business types to leather-clad latter-day hippies.

Jack frowned, then motioned Doc to follow him to the Information Desk. He smiled at the woman seated there. "I have an appointment with Mel Connors. My name is Jack Hatfield."

"Welcome to the Laboratory's Discovery Center," she said pleasantly. "One moment, please."

While she called over to Connors's office, Jack turned back to Doc, who was still surveying the crowd.

"They're having a lecture today," Doc informed him, nodding to a poster and banner located near the entrance to an auditorium. "Part of an open series, apparently."

Jack gave a small grunt in reply, busy thinking about how best to approach Connors—and how much to tell him.

"Excuse me, Mr. Hatfield?" the woman at the desk said. "His office has informed me that something has come up and Mr. Connors has asked for your patience. He'll be down as soon as he can."

"Do you have any idea how soon is soon?" Doc asked. Patience was not his greatest virtue.

"I'm sorry, I don't," the woman said behind a tolerant smile. "Please feel free to visit our exhibits while you wait, or we have a nice cafeteria in the building. I'll page you as soon as Mr. Connors is available."

Jack thanked her, resisting the urge to probe what the delay was. He turned to Doc with a sigh. "Want to go to a lecture?"

"Not especially," Doc admitted. He was the kind of guy who liked to learn by doing, not by listening. "But it beats sitting in a lobby."

Jack followed Doc to the signpost listing the lectures. Today's talk was Security in the 21st Century and the speaker was General Thomas Brooks.

Doc nodded in recognition. "Second-ranking officer in the U.S. Special Command," he informed Jack. Doc had seemingly been in every field of battle since 'Nam, and had an encyclopedic knowledge of the military. "On second thought, this might be interesting."

"Sure," Jack said, "if you don't mind the same old party line. You know, 'We're facing grave times and ominous threats, but give us carte blanche and trust us.' On second thought, you go ahead if you want to. I'll be in the café."

"We're like a married couple," Doc teased. "When I want to do something you don't and vice versa."

"I look at it as partners covering more ground," Jack said.

He started to walk away when a text came in on his smartphone. It was from Sammy. The message was **Getting close, sit tight** and the attached picture showed the online newspaper clipping from the Flower & Garden Show.

Jack looked at the clipping as he walked toward the cafeteria, his eyes absently taking it all in, then froze. He enlarged the photo's caption: "Son, Thomas, daughter, Brook."

Jack turned back toward the lecture series' poster. His eyes seemed to zoom in on today's speaker's name. "No," he said quietly. "It couldn't be."

He hurried over to Doc, who was filing in with the eggheads. Doc turned in slight surprise as Jack's hand clapped on his shoulder in the lecture hall doorway.

"I changed my mind," Jack said. "This might be interesting after all."

"You're definitely the female part of this marriage," Doc joked.

The lecture turned out to be very interesting. Far from being a bore, General Thomas Brooks was an electrifying speaker. While he didn't quite come up to the standards set by Patton, a man whose name he seemed to insert in every other sentence, Brooks was definitely the real deal—the sort of man who could look a soldier in the face and get him to run directly into enemy fire.

"The world doesn't realize that we're at war," Brooks was saying. "Iran is the tip of the iceberg. Islam and the West are on a collision course. The two *will* clash in a cataclysm of unprecedented violence and destruction. Whether the bomb comes from Iran, or Pakistan, Saudi Arabia—we are looking at Armageddon."

"He's playing your song," Doc whispered.

Jack shushed him. He'd never heard a general—one still in the army—speak so candidly and openly about the dangers of radical Islam. Generals these days were extremely wary creatures, kowtowing to the status quo and political COWARDICE.

Not so Thomas Brooks. He said everything Jack had said on *Truth Tellers*, but with three stars on his shoulders. They could label Jack a racist, they could hound him off the air, but here was this military leader, second ranking in the Special Command, and no one was coming after him, and no one was shouting him down.

As the general passionately continued, Jack forgot Mel Connors and began visualizing Brooks speaking to Montgomery Morton this way.

"This is the truth about twenty-first century security," the general concluded. "This is why we have the Patriot Act. This is why we have the NSA. I don't mind hearing people complain about wiretaps. I don't mind hearing people complain about security cameras. I've got bad news for those people. It's not enough."

The speech ended to polite, even shocked, applause. Several men and women—some of whom wore head scarves—had already walked out. Jack realized that many had attended to come away feeling safe, and were not expecting such a blunt call to action. But those people were not Jack Hatfield. He got up as Brooks began taking questions, and moved toward the side of the room. Doc followed.

"You got the digicam?" Jack whispered. Doc made a face as if to say "of course." He had already palmed it and turned it on.

There was a door behind the stage and a man in uniform stood there—undoubtedly one of the general's bodyguards. And there was Mel Connors, sitting at the end of the front row—the general's official host, no doubt, with two more uniforms to their right. Well, no wonder. This lecture, apparently, was the "something that came up."

Jack waited until the questions petered out, then moved up to the front, arriving just behind Mel as he congratulated the general on his performance.

"So," said Jack, loud enough to draw the general's attention, "as Patton said about Russia, war is inevitable and it's better fought sooner rather than later."

The general turned to see who was talking. He regarded Jack

over a crowd of supporters. The look in his eyes was part challenge, part query.

Jack pressed on quickly, fearing he might get muscled away.
"Once Iran has a nuclear weapon, it will be used. Whether by them
or by other Middle Eastern countries who feel that they need the
bomb as well. Because the Sunnis are not going to allow the Shia
to have one. Am I right?"

Brooks nodded noncommittally. His eyes were now fixed on
Jack's.

He knows more than he's saying, Jack thought.

"There's no evidence that Saudi Arabia or any other country
in the Middle East, outside of Iran, is interested in a weapon," Mel
Connors piped up, answering the group in general and Jack in particular.

"What about something nonnuclear?" Jack asked. "Know anyone out there who might be interested in trumping the Saddam
Hussein or Bashar al-Assad strategy of gassing their own people?"

"How do you trump that?" a voice in the group asked.

"Weaponized bacteria or viruses," Jack said. "Something
launched with a cold delivery system."

"A 'cold' delivery system?" Connors said mockingly. "Explosive
grout, you mean. It's used in demolition and mining to localize
damage."

"So far," Jack countered. "But you're avoiding the larger question."

"Not avoiding. This isn't the time or—"

"The Soviets played around with botulism, smallpox, anthrax,
and Ebola," Jack went on. "The Japanese terrorists Aum Shinri-
kyo sent people to the Congo during an Ebola outbreak in the
1990s to collect samples."

Connors chuckled. Jack thought it had a nervous rattle to it.
"You're just looking for a sensational headline," he said.

"Actually, sir, what I'm looking for is the truth."

Connors replied coolly, "We've been through this mistake in
Iraq, and it cost us dearly."

"I don't know that there's no evidence," said Jack, keeping his
gaze on Brooks. "Another country could obtain uranium much
more quickly than Iran did."

Connors scoffed. "Now come on, Jack. You don't understand the science."

"Don't have to. I understand robbery."

"What does that mean?" Connors demanded.

Brooks continued to regard Hatfield. "Do I know you?" asked the general.

"Possibly." Jack elbowed through the crowd that parted—not like the waters before Moses but like Romans before a leper. Jack stuck out his hand. "Jack Hatfield, formerly of *Truth Tellers*. I'm working on a documentary on weapons of mass destruction in the Middle East. I would love to do a formal interview with you."

Brooks looked intrigued, but only for a moment. "I'm not sure I'll have the time."

"At your convenience," said Jack, pulling out a business card. He handed it over and the general slipped it into his pocket. Jack knew it was a good sign because he didn't hand it to a subordinate or bodyguard.

The other members of the audience closed ranks again, pressing around Brooks to ask questions. Jack slipped back, listening to people talk as they filed out. The crowd around the general was astoundingly starry-eyed. "Shouldn't America use nuclear weapons first?" one man asked. "Why were Muslims more likely to use the bomb than Americans?" asked another.

It wasn't so much their extreme politics that struck Jack—he had espoused those very positions at various times, but as part of a larger policy of rebuilding national stature. Rather, it was the naïveté of the group that bothered him. They wanted satisfaction now. They had been brutalized by terrorists, by the economy, by their own ineffective government and were looking to lash out. All they needed was a ringleader. As the Germans had learned, that never worked out well.

Jack started to retreat with Doc, but backward, so Doc could keep the camera on Brooks and company. He caught a glare from Mel Connors, who must have noticed the video, but Jack just smiled. The PR man would get over it.

Normally Jack would already be planning to follow up with e-mails and calls to the general, but he was fairly certain those would not be necessary. The general would want to hear more.

No doubt he saw an ally in Jack, one who could help sell his vision of the future. Jack and Doc were about to slip out the main entrance just as Brooks was about to do the same in the back. The general kept going, but Jack froze. For, in that brief moment that the door opened just wide enough for Brooks to slip through, Jack, even from across the room, could see who was waiting for him.

General Montgomery Morton.

15

Brooks finally succeeded in escaping the small pack of sycophants and brown-nosers, ducking away with the media relations director, Mel Connors, and Morton. The latter started to lead the group to the Center's private parking lot.

"Hatfield's interesting," mused Brooks.

"That's not the word I'd use for him," Connors grumbled.

The general smiled at the publicity director. "And what would that word be?"

"It's actually four words," Connors confessed. "Pain in the ass."

Brooks chuckled. "Funny. That's what they call me as well."

By then they had reached the government black Suburban. The two generals got into the back of the car while the bodyguards got in front. The Lab men made their good-byes, and the bodyguards raised the soundproof glass between the front and rear seats, but Morton didn't speak until the car was well on its way back to San Francisco.

"Hatfield was the one questioning Schoenberg during the press conference," he said.

"I know," the general replied. "It's rare to meet a journalist who not only understands what I'm talking about but can reach the obvious conclusions."

"That doesn't concern you?" Morton asked.

"Not yet," said Brooks. "What else do you know about him?"

"He was a cable talk show host," said Morton. "He got kicked off the air for saying the same things you do. Only you don't have advertisers to answer to." Morton fleetingly thought about adding, *You have the entire population of the United States to answer to*, but thought better of it. He, too, had the entire U.S. population to answer to, plus-one: General Thomas Brooks, and that extra man made all the difference. "He asked you about stolen material," Morton reminded his mentor. "That doesn't raise any alarms?"

"He's a journalist with good sources and a good mind," Brooks replied. "Let's wait and see what he does with any suspicions he may have. More importantly, what's going on with the fusing system?"

Morton was looking out the window, oblivious to the sudden change in subject matter and the question hanging in the air. When had he changed from a general himself, with major responsibilities, to Brooks's adjunct? *When you agreed to help bomb Mecca, that's when.*

"Monty!"

"Yes?" Morton suddenly snapped to attention.

"The fuses?" Brooks repeated with smiling lips but unsmiling eyes.

"Almost there."

"The lens?" pressed the general.

"That's been in place for days. The fuses are the last pieces we need."

"Good. Is it going to work?"

The question caught Morton off-guard. "It's all new technology. The experts are agreed: in theory, nothing should go wrong."

Brooks settled slightly in his seat. "The A-bomb was new, once. All right. I can live with that. And Schoenberg?"

"He still wants to meet with you."

Brooks's response was cold, stony silence.

"I can't put him off," Morton complained. "He's not satisfied with me. He knows—everyone knows—you're the boss."

Brooks opened his mouth to say that he needed his second-in-command to be more assertive, then shut it again. Morton was right. He was the man in charge, the one people wanted to hear from. And that wasn't necessarily a bad thing. It meant that when they did get to see him, his word—brief, handed down like the laws from Moses—*was* law.

"Is there something in particular he wants to discuss?" the general asked.

"The operation, and something *new*," Morton replied. "As it happens, it's this reporter. Hatfield had some pointed questions about Der Warheit Unternehmen's earlier deals with Iran."

"I like him more with each passing minute."

"This could be pretty damning for Der Warheit Unternehmen."

"It *should* be damning," snapped Brooks. "Those bastards practically gave away the family jewels." *And a good thing they did, too,* thought Brooks—that was how they had blackmailed Schoenberg into selling them most of what they needed.

"Fine, but now he shows up today?" said Morton. "Connors tried to put him off when he heard about the scene at the press conference, and—well, you saw. Hatfield got in anyway."

"What are you saying, Morton? That he knows more than what he's let on?"

"My guess? Yes. How much? I don't know. He should be watched."

"By all of America."

"That's not what I meant," Morton said.

"Even if he does know what we're doing, Jack Hatfield might be the best thing that's happened for Firebird."

Morton stared at his commanding officer, speechless.

"If anyone could sell the necessity of Firebird to the American people," the general maintained, "it would be him. Frankly, after looking in those eyes and finding them as resolute as anyone I ever faced, I am seriously considering grooming him for just such a position—if and when the time is right."

Morton's managed to find words. "Sir, you've got to be kidding."

Brooks looked back evenly. "Funny, that's what I said when I heard about your whore."

Morton's mouth shut with an audible snap. He stared at his commanding officer, unblinking. "That situation is contained," he said when he found his voice.

"Oh? Is she dead? In our custody?"

"She is hiding," Morton said. "Or maybe she's still running. And as long as she *stays* hidden or running, she is no threat. We will find her soon enough."

"Is she unable to discuss what she heard with anyone else?"

"She heard a single word—" ·

"'Overlord' was a single word!" Brooks yelled. "Would Ike have wanted Hitler to know it? Would that have helped the D-Day invasion? You said she was with someone when your men found her. Who?"

"A neighbor, we think," Morton said. "His name is Sammy Michaels. We're looking into him, now."

"You're still 'looking into' him?"

"We have to be careful," Morton said.

Brooks didn't immediately bark back. He exhaled evenly through his nose and glared at the other man. "It's not the overheard word that concerns me, it's how you reacted once the word was overheard. A hit squad. And one made up of your own loyal but inexperienced coworkers from G-2. They were obviously not ready for an urban seek-and-destroy."

"They decided not to turn the streets of San Francisco into a battleground. It was the right choice to retreat before the police arrived."

"Another Operation Eagle Claw," Brooks said, referring to President Jimmy Carter's ill-fated attempt to rescue the hostages from Tehran. He stared out the dark window at the beauty of the city on the bay.

The general's incessant browbeating finally got the better of him. "Sir, I *do* know more. What would you say if I told you your reporter is the half brother of the whore's neighbor?"

Brooks turned slowly toward his companion. "Go on."

"What if I told you it was he who saved her and called for reinforcements, persons unknown—and that it's he who is probably hiding her, now?"

There was no explosion, no change in the general's demeanor. Brooks looked as if Morton had just relayed some interesting sports scores.

"What I'd say, Monty, is—'I know.'"

Morton gaped at Brooks incredulously.

"I saw the security footage, too," Brooks informed him. "Being a three-star general who enjoys a close relationship with the NSA has its advantages. Why do you think I would rather recruit Hatfield than have him killed?" Brooks let that sink in, then actually laughed at Morton's confused reaction. "How long have we known each other? Thirty years? I'm the godfather of your kids. You named them after me, for pity's sake!"

"Yes," Morton sighed, fighting to control himself. "Yes, I did."

"Why do you think I only shot a ricochet round at Captain Reynolds's foot?"

"I don't know, sir." His voice shivered at the memory.

"When you can't change what's been done you embrace it. You work on it from up close. Who had the most successful attempt at killing Hitler? Not the French Resistance, not Allied bombers—the men closest to him. We've come too far to go off the rails now. Just a few more days, and it will all be over. The truth is, no one can stop it now, not your whore, not the reporter. So we keep him close. We keep Schoenberg close by keeping him wanting to see me."

Morton nodded, feeling from Brooks's approach—and the general's own confidence—that the operation was unstoppable.

"So, what do we do with Schoenberg?" Brooks asked.

"He wants to talk to you in person. Tomorrow, if possible."

"Fine," said Brooks. "Tell him I'd like to meet him at the factory in the morning."

"The factory?"

"The factory, yes. The company we had Schoenberg buy for the nano switches. You know, the krytrons. Tell Schoenberg to be there at seven."

"But you've got a morning's worth of appointments," Morton reminded him.

Brooks's smile would not have been out of place on a jackal. "Just tell him to be there. And Monty?"

"Yes, General?"

"Make sure there's no record of the call."

16

San Francisco, California

Because Sammy had worked through the night the first day they were at the safe house, sleeping arrangements were not an issue. Today, they were. It was the first time Ana slipped into his safe house bed beside Sammy and he'd tensed. He'd assumed she would sleep with one of the other girls, though he realized they were already sleeping together in another bed. She embraced him from behind in the comfortable spooning position. Sammy tried to relax but comfort wasn't the foremost thing on his mind.

"You know you don't have to do this just because I helped rescue you," he whispered, not wanting to disturb the other safe house residents nearby.

Ana's softly accented words seemed to slip into his ear. "In my professional life, I do what I have to in order to survive. In my private life, I never do anything I don't want to."

For a few endless moments in the dark quiet of the night, they lay there together, wearing what had already become the standard safe house sleepwear: T-shirts and boxer shorts. But it was too good to last. Sammy couldn't just go with it. Innocent though this might be, it was still intimate. He could not just jump into it, even if 'it' was just sleeping close together.

"I'm sorry I wasn't able to find anything about Morton," he apologized quietly. "But military secrets are the best protected information in the world."

"Except when they aren't," Ana pointed out. "As when there is a working girl in the lavatory."

"Yes, loose lips still sink ships. But other than that, even on his home computer, the firewalls have fire walls."

"Don't *worry*," she softly reassured him. "Only one thing matters right now."

"What's that?"

She replied, "I feel safe here with you."

"I wish I could relax," he said apologetically. "I was just lying here thinking. I'm sure his wife and children have their own PCs."

She resisted a simple way to make him relax. "You think there may be information that is helpful?"

He shrugged. "We can hope."

Ana smiled. "My father used to say something about 'hope,'" she said. "It was from the Bible, Isaiah. 'But those who hope in the Lord will renew their strength. They will soar on wings like eagles; they will run and not grow weary, they will walk and not be faint.'"

"That's beautiful," Sammy said. "I thought most Russians were atheists."

"Many are, officially," she said. "We were not."

Sammy was still uneasy. "Listen, you know I'd like nothing better than to stay here with you, but now that I think of it I should get on this right away. Who knows how long it'll take?"

Ana touched him invitingly on the back with her right hand. "If you must go."

He was on his feet, backing away. "Yeah. I must. Don't wait up, I'll be back as soon as I can."

Then Sammy turned and headed for the computer console. Ana closed her tired eyes and pushed her face into the pillow. She didn't know what she had done wrong. What she didn't know was that Sammy was afraid of her sexuality; all women's sexuality. He was not gay, he was impotent.

17

The phone woke Jack at 5:30 A.M. He didn't have to check a clock. All smartphones showed the time and date whenever a call activated them. Jack fumbled for the device, noticing Doc's head and shoulders rise up from the apartment sofa like a mummy emerging from its tomb.

Jack saw, again from standard smartphone information, that it was Sol calling.

"Everything okay?" Jack asked.

"Guess who just woke me?" the crime boss said.

"It's dawn and most people are sleeping. But I'm guessing Schoenberg's office is on duty this time of the morning?"

"Nearly bingo," Sol said. "Not Schoenberg's office. Schoenberg himself."

Jack was totally awake now. "Schoenberg personally called you at five-thirty in the morning? What did he want?"

"Not me," Sol said.

"Me? How'd he know—"

"That we were *paisans*? He had eyeballs at the press conference where you and I got cozy. Guess he filed that away, like a good little paranoid."

"Right," Jack said.

"So how'd you like an exclusive, warts-and-all interview at 7:30 this morning? Being the nice guy he is, he wanted to make sure you had plenty of time to prep, shower, and breakfast."

"Where?"

Sol told him. The very address galvanized Jack. As he ran around getting dressed, Doc, who only needed a few minutes to slap cold water in his face and hair, shadowed him while shoving a granola bar in his own mouth.

"A dawn call to Sol means our German buddy was wrestling with this all night," he said from around the oat clusters and almonds.

"How do you solve a problem like Jack Hatfield?" Doc joked. "You got Kevlar?"

"No. You got the digicam?"

Doc gave him a look and the two hustled down to the Ford Escape. Doc got behind the wheel.

"Good thing this baby's got fog lamps," Doc commented as they pulled into traffic. "Where to?"

Jack passed on the information and explained the significance. "The professor told us that Iran was using uranium deuteride as a trigger."

"Yeah, *if* you're building a nuke. We still don't know that."

"True," Jack agreed. "But this is a helluva false trail to lay out. It's gotta lead somewhere that we want to be."

"Fair enough," Doc agreed.

"So, you need something called a krytron switch to work the trigger. And that stuff can be found in a special gas inside airport runway lights or in special 3D copy machines."

"Copy machines?" Doc asked.

Jack nodded. "In my research on Schoenberg and Der Warheit Unternehmen's holdings, I discovered they owned a small firm that made 3D printers and components. These included very high-speed switches. DR Incorporated had been purchased four months before for several times their earnings. Even *The Wall Street Journal* had written 'typical case of Europeans overpaying.'"

"And?" Doc prompted.

"Three months later, Der Warheit Unternehmen announced that it was contemplating a reorganization so production at DR was going to be shut down. Stock analysts called the purchase one of Schoenberg's rare missteps. DR's components were expensive; they couldn't compete with China on price. But they were also very good, far better than their competitors. The krytrons were at least ten times more precise than those used in the highest-end copy machines."

"Well, I'm sure that's all important," Doc said, "but you might as well be speaking Urdu."

"Don't you see?" Jack flatly stated. "Schoenberg bought a company whose technology could be used to make triggers for nukes and other explosive devices—then shut it down."

"Ah. The question is why," Doc pondered.

"It is indeed," Jack agreed. "When we get to DR, let's see if Herr Schoenberg can tell us."

The fog that typically shrouded San Francisco Bay was in a particularly surly mood, lying thick against the earth. That, and the usual city pre-rush hour traffic, made the going tougher than either man would've liked. So it was not quite seven A.M. when they arrived at the DR Incorporated parking lot. The place looked deserted. And if it weren't for the sign near the walkway, Jack would have thought they had the wrong place entirely.

While there had been no photos of the building that he could find, Jack still expected an ultra-modern structure in keeping with the Silicon Valley ethos. It wasn't enough to have the latest manufacturing technology, advanced robots, chip machines, and laser-clean rooms. The exterior design and landscaping had to proclaim the business a worthy depository of venture capital.

But this building was the blandest of bland. It sat on one side of an industrial park that, while well-kept, consisted primarily of warehouses. Long and flat-roofed, the gray-brick home of DR Incorporated wouldn't have impressed a mason, let alone an investment banker.

Concerned that he might have the wrong place, Jack checked the address again. Not only was this it, but there were no other addresses listed for the company. Jack got out, closing the car door gently. Doc stayed behind the wheel, just to be on the safe side, but clicked the digicam on and set it on the dashboard. It watched Jack as he peered through the front door. There was a reception-

ist's desk, a small waiting area, a low wall. He couldn't see anything else. The light was still dim, the sun barely able to fight
through the clouds, but when he looked through the window
around the corner he could see enough to make out a solid wall a
few feet from the window.

He went and peered in the next, then the next, slowly circling
the building. It looked like a corridor ran all the way around the
building—a building inside a building? He glanced at his watch;
it was two minutes past seven. Twenty-eight minutes until the
scheduled interview. Jack headed back to the SUV.

Doc's camera were not the only eyes on Jack.

Pyotr Ansky watched him go through the Nightforce scope of
an Accuracy International AX338 sniper rifle. When Jack had first
arrived, Pyotr had thought he might be Schoenberg, and had nearly
squeezed the trigger when he got out of the car. But he hesitated
just in the nick of time. The man who got out of the Ford SUV
man was younger, trimmer, and definitely an American.

Pyotr would still kill him, once he had Schoenberg. Why not?
The water tower where Pyotr crouched was precisely 1,108 meters from the front door of the building. That was hardly close,
but it was well within range of the rifle and its Lapua round. The
bullet had been developed as an alternative to the heavier and
larger .50 caliber ammunition, which consequently required a far
heavier weapon than the one Pyotr was aiming.

There was a light breeze. Pyotr ignored it; it was too variable
to factor into his calculations, and in any event he couldn't be sure
of either the direction or the speed at the moment he shot. His
Russian Army sniper teacher would have been appalled. He was
a man who lived by the textbook. His Chechen militia leader
would have nodded knowingly. The textbooks had little use on
the battlefield.

Another SUV came off the main road of the complex, and
headed toward the building. Pyotr slowed his breathing. He was
a machine now, every movement mechanical, everything pre-
ordained. A bodyguard got out of the passenger side of the vehicle, glanced around, began walking toward the car that had arrived
earlier.

A second man got out of the SUV. He glanced in the direction of the first man, then began walking toward the building. Pyotr drew a long, steady breath. He could shoot through the roof of the vehicle if he had to. But he would be guessing where the man was. He didn't like to guess. He would simply wait. If this wasn't the time to kill him, he would find another. Patience was important for a sniper. A bald head emerged from the truck. Pyotr knew before he found the man's face in his crosshairs that it was Schoenberg. He adjusted his aim, and pulled the trigger.

By the time Schoenberg fell, Pyotr had put a bullet into the neck of the bodyguard near the building, and was chambering another round.

Jack saw Schoenberg jerk in midstride, as if he'd been hit by a streak of invisible lightning. A moment later the air cracked as the sound reached Jack's ears. The German CEO fell to the ground, his head opening up like a bony, blossoming, cranberry-sauce-spewing flower. Jack had seen people die, but no matter how many and how often, nothing could prepare him for this sort of sudden, savage, assassination. The bodyguard who'd been walking toward Jack leaped forward and threw him to the ground. Jack yelled as he was slammed into the pavement.

He heard another sharp report, then realized they were still under fire. He crawled toward his car, slithering as low as he possibly could to get under the aptly named Escape. He looked for Doc. The man was nowhere to be seen. He looked back and saw the guard on the ground nearby.

"Come on!" yelled Jack. Then he realized blood was spurting from the man's skull. There was another shot. The SUV that had carried Schoenberg screeched into motion. Two more shots, and it crashed through the doors at the front of the building. It came to a smoking, squealing halt, and the horn began to blare.

Jack twisted around so he could get his smartphone and dial 911. He realized he had foolishly left it on the front seat of the Ford. Cursing himself, Jack dove toward it.

Pyotr had the man's spasming back in his sights and pulled the trigger. Had he tried to leap into the Ford's cab, as Pyotr had expected, his spine would have been shattered. Instead, the man was diving for the vehicle's undercarriage, so the bullet had torn into the front seat instead. Now he was sprawled under the vehicle.

Pyotr's lips peeled off his teeth in a wolf's deadly grin. *Clever fellow*, he thought. *But let's see how clever you feel in five seconds.*

In those five seconds, Pyotr used his bullets to start splitting open the Ford's lower lip.

"Jesus Christ!" Jack swore as the shells not only tore open a wedge in the vehicle's lower side, but smashed into the parking lot asphalt—sending shards of concrete and metal into the reporter's face. Even as he scrambled back, trying to avoid the shrapnel, he realized that with each shot, the bullets were edging closer and closer to the Ford's fuel line. Where was Doc? Did any of the subsequent shots nail him? Would he appear in time to save them both? The next shot tore open more of the car, its ricochet perforating the exhaust pipe. Jack immediately saw that it would only take two more bullets before the gas tank was hit. And then he might as well be in an exploding oven broiler.

The next bullet hit. Jack jerked to the opposite edge of the car. Could he run? Could the sniper hit him through the cover of the SUV? Did he have any choice but to attempt it? Jack was about to scramble up and start running when, suddenly, police cars, sirens screaming, came tearing into the parking lot from every direction—on the roads as well as through hedges and over grassy knolls.

Pyotr was already disassembling the rifle and securing it in a backpack. He could do that in less than ten seconds. He would slide down the tower's ladder in four seconds. It would take him exactly twenty-three seconds to reach the van. The highway was thirty-six seconds beyond that.

The last man he had been trying to kill clearly hadn't seen anything, and would therefore be of dubious value as an eyewitness. Still, the idea of missing a killing irked him. What is one death compared to the many to come? Pyotr allowed himself a grin, and made like the Ford SUV. He escaped.

Jack, meanwhile, found himself in the center of a police maelstrom. Armed cops seemed to appear from everywhere, like an never-expanding dartboard with Jack as the bull's-eye. Only one weapon was pointed at him. Every officer, save one, was fanning out, looking for the shooter and securing the scene.

That one, however, marched directly at Jack, his Sig Sauer P229 automatic in one hand, and his other hand out. It was Captain Daniel Jeffreys, with an expression that combined concerned and relief.

Feeling that same relief wash over him, all Jack's fear and tension also erupted.

"What is this?" he shouted in adrenaline-fueled defiance. "Have you been following me?!"

Jeffreys stopped in midstep, and nearly laughed in disbelief. Instead he boomed back, "You're damn right we've been following you!"

Jack stepped forward and grabbed the captain by the arms. "Thanks!" he exclaimed, a little too loudly, in the cop's face. "What took you so long?!"

18

"He got away," Doc said as he appeared from around the back of the DR building. "But I might have caught a glimpse of him on video."

"Let me guess," Jeffreys said drily. "About six feet tall, slim, blondish?"

Doc raised his eyebrows as he neared the pair. "They teach mentalism at the Academy now?" He jerked the digicam up. "I might even have got his van's license plate."

"I doubt it," Jack said miserably. "These guys have a way of obscuring their plates. I learned that at Sammy's apartment."

They were sitting on the back lid of a SWAT van at the edge of the parking lot. A uniformed officer handed Jeffreys some coffees, and Jeffreys handed them over to Jack and Doc.

"Why was Schoenberg killed?" the cop wanted to know, though he was really thinking out loud. "Were the Israelis catching up with him?"

"Or maybe the United States?" Jack suggested.

"That's a little paranoid," Doc pointed out.

"Someone's tried to kill me twice in as many days," Jack retorted. "I've earned my paranoia."

A squat EMT made a disapproving face as she tried to tend the cuts and scrapes on Jack's face, neck, and shoulder. Jack shut up, raised his chin, and let her do her work.

The forensics van pulled up. Jack and Doc watched as the two technicians got out. They moved to the back and donned protective gear.

"Come back to the station to make a statement," Jeffreys said.

"Can't I make it here?" Jack asked.

The captain smirked. "Sure. Then how do you propose to get back to town?" He motioned at the bullet-ridden Ford SUV. "Come on. I'll drive you. And I promise, not a single question until we get there."

Jeffreys was as good as his word. But once they returned to the captain's office, Jack and Doc saw why. Carl Forsyth and Dover Griffith were waiting for them. Dover came right over to Jack and studied his face with concern. Seemingly unconsciously her hand raised to tenderly touch the deepest cut on his cheek. Jack winced at the pain her touch of the wound elicited.

"You should see the bull that gored me," he joked as Jeffreys closed his office door and lowered the shades on his windows.

"Who was he?" Forsyth seethed as Doc sat on the edge of Jeffrey's desk.

"Your guess is as good as Jeffreys's," Jack said as Dover took a position between her boss and her boyfriend.

"Maybe better," Doc drawled, handing the digicam to Forsyth, with the video he made while trying to catch the sniper.

Dover and Jeffreys leaned in on either side of the FBI chief and all three watched the jiggling point-of-view shot as Doc had run toward the tower. Suddenly the image shot upward, and tried to zoom in, on a moving figure in the distance.

"He slid down that ladder like a circus acrobat," Doc commented. "And he ran like a gold medal sprinter. Even if I had my six-shooter, I doubt even I could have nailed him. I certainly couldn't catch him."

The others watched as the man, his head obscured by a hoodie, disappeared behind some hedges. Moments later, they could hear a van engine. The image seemed to burst onto another parking lot and Doc's camera just caught the van as it roared out the exit.

"Can I send this to our techies?" Forsyth asked. "They should be able to clean it up."

Jack seemed reluctant.

"You'll get it back, better than you left it," Forsyth promised.

Jack nodded.

"Even if they obscured the tags," Jeffreys said, "the van may have been a rental. That could give us something."

"Yeah," Forsyth said. "We'll find the car and discover that the renter paid in cash and used a fake name, while the security camera will only show a hood, sunglasses, and maybe fake facial hair." He shrugged apologetically. "At least that's the customary MO. Still, we've got to explore every angle." Forsyth looked at Jack. "You think this guy was one of the hit squad shooters?"

"I don't think so. This guy is in a different class entirely. The Levi Plaza guys didn't have the single-purpose mind-set of experienced killers."

"Yeah," Jeffreys agreed. "I don't know a pro hit man who'd ever let themselves be hit by a trolley."

"So?" Forsyth asked. "I know you, Jack. You're thinking something."

"Only what I've been saying all along," Jack said darkly. "You've got the same information we do. How's it adding up to you?"

"Two and two is equaling five, Jack," he responded, ticking off the facts, as he saw them, on his fingers. "Yes, a Russian plane went down. But we have no conclusive intel that it's connected to this magic word your 'friend' supposedly heard. And yes, another friend of yours says that something 'biotoxic' is missing."

"They said 'biotoxic' and not 'nuclear'?"

"That was the exact word they used," Forsyth replied. "On the alert scale, that's considerably lower than 'nuclear,' since it's considered, at best, a localized danger."

"As far as anyone knows *so far*," Jack said, emphasizing the qualifier.

"Fine," Forsyth agreed. "Point is we have no idea whether that's connected, either. See the problem I'm having, Jack? Anybody can take anything that happens to anyone anywhere in the world, then play 'six degrees' with it until it comes out just as circumstantial."

"But what about what just happened?" Jack asked, pointing at his facial wounds. "Are these just circumstantial?"

"Jack," Forsyth said, "both you and Schoenberg have plenty of enemies who wouldn't need a magic word to try deep-sixing you. In your case, every Muslim and Mexican in the Bay area. And that's just to start with."

"Uh-uh, Carl. That would be just too coincidental."

"Really? That makes more sense to me than dragging in decorated U.S. Army heroes into this tenuous, highly imaginative scheme."

Jack didn't agree but he had no evidence to dispute what Forsyth had just said. He looked to the other's faces, seeing concern in his friends' expressions, and conviction in the police captain's.

"My immediate concern, here, is that Schoenberg was assassinated," Jeffreys said. "I can assure you both that we will be investigating that without prejudice to where the trail might lead. And for the record: the general description of the assassin corresponds with the description of a man who has been looking for someone who fits Anastasia Vincent's description."

Jack's eyebrows raised at that revelation.

Jeffreys continued carefully, "But I think you would have to admit that, even if this attack was connected to the previous attack, it is more likely because of something else Ms. Vincent did, something she isn't telling you, rather than some sort of international conspiracy that involves the second highest-ranking officer in the United States Special Command."

Jack had to admit that when they put it like that, it sounded like he was lost.

"So give me one good reason I shouldn't lock you up, Jack," Forsyth said.

"On what grounds, sir?" Dover demanded.

"Obstruction of a criminal investigation, for one."

"'Whoever willfully endeavors by means of bribery,'" said a voice as the door flew open. "Emphasis on the bribery. Has that occurred?"

They all looked up to see Sol Minsky standing just inside the office with an extremely embarrassed police officer behind him.

"I'm sorry, sir, he barged in—"

"No problem, officer," Jeffreys said, putting his fists on the desk and slowly rising from his seat. "Our visitor knows this place better than all of us put together." He lowered his brow and pinned Minsky with his gaze. "And he knew it long before you were born."

Sol just smiled and glanced over his shoulder. "That means you're dismissed, sonny."

The desk cop made a face and left. Sol, resplendent in a perfect suit, calmly closed the door behind him.

"To what do we owe this rare public appearance?" Jeffreys asked evenly.

"I heard my partners in—"

"Crime?" Forsyth interjected.

"Documentary production," Sol corrected affably, "were being detained. I also heard that one of our company vehicles was damaged in an illegal attack on these innocent bystanders. So I thought I'd give these men a ride." He looked cordially from Forsyth's consternated face to Jeffreys's grudgingly impressed visage. "That is, of course, if neither of you gentlemen has something better than a half-assed charge."

Doc stood. "Are we free to go, Captain?"

Jeffreys nodded without taking his eyes off Sol.

Doc's own gaze shifted. "Are we free to go, Agent Forsyth?"

There was another moment of tension, but then Forsyth's shoulders relaxed. "Get out of here," he growled. The three men started to do just that, Jack and Dover exchanging a tender look as he walked by.

19

General Thomas Brooks waited impatiently for the call from the Army Chief of Staff to come through. He'd known General Horace Ortiz since West Point, when Ortiz was a firstie and Brooks a lowly plebe. Brooks's ability as a pitcher won him a spot on the Point's junior varsity baseball team that year, which ordinarily would have accorded him a modicum of respect from upper classmen like Ortiz. But apparently Brooks had beat out a friend of Ortiz's for the position, and the future chief of staff had ridden him all the harder. All these years later, traces of that original gulf lingered in their relationship; Brooks could have earned the Medal of Honor and he would still taste vinegar in his mouth every time he had to deal with the man who had become known as "Asskisser-Ortiz."

The service chief finally came on the line. Over the years his voice had lost most of its Hispanic twang—except when he talked to people he'd known back when.

"There he is," drawled Ortiz. "How are you, Tommy-gun?"

"I'm fine, General." Brooks made a point of showing his superior exaggerated respect.

"Ready for your new . . . assignment?"

So that was what they were calling being "MacArthured" nowadays. "Yes, sir, I am."

"Good." The pause that followed told Brooks that playtime was over. "I understand you gave a speech at Livermore last night."

"Yes, General. Part of my farewell tour."

"Huh," Ortiz grunted. "I'm told it was quite . . . provocative."

"It's nothing I haven't said before."

"Well, that's just it, 'Bomb-em Brooks.' You don't have a cotton mouth, like me. Yours gets you in trouble time and time again."

Brooks remembered one of those times in particular, when mouthing off to a certain firstie had earned him a good thrashing—for which he, Brooks, was then punished with a boatload of demerits and several hours of "walking the area"—essentially going back and forth with a rifle on his shoulder. Of course, somehow his punishment didn't interfere with his pitching schedule—a good thing for the Black Knights, as it came during his string of twenty-two innings of no-hit baseball.

"Frankly, General, you don't do yourself any favors by implying that America should go to war with Islam."

"I'm not in this to help myself and I'm not 'implying' anything," Brooks corrected. "The West is already at war with Islam. We've been under attack since the Beirut bombing during the Reagan administration, and you know it. Islam won't be satisfied until we're wiped out. There's an epic war going on in the Middle East right now. Egypt, Syria, Iraq—the radicals are marching. The problem is, most of the West has closed its eyes. And our leaders—"

"Damit!" Ortiz interrupted. "Now I know why you didn't get CENTCOM. Look, I don't care what you say in private. But you keep Tommy-gunning your mouth off in public while you still have those stars next to those huge chips on your shoulders, and you'll find out what the Chairman can do. Think we can't do worse than put you out to pasture? Think again. In short, Thom, this is coming from the commander-in-chief. Shut. Your. Big. Mouth. That's a direct order. Do you understand?"

Brooks thought of many things he wanted to say. But what he

did say was, "Yes, sir." Ortiz sighed, and took a more conciliatory tone now that the message had been delivered.

"Look, Tommy-gun, be reasonable. Keep your trap shut for the next week. Just one week. Then, once we shift you out of the army, you can say whatever you'd like and the public will be free to label you a lunatic crank on their own."

"Are we done here, General?"

"We're done here, General," Ortiz replied. "I have more important things to do than explain to everybody that one of my senior officers is trying to start World War III."

On that, Ortiz hung up. General Thomas Brooks looked at the phone and spoke quietly but distinctly.

"I'm not trying," he stated. "I'm doing it."

20

Montgomery Morton typed furiously on his smartphone, trying to get the message finished before the general came out of the office. They were going to be tight on time getting to the airport. There was too much going on, all of it bad: Pyotr, the last pieces of the device, a sick technician in Saudi Arabia—to say nothing of regular army business related to the turnover of commands.

On top of it he was trying to contain the damage he had caused from overreacting to the escort overhearing the wrong thing. His old G-2 friends, the ones who were ready, willing, and able to help him out, were back at their units, scattered all over the country. The wounded one's story about a car accident had been accepted. Morton was certain that none of them would ever betray him. All of them would rather forget the whole stinking SNAFU.

He rubbed his eyes and tried to switch mental gears. Brooks was full of last-minute questions about everything; the latest was on the aircraft. And there were payments due. Or missing— Morton couldn't keep everything straight. He was suspicious that the Russian mercenaries Brooks had hired had tried to double-deal with someone; there were communications on the website system they'd set up that he couldn't account for. But for some reason, Brooks didn't want to hear it. He trusted them, and their leader Pyotr Ansky, more than the people who'd been with the conspiracy since the beginning. Even more than he trusted Morton, it seemed.

Well, he deserved that, Morton supposed. If an underling had behaved the way he had, Morton might've done the same as Brooks. But it was best to stop dwelling on it. *That fiasco is over.* He concentrated instead on the fact that the Russians had been hired to deliver the material, which had been stolen and placed on the plane by two hand-picked former Special Forces members. He thought Pyotr's involvement was to end there. But it seems he was too talented to let go.

To top it all off, Morton's wife was almost as bad as the general when it came to his promised presence at his son's sixth birthday party. He wanted to go very badly, but didn't she understand it really wasn't up to him? Morton felt the beginnings of another headache coming on. He pulled the small case with his medicine from his pocket and quickly popped out another pill. He was about to shove it in his mouth when his peripheral vision caught a bulletin on his computer's 24/7 newsfeed alert.

"German Industrialist Killed in SF Attack," it read. All thoughts of the pill were gone. Morton leaned over and read on furiously. "Helmut Schoenberg, the CEO of German conglomerate Der Warheit Unternehmen was shot to death this morning in a bold attack outside a building belonging to one of his companies in Oakland, California. Police have questioned at least one eyewitness, identified as former cable television host Jack Hatfield."

Hatfield? Again? he raged inside.

"The murder occurred at approximately seven A.M., when Schoenberg was apparently inspecting a building owned by DR Inc., a subsidiary of the German conglomerate. The building has been vacant for approximately three months, following consolidation of their manufacturing operations overseas and the relocation of the business offices."

"Can I get you a glass of water?"

Morton jerked in his chair, his head snapping up at the sound of the quiet, lightly accented, voice. "What?"

"For your pill," said Peter Andrews solicitously, back in his handsome pinstriped blue serge suit. "Headache?"

Morton looked at the small white orb in his hand like it was an alien from outer space. "Uh, no, I mean yes, it is a pill, but no, you don't have to get me any water."

"Very well. I am here with the car to take the general to the airport."

"Oh. Great. I'll let him know."

"Thank you." Pyotr walked calmly away, but stopped just inside the office door. "Hope your headache goes away."

"Me, too," said Morton. Then, a moment later, Morton's headache went back to the general's car, and he finally got to take the pill. Even before he swallowed it, he felt better. If Brooks didn't harangue him further, all would go according to schedule, and he might, just might, be able to make it to his son's birthday party as well.

21

As they drove back toward Jack's secret apartment in Sol's newest car, a factory armored BMW—"This baby gives new meaning to 'auto erotic,'" Doc said admiringly—Jack filled the mobster in on the latest developments while Doc added his own detailed observations and insight.

"Do you think the Mossad killed Schoenberg?" asked Jack.

"Why?" asked Sol.

"For helping the Iranians," Doc suggested. "It's something they would do."

"The Mossad wouldn't assassinate someone on American soil," Sol decided. "Too risky."

Jack shook his head. "Two years ago, I would've agreed with you. But now is the idea any more outlandish than the Chinese trying to use San Francisco to poison the country, or turn the Golden Gate Bridge into ground zero for a dirty bomb?"

"Hmmph." Sol pressed his lips together.

"It's possible," said Jack.

"Of course it's possible," Sol complained. "Anything is possible."

"There's possible and there's probable. The Mossad killing someone they consider a traitor: that's possible. Radical Muslims trying to destroy this country: that's reality. See the difference? So, can you find out what is possible?" Jack pressed.

"Maybe."

The answer satisfied Jack more than a quick yes or no: it was honest, a word Jack never thought he'd apply to a gangster.

"What's your beef with the Mossad?" Sol inquired.

"How much did you hear before your dramatic entrance in the police station?" Jack asked.

"I thought I heard plenty, but now I'm beginning to doubt it," Sol admitted. "What did I miss?"

Doc cut to the chase. "The authorities are putting all their eggs in Ana's basket," he said.

"They're buying that she heard what she says she heard?" Sol asked.

Jack nodded. "So the question is, besides your instincts, how much can we really trust what she says?"

Sol chuckled. "You don't have to trust anything she says, Jack. That's not the point."

Jack tried to get it and failed. "What is the point, then?"

"You know a man or woman by the quality of their enemies, right?"

"So it's been said."

"Well, look who attacked her. In all my years working the underbelly, I've never seen an angry pimp or vengeful drug dealer marshal a team like that, or go after a German industrialist for that matter. Drug lords do it, but Ana would've told us if she were in with that crowd. Just thinking about them scares the words out of your mouth. It's a special kind of fear in their eyes because they all know what these guys do to people."

Jack nodded at the sense Sol was making, and was just beginning to find the right track again when his smartphone buzzed. He was expecting the call, so he answered immediately.

"Hey," he said softly.

"Can't talk long," Dover said, equally as softly but even more quickly. "The weapon that was used to kill Schoenberg was a high-powered sniper rifle. It's very expensive and rare, and the State Police and Bureau have already begun helping to check for recent sales. It uses a bullet that's a little larger than your normal hunting rifle and that is even rarer. They may be able to identify the actual gun model. My weapons expert has two candidates, but there may be more."

Jack nodded. Long rifles did not require a permit in California, but the gun that had been used could only have been bought in a few dozen places in the state. That gave them some hope that they might be able to identify the buyer. Dover quickly informed him that they were going over Doc's video as well as looking for other surveillance camera footage.

"You won't find any," Jack told her with certainty. "Whoever this guy is, he's better than the Levi Plaza gang."

"I agree, but we have to try."

Jack totally understood. "Are they really attributing all this to Anastasia's secrets?"

"I doubt it," Dover assured him. "Not by the way they acted after you left. These are very dangerous waters. I think they were trying to lull you into their confidence so they can keep you close."

"Bastards," Jack grumbled.

"Only sometimes, Jack." She paused. Jack imagined that someone was trying to get her attention. "Gotta go," she said, and then the connection was gone.

Anxious to get back to his workstation, he looked up to see where they were.

"Hey!" Jack complained as they pulled up to the safe house. "What are we doing here?"

Sol looked at him knowingly as he turned off the purring engine. The locals didn't think twice about the luxury car. Many luxury cars came to the neighborhood to visit their wayward children in the halfway house. "You wanted to know if the Mossad was involved in this."

"Yeah. And?"

Sol motioned for Jack and Doc to follow him. He led them into the public part of the halfway house rather than upstairs. He moved through the cafeteria to the far side of the counseling room. There they saw Ritu working with a young resident along with the safe house's manager, a ruddy, young, tall, brown-haired man.

Jack thought he saw the hands of the Indian escort and the manager touch, but he couldn't be sure. The man stood swiftly, almost as if coming to attention, at the sight of the halfway house's benefactor. Jack did notice Ritu smile before returning her attention to the resident.

"Boaz," Sol said to the man. "Could we see you for a moment?"

"Of course, Mr. Minsky," he said in a low, slightly accented tone.

He motioned toward a plain door in the corner. They followed him there, but Jack noticed a smile was growing on Doc's face.

"What?" he asked his experienced old friend.

"Wait for it," Doc replied, further noticing that the door looked wooden, but was actually metal.

The manager brought them into a plain room that reminded Jack of the police station's interrogation room, except that it had a fridge, coffee machine, and simple computer table.

"Please, gentlemen," the manager said, motioning toward the plain chairs around the plain table. Then, with a flick of the bolt, they were sealed in.

"Gents," Sol said as he sat, "May I introduce Boaz Simonson. Boaz, this is Jack Hatfield and Doc Matson."

"Good to finally meet you both," Boaz said, shaking each man's hand.

"Israeli, right?" Doc said as the two men shook, not bothering to check each other's strength.

Boaz nodded, grinning. "If the name doesn't peg me, the accent does."

"Hey, should we be talking like this in here?" Jack wondered, crooking his head toward the seemingly thin walls separating them from the recovering alcoholics, addicts, and prostitutes.

Boaz's smile widened. "You are now in one of the most secure places in the city, Mr. Hatfield. This building was basically built around this room. And this room took us years to secure, design, and build."

"Not to mention hundreds of thousands of dollars," Sol added.

Doc, his own smile widening, crossed his arms and sat on the table edge. "I'm guessing the money did not just go into soundproofing."

Sol winked. "Boaz, was the Mossad involved in the assassination of Schoenberg?"

Boaz shook his head. "Absolutely not."

"How would you know?" Jack asked dubiously.

Boaz looked to Sol. Sol looked at Jack. "Because Boaz is this region's central Mossad sleeper agent." Sol motioned sweepingly. "My entire staff is comprised of them."

Jack shook his head. "Sol, don't tell me—"

"Jack," said the alleged mob boss, "you are the first people outside of my organization I've ever said this to. This facility is not a front for my crime activities. My crime activities are a front for these people."

22

Doc acted as if he suspected it all along while Jack's face was infused with growing understanding.

"Genius," Doc drawled. "You needed a position where you could seed sleeper agents all over the world, but also a base where both the underworld and Feds would be watching your criminal activities so closely they'd miss the real operations."

"Hide in plain sight," Jack said.

Sol nodded. "We needed a Mossad presence here, especially after the events you were involved with over the last few years, so I moved my headquarters from the East to the West Coast—to find my reputation had preceded me. The move started bearing almost immediate fruit." He nodded at Jack, and then turned back to Boaz.

"The assassination of Schoenberg was not done by us," his top agent repeated.

"CIA?" Jack asked.

"Definitely not."

"No possibility?"

"Never say never, but we found no hint of it. And we're very good at finding hints."

"Who would kill him then?" Jack asked.

"Someone who didn't want him talking about the very special switches he 'sold' and shipped to Saudi Arabia."

"You stressed 'sold,'" Doc pointed out.

"The cost was so nominal as to be ridiculous," Sol explained.

"Further," Boaz added, "we found no evidence of even the bargain basement price having actually been paid."

"Meanwhile, we now know that what was most likely a biological agent was stolen from a Russian depository a few weeks ago," Jack said. "I'm guessing that the Russians had tracked it to an airliner that crashed in the Caspian Sea. They must have planted an agent on board to bring it down and reclaim the contraband."

"They didn't," Boaz corrected.

"Then who?" Jack challenged.

Boaz considered the question but said nothing.

"He doesn't answer unless he's sure," Sol said. "Or unless I don't want him to."

"Which is it now?" Jack asked Sol.

"I've got no secrets from my partners," Sol replied.

"So the toxin is still out there somewhere and no one is entirely sure who's got it," Jack said. "I thought Iran might be involved, but they are focused on uranium. So it wasn't a CIA operation, and neither the Mossad nor another Western intelligence was involved. That leaves the Muslims or the Russian mafia."

Boaz frowned philosophically. "Why not both?"

Doc lowered, and shook, his head. "I've worked with the Russian mob on just this sort of thing for years," he admitted. "They abhor the idea. None of them want anything to ruin their 'fun,' especially something that can wipe a city off the map. They bring me in to help prevent that kind of thing, not cause it."

"So," Jack concluded. "Al Qaeda? Those guys can't blow their noses anymore without us knowing it."

"I'm not sold on the Middle East being involved at all," Doc said.

"Why not? You know as well as I do that they'd love nothing better than to get another crack at killing thousands like they tried here two years back," Jack said.

"Saudi Arabia basically funded Pakistan's bomb. We looked the other way for a lot of reasons. The Saudis were allies, they weren't crazy about India being the only nuclear power in the region, and we needed Saudi oil. More importantly, the princes had an understanding that, if things got tough in the Middle East, they would borrow a few nukes from the Pakistanis to keep everyone honest. That lend-lease hasn't happened so obviously Riyadh isn't losing any sleep about the missing material."

"Not yet," Jack said. "Privately, they may be as concerned as we are. We don't know what's in motion there . . . or what they may know."

Sol and Boaz shared a look. "I think we may know someone we can ask."

Sol motioned for the others to join him behind Boaz, whose fingers were already flying over the computer keyboard. Like the room itself, the computer was deceptively simple-looking. But by the way it responded to Boaz's prodding, it was exceptionally powerful. The screen quickly filled with a face and a name. "Riad al-Saud."

"Member of the House of Saud, a small clan that runs Saudi Arabia," Boaz informed them. "He's the nephew of Prince Tirki al-Faisal, the ambassador to the United States and the country's spy chief, who publicly said in 2011 that Saudi Arabia would do more than borrow Pakistani weapons if Iran exploded its bomb. They'd make their own."

"And it wasn't an idle threat," Sol continued. "Interstrat, a website that tracks international relations, had published an article six months before ticking off a number of steps the country had already taken, including establishing bunkers and underground development areas. There was even the skeleton of an organization, known to Western analysts as the 'bomb committee.'"

"Riad al-Saud was a member of that committee," Boaz went on. "As the only one with family connections to the country's rulers—he had the right to be called prince—it was logical to conclude that he was the one in charge. He was also a government minister, whose portfolio included the ministry of minerals and resources, giving him ready access to funding and considerable power."

"Saudi Arabia with oil and nukes," Jack said. "Remember when we thought the Cold War was scary?"

"The spawning ground of Osama bin Laden armed with cash, weapons, influence, and idealogues," Boaz agreed. "And the United States dares to call Israel paranoid?"

"The problem we've had until now," Sol interceded, "was not who to ask or what to ask, but how to ask. As you can imagine, al-Saud wouldn't be interested in talking to me or the Mossad."

The light dawned on Jack's face. "My documentary."

"Exactly," Sol smiled. "The Saudis have a vested interest in assuring America that we have nothing to fear from them. They at least have to pretend to be an ally."

But the light faded quickly. "I don't know," Jack said. "Wouldn't my reputation for mistrusting Muslims proceed me?"

"Mistrusting?" Doc sniffed. "You issued a call to arms that got you thrown off TV!"

"All the better," Sol assured him. "To convince the great American devil of their sincerity would be a coup indeed."

"But what about General Montgomery and his cronies?" Jack asked. "How are they involved, and, maybe more importantly, why?"

"Oh," Doc said, elbowing Jack. "So now we're putting all our chips on our hooker again?"

"I believe whole-heartedly in the bullets that were shot at her, and me," Jack stressed.

By the time he looked back at the computer screen, Boaz had hacked Morton's office PC.

"How did you do that?" Jack marveled.

"No miracle," Boaz said humbly. "The day-to-day office computers are far less fire-walled than the interoffice communication devices."

Sol shook his head at his agent's false modesty. "We're hacked in now, and it only took us two weeks to get this far."

"Mr. Minsky," Boaz interrupted. "Look. We've got something new."

They all stared at what Morton had typed in before the end of the workday. It was General Thomas Brooks's "farewell tour" schedule.

"Well, that explains that," Jack said, his eyes on the glowing screen.

"What explains what?" Doc asked.

"General Thomas Brooks is due to leave his command in a few weeks. Maybe that's why he's been so willing to speak his mind."

Doc shook his head, his glower darkening. "No, Jack, that's not how it works. A retiring general protects his pension. The only sort of military man who acts the way Brooks did is one with nothing to lose."

Jack was struck by the gravity of his veteran military friend's words and was only distracted when Sol spoke.

"Look at Brooks's venues, Jack."

Jack looked. The general was going to the Dome of the Rock in Jerusalem, Israel, and then the city of Hejaz, in the capital of Makkah Province, in Saudi Arabia. "Mecca," he breathed.

Their realizations were like an elaborate domino maze clicking into place. All the disparate pieces came together in a nearly unbelievable whole.

"Jack," Doc asked slowly. "If you were Brooks, and you had a bomb, what would you do with it?"

It took a moment for his words to sink in. Then each of them, in turn, took the next step.

"Crap," Jack blurted. "Let's get Ana. She may have ladies who are on the tour route. Maybe they can help."

The four men barreled from the safe house panic room with Jack thinking that there was no way he would be able to convince any of his FBI or CIA contacts of what had occurred to all of them. Not in the short time before Brooks arrived in Mecca. Even he still didn't want to believe it, though it all now made perfect, albeit insane, sense. Still, they had to try.

Ritu looked up and her expression changed from kindness to worry at the sight of Boaz's grim visage. He came over to assure her everything was all right as Jack, Sol, and Doc headed for the stairs.

They all but burst into the loft apartment, only to find it empty.

"Ana?" Jack called. "Sammy?"

Sol was about to call their caretaker Ric when the man appeared in the door of the bathroom, soaking wet, a towel around his waist.

"Where are Anastasia and Jack's half brother?" Sol asked his assistant.

Ric looked around the room, blinking, as if expecting to see them there.

"Don't tell me they're gone!"

"I don't know, Mr. Minsky. We were doing research on the computer, then I took a break—"

Sol started, before shouting, "A break? We don't take breaks here!"

"Sorry, sir."

"Did you lose the Asian girl, too?" Sol yelled. "This isn't Hebrew school where you push and shove and knock a yamulka off the other kid's head! These bastards play to kill."

But then Miwa was there, also soaking wet, standing sheepishly behind Ric.

Sol looked from one to the other. "Screwing? On my dime?"

Jack was in no mood to reprimand. He just had to know that the others were okay. "Miwa, do you know where Ana is?"

"They were there just a minute ago," she maintained, gripping Ric's shoulders. "I swear."

"What kind of research were you doing?" Jack asked Ric.

"The generals. We found a way into a computer. Got information about their private lives. Sammy said something about a function this afternoon."

Jack looked from one face to the other, as each tried to figure out what had happened. Jack felt like his head might explode. "Ric, show me the computer they were working on. And I better find out he was looking to buy a clown nose with a gas filter built-in!"

23

Montgomery Morton slid his cell phone into his pocket as he got out of his car. Shoulders hunched, he continued across the lawn to his front door, moving as swiftly as he could without running. The sun was hurting his eyes, and he could taste metal in his mouth—sure signs of an impending migraine.

He had no time for that now. The general would accept no excuse for not accomplishing his orders. There'd be no relief afterward, either—Morton had a long daily list of things that needed to be done. The private contractor he was using in San Francisco to transport items had asked too many questions, for starters.

It all came back to the decision to relieve the general of his position three months earlier than originally scheduled. It had forced them all to scramble—a mad rush after years of methodical planning. And now he wants to go to Israel and Riyadh for the show? Why not just drive a tank personally into the Kaaba and be done with it?

Because Brooks has his own way of doing things, that's why, he reminded himself.

Morton quickened his pace to the door. He had a new bottle of Sumatriptan inside. Relief. The outside door was locked. He pushed down on the latch, confused. *Wasn't Cynthia home?*

Damn. Morton fumbled in his pockets for his keys, but when he couldn't grab them in a second, he suddenly started marching around the side of the house, the anger in his throat, and the pressure in his head, building with every step.

He was about to chew out the first person he came to, be it spouse or offspring, when he stepped around the corner into their well-manicured backyard. It was as if he had stepped into a circus. The music, which he had thought was just additional pounding in his head, leaped laughing into his ears, and the sight of streamers, balloons, and banners assailed his vision. Had it been a few years before, it might have even set off Afghan flashbacks. His son's birthday party, of course! Hadn't he been racing back to get to it in time? All his other responsibilities and worries had crowded that priority out, but now it all came back to him. Even through the pain, he felt his lips widening in a smile. Cynthia had really gone all out on the event. There was a bouncy castle, a Slip'N Slide, a big table of food, another for desserts, and another for presents. People in outfits depicting popular cartoon characters were walking around, and there were lines for places where kids could have their faces painted, caricatures of themselves drawn, and even a roving clown making balloon animals.

"Daddy, Daddy!" he heard from two different directions, and then his daughter, Brook, and the birthday boy himself, Thomas, were running at him, their arms wide. They embraced him at the same time, and Morton was nearly overwhelmed by the rush of pleasure he felt. *This is what I'm doing it all for,* he thought. *So they'd be safe. So they'd have a future to build upon.* It almost made him forget his headache. Almost.

"You made it!" Tommy, his son enthused.

"Mommy said you might not," Brook pouted.

"Well, Mommy was wrong, wasn't she?" Morton grinned, kneeling down to get on their level. "I'm here, and I'm staying here until it's all over."

His children laughed and clapped and cheered as Morton stood back up. "I'm just going into the house for one thing, and then I'll come back out with a big surprise!"

"Oh, boy!" his son cried, hoping it was a big present.

"You just wait. I'll be right back." Morton kissed his daughter on the top of her head and patted his son on the shoulder, gently pushing him out of the way so he could go inside and get the medicine he needed.

He stepped into the kitchen, relief flooding through him as the noise and music and activity was quieted behind him. He then started a quick march to the master bedroom's medicine cabinet. He just got to the living room when he nearly collided into another obstruction.

"Monty?" His wife Cynthia stood in the hall.

"Cyn!" he said, moving quickly past her. "Great party, great job, I just have to . . ."

She knew the routine. In the last year, his first stop, whenever he did make it home, was the medicine cabinet. She followed him to their bedroom. She could tell by his face and manner that this was a mean one. His pain had been growing exponentially.

"Bad?" she asked as he pulled out the container where he kept the pills.

Morton dumped four pills into his hand—twice his normal dosage, which itself was twice the prescription—and swallowed them dry. They tasted like aluminum crackers. Suppressing a gag reflex, he closed his eyes and lowered his head, praying the pills would work quickly.

Before the kids were born, his wife would have come over and rubbed his shoulders. It did nothing to relieve the pain, but it felt good nonetheless. Now she remained standing across in the doorway, just as she had for the past seven or eight months.

The pills would take a few minutes to work, but just swallowing them made Morton feel better; he knew the pressure wouldn't get any worse. The lights would go away, and after a while he'd start to feel light-headed, and a drink of bourbon—absolutely forbidden by the doctor—would make him care a lot less about how much pressure he was under.

"You're not going to lock yourself in your office, are you?" asked his wife.

"No, no," he said. "Not yet." Morton kept his head tilted toward the tub, trying to relax his muscles. What he needed was a good orgasm—after the bourbon. He doubted he'd get it with Cynthia. That, too, had declined over the year. "Just have to double-check a few things. But it can wait. I swear."

"Why don't you just tell the general you have a headache?" Cyn dared to suggest. The success of the party had emboldened her.

"Right," Morton snorted. "To a man who gives them but doesn't get them. He doesn't even know I get migraines."

"Or tell him it's your son's birthday."

"He knows," Morton sighed. "He'd just say that we're insuring that he'll have many more."

"It's not going to affect your career."

Morton almost laughed. If only that were true. He raised his head and looked at his wife. High school sweetheart, mother of his children. He loved her more than he could even describe, yet he had been unfaithful to her. He was doing all this for her, and his children, and yet he couldn't tell them what it was.

He watched as her face became concerned, and then even a little scared. "Oh, Monty, don't look at me like that."

"Like what?"

"You look so sad." She came over and embraced him. "Like our sad clown."

He felt her warmth and caring against him, and suddenly knew it was going to be all right. He was doing the right thing. Even his migraine was going away. "What sad clown?" he asked.

"You know, the sad clown and the happy clown. The happy clown does the magic tricks and the balloon animals. The sad clown gives all the kids red clown noses that honk. She honks their noses and they honk hers."

"Hers?" he echoed.

Cynthia kept hugging him but leaned back to look up at his face. "His and her clowns. He does this thing with his ears and she does this thing with her eyes. I told them I'd give him a good review. I bet the DiCarlos would really love him for Tanya's birthday. Where did you hire them?"

"Me?" he said, the migraine beginning to chime again. "I didn't hire them. Didn't you?"

Cynthia frowned, thinking. She had hired a lot of people in

the past few months, but among the caterers and the entertain-ers, she didn't remember asking for any clowns.

"Maybe the agency sent them," she started doubtfully.

"Where are they?" he suddenly snapped.

She was taken aback by his sudden change in tone. "I don't know," she said. "In the backyard with the children, I suppose."

Morton raced back there, ignoring the way he had broken his wife's embrace. When he slid open the kitchen door, the party noise and brightness and activity assailed him again, as did the migraine. He looked to where he remembered the clown doing balloon animals. He wasn't there. He looked to the bouncy cas-tle. Not there. He looked toward the food and presents table. Not there. . . .

"Daddy!" His son had come running back, jumping up and down in expectation.

"Yes, Tommy, yes," he said, absently patting the boy's head.

"Where's my big surprise?"

"Oh, soon, Tommy, really soon. I, uh, worked it out with the clown. Have you seen the clown?"

"Oh," Tommy responded, at first disappointed, but then get-ting even more excited. "The boy clown or the girl clown?"

"Either," Morton said, peering everywhere he could for a glimpse at them.

"I don't see the boy clown," Tommy frowned, then brightened. "I saw the girl clown, though!"

"Where?" Morton looked quickly down at his son. "Where do you see her?"

Tommy pointed at the house. Morton's gaze followed his arm. He was pointing at Monty's office window.

"Be right back!" Morton said, then raced for the kitchen door.

"But we're having cake soon!" he heard his son call after him.

He raced past his wife, who had to step quickly out of his way. "Monty?"

"You let them in the house?" he yelled back at her.

"What are you going on about? Just the bathroom," she main-tained. "They needed to freshen up their clown makeup and didn't want the kids to see!"

But by then he was in his office. His desk was L-shaped, with a computer at the side. The phone charger and the back-up battery were on the left side of the computer, near the back-up hard drive and small stack of flashcards. Only one thing was wrong with the picture. The back-up drive and the flashcards were gone.

When Cynthia stepped into the office doorway, her husband was briskly rooting around in his top left drawer—the one he always kept locked . . . the one the rest of the family was forbidden to touch.

"Monty, I—"

"Cyn, find the clowns for me? Right now. They're not in the backyard. You take the left side of the house, and I'll take the right."

"But—"

"It's important, Cyn," he said, walking up to her, his left arm stiff and slightly behind him. He gripped her right arm and kissed her on the forehead. "Right away, okay?"

"O-okay," she stammered, but he had already quick-marched beyond her and was out the side door by the time she had turned.

Cynthia Morton blinked a few times. She drew in a big breath, and then let it out again. She started to think about how her husband had changed over the last few years—how he was becoming more distant and increasingly ill—but then supposed she had better do as he had asked.

But before she turned, she noticed the open top drawer. Inside was a burnished wooden box that was also open. In it were red-cloth-padded sections that were also now empty. One was in the shape of a small cylinder. And the other was in the shape of a pistol.

24

General Montgomery Morton spotted the pair of clowns from the front door of his suburban house. There were so many guests that the driveway had filled up quickly, forcing many motorists to park along the street. The man clown and the woman clown looked to be heading for a minivan wedged in among the many other vehicles.

"Monty . . . ?" It was his wife, coming from around the side of the house.

"Go back to the party," he instructed tersely. "No matter what happens, keep the kids there."

"Monty?" she repeated hollowly.

But he was already running. "Do as I say!" was all he left her with.

The front lawn was large enough, the grass thick enough, and the clowns were so intent on reaching their vehicle that they didn't hear or see Morton coming.

"Don't move," he said from behind them.

The man clown did as he was told, his shoulders stiffening. But the woman was obviously not used to being caught. She turned slowly in place, her eyes wide and fearfully defiant.

Her eyes.

Morton knew instantly who she was, and by extension, who the man clown must be as well. He fought the mix of guilt and rage that splashed inside him as he glared at them from inside his pounding head.

"I believe you have something that belongs to me," Morton said, trying to keep his voice from succumbing to the rage he felt.

Finally the man turned to face him. The tag from the Fantasy Fetish Wardrobe store where they'd stopped en route was still hanging from his sleeve.

"We don't know what you're talking about," the man clown said.

The man clown took a step toward him and Morton raised the suppressed Sig Sauer MK 25, keeping it close to his stomach and shifting his body so it would still stay out of sight of the house and any snoopy neighbors.

"Stay there," Morton commanded. "And you know exactly what I'm talking about, dammit. Return it and you might still walk away."

"You wouldn't kill us here," the man clown guessed, his lower jaw stiffening.

"Do as I said or you'll be dead in a second. The police would find you on my property *with* my property," Morton went on. "I wouldn't even be arrested."

Sammy and Ana both hesitated.

Morton held out his free hand. "Give me the drives."

The woman clown took a step forward but her partner put his arm out to stop her.

"Not gonna happen," Sammy said. "Your move. The cops might let you off but what about your boss or your partners."

"Worse for me if I let you go," Morton assured them. "Last chance."

Ana clung to Sammy, her frizzy-wigged head bizarrely buried against his puffy, striped shoulder, as a silent Ford C-Max Hybrid came to a stop parallel to them.

"Or what?" came a voice from the passenger window of a dark, 190 horsepower sedan parked by the curb just yards away.

Morton immediately lowered his gun out of sight and stepped back, his eyes widening at the voice who had just interrupted. He couldn't see the speaker through the open window. Then the man leaned out.

"You again!"

"Or what, General Morton?" Jack Hatfield repeated from the window, holding nothing more dangerous than a digicam. "Let the world know what you're planning!"

How did he get here? Oh, course, he's this clown's half brother! Was it all a trap?

"These people are thieves," Morton declared, as the driver's side door opened and a stocky, yet aristocratic, man in a fine suit emerged.

"So call the cops," the man suggested casually, as a taller, lankier, slimmer man emerged from the sedan's rear seat and took the first man's place behind the wheel. At just one quick glance, Morton thought the second man might've been Dirty Harry.

By then Jack Hatfield had also come out of the car and the two were approaching him slowly as he, most obviously, was not calling the cops.

"General Morton," Jack said calmly. He motioned toward Ana. "You tried to have this woman killed after she overheard you planning 'Firebird,' didn't you?"

Morton was shaken. But he was not so shaken as to utter anything even stupider than what he had already said.

So maybe Hatfield does know, he thought. But if he did, why weren't the military police, the CIA, and secret service crawling all over him? It came to Morton in a flash, and not a flash drive, either. *They have no proof. This is a fishing expedition.*

"Turn off your camera," the general ordered. He waited. Jack didn't even look at any of the others before he did what Morton asked. "You won't find anything on what they stole," the general insisted.

Sol Minsky and Hatfield shared a look. "Maybe we will, maybe we won't," the aristocratic man commented blithely. "But now, on the occasion of your son's sixth birthday party, why don't you grow up. Just come with us and confess to the proper authorities?"

"Aren't you the 'proper authorities'?" Morton said sarcastically, starting to feel out the upper ground.

"You knew we weren't when we drove up without the cavalry," Sol said drily. "We're just a few sane people trying to prevent World War III. Why don't you join us?"

Morton looked from one to the other of them. They all looked back at him with different degrees of imploring. But then he remembered everything that had been said and done by the conspirators during the last few years. He, too, then lowered his head.

"No," said General Morton. "It must be done." He looked up beseechingly at Jack. "You, of all people, know this must be done."

"Not like this," Jack responded. "Not with us taking first blood."

"That's not what you've said in the past!' Morton accused him. "Why must thousands of us die first before we take action? Why can't we take action—action that must be taken—after thousands of them die? Why is it always our blood?"

"Fitting you should use that word," Jack said. "Blood. That's where you're hitting them, isn't it?"

The other man was silent.

"What is it? Smallpox? Ebola? Anthrax?"

"Does it matter?" Morton replied. "All that matters is an end to the madness of jihad. You can't disagree with that. You said so on television!"

"My question was about justice. It was about self-defense," Jack defended himself. "It was about heroism."

"And what is this?" the general asked.

"What you're doing is what *they* would do, what those sick Jihadists belonging to ISIS want to do."

"For the right reasons, though. That's a big difference, wouldn't you say?"

"No, General. Anything that would align our tactics with their tactics merits a big, fat second look." He put his hand on Morton's shoulder. "General, you know this is wrong. You know bringing down that passenger plane was wrong. You know trying to kill us was wrong. For God's sake, stop this now before it's too late."

Morton looked at Jack, then looked away. He didn't answer, which was his answer. Finally he all but whispered, "Get off my property."

The four other people on the sidewalk looked at each other, and then, as if in a funeral march, moved toward the minivan.

Jack was the last one to enter. He looked back at General Morton, took out one of his business cards, and tossed it on the front lawn. It looked very small, and Morton looked very alone, in front of his house.

"Tell your commanding officer I'd like an interview," Jack said. "Anywhere, anytime."

That, of all things, brought a small, irony-filled, smile to Morton's lips. "You know what's funny? He'd like that," the man said softly. "He wanted that."

Jack nodded. "Good. And, sir?" He waited until Morton met his eyes. "Another rhetorical question. What if you do this and we lose? What would the world look like then? Think about that, okay?"

"I will," said Morton stiffly. Then under his breath, he added, "I have."

"Good," Jack repeated. "Call me anytime, from anywhere, but make it soon. I'd rather settle this than go public with the data and this video." He nodded toward the man's house. "There are other lives to consider."

Morton said nothing, waiting until the minivan, and then the silent hybrid sedan, pulled away, and disappeared around the corner. He stood there for a few moments more, then wearily retrieved the business card and trudged back to his house.

As he entered the foyer, he could hear, and partially see out the windows, that the birthday party was still in full swing. It made an incongruous dichotomy with what had just happened. Morton sighed and went to his office to return the gun to its place in the "forbidden" desk drawer.

He placed the silencer back in its red velvet place, but paused with the gun in his hand. He looked at the powerful automatic, the favorite of SEAL teams everywhere, and thought about the good it had done all over the world. He thought about all the heroes who held it and used it to accomplish honorable goals. He heard the pleading of all the evil people it had vanquished.

And then, mixing in with the begging, he heard the voices of the people on that Russian passenger plane they had brought down, growing louder and more pitiful, until it drowned out all the rest. Morton looked at the gun as if hypnotized.

Hadn't there been a rumor that the commander-in-chief had known of the December 7, 1941 attack of Pearl Harbor, but had let it happen so the entire country would support our entering World War II? In that case, weren't those heroes who died in the attack the same as the plane passengers?

No. Even if the rumors were true, the commander-in-chief simply didn't relay the information to Pearl Harbor authorities. They didn't plan, or hire someone to carry out, the attack.

The cries grew louder in Morton's head as he brought the gun up, rather than place it down in its case. He found his mouth opening and his eyes closing. He felt the bite of the muzzle against the top of his mouth's palette. The screams of the dying filled his head until he thought he'd hear nothing ever again.

"Daddy!"

Morton's eyes snapped opened.

"Where's daddy?" he heard from outside. "He said he was going to give me a big surprise, like, hours ago!"

Morton blinked, the gun jerking from his mouth. His lips twisted into a shocked grin, and a voice deep inside his head, over the now silent screams, said, "Yeah, this would have been quite a big surprise for your son, wouldn't it?"

Morton snapped the gun back into its box and slapped the lid shut with the finality of a coffin. He had done this, all of it, for them, his children. To give them a better world upon which to build. Suddenly he saw it all clearly. It would all be over in just a few days. A matter of a few dozen hours, really. It was too far along to stop.

Let the clowns and their friends try, he thought. One way or another, Morton had done his job. He had done what he thought right. He had done it for his family, and that, at the end of the day, or at the end of the world, was always what he would do.

General Montgomery Morton closed and locked his desk drawer, then went out to hug his children. The setting up of an interview, desired by both sides, between Brooks and Hatfield, could wait until after the party.

25

"Kinky," Doc said when he noticed the tag on Sammy's sleeve.

"How did you find us?" Sammy asked breathlessly.

Jack tried not to come down hard on his brother's foolhardiness. Not now. "Sammy, you knew that the safe house had cameras all over the place. Also, you didn't erase your cache. We looked where you looked."

"And strike three," Sol explained from the driver's seat. "All my vehicles have tracking devices that only we can follow."

"Wow," Sammy said. "You're harder to trip up than the FBI."

Neither Jack, Doc, or Sol told him why.

"I'm gonna kill Ric for this," was all Sol said.

No one was sure whether he meant it literally or figuratively.

"Did you tell Miwa to come onto the poor guy?" Jack asked Ana, in case it was the former.

"No!" Ana insisted. "She already liked him. She likes nerdy types. She did it on her own." She looked at Sammy. "We didn't even think about crashing the party until after they both went to shower."

"Did you even have a plan?" Jack pointedly asked.

"Of course I had a plan!" Sammy answered resentfully. "When we saw on Mrs. Morton's social media page that she was having a big birthday party for her son, I realized that nobody would question a party clown. It was too good to pass up. By the time I realized that, the party was just about to start. I knew that if we waited and went through the chain of command, we'd miss it."

"So you just took off on impulse," Jack countered.

"Yeah," Sammy said proudly. "I suppose you've never gone by your gut?"

"Sure, when there was just me at risk," he said with a telling glance at Ana.

"That was my choice," she insisted.

"Boys, boys . . . girl," Doc said from the backseat. "You can have your pissing contest later. We got bigger fish to fry right now. And data to analyze? Data Sammy and Ana got for us?"

Jack mentally kicked himself. "Right. Sorry, Sammy," he quickly apologized. "These guys could tell you, I was so worried when I found out you were missing."

"That's true," Doc said.

Sammy's face shifted from defensiveness to surprise. "Yeah, all right. I'm sorry, too, Jack. It's just that I thought, carpe diem and all that."

"And *vestis facit virum*," Doc winked.

Ana laughed. The others gazed blankly.

"Clothes make the man," she chuckled, rocking her thumb between her getup and Sammy's.

Everyone smiled at the tension breaker, after which Jack asked to see what they recovered. Ana may have actually blushed, but it was impossible to tell with the clown makeup. Still, she shoved one arm down her pants, rooted around, and her fingers emerged with both a wallet-size, armored, orange, black, and silver hard drive as well as two small flash drives.

She held out all three to Jack, but he waved them toward Doc. "I wouldn't know what to do with them."

Ana gave them to Doc, who winked at her disguised face.

"So, from the beginning," Jack said to them. "Tell me."

"I—*we* thought we might be able to find out what Firebird was, exactly," Sammy said. "So I came up with the party clown gambit. No way I was going back to my place—"

"Smart move," Sol said.

Sammy beamed.

"So we went to a place I know on Haight," Ana said, "one that caters to the fetish market."

"I know the place," Sol commented. "Fairly close by. One of my mob buddies owns it."

"There are clown fetishists?" Doc asked.

"There are all kinds of men with all kinds of interests," Ana said. "We cobbled these together from several costumes, actually."

"Anyway, we put on the makeup, suited up, and still got to the party in plenty of time," Sammy said.

"I snuck in while Sammy performed," Ana told them.

The tale she told—Anastasia breaking into the house while Sammy did his clown act—was inspired, completely irresponsible, and criminal, all in one big bite.

It was also vintage Sammy. Jack could cite a dozen different episodes from childhood where Sammy had gone off with some older kid to pull some prank. He hadn't been a bad kid, but at times he seemed to have exactly zero judgment. When he had a nutty or ambitious goal in mind, he was a car without brakes.

"Hopefully, it will have been worth it," Sammy said. "Maybe one of these things'll tell us what Firebird really is."

"Morton said it wouldn't," Jack reminded them.

"But he has no good reason to tell the truth at the moment, either," Sol added.

Sammy had frowned at his half brother, but brightened when Sol spoke. He lunged forward like an eager-to-please sheepdog so he could better engage the mobster.

"So why don't you send a bunch of your guys in there and beat a confession out of old Monty?" When no one replied for a moment, Sammy sat back defensively. "I mean, you do that all the time, don't you?"

Jack gave Sol a look, which said, "If you want to tell him everything, that's up to you."

"Yes," Sol said evenly, "when one of our own betrays us, we'll have a friendly little 'talk.' But it would be a different story to confront a highly ranked, decorated member of the U.S. military that way, especially on American soil."

"Oh," said Sammy. "Yeah, right. Of course."

Jack exhaled through his nostrils, trying to think of something to say that wouldn't kick-start his half brother's defense mechanisms, when Sol put them all in their place.

"And, on that note, I think we should table this discussion until we arrive back at a location where it is totally safe to speak of such matters."

"Wouldn't you know if your car was bugged?" Sammy asked. "Aren't there safeguards?"

"You brought several items with you that haven't been vetted," he pointed out.

Sammy shrunk back like that same sheepdog who had just had his nose whacked with a rolled up newspaper.

"Speaking of my security arrangements," Sol concluded for the moment, "I would like to inform both of you that if you even so much as think about doing anything as bold or cavalier or reckless as this again—take your pick—your safe house will instantly become a dungeon. And I can assure you, we are very good at dungeons."

The two clowns looked at him, one big red mouth smiling incongruously, the other frowning as it should have been.

"What you don't know," Sol said, "is whether there are eyes on the general's house. Maybe he has private security. Maybe the FBI or the CIA or the SFPD has drawn the same conclusions we have and are watching him. Maybe they decided to tail us. And you're not exactly inconspicuous, even with smoked windows."

"I thought that's why you took the circuitous route you're taking," Doc said. "Stopping at lights, racing through others, going up and down hills so you can check the rearview mirror."

"Exactly," Sol said. "They were as underprepared as our team on this one." He looked at Sammy and Ana in that mirror. "Do we understand one another?"

"Yes, sir," Sammy said, his Marine training taking over.

"Understood," Ana agreed.

And then they all fell somberly quiet until they were back at the safe house again. The clowns' darkened moods were broken by the delighted reaction of Miwa and Ritu, who excitedly laughed and talked and made fun of the makeup and outfits.

"Oh, you should get out of those things!" Ritu chided. "You will attract attention."

"So we've been told," Ana replied.

"Yes," said Miwa. "You should take a shower. The shower is very nice!"

She looked over at Ric knowingly, but Ric only looked at Sol with a combination of apology and a willingness to take any reprimand required. When the Asian girl saw the look Ric and Sol shared, she quickly added, "I will help, Ana, if you need me somewhere else."

As the girls and a slumping Sammy retired, Sol glared at his assistant. "I don't have to say anything, do I?"

"No, sir," Ric replied with conviction. "You don't."

"Good, then come on." He motioned for Jack and Doc to follow him as well. As they all neared the secure room, Boaz broke off from what he was doing and joined them. Once they were all inside and Sol had locked the door, he turned, his expression grave.

"We have a phrase in Israel. '*Ziyun moach*,'" he told them, moving to the coffee machine. "That's what we're in now, so you can imagine what it means."

"You were wise to point all the pitfalls out to Sammy," Jack said to Sol. "Sorry, and thanks."

"It's okay," Sol said. "Actually, it was a decent gamble, kind of ballsy. And I'm sure we weren't followed. Anyone who saw what went down would be way more interested in the general than in us."

"I've been thinking," Doc said. "What *about* Sammy's idea? Interrogating the general, I mean."

Sol shook his head. "It's one thing to interrogate one of our hostile neighbors, it's another to question an American. Even though we know what we know, and worse, fear what we fear, the Mossad cannot risk jeopardizing Israel's relationship with the American government no matter how correct we turn out to be. I may even have been taking too great a risk just talking with Morton in public. If anyone was to ever find out who I'm actually loyal to. . . ." His voice trailed off.

Doc and Jack shared a glance. "You feel like reaching out and touching someone?" Jack asked his old friend.

"I was just thinking that," Jack said. "We don't have the same restrictions as these guys."

Doc leaned back in a chair and put his cowboy-booted feet up on the table. "Brother, I don't have *any* restrictions."

Jack asked Doc to give Boaz the items Sammy had retrieved. He handed them over.

"Why don't you and Ric get everything on those drives?" Jack asked. "And I mean everything. I don't care if the encryptions have encryptions, I want to know everything possible as soon as possible."

It only took a glance from Sol before the two men were heading upstairs. Jack then turned his attention to the others. "If Riad al-Saud and Thomas Brooks are in the Middle East, it looks like we'll have to corner the tigers in their lairs."

Doc shook his head with mock regret. "Too bad we couldn't just plug the guy and have done with it."

Minsky yelled, "No. You don't just crush someone with a steamroller. I worked in Vegas and saw what happened when some lawyer said 'get rid of him.' You make a lifetime of trouble for yourself. . . ."

The glint in Doc's eye when he looked over showed he was just kidding . . . sort of. "Unlikely Brooks'll be pulling the trigger himself."

"Yeah, I figured the process is too far along by now, too," Jack agreed. "I just think he wants to be there when his life's work blows sky high. So our job is to stop the bomb before it reaches him." Jack shouted after Boaz. "Anything new on how the switches got to Saudi Arabia?"

The safe house manager came halfway back. "We were able to check the shipping manifests at DR Inc., which turned up a listing to the Middle East. One hundred and twenty copy machines are due to be delivered aboard the Malaysian-flagged *Flower of Asia*, scheduled to dock at Yanbu' al Bahr."

Jack looked from Doc to Sol. "Any way we can beat it there?"

It was Sol and Doc's turn to exchange looks. "We can try," said Doc, getting his boots back on the floor. "We'll need transport and translation, ground intel as well if that's possible."

"It's possible," Sol assured them. "Let's confab on transport,

Doc. I think, between the two of us, we can come up with something fast and secure for all concerned."

"What about translation and ground intel?" Jack asked.

"I got that covered," Sol promised as he approached Doc. "Give me two hours."

"Good," said Jack, heading for the door.

"Hey!" said Doc. "Where are you going? While we're doing all this, what are you going to do?"

Jack stopped at the door, his hand on the latch. "Me? I'm going to find out everything there is to know about dismantling a bomb in two hours flat."

26

Jack drove along the 101 toward the airport in the Ford C-Max to the gate at Coyote Point Park. He didn't have to stop, or even speak. No visitor had to. He gave the uniformed young ranger a wave, then turned right, drove past a gigantic playground that was dotted with laughing children, and parked at the far end of the huge lot beyond it.

Just as he was told, there was a run-down, rarely used path below it. Checking his watch, Jack started navigating the crumbling, decrepit, otherwise empty trail deep into the park—over and down to one of the most macabre beaches he'd ever seen. He walked carefully around the carcasses of dead crustaceans, bones, broken shells, crushed cans, stubbed cigarettes, and single shoes until he reached the man waiting for him.

Professor Peters smiled as Jack arrived at the very edge of the fetid water. Jack opened his mouth to speak, but Peters held his right forefinger up while checking his own watch.

"Fifty-seven, fifty-eight, fifty-nine," he counted. "Sixty." And, at that moment, a jumbo jet at the end of its descent to the neighboring airport appeared overhead like a parade balloon, seemingly floating, as well as hovering, above them. Its roar was so loud it seemed to drown out even Jack's thoughts. A moment later, it was gone.

"Every three minutes," Professor Peters said proudly. "Let's see anyone record our conversation now! Can you imagine someone in a van trying to establish an audio baseline with *that* bass roar?" He chuckled. "It will blow out their ears and equipment on the first pass!"

Jack grinned. "I like your style."

"Thanks," the physicist replied. "Sometimes, simple solutions are the best."

It was quite the talk. Jack asked for everything he needed to know about making a nuclear bomb, and Peters was just the man who wanted to tell him.

"Airport lights," he said. "Why would the Kingdom need so many runway lights?"

Even though a seemingly incongruous statement, Jack knew that there was method to the prof's seeming madness. In addition to foiling any listening device, real or imaginary, the rendezvous point he chose had an additional meaning.

"Because there's a gas inside runway lights —decay energy 18.6 keV, also known as tritium, also known as hydrogen-3, which is a radioactive isotope of hydrogen—that can be used to increase the yield of nuclear devices."

Peters turned to smile at the runway lights in the distance. "The emitted electrons from the radioactive decay of small amounts of tritium cause phosphors to glow, so as to make self-powered lighting."

"What about nonnuclear explosives?" Jack asked. "What could it do for those? Biological agents, for example."

Peters thought for a moment. "If you were proficient in its application, an explosion involving tritium could alter the structure of any agent you're delivering."

"Meaning?"

"Let's say you have a virus that affects the circulatory system," Peters said pensively.

"Like Ebola," Jack said.

Peters nodded. "What if it has been genetically manipulated into a pathogen that impacts the respiratory system."

"So that it's airborne rather than carried in bodily fluids," Jack said.

"Exactly. The Russians, the Israelis, the Germans, the United States have all worked on creating mutated forms of such diseases to which normal methods of treatment would not apply."

"Okay, I've reported on all that. But the tritium? Where's that come in?"

"Suppose the virus isn't weaponized until it's irradiated? What if the tritium begins the mutagenic process? Or, worse—"

"What could be worse?" Jack demanded.

"What if the tritium does something else? What if it irradiates the environment around the new strain and destroys any incoming curative?"

"Hold on," Jack said. "I thought radiation *kills* disease germs. Hell, exposure to just ninety seconds of ultraviolet light stops Ebola from reproducing."

"That is true," Peters agreed. "But you're talking about the traditional form of the disease. A nation that has created a superbug would want a very special key to unlock its potential. Tritium could be it."

He kept talking but Jack didn't hear because another jumbo jet appeared overhead. Once it was on its way, Peters turned back to Jack with an even wider smile, but troubled eyes.

"The isotope is used in very high-tech runway lights," the scientist went on. "But how many do you need? Check to see how many were delivered to Saudi Arabia in the last six months."

Jack held up his smartphone. "May I?"

Peters nodded, then checked the skies. "Be quick."

Jack called Sol, who passed on the question to Boaz and said he would get back to Jack. Once Jack hung up, the next plane was there, seemingly close enough for Jack to reach up and scratch its belly. When it, too, was past, Peters took up his lecture.

"Saudi Arabia has purchased a large number of perfectly legal items that could, under the proper circumstances, be taken apart and modified for something that could be used as part of a nuclear weapon. There are several ways the isotope could be used, depending on the exact type of bomb." Peters checked his watch. "Bottom line: tritium could be used to make uranium far more dangerous. The material increased yields and made detonation simpler. As for its effects on other agents, that remains pure speculation . . . none of it good."

They waited through the next plane's descent.

"What about krytrons?" Jack asked.

"You asked about those last time."

"Remind me," Jack said, trying to keep everything straight.

The professor sighed. "High speed switches—the kind used in bombs—are pretty rare. Only certain copy machines use krytrons any longer, and even those machines didn't use the same ones that bombs used. You need someone who supplies 3D copy machines."

"Right," Jack said.

The next plane appeared, giving Jack time to think. He now had another trail to follow—one figuratively lit by runway lights.

When the plane disappeared, Jack put his arm around Peters's shoulder, and gently led him back toward the path. "Tell me, Professor," he said. "If ever I was ever to come across these switches, these runway lights, or even a completed bomb, what's the best thing to do?"

"Duck and cover won't work," he said glibly.

"I know," Jack said.

"If you're asking how to defuse a bomb, remember what I said before? About simple solutions being the best?"

"Yes?"

The professor shrugged. "Pour a bottle of water on the device. Hose it down. Or pee on it."

It took a moment for Jack to realize that he was serious. "Can you elaborate?"

"If you don't happen to have a robotic bomb disposal unit and experienced technician, just wet the damn thing down and chances are pretty good you'll short circuit something, anything."

" 'Pretty good,' huh?" Jack muttered. "Can you be more specific? What are the odds of that working?"

"A little better than fifty-fifty," the scientist told him. "The good news is, if it doesn't work you'll never know."

Jack had hoped the physicist would come up with something a little more practical, a little more scientific. But as stopgaps went, he knew he would always have access to at least one of those options. . . .

27

U.S. Radar Station, Mt. Keren, Israel

Colonel Tristan Q. Ashlock was not a lunatic by any means. He was not criminally insane or pathological in his views of the world. He was an ardent American patriot who had spent his entire adult life wearing the uniform of the United States Army. Every male member of his family on his mother's side had worn that same uniform, dating back five generations to the Civil War, all of them graduating from the Virginia Military Institute near the tops of their classes. Not one of his line had ever graduated at the very top, however, until Tristan did so in 1977. His great-great-grandfather, William J. Smith, had been on the verge of doing so when the Commonwealth of Virginia voted to secede from the Union in the spring of 1861, but this was as close as anyone else with his blood had ever come to matching the achievement.

Upon leaving VMI to fight for the Confederacy, the young Lieutenant William "Bill" Smith had served briefly under General Barnard E. Bee before both were killed in action on the 21st of July at First Manassas. In death, Bill Smith left behind a pair of infant twin daughters, Eleanor and Sarah. It was from Sarah's line that Tristan Quentin Ashlock would emerge four generations later as the youngest of four sons, his older brothers all destined to give their lives either in the jungles of Vietnam or in clandestine military operations carried out during the Cold War. Their deaths, along with Tristan's genetic infertility, had assured that he would be the last of Sarah's line. Such were the laws of primogeniture.

Today, Colonel Ashlock was fifty-seven years old with thick gray hair that he still wore closely cropped to his head. His penetrating eyes were the color of steel dust, and though his facial features had begun to sag a bit, he maintained the distinguished, chiseled visage of the handsome warrior he had once been. He was a veteran of both Gulf Wars, the ongoing debacle in Afghanistan, and the recipient of the Distinguished Service Cross. Though his service career had been well distinguished as a commander of troops in the field, he had made some socially critical errors during his climb up the chain of command, errors in the form of failing to keep his mouth shut at the appropriate times and failing to kiss the butts of the appropriate generals when it would have been prudent to do so, thus giving offense in all of the wrong military circles at all of the worst times. As a result of these social blunders, he had never been able to attain a board selection to attend the prestigious United States Army War College, and would therefore, in all likelihood, never attain the coveted gold star of a brigadier general.

To say that Ashlock was resentful of his circumstance, was to say the very least. He was a soldier, not a sycophant. His job was to close with and destroy the enemy, either bodily or through the extension of the men and matériel at his command, and he had done exactly that, with distinction, for the past thirty-five years. Now that he realized he was to be permanently passed over—left to ride out his final years of service either accepting minor commands or marching the halls of the Pentagon as a glorified dog robber for generals who had never been on a battlefield—he had decided to go forward with his retirement plans.

The upper echelons of the United States Military, from the president down through the entire General Staff, had forgotten their collective duty. They had grown soft and indecisive in their misguided desire for peace at any cost, satisfied to let the tide of Islam slowly envelope the world. How many Middle Eastern governments would have to fall to Muslim extremists before America's leaders woke up and realized the folly of their *peaceful* ambitions? First the Egyptian government had been overthrown and taken over by Hamas. Then Gaddafi was deposed with the help of American air support, only to see Al Qaeda move in and set up house. And now it looked as though Syria would be the next to fall. Ashlock believed that something bold and decisive had to be done to cauterize the growing malignancy of Islam, and since no one in the upper echelons of any Western government possessed the resolve to take this decisive action, it appeared that he would have to do it for them.

Checking his watch and seeing that it was time to go, he got up from his chair and reluctantly left his air-conditioned trailer where was stationed atop Mt. Keren just five miles over the border from Egypt into Israel. He instantly felt the oven-like desert heat on his face as he gazed out over the Israeli terrain spread out far below him in all directions, reminding him briefly of the view from Masada. For the past year now, he had been the commander of a highly classified American-run radar installation with 120 American technicians and combat personnel under his command. The only foreign troops stationed on Israeli soil, their mission was to maintain a close radar watch on Tehran one thousand miles away to the northeast. The classified X-Band radar they used to perform this mission was so powerful that it could detect a soccer ball kicked into the air from nearly three thousand miles away.

The two portable, school bus–size radar units were painted in desert khaki and discretely positioned behind protective concrete blast barriers on the far northern side of the base where they were monitored constantly by American technicians in bulky radiation suits worn to protect them from the extremely heavy radiation generated by the radar units.

In the event the Iranian government ever made the fateful decision to launch one of their Shahab-3 missiles at Tel Aviv, this radar installation would detect it within seconds of launch, allowing for effective countermeasures to be taken before the missile ever reached Israeli air space. The Israelis' own radar would not pick it up for a full seven minutes, far too late for an intercept. So this significant time difference in detection made the American

early warning system an invaluable asset to the security of Tel
Aviv, as well as a powerful bargaining tool for the United States
to use in curbing the aggressive natures of many hard-line First
Strike advocates within the Israeli government.

Ashlock got into his car and drove across the small base to the
gate were he was passed through by a pair of American soldiers
armed with M4 carbines. He drove down the mountain and headed
out into the desert. Within the hour, he pulled up to a large government garage used to house earth moving equipment, eleven
miles south of the Negev Nuclear Research Center. He parked near
three other civilian vehicles, all of them bearing either diplomatic
or government license plates, and went inside.

Standing around a battered contractor's table near a dirty D10N
Caterpillar track hoe were six pensive looking men, four Israelis
and two Americans. Both of the Americans were CIA agents in
their forties. Two of the Israelis were of the same age, both agents
with the Israeli Mossad. But the other two Israelis were ten years
younger than the rest, both of them nuclear physicists working
for the Israeli government. They were also brothers, though this
wasn't immediately obvious to look at them with one of them being Orthodox while the other was clearly a Hasidic Jew with the
curled sidelocks of hair hanging down in front of his ears. Both of
them worked at the Negev nuclear plant where the entire world
understood that Israel had probably manufactured close to two
hundred nuclear weapons since the plant had first gone on line in
the late 1950s. In a basement of the plant, several levels down,
the Israelis also ran chemical and bacteriological weapons programs. These were launched in the middle 1960s when there was
concern about the widespread destruction the high yield bombs
would cause as well as decades of lingering radiation. Nerve agents,
blood agents, and choking agents were produced here along with
disease agents ranging from anthrax to Ebola. There was a secondary reason for producing these other weapons: in the event of
an attack from any of its neighbors, the bomb runs would release
these toxins and cause untold devastation in those border nations.

"I take it we're all here then," Ashlock said, "because we've decided to go through with this?"

One of the CIA men, a gruff looking fellow wearing a Yankees cap with gnarled hands and a sunburned face shook his head, jerking his thumb at the Hasid. "Curly here's got cold feet."

"Watch your mouth!" said the Hasid's older brother. "He has valid points!" The older brother was tall and thin, scholarly looking with a prominent nose and thick black hair. His name was Kolton.

The CIA man chuckled. His name was Chevrier, a former Navy SEAL from the first Gulf War. He glanced at his partner, a thinner man with a hatchet face and dark sandy blond hair. "Hear that, Parks? He's got valid points."

Parks smirked and shook his head, trying not to laugh. If Chevrier was the muscle in their little CIA team, Parks was definitely the brains.

Kolton took a step around the table, but one of the Mossad men, another military looking man named Laidlaw with a shaved head and goatee, put a hand on his chest to stop him. "You'd better grow a thicker skin, boy, or you're likely to get your neck broken."

Ashlock stared at Chevrier long enough to make sure the CIA man felt the weight of his gaze then turned to the younger brother who stood looking defiant on the far side of the table. "What's on your mind, Isaiah?"

Isaiah was the smartest man in the room at twenty-nine years of age. He wore wire-rimmed glasses and looked like the classic Jewish nerd. "The target is wrong," he said simply.

"Wrong how?" Ashlock asked, wondering if he had judged the younger man correctly.

"Destroying Mecca will leave no center to the Muslim faith," Isaiah said. "The war will never end because they'll have no reason to ever quit. We'll have to kill every last one of them."

"Ha!" Chevrier said with a sneer. "What's wrong with that? Isn't that the idea?"

"No, it isn't," Isaiah said, mater-of-factly, pushing his glasses up onto his nose. "The idea is to eliminate the extremist threat to the civilized world, but by destroying Mecca you instantly turn every single one of the peaceful into another warrior extremist. You fill him with hatred and you force him to fight. It's obvious if you take a moment to think about it. It's a total war, a war of complete annihilation."

"Which is exactly what we want," Chevrier said.

Isaiah looked around the room at the others. "I can't agree to that," he said, shaking his head. "It's not a sound strategy. Look at it another way . . . if you want to control a man, do you murder his entire family? No. You murder one child and leave the rest alive, making sure he knows the lives of others depend on his co-operation. After that, he has no choice but to do as he's told. You can only destroy Mecca one time, gentlemen. After that, there's nothing left to threaten them with. You'll have to kill them all, and I don't think we can count on the Western powers to do that. There will be too much guilt. They'll fight the war halfheartedly—just as they're doing now—and it will drag on forever . . . just as it has for two thousand years."

Chevrier grumbled, mumbling something unintelligible under his breath.

Colonel Ashlock stood watching the others, his arms crossed as he waited to see who would speak next. He had already decided what had to happen, but he was counting on one of the Israelis to do the actual dirty work for him.

Laidlaw lit a cigarette, tossing the pack onto the table with a sigh. "Listen, I understand what you're saying, Isaiah, but there are no compromises that work in this situation. None at all. When big guns are available, you don't use peashooters. You of all people know this. Otherwise, why bother to use it? We have to hit their biggest target and kill as many as we can because after the war begins, the West will have to keep it conventional, and that means—"

"Is that what you think?" Isaiah interrupted. "You honestly believe the already dangerously unstable Muslim government of Pakistan will sit on their own nuclear arsenal if Mecca is hit with a weapon of mass destruction? Allow me to remind you . . . after the remains are finally analyzed, the source of the components used to make the bomb will be traced right back here."

Ashlock held up a hand to caution him. "That's not necessarily so. Only the U.S. has the requisite data to trace the source back to Israel, because nobody else even knows for sure you people have weapons of mass destruction, and the U.S. isn't going release that kind of information to the Muslim world . . . for very obvious reasons."

The other Mossad man cleared his throat, speaking up for the first time. His name was Frank, and he looked more like a banker than a Mossad agent. "Which site do you propose we hit instead, Isaiah? I ask, because even hitting Medina feels like a half measure to me. You make the Islamists every bit as angry, but you kill maybe half as many. My problem is the mathematics of the thing."

Isaiah crossed his arms, glancing furtively at his brother before he spoke the words they had agreed on the night before. "I propose we hit the Dome of the Rock."

"You're insane!" Laidlaw blurted. "Destroy one of our own cities?"

"Think about it!" Isaiah urged. "Isn't it clear to you? Hours before the detonation, Al Qaeda announces to the world they've stolen a weapon of some kind from Israel. People will be afraid, but no one will truly believe it because they're such liars . . . but then when it actually detonates—Oh, my God! Can you imagine the mutual rage and panic? Both sides will blame the other, and both sides will rush to war in earnest." He looked at Ashlock in the hopes of finding a supporter. "And *your* country, Colonel, will *have* to come in on Israel's side or risk seeing the world's oil reserves fall into the hands of God knows who. Not to mention the Jewish American community will demand it!"

Ashlock was hard pressed to keep the smile from his face as he stood pretending to think it over. "Well," he said carefully, "it does rather lessen our concerns over the isotopes, doesn't it?"

Laidlaw drew from the cigarette and stood staring at him. "You're saying you agree with this insanity?"

"Don't look at the colonel!" Chevrier said. "Hitting Jerusalem was Curly's idea over there, but I have to admit I like it. Wars are won by the will of the people. If we hit Mecca, we definitely start a war, but who knows how much motivation the West will have to finish it? On the other hand, if we do hit Jerusalem . . . well, hey, we piss off every Christian and Jew on the planet . . . and you know damn well they'll take action then! Hell, we might even find a way to get Iran blamed for the whole damn thing! Nice thinking, Curly. I had you all wrong." He laughed and bummed a smoke off of Laidlaw.

Kolton stood tapping his chin, preparing to deliver their closing argument. "Some kind of a strike against Israel is probably inevitable, anyhow. This way we control the yield of the explosion." He looked at Ashlock. "What do you think, Colonel?"

Ashlock nodded. "I think your brother is right . . . and wrong."

"How so?" Isaiah said, a shadow creasing his face.

"I'm saying what if we hit both targets?" Ashlock suggested, fascinated that Isaiah had stepped so willingly into the trap he'd been patiently laying over the past few weeks. No way could he have been the one to suggest striking the Dome of the Rock without giving a great deal of offense to his Israeli counterparts. "If we hit Jerusalem and *then* Mecca, both within a couple days of each another, I think we can just about guarantee a full-fledged holy war with very few prisoners taken by either side . . . a genuine fight to the finish."

Laidlaw eyed him disdainfully. "Then why not hit New York while we're at it?"

Ashlock eyed him right back. "Because New York's already paid her pound of flesh in this godforsaken war, Mr. Laidlaw . . . or have you forgotten about that?"

Laidlaw looked away, stubbing the cigarette against the tabletop. "So I guess it's time we took a vote then."

The vote was unanimous.

28

Jerusalem, Israel

It was hot, in every sense of the word.

And, as always, it was a heat unlike that of anywhere else in the world—dry, penetrating, searing. *The heat hangs in the air like needles*, General Thomas Brooks thought.

He imagined that, if he made any sudden movements, it might scratch him.

The sun burned away the sweat beads as they emerged from his pores while he strode away from the helicopter that had taken him south into the desert hills from Tel Aviv. His legs were stiff, the muscles deeply knotted. His neck and shoulder muscles had atrophied into rocks. His eyes, dried out from the plane ride, sat deep in their sockets like hardened raisins.

He'd tried to sleep on the plane but one thing after another had kept him awake: details about the plans, yes, but also an annoying article that *The New York Times* was planning to publish about him in a few days. It wasn't actually about him. In fact, of the three thousand or so words in the advance copy the Army Press Corps forwarded, only about one hundred and fifty were directly related to him, and a good portion of those might even be said to be neutral.

But the intent was clear: the writer declared Brooks "one of the new old-guard, a contemporary replica of obsolete neo-liberals, neo-conservatives, and borderline lunatics who believe religion is the greatest threat to life in the 21st century." The writer then quoted from a Brooks speech several months back. "Islam is at war with the West, whether we want to realize it or not."

It was an accurate quote, and though presented in a way meant to make him seem like a borderline lunatic, was in fact probably the truest thing in the story. Brooks inwardly sighed. *If only the fourth estate was filled with more people like Jack Hatfield*, he thought. Hatfield would have communicated the fact that Brooks was not a lunatic, borderline or otherwise. Hatfield would have known, and reported that, while Brooks had spent his entire adult life in military uniform, he had worked hard to keep his perspective as wide as possible. He'd studied art and voraciously read history. The final stages of the Eastern Roman Empire were a special interest, and had been since his second year at the Virginia Military Institute when he was fifteen.

He had written a paper on the fiasco of the Angeloi dynasty for an independent study project at West Point. Later, at command school, he had produced a three-hundred-page report on the Fourth Crusade—analyzing the social aspects as well as the military ones. He was equally at home talking about how a Roman sculptor carved a statue as how a modern army moved to battle.

This broad background made Brooks acutely aware of the danger Islam posed to the West. The administration was particularly blind and stunningly inept, but even the president's firmest critics were mostly unaware of the deep movements of history that were taking place. Analysts focused on regime change in one country and popular movements in another, while completely missing the deep radicalization that had swept Islam and informed every aspect of Muslim life. Jack Hatfield would have understood all that.

"Sir?" came the softly accented voice of his event coordinator.

Brooks looked to his right to see Peter Andrews, whose pale skin, blond hair, and gauzy white suit almost blinded him. Brooks said nothing, just kept walking. The sooner he was out of this direct heat, the better. Even though he wore his summer uniform, there was just so much it could do to counter this sort of intensity. There may always be a breeze in Jerusalem, but it was *hamsin*—hot wind from the desert.

"General Morton returning your call, sir," Andrews said lightly, his eyes veiled as he handed up the military smartphone.

At first Brooks considered playing tit for tat—making Morton call back again since he wasn't there for the original call. But considering the reason for Brooks's call, he decided to get it over with.

"Thank you, Peter," Brooks said, taking the rectangular, armored device. It looked like many other smartphones, but was far more powerful and protected. It looked, in fact, like a small war turtle. "Stay close."

"Of course, sir," Andrews responded, his voice teetering on the edge of obsequiousness, before lowering his head and slowing in step so he seemed to melt away from Brooks.

"Monty," Brooks said, using the nickname only he used, with just a touch of forced bonhomie. "What took you?"

"Your call surprised me, sir," Morton replied, sounding like he hadn't slept for days. There was, after all, a ten-hour time difference, and Andrews had called at three A.M. San Francisco time. "I wanted to make sure I hadn't missed anything on the list you gave me when you went to the airport."

"And had you?"

There was a pause. Brooks imagined Morton wracking his brain. "Not that I could find, sir."

Brooks smiled. It was a somewhat sadistic smile, but it was a smile nonetheless. "Good man. No, I didn't call to say you missed anything, or even to add anything to the list. I just wanted to tell you 'good job.' "

There was another pause. Brooks could imagine Morton reacting as if the ranking general had given his subordinate a "playful" punch in the gut. "Oh. Uh. Well, thank you, sir." Brooks continued as if Morton hadn't said anything. "And to say, since I'm on my farewell tour, farewell to you." Brooks imagined Morton's face going ashen.

"I-I beg your pardon, sir?"

"You've done a good job in extraordinary circumstances, Monty, but since I'm off-site I wanted to let you know that your services will no longer be required. We'll be taking it from here."

Morton knew what this meant. It was the big kiss-off. The words were grateful-sounding, but their meaning was we don't trust you anymore, so you're on your own. After the Levi Plaza fiasco and what triggered it, he supposed he had it coming, but still. . . .

Morton's next words were dull, painfully flat. "Of course, sir. Whatever you say."

"Good," Brooks concluded briskly. "You're part of history now, Monty. Congratulations, and good luck."

"Thank you."

Brooks was going to end the call in the middle of Morton's comment, but then he heard, "Oh—excuse me, sir?"

Brooks brought the phone back to his ear. "Yes?"

"After you left, Jack Hatfield contacted the office, requesting an interview."

Of all the things Morton could have said, this was the only one that kept Brooks listening. "Hatfield. Really?" That appealed to Brooks, not just the platform but the interest of a man like that. Then he remembered where he was and what he was doing. It wouldn't work. Not now.

Sensing his hesitation, Morton pressed, "He said, 'Anytime, anywhere. Even there. Even tomorrow.' He left a number."

"Did he? Give it to Andrews," Brooks snapped. "We'll take it from here. And again, Monty, thanks."

"Thank you, sir," Morton said, but Brooks might not have heard it, since he was already handing the phone back to Andrews.

"Take down the information," Brooks instructed. "Arrange it. Anytime, anywhere possible within our schedule. I must talk to this man before the main event."

"Yes, sir."

Andrews took the phone. He listened to Morton. Andrews's eyes only glanced sharply at Brooks when he heard who it concerned. Even if Andrews were bold enough to debate the wisdom of this, now was not the time. Colonel Tristan Ashlock was already greeting Brooks at the edge of the helipad.

"General, good morning sir," Ashlock said, saluting.

Brooks returned Ashlock's stiff salute, then nodded and gave him a warm smile. He liked the colonel a great deal. Ashlock was from a long line of American patriots—the sort of man, who, in an earlier generation, would have at least a general's star on his shoulder by now, if not two. He had served in Bosnia, Iraq, and Afghanistan, but, though he had several medals—including a Bronze and Silver Star for valor—he had committed the unpardonable sin of speaking his mind to his superiors, and had languished until Brooks found him two years ago.

Ashlock was now the commander of Brooks's special radar unit at Mt. Keren in Israel. His X-Band Radar was aimed at Iran, keeping a watch on the missile launching area some two thousand miles away. The base, five miles from the Egyptian border, represented the only American ground presence in the entire region. Or at least the only acknowledged one. Special operations units were, in fact, working in every country—some with the governments, some decidedly not.

Ashlock had an important role as the plan went into effect; he would report a contact made by his X-Band Radar. Brooks believed he would be even more important in the months and years that followed. Unlike the now-discarded Morton, he was exactly the sort of officer who excelled in war. If anything happened to Brooks, Ashlock would pick up the reins.

"They're here," said Ashlock, nodding past Brooks. "I gather there are problems."

"There are always problems, Colonel," said Brooks. "Where's our car?"

"This way, General."

Ashlock led Brooks across the sand-swept macadam to a trio of command trailers. The hum of their air conditioners was so strong the ground vibrated. Brooks, already soaked in sweat, considered going inside for a few minutes to cool off. But he was already running late and had much to do. A Humvee and a white suburban stood on the far side of the trailers. Brooks told the two men he'd brought with him as his security detail that they would take the Hummer; he, Andrews, and Ashlock would ride in the SUV alone.

Ashlock drove out of the small base down a series of switch-backs onto a hardscrabble road that ran in the general direction of Egypt. After about five miles, he turned onto a dirt road that paralleled Route 90. Though they could have made better time on the highway, video cameras monitored the road and Brooks pre-ferred to have as little record of his movements as possible.

Somewhere north sat the Negev nuclear plant. The entire world knew that Israel had used it to manufacture nuclear weapons but pretended they didn't for the sake of peace. Self-delusion was a wonderfully powerful drug with only one known antidote—reality.

As they climbed through the hills, Brooks caught sight of a pair of flatbeds parked along the nearby highway. The trailers had car-ried tanks, which were maneuvering somewhere farther south. It was one more reminder of how serious his business was. A series of cutbacks brought them up to a hilltop crowned by a dirt park-ing lot. Half a dozen vehicles sat in the lot—a Renault Duster, a pair of pickups, a Mercedes sedan, two small Toyotas.

Ashlock parked, the tires of the SUV nudging against the white rocks that marked the lot's boundaries. Brooks got out of the ve-hicle and the trio all started down a winding dirt path at the east-ern end of the lot. There was no need to tell the guards to wait in the lot; they had been here before and knew the drill.

An archaeological site sat about fifty yards from the sum-mit. A sideless tent was located just below it, adjacent to a small cave carved into the hill many millennias before. The men Brooks had come to see were waiting beneath the canvas top. Three were European—one from France, two from Germany. One was Chinese—Taiwanese to be more specific—though he claimed he did not recognize the distinction, let alone admit the legitimacy of the government currently occupying Beijing.

Two others were Israeli—Isaiah Varda, who had met Brooks and asked for the meeting, and his brother Haisd Varda. Each rep-resented about a dozen or so other members of the conspiracy, all personally recruited by Brooks, and all working toward the same end for years.

Brooks glanced at Andrews and gave him a slight nod. Andrews nodded back, smiled slightly, crossed his arms, and stayed where he was. Brooks then looked to Ashlock with an expression that said, "Here we go into the lion's den."

"Gentlemen, so good of you to come on short notice," declared Brooks as he stepped over to the pockmarked table in the center of the room. The only seats were two folded canvas camp chairs on the ground. Brooks wasn't about to take one if no one else did. "I understand Rabbi Varda has some points he wishes discussed at this very late, very critical date." Brooks examined the faces one by one. All met his gaze, but only the Frenchman, Lepeur, was anything but dour. "So tell me, Rabbi." Brooks fixed his stare on Haisd. "What do you want?"

The rabbi got right to the point. "Israel should not be bombed. Nor should Mecca. Strike Riyadh and Tehran."

"Riyadh?" asked Brooks, registering surprise. He'd expected Tehran, the capital of Iran, but not the Saudi capital.

"The two government centers," continued Haisd. "Destroying Mecca will leave no center to the Muslim faith. The war will never end. They'll have no reason to quit. We'd have to kill every last one of them."

"That does not sound like a problem to me," said Lepeur. "It's our goal." The Frenchman was a physicist—the one member of the inner circle who was. Perhaps because of his scientific background, he tended to see things in a very binary fashion; they were black or they were white. It was a refreshing worldview.

"It's not our goal," counted Isaiah. "The idea is to eliminate the extremist threat to the civilized world, but by destroying Mecca we instantly turn the peaceful into extremists as well. By destroying the center to their religion, you're telling them it's total war. A war of complete annihilation."

"Exactly what we want," repeated Lepeur.

"I don't agree," said Haisd, shaking his head.

"I too understand your point," Brooks contended. "But there are no half measures with a weapon of mass destruction. You, of all people, know that. Otherwise, why bother to use it? We have to hit their biggest target and kill as many as we can because, after the war begins, the West will have to keep it conventional."

"Is that what you think?" Isaiah said. "You honestly believe the Muslim government of Pakistan will sit on their own nuclear arsenal if Mecca is destroyed?"

"They can deliver their weapons no farther than India," said Herman Friedrich, one of the Germans. "They will be bit players in the war that follows."

"And Riyadh and Tehran will be destroyed at that time," said Ashlock.

"If it comes to that," said Friedrich.

Brooks studied him, trying to decide whether he had changed his mind about siding with the Israeli brothers or not.

The rabbi resumed his argument. "During the Second World War, Americans avoided bombing the Japanese emperor's palace in order to avoid destroying the cultural center to their lives. It was a wise move."

"Japan is an island," said Brooks. "The United States was looking to end a war. We're looking to start one."

This fact, stated bluntly, shut the others' mouths. As always, Brooks took advantage of the situation.

"This war must involve everyone, or it will not be decisive," he went on. "Israel will not stay on the sidelines."

"We will not," said Isaiah. "But we have already borne the brunt of Muslim aggression."

"Finally, the main point," said Lepeur. "You are not willing to make the sacrifice."

"I am willing to make any sacrifice," said Haisd.

The Frenchman looked at Ashlock, then at Brooks. "And I have said it before, General: America will have no choice but to support Israel in this or risk losing access to oil reserves and to the good will of American Jews."

"By your logic, there is no reason to strike Mecca," countered Isaiah. "Who will get the blame for that, but Israel?"

"No one will blame Israel," said Brooks. He needed to take better control of the argument. "Israel will remain the victim. The bomb will be Al Qaeda's second, blown up prematurely in the airplane shortly after it takes off with Tel Aviv as the target. They wanted to circle the pillar of Islam before setting out. We worked this plan out long ago, Rabbi," Brooks added, looking at Isaiah's brother. "If you had objections, you should have voiced them then. Now is too late."

"It is not too late. Don't hit Jerusalem. Or Bethlehem. Or any other site. That is easy."

"If we hit Mecca, we definitely start a war, but who knows how much motivation the West will have to finish it?" said Tong, the Taiwanese. "On the other hand, if we hit Jerusalem, every Christian and Jew in the world will take action."

"Maybe we should hit Beijing instead and get Asians mad," said Isaiah.

"That's enough," said Brooks, realizing things were getting out of hand. "Some kind of a strike against Israel is inevitable."

"There should be a vote," insisted Isaiah. "We demand our say. As contributors and planners."

"You had your say," Brooks said firmly. "This is not a democracy, gentlemen. I brought you into this for your help, and, for that, I am truly grateful. I have asked for your advice and guidance, and even your opinions. We discussed these same issues, practically word for word, a year ago. The decision was made then. You all agreed to it, unanimously." He smiled grimly at each and every one of them. "I did not bring you here for a vote. I brought you here to say that I will give you eight hours' notice. In the meantime, I suggest you make good use of these days of relative peace. They may very well be the last ones you know in your lifetime."

29

San Francisco, California

When Jack got back to the safe house, all he saw was hunched shoulders.

Boaz, Ric, and Sammy were bent over their respective computers; Sol and Doc were tucked over their phones; and Miwa, Ritu, and Ana were leaning over the stove, the chopping block, and Eddie's doggy dishes.

When in Rome, he thought and, with nods of acknowledgment from everyone who looked over, Jack went to his own laptop, hunkered down, and tried to track Brooks.

He wondered why Strategic Command was even involved in anything like this. Various elements of America's strategic forces—nuclear weapons, satellites, and cyberwarfare units—were all organized under its umbrella. It was a combined command, with units from each service answering to the four-star general in charge. Brooks was the number-two man, and the army's representative in the leadership. As such, he was essentially untouchable. The perfect person to lead the world into war.

To Jack's surprise, Minsky's powerful Wi-Fi allowed him to access Morton's history as well. He'd been liaison officer at Livermore and several other labs for about two years. His assignments before that tracked Brooks's almost to the month. It seemed clear that he had hitched his wagon to Brooks's stars, and was moving up the ladder with the general's help.

That, of course, was interesting, but not exactly helpful at this juncture.

Jack was about to look over the others' shoulders when his smartphone buzzed. It was from Dover.

"Hey, hon, what's up?"

Dover dove right in; he could tell that she was on the move, probably making the call while hustling between offices.

"There's a lot of traffic—a *lot* of it—coming out of the Middle East."

Traffic meant communications, and if this sort of traffic reached the FBI it wasn't just one person saying "hi" to another person. The NSA routinely snagged messages on the Internet and from phone lines, decrypting them by the millions. Specific messages, however, rarely provided direct intelligence—few terrorists were stupid enough to say, we are going to bomb point x at time z, even if they were encrypting their message.

Code guessing—interpreting the meaning of code words—was still an art akin to crystal ball gazing; it was one thing for a psychologist to declare that action words were used as coded commands ninety percent of the time, and quite another for a program to pick the right words out, let alone correlate them to a specific action.

But patterns in the messages sent—time, volume, length, direction, etc.—were much more easier to detect and interpret. In the years following 9/11, the intelligence services had become increasingly adept at measuring upticks in "traffic," to name one of the simpler metrics, and interpreting their importance.

"Terrorist attack kind of traffic?" Jack asked.

"Nothing definitive yet. I just wanted you to know people are concerned because of the amount of traffic. And . . ."

"And?"

Her next words came in a rushed whisper. "The Agency has ramped up its efforts to find the missing toxin, and is concentrating on Saudi Arabia. Gotta go."

"Texting you the code to Sol's sanctum," Jack said. "In case you need a safe place to work."

The call was disconnected just as Ana announced that the meal was ready. Jack looked around at everyone else's reactions—they were all standing and stretching—then quietly said into the dead phone, "So do I."

The team gathered around the simple, yet elegant, rectangular table: Sol and Jack in the end chairs; Sammy, Ana, and Ric on one side; and Boaz, Ritu, and Miwa on the other. The ladies had made their specialties; fish stew, chicken curry, and sesame noodles. Although stereotypical, they were delicious. Jack and Doc especially savored it. It might be their last solid meal for the foreseeable future. But even before they had all swallowed their first bites, the progress reports began.

"Got the transport," said Doc, reaching for some rice. "Someone who owes me a favor has someone else who owes him a favor. We can fly to Saudi Arabia on a private jet. Gulfstream. Very fast, very sleek. And very private."

Jack opened his mouth to ask how he pulled that off, then decided he didn't want to know. He shoved a piece of white fish in instead. As he chewed the surprisingly delicious halibut, he asked, "When?"

"Tonight," Doc said around a piece of chicken.

"Got the translator," said Sol, twisting some noodles around his fork. "You'll be met at the airport."

"And I've got the Riad al-Saud interview scheduled," Boaz continued. "Tomorrow afternoon." He checked his watch. "About six hours after you land."

"That should give you enough time to check out the *Flower of Asia*," Ric reported. "It's scheduled to dock around two hours after you arrive."

Jack was impressed and pleased at the team's ability. If all went well, they might even be able to, in Doc's favorite parlance, "cut the shipment off at the pass" and nip the entire conspiracy in the bud. He looked down to see Eddie happily awaiting any table scraps. The sight of the little guy made Jack happy, as well as wistful. Who knew when he'd be seeing man's best friend again? At least he knew he was leaving Eddie in many good hands.

"What's the progress on Morton's hard drive?" Sol asked.

Suddenly all eyes were on Sammy. He looked back at them with embarrassment. "So far, what I've got is just a lot of pictures of his kids," he mumbled. "It's not easy you know. It's a military hard drive, there's all sorts of firewalls."

Just then there was a sharp sound that hurt their ears and made everything on the table jump. They all looked over in surprise at Sol, who had slammed one meaty paw on the table. But he stared only at Sammy, and waited until Sammy stared back.

"The only person who doesn't know you're a valued part of this team is you," Sol said, pointing between Sammy's eyes. "That ends now. We don't have time for it. No more apologies . . . just do the job you know you can do. Get me, Sergeant?"

Sammy looked shaken and glanced at Ana. It was her look of caring encouragement that caused his jaw to set and his brow to darken with determination. He looked back at Sol, seemingly a changed man. "Yes, sir."

That was when Jack's phone rang. Looking down at it, he was expecting Dover's number, but it was one he didn't recognize—one that was obviously coming from overseas. He vaguely recognized the international codes. Then it hit him.

"It's from Israel!" he blurted.

Ric was up like a shot, and grabbed the device from his hand. "Over here, over here," he said, all but running to his computer console. "Quick!"

They all followed, Jack in the lead, as Ric frenziedly searched through the desk's many wires until he found the one he was looking for. He shoved it into one of the phone's receptors, and thrust it back to Jack.

"Hurry," he said. "Before it goes to voice mail."

Jack accepted the call. "Hello?"

"Is this Jack Hatfield?" came a lightly accented voice Jack could only describe as coolly condescending. "From the television series *Truth Tellers?*"

"It is," he answered, seeing all the others looking at him, except Ric, who only had eyes for a program that was running on his screen—recording, analyzing, and tracing the conversation. "Who is this?"

There was a slight pause, as if the caller was deciding what to say. "I am on General Thomas Brooks's staff. You requested an interview?"

Ana put her hands over her mouth. Sammy put his arms around her. Boaz put one hand on Ritu's shoulder. Miwa quickly stepped over to stand beside Ric. Jack shifted his gaze between Sol and Doc.

"Yes," he answered. "I did."

The next words were not what anyone was expecting. "This is your lucky day," said the caller. "Can you be in Riyadh, the capital city of Saudi Arabia, tomorrow?" He said it like he was expecting Jack to say something like "that's impossible." But he seemed unfazed when Jack replied in the affirmative—while looking incredulously at Doc and Sol.

"Yes. I think I could arrange that."

Sol gave him a thumbs-up, appreciating that Jack was sharp enough to say "I" and not "we."

"What time?" Jack asked, hoping it wouldn't conflict with the prince's interview. It didn't.

"The general is busy all day," came the reply. "Would you be willing to interview him in the evening?"

"Of course," Jack answered. "I know how busy he is. I serve at the general's pleasure." That seemed to charm the speaker. "Excellent. Can I reach you at this number?"

Jack looked quickly at Ric, who nodded and gave him the thumbs-up. "Yes."

"Then I will call you with the exact time and location."

"Thanks," Jack said quickly. "I'll be bringing my cameraman and interpreter, if that's all right." Jack nearly smiled when he saw Sol silently celebrate Jack's quick thinking.

"I don't see why not," said the man. "If for any reason you don't hear from me by tomorrow afternoon, call me at this number."

"And who should I ask for?"

"The name is Andrews," came the clipped reply—the speaker hitting every syllable of his name as if saying it for the first time. "Peter Andrews. I am the general's event coordinator."

"Thank you, Peter," Jack replied.

"Bon voyage, Jack," Andrews replied frostily in kind. "See you tomorrow. Fly safe."

30

Jerusalem, Israel

The golden Dome of the Rock stood out from the light clay and dark green colors of the area around it like a half moon in the night sky. General Thomas Brooks stared up at it, letting its beauty and significance bathe him. It was an indulgence, he knew. He really didn't have time for it. But, deciding to make a virtue of his hardship, Brooks indulged himself in a last-minute visit. There was a very good chance it was the last time he would see the site—sacred to all three major religions—during this lifetime. There was also a distinct possibility it was one of the last times anyone would see it.

It had been years since Brooks had visited any part of Jerusalem, and he let Colonel Ashlock act as his tour guide, channeling his own indulgence onto the colonel and even his event coordinator as Ashlock pointed out various historical and archaeological highlights. The colonel knew a good deal about the Rock; he knew much more.

The long history of the site was as complicated and symbolic as any part of Jerusalem. Believed by Jews to be the site where Abraham offered to sacrifice his son Isaac, it was also believed to be the site of Solomon's Temple—though firm archaeological evidence was lacking. The Jewish Second Temple, the holy structure built after the Jews returned from the Babylon Captivity, was known to have been built here. Reconstructed by Herod, the temple was destroyed by the Romans during the Jewish revolt. Later, its place was taken by Christian churches and a basilica. After Jerusalem was conquered by the Muslims, Caliph Abd el-Malik decided that a shrine would be built on the location to protect the site, said to be the rock where Muhammad had undertaken the holy Night Journey, ascending to heaven and speaking to God.

General Brooks knew that, religious significance aside, the story of the Night Journey taking place at the site was total fiction; Muhammad's journey to heaven almost surely originated much closer to Mecca. But people needed their fictions, large and small; disturb the small fiction of where an incident took place, and the larger and more significant belief would be questioned as well.

Brooks did not believe that religion, even Islam, was fiction. It was something that answered a deep need in the human race. Its power was proof of that. But that power was also its undermining—if enough people were caught up in the surface fictions, the result would be traumatic. For when death and destruction were applauded by religion, there was no stopping them. History made that clear.

No matter the beliefs about it, there was no question that it was a beautiful building. Not a mosque, but a shrine—the dome exterior and the structure's interior glowing with gold. The interior circle wall seemed like a golden halo, sitting over the gray sandy color of the rock where Isaac nearly died and Muhammad was said to have gone to Paradise. *How much more appropriate that this be the target*, Brooks thought. For the symbolism. It could have worked both ways—the intention was to anger the Jews and Christians— but striking the Rock would have angered Muslims as well. That could have made it an ambiguous symbol, and so he had dropped the idea.

There was no way of knowing precisely how much damage would be done by the bomb intended for Jerusalem. As Brooks had said at the meeting, it was the smaller of the two weapons.

The air-burst weapon's initial blast radius would extend roughly five miles in all directions. The poisonous effects would be most severe within about a half mile of ground zero, though ultimately would extend much farther, depending on the wind and the vagaries of chance . . . such as where people would go before they knew they had been infected with a super-Ebola virus. How many people would they breathe on? How many people would become infected and then infect others? There were too many intangibles, including how much destruction would be caused by the explosive component itself. Although the bomb would be set off above the site, geography would still play a role, absorbing or amplifying the shock wave.

Brooks himself thought the zone of destruction might extend to the outskirts of Jerusalem, roughly five miles to the north. There was a chance the airborne Ebola itself, not just the inhaled supervirus, would spread all the way to the Dead Sea, some fifteen miles to the east. In any event, the center of the city, the birthplace of Christ, would surely be destroyed.

Of course the Israeli conspirators had objected. They would lose many of their countrymen. But they had been the ones to make the argument for the strike in the first place, when Brooks was only talking of destroying Mecca. Without a Jerusalem strike, they persuasively argued, the result would simply be a meandering war—simply a bloodier version of what was happening right now.

It would be like Iraq in 2007, General Brooks thought. Car bombs and IEDs every hour, in every major city across the United States and Europe. "Rules of Engagement" that handcuffed American soldiers, European governments that decried the sight of blood—but only if it belonged to Muslims, not their own people. A war like that would continue for a hundred years, until the Muslims won.

"Hit both sides," the brothers argued. And at that point, at least, they were willing to strike Israel, and had even offered up Jerusalem.

Brooks walked through the shrine, fighting off the memories of Iraq. He'd led an army corps during the invasion. The assault was a piece of cake. The aftermath was ecstasy—for a few months. Tired of Saddam, tired of the depression caused by misrule and the UN sanctions, the Iraqi people had welcomed the Americans as liberators. It was like Europe in the summer of 1944.

And then, somehow, somewhere, someone threw a switch.

The first IED in his area went off on a highway a few minutes after a supply convoy passed. It caught everyone by surprise. One of his divisional G-2s thought it was a Saddam-era bomb whose fuse went off by accident.

Brooks had removed him within a month. By then, the mujahideen had become much better at both creating IEDs and setting them off. His forces were taking a dozen casualties a week. The next month, it was a dozen a day.

Military targets weren't enough for the bastards. By the end of the year, civilians were being slaughtered in marketplaces, bazaars, main roads. It had become a religious war as well as one against the United States: Sunni versus Shiite, and vice versa.

Iran was fanning the flames, and American troops were a target for both sides. But the core of the problem was Islam itself: a pre-Medieval religion that had not only never adjusted to modern realities, but was now being driven back to its most violent roots by ignorance and strife.

Brooks saw then that there was no hope for redemption—no chance that the religion would purge itself of its worst attributes and become a positive force for its adherents. It had entered a fatal downward spiral, like the Byzantine Empire or the American Indian ghost dancers or the German Nazi Party. There was no hope except for self-annihilation.

The reasons were complex, but one look at the center of the Dome of the Rock provided the most obvious clue: superstition and ignorance were ridiculously hard to overcome. Once they reached a critical mass, there was no hope.

The only question was how much of the rest of the world would they take with them. Strike now, and at least there was some hope that the United States and a portion of Europe would miss the worst of it. Wait five years—when Iran would have nuclear weapons, when Saudi Arabia would have clandestinely imported some Pakistani bombs, when perhaps even Al Qaeda or Hezbollah would have access to them—and the toll would be far, far greater. The war had to start now, and it had to start on the West's terms. If the West would not take preemptive action—and not even a competent administration was ready to contemplate it, let alone the boobs they were saddled with—then it would have to be started for them.

Still deep in thought, Brooks walked outside the building. There was much to do, and yet he felt the overwhelming urge to reflect and contemplate. There were two parts to him; he was a man of action and yet a thinker as well. The two sides were constantly at war. It was that way for Patton as well. His diary showed it clearly.

"General, you're going to want to leave for the airport soon if you want to stay on your schedule," said Colonel Ashlock.

"True," said Brooks. "Peter, why don't you go on ahead and make sure the vehicle is ready?"

Peter Andrews considered pointing out that the vehicle would certainly be primed and ready to go. Instead, as always, he looked behind and beneath Brooks's words to see what the general actually wanted him to do. The event coordinator smiled thinly, turned, and engaged the security detail—six soldiers from Ashlock's command, and two from Brooks's—in a detailed conversation as to what their duties were here, on the way to the airport, and then at the plane.

Even so, Brooks kept his voice so soft Ashlock had to lean toward him to hear.

"We're at T-minus two days," Brooks reminded him. "Are you sure your command is ready?"

"Absolutely, General."

"Arrange for a helicopter to be at your base," added Brooks. "You'll need to be mobile."

"I have a pair of Chinooks coming for an exercise the night before," said Ashlock. "They're due to arrive at 1300."

"Push them forward to the morning, no later than 1100," said Brooks. "I want a margin for error. I'm not sure how far to trust the Israeli brothers."

Ashlock gave him a look of concern, but then nodded.

"If anything happens to me," added Brooks, "enact all of the contingencies, one by one."

"I will not fail you," said Ashlock.

"Good. Now let's move it along, Colonel," said Brooks loudly. "I'm due in Riyadh in a few hours. I'm having cocktails with the ambassador. I never realized how much work it was saying good-bye to an old command."

31

Fifty Thousand Feet Over the Atlantic
Heading East

Jack had too much time to think, plan, work, and worry on the flight to Riyadh, but at least the time was spent in comfort. Doc had secured a Gulfstream 650, which had already set around-the-world speed records. So the powerful engines on this sleek beast would cover the eight thousand miles at nearly the speed of sound.

Jack sat at one of the four comfortable workstations. The cabin was the longest, widest, and tallest of any private business jet he was ever in, and normally he would have enjoyed it, but its details weren't as important to him as their mission. Thankfully, the time passed quickly. Jack saw to a hundred details, but fretted over missing a hundred more.

He was stepping into the heart of darkness, filled with people who'd like to see nothing less than America in ruins. That and their God was all they lived for.

A God they didn't understand any better than they understood respect for women, Jack thought.

But, for now, they worked, watched, and waited for the red, white, and blue to lower their guard . . . just enough. . . .

Sol had arranged for a line of credit and Jack took a medical insurance policy in case any of them were injured or something went seriously wrong. He then discovered that to get a visa to visit the Kingdom of Saudi Arabia, he needed a sponsor. That was not as easy for him to arrange. Who was he going to use: a journalist, a cop, an FBI agent, or an ex-CIA man? But Sol just smiled, said "Leave it to me," and paid a considerable bribe to take care of the paperwork.

"Not that it's called a bribe," Sol told him when Jack pointed out the unfairness. "It's an 'expediting fee.' That looks much more comfortable in the company books."

When Jack still shook his head, Sol had just shrugged. "Makes the world go round, Jack, and you're going halfway around the world. Better be ready for anything." Jack hoped he was, and went over every contingency he could think of. He thought so hard and so long about it, in fact, that it ultimately put him to sleep, visions of mushroom clouds dancing in his head. When he woke up with a start, he found Doc leaning over him, his big paw on Jack's shoulder.

"Glad you could catch some shut-eye," his lanky old friend told him. "You'll need it. We're starting our descent into Riyadh."

Doc was wearing a dark tan suit made from a linen/silk weave. As per Boaz's instructions, he wore a long sleeve shirt and tie, which was considered appropriate in Saudi Arabia. Under no circumstances should they show their knees, sport gold chains, and certainly not wear crosses. Since neither had any intention of doing any of that, they felt safer.

Jack glanced out the nearest window to see Riyadh's domed, octagon-shaped airport looking like a fried, sunny-side-up egg on the flat desert surroundings below. He quickly headed to one of the sleeping quarters to change into his own dark poplin suit, and slip on the versatile leather shoes Ric had acquired for him.

"You'll need to be ready for anything," Sol's assistant had told him, "yet still dress according to the Saudi dress etiquette. So the suit can breathe, is very durable, stain resistant, and there are eight interior pockets for security."

By the time he was ready, the jet was ready to land. Jack strapped himself in next to Doc, and they exchanged a look of determination and support.

"Stay loose," Doc advised.

Arriving in Saudi Arabia on a private jet was nothing like coming in on a commercial airliner. Jack and Doc were met on the tarmac by a plainclothes customs agent, who treated them as if they were potential clients looking to spend millions. The check of their bags—one each—was perfunctory. Doc's camera was removed but not turned on, and Jack's laptop wasn't even acknowledged. Jack barely had time to taste the tea the man's assistant offered in the customs office before they were cleared through.

"Pretty nice to a bunch of foreigners whom they don't know," Jack murmured as they followed the customs agent to the exit.

Doc smiled. "The prince's people probably told them who you are," he theorized. "They're going to roll out the red carpet so you make him look good."

The men stepped out onto the bronze stone of the airport's handsome interior, admiring its gold-paneled columns and the many sunlight-infused cathedral ceilings.

"Our car will take you into the city, if you wish," said the customs official.

Before Jack could reply, Doc nudged him, then pointed at a small, nut-brown man wearing an immaculate white robe that covered him from neck to ankles; brand-new leather, open-toes sandals; and a red-and-white checked headscarf with a neatly knotted rope holding it fashionably in place. The man—in what was called a thawb robe, a ghutrah scarf, and an agai head rope—was holding a small, beautifully lettered sign reading HATFIELD.

Jack raised his eyebrows at the long and powerful reach of Sol Minsky. "Thank you," he told the official, "but I believe our ride is here."

"As you wish," replied the customs man, who almost bowed as he took his leave—watching the three until he disappeared back into his offices.

The diminutive, nut-brown-colored man put his hand out as if it were a spear when the two Americans approached. "I am Jimmy," he said in a deferential, accented tone. Jack shook it, impressed with his solid muscles. "You are Mr. Hatfield." Jimmy looked at Doc, sticking out his hand again. "And you are Mr. Matson."

Doc shook, while placing his other hand on Jimmy's shoulder, then his elbow, while looking deep into Jimmy's dark eyes. The Middle Easterner seemed to be made from solid, petrified wood, and by the crinkles around his eyes and mouth, could be any age from forty to a hundred and forty. "That's right," Doc told him as he leaned down and whispered, "and your reputation precedes you."

Jimmy grinned. He was missing a tooth at the front. "My brother, Doc—he says you need translator. I am best terp around."

"You are, huh?" Jack said dubiously.

"Ask SEALs," Jimmy told him. Jack looked at Doc, who nodded.

"If Doc says you're good, that's good enough for me." Jack checked his watch, and started toward the airport terminal exit. "Let's go."

"Wait." Jimmy took hold of his arm and held him back. "Let me go first. My brother says you have trouble. You don't take chances. I go first."

The translator began walking. Jack looked at Doc, his face impressed.

"I think he's going to work out pretty well," Jack decided.

Jimmy led them to a big, light tan Toyota Sequoia SUV.

"Isn't that a little obtrusive?" Jack wondered.

"We'll be going all over the place," Doc reminded him. "Best to be ready for anything."

"You wanted unobtrusive?" Jimmy asked, beaming as he opened the back hatch with the key fob. "I was offered a Hyundai first. I got this for same money."

"Did you bribe the salesman?" Jack asked as he went around to the passenger seat while Doc stretched out in back.

"No, no. Not a place for bribes," said Jimmy. "I just say I get good car or I cut his balls off. Easier than bribe. Where to?"

"We're on a tight schedule." Jack said. "We have to get to the port before the *Flower of Asia* docks."

"Good idea," said Doc. "But I think we have enough time to make one stop first." Jack looked at him with a raised eyebrow. "You sure?"

Doc nodded solemnly. "I'm sure."

Jimmy nodded, started the engine, and made their way out of the airport. Jack, who had never been to Riyadh before, found it interesting, to say the least.

"What's the giant bottle opener?" he asked, crooking his thumb at the big building in the center of the city.

"The Kingdom Centre," Jimmy informed him. "Biggest skyscraper in Riyadh. Third tallest building with a hole in it in the world."

"With an A-hole in it?" shot back Doc. "I find that hard to believe."

Jimmy laughed. He might not understand all of the subtleties of English, but he had a good command of curse words and off-color humor, thanks to the SEALs.

He was also a good driver, navigating Riyadh's streets with ease. The traffic was far sparser than Jack had imagined—lighter even than the financial district in San Francisco on a Saturday afternoon in February. Jimmy made his way to a residential section on the eastern side of the city where the narrow, tangled roads made it easier to make sure they weren't being followed.

Then he scouted Doc's directions to a faded yellow house about midway down a block of clay-brick buildings. It was in a dim corner of the city, south of the Ad Dar Al Baida district. Two kids were playing with a soccer ball in the dusty front yard. Their faces were smeared with sweat, but they wore brand-new Reeboks and shiny basketball shorts in the latest U.S. style.

"I need Ahab," Doc told them in English.

Jimmy started to translate, but the kids had already heard what they needed to hear. They darted into the house. Less than thirty seconds later, a thin man with a grizzled face came out. At least two decades older than Doc, which was saying something, his shoulders were stooped and his leg dragged. He held a small gym bag like a football against his side. Doc went over and hugged him. They said a few words that Jack couldn't hear. Doc reached into his pocket and pressed a wad of American money into Ahab's hand. Ahab nodded, and handed off the bag.

"Acchay," said Doc. "Thanks, and good-bye."

He went swiftly back to the car. "Go," he told Jimmy.

Doc opened the bag as Jimmy drove. There were two pistols, both .45 caliber Glock 21s, along with six filled magazines. There were also fake passports and other documents.

"Just in case," Doc explained as he divvied up the contents.

Jack told Doc to give Jimmy the pistol. "I'm sure he's a better shot than I am."

Doc quickly agreed. "What, you think these were for you?" he joked. "There are licenses for the guns in the paperwork that each one of us has," Doc noted, "but you have to be careful. If you're carrying them in a mosque or a government building, the penalty is only slightly better than getting caught with one in New York City."

"What penalty?" asked Jimmy.

"They'll chop off your hand," said Doc.

Jimmy laughed. "No, no, actual penalty here is eighty-thousand-dollar fine and a month in jail," he corrected, then shrugged. "But life in Saudi prison? Losing your hand might be better."

Jack steered the subject to something that intrigued him. "Who's Ahab?"

"Fellow merc," Doc told them. "Originally from Delhi."

"Yes, yes," Jimmy piped up. "You say good-bye to him in Hindu, yes?"

"Yes," Doc continued. "Ahab had been a cook for one of the larger mercenary outfits in Iraq, but was kicked out after he voiced suspicions about a young boy on his crew. The young boy was apparently a 'special friend' of the local supervisor. Week later, the kid walks into the mess tent, and blows himself up. Kills about two dozen locals, and two U.S. servicemen. Turned out the whole thing was an Al Qaeda setup."

"Let me guess," Jack interjected sourly. "The supervisor remained in place. Firing him would have been 'politically incorrect.'"

"I would do more than fire him," said Jimmy.

"Someone did," said Doc. "Not a week later they found him hanging from a rope. His face was battered and two ribs were broken, fingers, too. They called it suicide. I guess they were right in a way."

They stayed silent for a time as Jimmy drove to Abi Bakr As Siddiq Road, one of the main arterials in the city. This was a broad highway that took them from the business area to a section of sand-strewn lots that reminded Jack they were in the middle of a desert.

"Reminds me of Baghdad," said Doc as they passed a large expanse of open sand.

"No checkpoints," said Doc.

"No IEDs, either," said Jimmy.

The buildings they passed were mostly new, and if you made allowances for the Arabic lettering, would have fit in the suburbs of any southwestern U.S. city—low-slung offices interrupted by the occasional condo complex and a smattering of stores. A more crowded residential zone lay to the west as they found King Fahd Road, but at least from the distance it didn't look anything like the poor, crowded urban area Jack had envisioned. Riyadh was, in fact, a far cry from Baghdad, which Jack had visited twice as a cable host. Far more modern and far less crowded, it was as different from the Iraqi capital as the countries were.

Part of the difference, Jack knew, had to do with oil revenue; Saudi Arabia had been blessed with massive oil reserves that made the gas cheap and the Kingdom better off than many other countries in the region. But it was not simply that; it was education and a willingness to accept some aspects of modernity. What might other countries achieve if they weren't blinded by hate?

And what might Saudi Arabia achieve if it weren't hamstrung by medieval attitudes toward religion and society? There were no women drivers, and Jack was well aware that business and even everyday life was hamstrung by strictures that had become self-defeating hundreds of years before. But he wasn't here to change the world. Just, hopefully, save it.

"Come on, Jimmy, step on it," he said. "We got a boat to catch."

Jimmy's reaction took Jack completely by surprise. The driver made a sharp U-turn across seven lanes and headed back toward the intersection. None of the other cars on the road beeped or even moved out of the way.

Jack turned to look at Doc, but Matson was intently talking on his phone. Then, to Jack's increased agitation, Jimmy floored the accelerator and directed the Sequoia right back to where they started: the airport.

32

Riyadh, Saudi Arabia

The Gulfstream was refueled and waiting for them.

"The port city of Yanbu' al Bahr, five hundred and fifty miles to the west," Jimmy explained, pointing as they headed for the G650's door. "Six hundred and seventy miles via highway."

"Almost a ten-hour drive," said Doc. "Minimum."

Jack looked at Jimmy in surprise. "Couldn't you do it faster than that?"

"Me?" he said, pointing at himself and smiling. "Yes. With you in car?" He pointed at Jack and Doc. "No." He shook his head. "Not a good idea."

Jack looked to Doc in confusion. "This place has one of the highest accident rates in the world," Doc explained, checking the new flight plan manifest that the pilots needed to negotiate once they had landed. "And if a foreigner is involved in one, they'd be dropped into a legal system that would make both Kafka and Escher blanch." Doc handed the clipboard back to the pilot. "Driving, ten hours or so. Flying? About an hour. Welcome aboard, Jimmy." Doc let their interpreter enter first.

Unlike Jack, Jimmy was ebullient with his appreciation of the private jet's amenities. Even so, they managed to get him belted in before they took off. The desert spread around them as they flew north, and within a few moments it was all Jack could see—open brown space—a harsh environment where even the smallest patch of green seemed a miracle. Farming was out of the question.

Below they could see that the highway traffic was mostly tractor trailers. Even though the jet cut their travel time enormously, there was still almost an hour to sit. Rather than worry, Jack let his reporter instincts lead him. He turned to Jimmy.

"How did you start working for the SEALs?" he asked.

"Didn't know they were SEALs," the man answered, eyes still looking out the window. "Working for army. One day sergeant asked if I wanted to make more money. I said yes." He gave Jack a big grin.

"Don't be so modest," said Doc, turning to Jack. "He was always more than a terp." He turned back to Jimmy. "Tell him about the smugglers."

"Oh, nothing big," said Jimmy. When he stayed humbly silent, Doc took up the story. "There were these black-market guys, hijacking trucks north of Baghdad," Doc told Jack. "Jimmy was an interpreter with an Army MP unit. One day they went to make an arrest and no one was there. The captain was pissed. Jimmy told him if he wanted to catch some bad guys, he should go to this market north of town. They got there around midnight, just as the operation was in full swing. The smugglers, who, as far as Jimmy knew, weren't actually terrorists, just criminals, were unloading their latest prizes—a pair of tractor trailers loaded with cigarettes and booze. The MPs pulled up in a pair of Humvees, and immediately came under fire."

Doc looked at Jimmy encouragingly, but the man just kept looking out the jet window.

"The sergeant Jimmy was with went down, shot in the leg," said Doc. "Jimmy grabbed the guy's MP4 and ran at the bad guys, blazing away, so others could come and drag the sergeant to safety."

Finally Jimmy spoke. "Stupid move," he said without turning from the window.

"Killed two bandits," said Doc. "The rest ran away." Doc glanced at Jimmy again, but the man wouldn't take the bait. Jack realized that Jimmy wasn't about to toot his own horn. That would be arrogant and unseemly. That only made him more impressive in Jack's eyes.

"After that," Doc continued, "the MPs loved him. He went on all their tough patrols. Two months later, when the SEALs needed a terp to go on missions, the MPs recommended him. Interpreters weren't supposed to be armed, but Jimmy always seemed to have a weapon with him. He'd ended up becoming one of the SEALs' most valuable assets, passed from unit to unit as the Americans rotated in and out of Iraq. Several men credited him with saving their lives."

"Maybe I save someone there," Jimmy quietly admitted, as if convincing himself. "Explain to people SEALs only look for bad guy. People excited, worried. They don't know what is going on. I warn. I help."

"As a rule, interpreters stayed in the back of the 'train,'" Doc went on. Jack knew that the "train" was an informal term soldiers used to describe the lineup of men who made the first entrance into a terrorist's house or stronghold. "Jimmy always managed to be near the front. His work earned him enough respect with the SEALs that the terrorists honored him by putting a price on his head—ten thousand American dollars."

"I think sometime I turn myself in for that," Jimmy said, silently chuckling. Then Jack noticed that, while his head didn't move, his face grew dark. "Okay, you make Jimmy big hero," he said quietly. "Now you tell him the rest."

Doc's smile also stopped when he remembered the rest. "His family had been moved for their safety," he said, even as Jack knew what was coming. "They had a safe house in a very quiet area of Baghdad. . . ."

"Quiet street," Jimmy echoed hollowly. "Safe, they said. The bad guys, they kill my wife and daughter if they find them." Jimmy shook his head. "They don't find them. Not on purpose. They killed by car bomb at market, with twenty others. Accident, not assassination."

"Murder, by any name," Jack said grimly. He glanced at the reflection in the jet window to see Jimmy's face. It was pained, his eyes narrow slits. But he didn't cry. Jack guessed he had no more tears left.

"Jimmy kept working," said Doc. "Another year. Two. A couple of attempts on his life. He kept going out on missions. The SEALs tried getting him a visa to come to the States. They knew it was just a matter of time before somebody got him. No luck. But they kept finding ways to move him around the Middle East. It's our good fortune that Sol got him assigned to us. . . ."

"Look," Jimmy declared, pointing. "We close now."

Jack looked out the other window to see the same green-spotted expanse of dark brown and tan countryside, only this time knifed in the center by a swath of dark blue and light green-blue.

"Yanbu' al Bahr means spring by the sea," Jimmy explained. "Because it's an oasis, with water. Green in the desert."

"I see," said Jack. "I do, indeed."

"Saudis all rich," Jimmy added. "But like rich uncle, not give money freely. You work here, you are slave. Most workers, not Saudi."

With that knowledge rattling around his brain, Jack was glad that his prince-driven fame held him in good stead here as well, despite the airport not being nearly as grand as the one in Riyadh. It was far smaller, in fact, than a comparable facility in the United States. Instead of the massive fields of parking lots and garages, there was a single lot that wouldn't have impressed a McDonald's restaurant back home.

The three were out of the airport and over at the car rental stands within minutes. The man there wanted to give them a Chevrolet Caprice but Jimmy came away with a Mercedes E-Class.

"Shouldn't we keep a low profile?" Jack wondered once more.

"Here, Mercedes is low profile," Jimmy assured him with a big grin. "With Chevy we stick out like . . . what you call it? Shore thumb."

Neither man bothered to correct him. In this port city, "shore thumb" worked fine. They hadn't gone two blocks before Jimmy spoke up again.

"Someone following," he said.

Both Americans knew better than to turn around and look, but Jack couldn't keep himself from saying, "You sure?"

"I go back and forth, they go back and forth," said Jimmy. "I twist, they twist."

Doc slid down in the seat so he could see out the side mirror. "White Opel. Ten years old."

"Too old for a government car," said Jack.

"Not here," answered Doc. "It's not like America. Bureaucrats don't get a new car every year."

"Qaeda used cars like that in Iraq," said Jimmy, glancing at Doc.

Doc shook his head. "The Saudis aren't going to let Al Qaeda operate here. Two men in the front seat. Can't make out their features. My guess is it's local cops."

Jimmy didn't answer. Jack thought Doc was probably right—the car more than likely belonged to either the local police or the interior ministry's notorious Mabahith—the central government's secret police. They routinely kept track of foreigners. This was better than being trailed by terrorists, though he wasn't sure by how much.

"The question is, why did they decide to trail us?" said Jack. "Just because we're strangers in town? Or do they know who we are?"

"The first," answered Doc. "Routine in Saudi Arabia."

"I can lose them," said Jimmy.

"I doubt that," said Doc.

Jimmy mashed the gas pedal. Jack put his hand on Jimmy's shoulder. "No. Take it easy. If it's the police, we're not going to get very far. They'll call for help and then we'll have other problems. We have a lot to do here. Play it cool. If they stop us, just be honest and up front."

"We say we look for weapon of mass destruction?" The interpreter took his foot off the gas. The other car had not sped up appreciably.

"Not that honest and up front," Doc said.

"We're working on a documentary about Saudi Arabia," Jack fudged. "We're here to look at the port because it's an important place."

Jimmy glanced at him. "You do not have a lot of camera equipment."

"We're guerrilla filmmakers," Doc explained.

Thankfully, their contingency plans were unnecessary. Within minutes, the Opel had veered off, and disappeared into the surrounding roads. Jimmy raised his eyebrows, surprised.

"Gave them time to check with the airport authorities," Jack guessed. "They probably found out I was in the country to interview Prince Riad al-Saud."

"If it's government, true," said Jimmy. "Al Qaeda different."

"Doc said that's unlikely."

Jimmy shrugged.

"You don't agree?" asked Jack.

Jimmy shrugged again. Just then, the call to prayers sounded from the minaret of a nearby mosque. The recorded message sounded both mechanical and lyrical at the same time—the Arabic reverberating in the stillness of the dawn. It had no effect on Jimmy, who seemed completely oblivious as he steered the car toward the port area to the south. Jack wondered what Jimmy's attitude toward Islam was. But asking felt like violating the man's privacy. Jack remembered a snippet from a show he'd done with a minister. It was easier to talk about how much someone earned than how he worshiped God. Maybe that was part of the problem.

"What name the ship?" asked Jimmy as they neared the port.

Jack looked out the windshield, scanning the area for every detail he could retain. The port was an interesting mixture of the old and new, the small and the large. There were slips for pleasure and fishing crafts as well as piers for container ships and tankers. On the basis of their research back in San Francisco, the boat they were waiting for was somewhere between the two extremes.

"*Flower of Asia*," Jack told Jimmy. "Don't worry. We've got plenty of time. . . ."

"No we don't," Doc interrupted. "Look."

Jack stared out the windshield to see a smallish cargo ship docked at the pier Jimmy was approaching. Its containers were being off-loaded. The name on the side was in both Chinese and English. The English letters read FLOWER OF ASIA.

The ship had arrived hours, if not a full day, early.

33

"Bastards," Jack exclaimed. "Probably filled out the manifests wrong to throw off the Mossad, let alone us. Should've thought of that."

"Nothing we could've done," Doc assured him. "We were already behind the time gun when we started. Could not have gotten here any sooner."

Jack bit his tongue as he thought about the time they could've saved if they hadn't gotten the illegal guns, but he was thankful that Doc and Jimmy had them. "So what do we do now?" he finally said. "How do we find out whether the switches have already been off-loaded?"

"No problem," said Jimmy. "We go see."

"But—" Jack started, then fell back as Jimmy accelerated toward the pier. He drove directly to the gate, and after an animated conversation with the guard completely in Arabic, filled with gesticulations and several direct pointing at Jack and Doc, they sped through.

"What did you say?" Jack asked.

"You are representative of company, check to make sure shipment correct."

"But what if they check?"

"SEAL rule: we deal with problem if it is a problem." Jimmy flashed a smile—the first of the day. "SEALs always say, 'Do until you are told no.'"

They drove up to the control booth where the unloading was being supervised. The glass-enclosed booth stood at the top of a steel grid about five stories high, giving the men inside a good view of the ship and the machinery that grabbed the containers. They were large metal prongs—they reminded Jack of the Erector toy sets he'd loved as a kid.

Jimmy led them up the steel stairs to the booth. Jack had to trot to keep up. The air-conditioned room looked very much like the control tower of a modern airport. A desk-like panel, surrounded by large display screens, covered three quarters of the space—running just under the large windows. Tinted screens sat at various heights to deal with the sun.

Three men in white shirts and dress trousers sat in Aeron chairs. They were so intent on their screens that they seemed not to notice the trio when they entered. Jimmy walked to the nearest man and began haranguing him—not too politely, Jack noted. A second man came over, and Jimmy turned his attention to him, talking even louder and gesturing with his hands.

The second man seemed to be in charge, though his only noticeable sign of office was a Western-style tie dangling from its clip on his unbuttoned collar. The man perspired profusely; sweat rolled down his cheeks despite the fact that the air-conditioning was blasting and even Jack, no fan of the heat, felt cold. The supervisor held up both hands as Jimmy's harangue continued, trying to calm him down. Finally the Saudi glanced toward Jack, appealing to him for calm, but Jimmy stepped in front of him, continuing to speak in nonstop Arabic.

The supervisor said something to the first man Jimmy had talked to. The man picked up the phone. Jack thought he was calling security and braced for a confrontation. Doc's hand on his shoulder reassured him. Sure enough, Jimmy began nodding. He softened his tone, and, after a few more minutes of conversation, everyone was smiling. The supervisor went to a printer at the far end of the booth. Fetching a piece of paper, he headed toward Jack.

Jimmy cut him off, his hand out. The man gave him the paper. The little terp nodded approvingly

"Come on, bosses," he said loudly. "Problem solved. Good job here. All good job. Very efficient."

Jack and Doc followed him out to the stairs. "Did I just promise to give them my first born?" Jack asked as they started down.

"What do you mean?" asked Jimmy.

"Did you bribe them?"

"Not at all. The container left the yard a half hour ago. Here is the registration of the truck and the destination."

The remarkable terp led them back to the car as Doc leaned down to speak quietly in Jack's ear. "Notice all the bribing was done Stateside?" he asked. "Get your head into the Middle East, Jack. You're in 'The Kingdom' now."

Jack nodded grimly. "Yes," he grunted. "That's what's worrying me. I can almost hear them thinking how my head would look on a stick, like Gordon of Khartoum. Get rid of me, weaken my country's safety a bit more."

"Starting to hear voices like a desert prophet, eh, Jack?" Doc joked.

"No," Jack replied gravely. "I'm mentally replaying the tapes of my old show, the hate-calls from the radicals."

The men bundled into the car, and Doc leaned forward to confer with Jimmy.

"Where to?"

"Warehouse," Jimmy reported, starting the car. "Other side of city. Six miles away. Time me—see how fast I get you there."

It was less than ten horrifying minutes. Some of Jimmy's turns and weaving brought them to a hair's length of other vehicles, the sidewalks, and even buildings. But they got there in one piece, and stared at the warehouse, which was nestled between what looked like a small chemical plant and an agricultural wholesaler.

A nondescript truck had just dropped off its container when they arrived. It rumbled out of the lot as they passed, leaving the large gray metal box near the loading dock of the one-story metal building. Jack craned his neck as they passed the building. It looked deserted.

"Let's take a look," Doc said.

"What are we going to say if someone comes along?" Jack asked.

Doc grinned at him. "In Jimmy we trust. Haven't you learned that yet?"

Jack looked over at the driver, whose smile and crafty eyes made him feel certain he was in good hands.

Jack studied the area as Jimmy studied the gate. Doc, meanwhile, watched their backs. The buildings flanking the roads were all fairly new mixtures of warehouses and small industries. A massive storage yard for containers filled the area on the north; its roughly two hundred acres was dotted with clusters of large metal boxes. There was no sign of anyone in the buildings.

Nodding, Jimmy marched right up to the container. Jack went right along with him. They checked the markings. Sure enough, it was the one.

"Inside that container are switches that could help trigger a bomb and kill God knows how many people," Jack told the others.

"Too big for car," Jimmy fretted. "What we do? Drag it behind car with chain?"

Jack looked around. Still no sign of anyone. "We've got to keep it out of Brooks's hands," he decided. "Let's just sabotage it." He looked at Doc for feedback or even approval, but the man just looked pensive. "What, you don't like the idea?"

"I like it fine," Doc rumbled. "I'm just asking myself: considering what's in that box, why isn't anyone here to collect it?"

Suddenly Jack felt very vulnerable and exposed. He looked around quickly for any sign of an ambush. "Good question," he said shakily.

Now both Doc and Jimmy were looking off in different directions.

"No snipers," Jimmy said with a certainty borne of experience.

"And I can't see anyone lying in wait," Doc reported. And if Doc didn't see them, there was no one there.

Jack began to get a very bad feeling of being led around by the nose. The docking time of the ship had been purposely changed. And now the switch shipment had been dumped in no-man's-land. He turned back to the box, which, in an extremely strange way, now felt as if it were mocking him.

"All right," said Jack. "Let's get this over with." He turned to Jimmy. "You got a tire iron?"

Jimmy held it up as if he were both a mind reader and a magician.

Jack turned to Doc. "Got the digicam?" Doc held it up the same way as Jimmy had produced the tire iron—only with the same expression he always reserved for that question.

Jimmy eyed the digicam suspiciously. "That's your equipment?"

"This cargo container has just arrived in Saudi Arabia from a small company in Oakland, California," Jack said tightly, as he pried at the crate's nails and slats. "A company that makes copy machines and electrical parts—very special electrical parts. . . ." Jack continued to narrate as he pried off the locks. "Key components for a sophisticated bomb, hidden in an office shipment. In just a few moments, we will make sure that they cannot be used in any weapon of mass . . ."

A section of the crate gave way. It fell onto the ground with a hollow clatter. Jack stopped speaking. There was no reason to continue.

The container was empty.

34

Riyadh, Saudi Arabia

General Brooks checked his watch. He was due at the ambassador's residence in three hours for a cocktail party in his honor.
Ordinarily he disliked attending fancy diplomatic shindigs—
"pretend balls" he called them—but he was going to relish this
one. The American ambassador to Saudi Arabia hated his guts,
and the feeling was mutual. Brooks would savor the pleasure of
smiling into his smile.

If only there was some way to get him to Mecca when the bomb
exploded! Brooks indulged himself in the image for a few moments, then turned his thoughts to the matter at hand. His man
at Yanbu had sent him a message; he needed to find a private place
to read it. He continued walking across the installation, nodding
at the salutes of the men he passed, heading toward the large
double-wide trailer used as the command's headquarters.

During the First Gulf War, the stationing of so many American troops on Saudi soil encouraged some extremists—most notably Osama bin Laden—to oppose the Saudi leadership and claim
that it should be overthrown. The issue of "infidels" on Saudi soil
was still very sensitive.

While the long-distance X-Band Radar here protected vital
Saudi assets—including the holy cities of Mecca and Jeddah—
Americans were nonetheless under orders to keep a very quiet
presence. The base was a small, self-contained area in the corner
of a Royal Saudi Air Force installation some thirty miles south of
Riyadh. Personnel were practically restricted from leaving, and
when they did leave, they had to wear civilian clothes. Very possibly these men would have to be sacrificed at the start of the war.
The thought sobered Brooks, and he gave each man a respectful
nod as well as a formal salute as he passed. Finally he reached the
command trailer. He pulled the door open and went in, luxuriat-
ing for a moment in the cool hallway.

The men's room was on the right. Brooks ducked in, and locked
the door behind him. It was one of the few places on the base
where he could absolutely count on being alone. He took out his
private satellite phone and began entering the series of passwords
that prevented anyone but himself from using it. Then he entered
the encryption key of the day. The last barrier was a retina reader
app, which required a photo of his iris. This was actually the trick-
iest step—General Brooks had developed a bad habit of blinking
as the flash went off, spoiling the shot.

It took two tries today. Better than normal.

He went to the web browser and called up the program where
the message was stored as a video. Leaning back against the wall,
he pressed PLAY.

Rather than the text he assumed he would see, an actual video
came on the screen. The image was in bright, sharp color. It showed
a Mercedes driving ahead of whoever was taking the video. The
unusually sensitive camera zoomed in and waited until the man
in the Mercedes passenger seat turned his head into profile. Then
the image froze, and zoomed in even more.

It was Jack Hatfield.

Brooks smiled. The general had been right. Hatfield was exactly the sort of man who could see what was coming and explain
it to America. Brooks had watched some episodes of *Truth Tellers*
on YouTube. While some of the broadcasts were not as unabash-
edly patriotic as he might have liked, on the whole Hatfield provided a clear and refreshing view of what was really happening in

the world. The fact that he was far outside the Washington Beltway was one factor, but Brooks was convinced that it was more than that—if every generation produced a finite number of people with clear vision and perceptive minds, Jack Hatfield was among them.

And now here he was in Saudi Arabia, not just preparing for their interview, but, as Peter Andrews suspected, tracking down the operation. Too bad he was wasting his time. The last pieces of the bombs were in place; in two days, Jerusalem and Mecca would be completely destroyed.

Brooks heard someone outside in the hall. He closed the program, exited out of the security barriers, and returned the phone to his pocket. Then he went to the commode, flushed the toilet, and washed his hands.

The base commander's chief of staff, a Chinese-American who'd recently been promoted to major, was waiting in the hallway when he emerged. "Sorry to bother you, General," said the major. "Your event coordinator wants you to call him right away regarding an interview. Colonel Hall's phone is available," added the major, pointing to his boss's office.

"Thank you, Major."

Brooks walked quickly up the hall, nodded at the secretary, then stepped into Colonel Hall's office. The call went through quickly.

"General," came Andrews's frosty tone. "It is time I tell your precious Mr. Hatfield the time and place of your meeting."

"Set up an appointment at the Four Seasons," said Brooks, revealing the hotel where he was staying in Riyadh. "Make it for dinner."

"That late?" Andrews countered. "Who knows what mischief he and his friends might get into by then?"

Brooks glanced quickly around, just to make sure he had complete privacy. "I told you before," he said tightly. "He is not to be touched. He may become very important in the mission's aftermath."

"Yes, sir," Andrews said in his unique way of making "yes" sound like "oh, very well." The event coordinator continued blithely. "And he will not be. Does the same go for his associates?"

The question brought Brooks up short. For a moment he considered how Hatfield being isolated from his support team might affect him. Would it make him easier to deal with? It could go either way.

"Yes," he told Andrews, "but only if they do not prove a direct threat to the operation."

"And if they do?"

"Hatfield is to be protected," Brooks ordered. "The others should be dealt with as you deem necessary."

Andrews appreciated the vote of confidence. "Yes, sir. Thank you, sir."

"You've earned it, Peter. Keep up the good work."

"I shall, sir," Andrews replied sincerely. He was about to disconnect the call.

"Peter?"

"Sir?"

"Tell Hatfield I'm looking forward to our interview," Brooks said. "I'm looking forward to it very much."

"I will tell him that, sir," Peter Andrews said into the phone.

35

Yemen, Saudi Arabia

It was Peter Andrews who spoke to Brooks, but now it was his alter ego, Pyotr Ansky, who disconnected the call.

Standing in the middle of the desert on the border, Saudi side, the killer adjusted his headscarf and then folded his arms in front of him. He had parachuted here ten minutes before, precisely as planned. After burying his parachute and helmet, he stood and waited. He smiled at the military-grade communication device in his hand. By all rights, it should not have worked here.

Communication towers? he thought. *Who needs them?*

Pyotr was not impatient. He had learned patience the hard way—spending time in the prison "box," where his only companions were the rats that gnawed at his toenails while he slept. He smiled thinly as he heard the sound of a motor in the distance. He took a slow, deep breath and waited.

A Range Rover appeared from the direction of the hills a few moments later, riding over the undulating dunes at a speed that had to be close to a hundred and twenty kilometers an hour. A vast cloud of dust and sand rose behind it. *The angry fist of God,*

Pyotr thought. Then he cleared his mind of metaphors. They were distractions.

The truck didn't slow until it was almost upon him. Then the driver hit the brakes so hard that Pyotr thought it would surely roll over and crush him. But he remained calm. He stood still even as the grit caught up with the vehicle and spread over him.

The truck stopped a few meters away, without rolling over. As the dust cloud settled, its driver and two other men got out. They had the Kalashnikovs, as Pyotr had suggested. The small group separated; two stayed near the truck; the other came forward. He held his gun in one hand, finger pointed parallel to the barrel, just as Pyotr had taught him. It was the man who had nearly fallen in the rigid-hulled raft after Pyotr had brought down the airliner. The remaining pair were his other men—the one who had worked the engines, and the third who served as their backup. Pyotr had trained them well, and they had proven capable and worthy.

The man who nearly fell when Pyotr had thrown the container at him had never faltered again. He now reached into his pocket and took out a USB drive. "The location is in the document."

Pyotr took the flash drive. "Good." It was time for the next phase.

"The Americans are getting closer and closer," his second-in-command blurted. "We could kill them easily."

Pyotr snorted. "A child could kill them easily." He looked up at his associate. "Are you a child who needs to have such a tantrum?"

The man swallowed, his lips tight. "No, sir."

"Then you will continue to do as you are ordered."

"Yes, sir. We will have the Jerusalem bomb in hand by the time you make your attack." He swallowed again. "As ordered."

"Good," Pyotr repeated. He turned to look everywhere around him, savoring the sight . He wondered what the sands would look like when a nuclear response turned them into glass. When he turned back, his second-in-command had never seen his smile so wide or his eyes so bright. "Now drive me back to the airfield," Pyotr Ansky commanded.

36

Yanbu' al Bahr, Saudi Arabia

"Brooks is playing with us," said Jack in frustration. "He knows we're here, he knows we're trying to stop the bombing, and he's playing with us. The cat-and-mouse mentality of the Islamists is rubbing off on him."

"How are *they* cat-and-mouse?" Doc asked. "Terrorists are more like mice, hiding and then running after they bell the cat. Or in this case, bomb him."

"Those are the foot soldiers you're talking about," Jack said. "I mean the leaders. The ones who plot, who want to instill fear until you're too paralyzed to act, would rather capitulate."

"Ah," Doc nodded. "I see your point. Well, we have to get ahead of this, that's for sure."

Jimmy watched the two, moving his head back and forth, as if they were tennis players.

"But how?" asked Jack. It wasn't really a question; he was thinking aloud.

"There's got to be another container, to start with," Doc surmised. "This crate had been switched for another one, probably right under our noses. Look." Doc held up the shipping records from San Francisco, and the record Jimmy had gotten from the shipping yard master. The number on this crate matched the shipping yard records. It did not match the San Francisco manifest.

"What we have to do is find the right one," Doc concluded. "We'll go to the yard and look for these numbers."

"Assuming it's still there," Jack added.

"Got a better idea?" Doc asked.

Jack didn't, so they went, Jimmy getting them there faster than before. They found a lot more activity at the dockyard, but if anything security was even laxer, with the guard simply waving as they came in. They began a search, but soon realized it was in vain. The place was bustling, and the odds of finding anything out of sheer dumb luck were about the same as hitting the lottery Powerball.

"Jimmy," Jack suggested. "Go talk to the men who unloaded the *Flower of Asia*. See if they can tell us anything."

Jimmy went to work, and ultimately wound up with a group of truck drivers who were waiting for their loads in a bullpen-type area near the entrance. It took him a few minutes and some cigarettes to find where the cargo containers that had come off the *Flower of Asia* were being held for pickup. Only a dozen trailers were stored there. None had the right numbers.

A few more cigarettes took Jimmy to the foreman of the crew responsible for unloading *Flower of Asia*. He was from Indonesia; his Arabic was poor, but his English nearly perfect. Doc took over, and managed to persuade him to check the records on what containers had been shipped out already.

The man wanted a hundred bucks. Jimmy frowned on that, but Jack supplied the cash. "Look for where this one went in particular," said Jack, handing over a piece of paper with the number of the container they'd found.

The man fiddled with the slightly oversize tablet computer that provided access to the records. It looked like an iPad with an antenna. He came up with an address two towns over.

Jack walked away with a cunning smile, but Jimmy was frowning.

"What's up?" asked Doc when they were far enough away from

the bullpen. The three were framed in a huge square doorway of the cavernous place.

"Man no good," Jimmy said. "Man lying. Sending us on wild moose chase."

"How do you know?" Jack pressed, hoping he didn't waste the hundred.

"Man took bribe," Jimmy explained. "Ask for too much. Man who take bribe dishonest. Man who ask for too much think you a . . ."

Jimmy didn't want to finish the sentence in deference to his manners, but Jack saw the truth in what Jimmy was saying.

Jack lowered and shook his head. He realized he wanted to defeat Brooks too badly. He looked up at a sympathetic Doc. "Should've listened to you about getting my head in the Middle East game. I keep thinking this is America with Saudis in it." He looked back to Jimmy. "How do we get the truth out of him?"

"Him?" Jimmy echoed. "We don't."

Jimmy looked around until he saw a group of Arab women and children in the far corner. The kids were playing, but only near the small circle of women, who knitted, cooked on small hot plates, and talked. The women were all wearing niqabs—the body covering garb that only revealed their eyes. To Jack's eyes, it looked like a small section of a Middle Eastern village moved inside an expansive hangar.

"Them?" Jimmy said with a wide smile. "We do."

He motioned to the two Americans to stay back, then casually approached the conclave of women and children.

"Probably wives and kids of the truckers," Doc surmised. "Who knows how long they have to wait here for an assignment, so the women come along to make them food or tend to whatever needs they require. And since they probably can't afford, or don't want, babysitters . . . !"

Jack watched as Jimmy chatted with the women. Since he was wearing nice Arabian clothes, they showed him respect, but soon there was more than that. He reminded Jack of certain perceptive, persuasive stand-up comics, and sure enough, the women started laughing and nodding to each other.

Eventually Jimmy made his farewells and returned to Doc and

Jack, motioning for them to follow him. "Those men would never betray their bosses, no matter how much you pay them," Jimmy explained. "You gone in a moment. Hundred dollars not enough to retire on. You never know the truth from them. Ah, but their wives . . . ! Wives know what men say about bosses behind bosses' back."

Doc smiled in appreciation and admiration as they all got back into the car. "So you commiserated with them, right?"

"What is commiseration?" Jimmy asked, starting the car.

"Sympathized with them," Jack translated. "Understood what they were going through, and joked about it with them."

"Yes, yes," Jimmy said as they drove away from the pier. "Co-mis-er-ate." He nodded. "Good word."

"What did they tell you?" Jack asked.

"Saudi Air Force," Jimmy reported, heading away from town. "The place they sent the truck was Saudi AF base."

"Around here?" Doc asked. "I don't know any Saudi Air Force Base around here."

"No name," Jimmy revealed. "Strange. But I have directions."

Doc frowned. "This does not sound good," he decided. "Take it nice and easy, Jimmy."

Jack looked to his tall, experienced friend with a question on his face.

"If the truck driver told his wife that he was sent to an Air Force base," Doc explained. "I figured it was because they wanted that driver, as well as the others, to stay away."

"No, no," Jimmy countered. "Wife say air force base okay. Got nice little town there, helping soldiers."

Doc's face registered surprise, then concern. "Interesting. Still be careful, Jimmy."

"Always careful, Doc," Jimmy assured him.

The landscape changed dramatically several times before they'd gone five miles. The port buildings gave way to a thin green belt of lettuce and other sunflowers, which promptly melted into total desert, then a fog of sand, and finally a hardscrabble collection of low hills and canyons that clustered beneath the horseshoe peak of Jebel Jar, a nearby mountain.

Jack studied the area. The only sign of life was a small group of Bedouins camped in the middle of the desert to the east as they drove. But no matter how hard they looked, the terrain in front of them looked just as empty and uninviting. Then Jimmy spotted a pair of large rocks at the side of the road. They had been painted with white swirls.

"We turn here," he said.

"There's no road," Jack pointed out.

"Rocks mark something," said Jimmy.

"What did they say?" Doc asked.

"'Praise Allah.' Out in the desert? Must be sign."

They fishtailed onto a pockmarked dirt road, skidding in the loose sand. Jimmy kept going, keeping his momentum up until they reached a harder packed section that headed them toward a set of low hills. The firmer surface of the road was a mixed blessing; the path was studded with holes deep enough to hide a dog in.

"I hope you know where we can get some good shock absorbers," said Jack as they thumped along.

"You be sterile for week," said Jimmy. "SEAL joke. Get it?"

Try as he might, Jack couldn't. He looked to Doc for help. "Damn squids never could come up with a good punch line," his friend grumbled. "Does this match up with what the trucker's wife told you?" he asked.

"Close enough," Jimmy assured him.

Jack realized that they were all at the mercy of a Middle Eastern game of "telephone." The husband told the wife, the wife told Jimmy, and now they had to live with the result. Five minutes later, they came across what looked like an abandoned oil well head. A concrete platform, half covered by sand, sat on a small rise just off the road. Jimmy turned again, nearly losing control of the car in the dirt. They quickly found a hard-packed road—and this one was much smoother than anything they'd been on since leaving the highway.

"That's a good sign," Doc determined.

Half a mile later, the road took a sharp turn to the left, then back to the right, entering a canyon. There Jimmy slowed the car down even more and he looked confused.

"What's up?" Jack asked him.

Jimmy looked in every direction, craning his neck. "Woman say village here."

Jack stared into the blankness of the area. "You sure?" Jimmy nodded. "Maybe we took a wrong turn at those rocks?"

"No," Jimmy said with certainty. He drove down the road slowly, his eyes checking both sides of the road.

Jack followed his gaze but could see nothing unusual. Even so, given the driver's concentration, he didn't want to distract him. "What is he looking for?" he whispered to Doc, who was leaning forward in the backseat.

"Booby traps," Doc murmured back.

Jack was bewildered. "Here?"

"If Jimmy is checking for booby traps, he has good reason. Shush."

They both watched the driver study the seemingly benign area, until Jimmy stopped the car as they reached a flat plateau. He turned off the engine and stepped out. Jack and Doc got out shortly after, watching as Jimmy moved around in a widening circle.

"Half-dozen shacks," Jimmy told them. He pointed between his feet. "Here."

Jack looked, and saw nothing.

Doc looked, and kicked at rocks on the side of the tire path. "Look," he told Jack. "More treads. Heavy machinery. And they were trailers, Jack. Easily moved."

Jack came over and saw the marks in the ground. "What'd they do with them?" asked Jack. "Haul them away?"

"I think so." Doc walked across the open area where the trailers had been. "The question is why."

Jack walked around the flattened area, his shoes sinking into the sand. He kicked down a few inches, scraping the dirt with his foot until he came to harder ground. Whoever had moved the trailers had simply dumped sand to make their work harder to spot. Why would anyone create a shanty town by a secret air force base, then sweep it away as if it never existed?

"They're done with the bomb," Jack realized. "That's why the village is gone." Doc didn't answer. He was too busy poking around the edges of what had once been a settlement. Suddenly he barked, "Here. Quick."

Jimmy and Jack raced over to find that Doc had uncovered some boards beneath the sand. Without exchanging another word, they all started digging at it with their hands. Jimmy found something. At first Jack thought it was part of one of the trailers—had they buried them here? Then he saw it was smaller, narrower. He looked closer.

It was an arm, sticking out from a pit below.

37

San Francisco, California

Sammy was alone in front of the computer console upstairs at the safe house. Ric was taking a nap, spooning Miwa, who was napping beside him. Sammy didn't begrudge them. They had earned it. Ric had been monitoring the situation nonstop since Jack and Doc had left, and was keeping both sides informed of any progress.

Sol was God-knew-where, doing God-knew-what. Probably getting more new cars, Sammy thought. Boaz was down in the secure room, monitoring Middle East chatter while Ritu served as night watchman for the residents. Sammy hoped that Boaz was doing a better job than the authorities. Dover could fret and suggest all she wanted, but any ex-Marine could tell you that the U.S. government was a sleepy giant, who only moved when it absolutely had to.

Sammy blinked. He realized he was a sleepy giant as well, entering his twenty-second straight hour trying to find golden needles in the sad haystack of Montgomery Morton's hard drive. Who else was Morton working with? Was the whole Strategic Command involved? Was Al Qaeda or some other terror group involved?

The questions were ghosts haunting Sammy as he picked through the digital puzzle pieces. It was an obsession, and more than that. There was a plan, a big plan, something worth killing over. That was why Schoenberg was dead. That's why Morton had tried to kill them. Maybe he'd stumbled onto it. Maybe he'd been part of it from the beginning. Sammy was convinced that it had something to do with the documentary his brother was working on, but far more serious.

That was the difference between them. Jack had the head of a journalist. Sammy had been a warrior. Jack and Sammy had the same mother, but their fathers had made all the difference. Sammy's father was old school with a vengeance, a strict disciplinarian who expressed his love for his only son with a constant stream of criticism and harsh words. Over the years, Sammy had come to understand that his father had been trying, in his own way, to help his son become successful. But growing up, Sammy had only felt the harshness. Jack had a different father, far more laid back and easygoing—probably too much, at least in Sammy's opinion. He doted on Jack, praising him to excess. Partly as a result, Jack felt free to pursue his dreams. Sammy was caught in a never-ending cycle of trying to please an unpleasable father.

As a result, Sammy was always one to push things, whether it was a teacher's patience or the red line on his motorcycle's tachometer. He surprised the family by joining the Marines in his senior year of high school, but in retrospect the move was typical Sammy—impulsive, honorable, and probably for the best. The Marines did little to tame his impulsive side, and certainly didn't hurt his confidence, but they added a discipline and a smattering of skills.

Sammy learned to use a rifle well enough to be recommended for sniper school. He turned the offer down, wisely knowing that while he might shoot well, he didn't have the patience to complete the scout portion of the training, which to the Marines was as important as marksmanship. He served instead as an intelligence specialist, where his daily interactions with computer systems sparked enough of an interest that he taught himself to program in C++.

He was home on leave, reacquainting himself with his motorcycle when a Prius driver yakking on a cell phone sideswiped him on a curve coming out of the Sausalito tunnel a few miles outside the city. The accident left Sammy physically disabled, and effectively ended his Marine Corps career. He bought the apartment with the insurance settlement, started going to school for computer science, but dropped out midway through his third semester. Various career plans had fizzled before he took up his latest: a clown.

Why a clown? Jack hadn't been able to fathom it. Becoming a Marine, studying computers—those were decisions that made sense. Putting a red ball on his nose and blowing up balloons for bratty five-year-olds didn't. But, he realized, with each balloon, Sammy knew there was something about being a clown that satisfied his soul. The kids' smiles and applause were part of it, but there was much more to it that he could never explain.

Sammy knew that his brother and the rest of the family were disappointed in him, but they didn't understand how being a clown made him feel. For forty-five minutes he was immersed in what could only be called paradise. And he was good at it.

The tap of a coffee cup hitting the desk beside him made Sammy jerk in place. Then the soft hand on his shoulder and light laugh behind him told him Ana was there, as always, anticipating his needs and backing him up.

She buried her face in his shoulder. Sammy craned his neck to kiss her ear and touch her hair.

"Are you all right?" she asked quietly, so as not to disturb Ric and Miwa.

"No," he admitted.

Her head came up, honest concern on her face. "What's wrong?" Her caring for him made him feel even worse, but still, somehow, stronger.

"Do you know why I'm working so hard on this?"

"Of course. You want to show us all what you can do. What I know you can do."

He shook his head, then nodded, seemingly confused. "No, I mean yes, of course, but beyond that." He looked deeply into her extraordinary eyes, trying to feel worthy of them.

"Because, if I figure it all out before Jack, then I'm the smart one. Not him. Me."

Her expression made his heart swell, because she didn't look at him with pity. She looked at him with understanding.

"It's so petty and venal, I'm ashamed of it," he confessed. "I need to best my brother . . . in the worst way."

"Oh, Sammy," she said, almost as a sigh. "Come here," she continued, gently turning his chair and wrapping her arms around him. "I know, I know. . . ."

He let her embrace him as his arms came up to hold her in return, but as he set his head against hers he mumbled bitterly into her silken hair, "How can you know? How can you?"

"Just hold me," she said. And he did, for what seemed like hours. He folded his arms around her, gently pulling her breasts against his chest. He lowered his head down into her hair. Her perfume entangled him, an exotic scent of flowers and spice. She began to rock very gently, as if he were a baby. And, like a baby being lulled to sleep, she told him a story. "I know because I, too, had a father," she went on. "My father was impossible. *Impossible*. The most impossible man ever." He heard in her voice her love for her father, but also her hate, and, ultimately, her acceptance, empathy, and understanding. "He was married to my mother, yet he wasn't. Not fully. He could never be. It wasn't because he didn't love just her. He didn't love women."

"You mean he couldn't love?" Sammy inquired.

She shook her head.

"Oh," Sammy replied.

He wasn't a gay-basher but he wasn't comfortable with the idea of homosexuality, either. It was one thing to say he didn't have a problem with it, and quite another to actually understand. He knew he should understand; he'd known three gay Marines, who of course were closeted though it was an open secret to the unit. He also knew they were good Marines—one was the second-ranking NCO on his first fire team, and Sammy would surely have followed him through hell. And living in San Francisco, it was impossible not to know someone who was gay. But Sammy had never had a real discussion about homosexuality with anyone he could think of.

But Anastasia wanted to talk about it, and so, maybe for the first time in his life, certainly for the first time since the accident, he wanted to listen.

"My father was in the closet when they got married," she whispered. "They were young. Well, I don't know. Maybe he didn't know. He claims he didn't know. My mother certainly didn't. I think maybe he wanted just to conform, but it's impossible to read someone else's mind, you know? Especially on something like that. But one day my mom came home and there he was . . . with someone else. It was a bad way to find out—a big shock. I was in the other room, a year and a half old. It was chaos. I didn't remember a thing, except . . . except my father was not there. I grew up without a papa, yet I still had one. In all the dirty whispers and all the pointed fingers, I still had one."

Sammy held her tighter. *What was worse?* he wondered. Growing up with an abusive father, or with an absent father and abusive neighbors?

"It wasn't like today," Anastasia continued as if it were a fairy tale. "There was still a stigma, and—and gays weren't considered good parents. That's nonsense, but that's what people said. But I didn't blame the whisperers and pointers. I blamed him. I blamed my dad." She stopped and took a long breath. "We didn't talk about him. I tried a few times. But my mother . . . her heart was closed. Years go by and I moved out to L.A. I was going to be a model and an actress. But too short here, too round there, blah-blah-blah. And your eyes . . . my God, what is it with your eyes?"

Anastasia gave a small, throaty laugh, which made Sammy feel better than he had since Jack and Doc had left.

"Then one day I get a phone call. It's him. In San Francisco. Of course, San Francisco. We met for coffee. We tried to patch things up, but I was too hurt. In his absence I let him hurt me. It was all my fault, you see? In my mind, he left because of me. And I cursed him for that fantasy."

Sammy felt a single tear reach his forehead. He was going to wipe it off for her, but then she continued.

"I couldn't get over the hurt I had built up. I couldn't move on. I was embracing my imagined hurt so I couldn't hold him. I had nursed the hurt so long I thought it was a better friend than he could ever be. He was a bartender in a gay club here. Cliché, right? But that wasn't the only one. I never visited . . . too busy, right? But then, two years later, a hospital calls. They say, 'Your dad's dying.' AIDS. AIDS! Of course."

He felt more tears, but her soft voice continued, telling him it was more important that he listen than console. "That is why I came to San Francisco. It wasn't that the modeling dried up. It was because I wanted to look after him. I could have stayed in L.A., but no. I couldn't leave him the way he left me. Not anymore." She was silent for a few moments, and he felt the tears stop. "I nursed him the way I had foolishly nursed my pain. It wasn't enough. He died within a month. It was only afterward that I found out he didn't get the drugs. He didn't want them. After all he had done to me, he didn't want to linger. . . ." She let go of Sammy. He sat up and looked into her wet eyes that were now shining like beacons. "You see?" she asked, her voice cracking. "You see what blaming your father does?" Sammy drew her to him, holding her more firmly, yet more tenderly than he ever had before. He wanted to protect this woman for eternity. He wanted to make her happy and safe more than he would ever want to best his brother. She had heard the word "Firebird." It had tried to destroy her. He would stand up to it and bring it down if he had to tear off every one of its fiery feathers with his teeth!

Samuel Michaels's eyes snapped open. He found himself staring at the computer screen, but dancing in his mind's eye was a pattern from an exercise he'd done for a class way back in the Marines . . . a byte dump . . . a website sign-in . . . a you-build-it template at an Internet provider creating a simple webpage. He stared at it now. All it consisted of was a template for a plumbing business. . . .

"Oh, my Lord," Sammy breathed. He took Ana's shoulders and kissed her more passionately than he ever had anyone in his life. Then he stabbed at the computer keyboard to access the plumbing site's activity log. Ana looked up at his face, saw his energized expression, and turned her own head to see what he was doing.

The webpage had first been set up over a year before. There were multiple log-ins, but mostly from five separate providers. Sammy checked the sign-in data to see where they were located.

Two were definitely local, and Sammy guessed they were providers whom Morton used to connect to the web. The others were from overseas. From the timing of some of the sign-ons, he guessed that they were being done by at least three different people, not simply one person traveling across the globe.

Now that he had found one website provider, he went back to the various hexadecimal dumps and looked for others. There, he found another website builder, this one from a place in Spain called Ariba!Go.com. Once more he found a bare-bones website, but this one's home page had something on it: a link to Google Maps. At first glance, there appeared to be nothing there—the middle of the desert in Saudi Arabia.

Sammy switched to the satellite view and zoomed in. A long strip of concrete sat in the desert, next to a building and a road. The place looked abandoned. There was a date under the link. It was from a month before. It didn't relate to the satellite image, which was marked as having been taken nearly a full year prior to that.

Once again, Sammy found a log of activity. The log-ins were from the same ISPs he'd found earlier. This site also kept backups of pages that had been worked on. Sammy went through the list. The oldest was the docking time for an Indonesia-registered ship in Saudi Arabia three months before. Sammy made a note of it to research later and scrolled on. There was another shipment, and a passenger plane schedule. Then a page with only three words buried in the description of available services: "Firebird alt feint."

"Jesus!" Sammy exclaimed, rousing Ric and Miwa. "It's a double blind!"

38

Outside Yanbu' al Bahr, Saudi Arabia

Jack's phone buzzed as Doc found the eleventh body in the pit. He looked at Doc, who glanced up from a dirt-covered corpse with slit eyes and a clenched jaw. The smell was not pleasant. Jimmy had already tied part of his headscarf over his nose.

Jack glanced at the smartphone screen. It was from Brooks's event coordinator. "Yes?" he said quietly.

"Mr. Hatfield."

"Yes."

"The general wishes to meet you for dinner at his hotel this evening," said Peter Andrews. "I will text you the exact time and address. Will that be satisfactory?"

"Yes," Jack said for the third time. "Thank you. Tell the general I look forward to talking with him."

"I will—" Andrews started, but Jack had already ended the call. He slipped the device back in his pocket as he looked at Doc.

"Rigor not completely set in," the old soldier intoned. "But they didn't die from natural causes."

"Why am I not surprised?" Jack said tightly. He looked at the sun. "So they were recently killed. And now we have a deadline. First the prince, then the general."

Doc nodded. "Which means we better find who killed them fast."

Jack nodded in return, waved Jimmy over, and the three began shoveling the dirt back over the dead men. Though the temperature was still in the low eighties, Jack's hands were cold. The back of his neck froze and knotted. Rising when he was done, he felt every muscle stiffen. His legs trembled as he walked to the car.

"We go now?" Jimmy asked as he opened the driver's side door. "We get help?" The look on Jack and Doc's faces gave him his answer. His own expression changed to one of understanding. If any justice was to be found in this godforsaken place, it would be found by them.

Incongruously, Jimmy smiled like a panther spotting his prey. "We go on, then," he said, starting the car. "To the Air Force base."

Jimmy piloted the car beyond the village of the dead. On the way, they grimly went over what they knew and what they feared.

"Those men helped Brooks's people make a bomb," Jack said. "Then, when the last pieces came in—the switches—they were killed."

Doc nodded once, gravely.

"You think the cops will find the bodies at the village?" Jimmy pressed.

"Probably not," Doc said. "Who will tell them? And the bodies will be gone in a few days. Scavengers'll pick them apart."

"Under the sand?"

"It was a shallow grave. Wind will blow it off. That's why we use rocks in the field, not—not like this. I'm sure they did it on purpose."

Jack considered making an anonymous call to the Saudi authorities, but quickly realized there was no sense in taking that risk. Even if the local police recorded what they found, it was likely to be suppressed.

"You're thinking," Doc noted.

"Yeah. So their killers can't be far," Jack decided. "No way they'd set the workers' village miles from the base."

Sure enough, within minutes, the car reached a large platform, covered with sand but perfectly flat, spread out by the side of the road. Jimmy quickly turned, and they found themselves at the top of a hill. Jimmy stopped the car behind the nearest dune, then the three scurried out to lay at the crest of an overlooking bluff.

Doc used the digicam. Jack used his smartphone's camera zoom. Jimmy just used his dark eyes to seemingly see for miles. All of them saw a trio of small buildings set in a little cleft between two hills, about five hundred yards below them. The largest of the three structures looked like a stretched one-car garage—maybe four or five car lengths long and barely much wider than one. It had had an overhead door at its face, and another door near the corner at the side, but was otherwise without openings.

One of the smaller buildings looked like a cottage, albeit one that might have only two rooms; the other was bunker-like, short and squat. They seemed to be made from concrete, though from this distance, even with the camera at full zoom, it was difficult to tell.

The small complex was surrounded by razor wire and two very large fences. Two heavily armed men patrolled the perimeter. The guns were HK G36s, easily recognized because of the launcher below the barrel. They were good guns, but definitely not Saudi-issue. The Saudi regular forces were mostly armed with Steyr AUGs; some elite forces used M16 and AR15 variants.

"Why would they need the grenade launchers?" Jack asked softly.

"Slow down an attack," muttered Doc, eye still glued to the soft rubber eyepiece of the digicam. "Blow stuff up. The usual reasons."

"Maybe projectile blow up vehicle," offered Jimmy.

There were two minivans in the parking lot, along with a pair of white pickup trucks. And a cargo container.

"There are no guards at the back," Jack realized. But the gate there was wide open, leading to a driveway that connected to a long runway etched out of the sand. Pointed toward the horizon was a small plane.

"Man moving," said Jimmy, pointing at a person leaving the building.

Doc zoomed in on the man. "Not Saudi."

"Westerner?" Jack asked.

Doc shook his head. "From the facial structure and light hair, I'd say Eastern European."

"Russian?"

"Maybe. The two guards as well."

Jimmy tapped Jack quickly on the arm. "He going to truck."

They watched intently as the man started the truck's engine and the vehicle started lurching toward the exit driveway, and the plane. The hair on all three men's necks stood up. It was as if all had been hit by the same thought at the same time.

"Can you see what the truck is carrying?" Jack asked. As he was speaking he used every pixel his smartphone's zoom had. He thanked the Lord that the truck was an older one, with just a canvas cover that was rolled up at the back.

They could all see a crate there, but there was no way Jack could discern the number from this distance.

"Anything?" he asked Doc intently.

By all rights, the old soldier's vision should have weakened by now, but somehow it had only gotten stronger. Even so, even he couldn't make out anything specific on the crate.

"No," Doc said, thumbing the digicam's zoom repeatedly, hoping against hope that somehow he had missed its optimum level.

Both men broke from staring at the back of the truck when they heard the trunk of their own car open. They looked over to see Jimmy taking an old-fashioned, nautical, telescoping spyglass out of the compartment. He ran back, and plopped down between them.

"Gift from SEALs," Jimmy grunted. As he pulled the object out to its longest setting, Jack saw the inscription on the side. *To ol' Eagle Eye, from a Grateful Crew.* Jimmy used it to target the back of the truck as it bounced toward the plane.

Jack held his breath, but he was already certain that it was the container they had been looking for. What else could it be? What else was worth killing all those buried men for?

"No numbers," Jimmy said. "Too bouncy. But crate from same ship. *Flower of Asia*, yes?"

"Christ Almighty!" Jack hissed. "They have the bomb, they covered their tracks, now they'll destroy the base and fly it out. What are we going to do?"

"Two Glocks against G36's?" Doc grunted. "Close to suicide."

"Close?" Jack snapped back. "But if we don't try, maybe millions will be . . . !"

Jimmy decided the matter for them. Both men's heads snapped right as they heard the throaty roar of the car. They ran toward it, seeing Jimmy's smiling face in the driver's window.

"Enough talk!" he cried as they leaped in and the car vaulted over the hill.

39

The road to the runway didn't exist. Any driver who wanted to remain alive would have told them that the hill was too steep to go straight down, but Jimmy didn't care. He piloted the car like a bobsled—Doc and Jack hanging on for dear life. They took one jarring jump, then another, and started sliding to the side.

"We're going over!" Jack shouted. He saw what would happen. The car would fishtail, then start rolling, top over bottom, as they were all mashed into pulp between the roof and floor.

"No!" Jimmy boomed, tromping the pedals and wrestling the wheel. "Never . . . over . . . !" Suddenly the car was level and surging ahead. Jack kept his eyes on the plane, but Doc and Jimmy's eyes were on the front gate's guards, who had managed to snap their stunned jaws shut and start leveling their compact carbines at the barreling auto.

Both Doc and Jimmy had their arms straight out from the driver's side windows, and were pinpointing their aim despite the car's movement. Doc cursed himself for missing the guard to the left on his first shot, but he knew it had been close, because the guard turned and kneeled. He wouldn't have bothered if the bullet hadn't been so near that the man had heard, or even felt, it.

Jimmy bellowed with rage and glee as he pulled the trigger

twice, making the guard to the right fall back. Jack studied the plane as the man in the truck jumped out of the cab and started waving and shouting. The high-winged plane had a sleek turbo-prop engine on each side, and with its long, cone-like nose looked a bit like an aerodynamic flying troll. "Czech plane," said Doc, catching a glimpse as he repositioned himself. With the guards running, he and Jimmy could no longer get a clear shot. "It's an Evektor-Aeotechink, for short runways."

"Helpful," Jack shouted sarcastically over the roar of the car. "Thanks! How do we stop it?"

"There's no way that's a bomber!"

"All it has to do is fly over its target."

Doc tried to find a shot to stop either the plane or the men, but he knew, at this distance, he'd only be wasting bullets. "We can call the Saudis and tell them to shoot it down," he yelled back to Jack.

"And they'd believe us?!" Jack countered. They had no right to be here, no real evidence, and neither thought a prince-approved interview was going to carry much water in this case.

"Damn!" yelled Doc, and they watched as the first man started the plane up while the other two disappeared into the main building.

"They're running for cover!" Jack enthused. "We got them! Now all we have to do is get in front of the plane, and . . . !"

"No!" Doc yelled, pointing. Jack's eyes followed Doc's arm, and his blood ran cold. Coming out of the building, charging at them, were now four armed men. "Jimmy . . . ," Doc started, but he didn't need to say more. Their driver, grinning like a death's head, stomped on the accelerator.

Thrown back in his seat by the acceleration, Jack didn't realize what was happening until something thumped hard against the car two seconds later. He ducked involuntarily as something else pounded the roof above him. There was a second thud, and the car skidded to a stop. They'd hit not one, but two people.

Doc leaped from the car. Jack did the same. A rifle lay in the dust just beyond the door. It was a 7.62mm ARM version of the Galil, a sturdy, Israeli-built assault rifle that in this case was con-figured as a light machine gun. A 25-round box hung from its belly.

As Jack grabbed the rifle, he saw something moving on his left out of the corner of his eye. He swung the gun like a baseball bat, connecting with the head of one of the men they'd just knocked over. The man, already battered by the car, fell to the side.

Jack tightened his grip on the gun and smashed him again, this time on the top of the head. A geyser of blood spurt from the fissure; Jack sent another blow to the man's chest, then stumbled backward, shocked at what he had just done.

"Check him for a radio," Doc yelled, running up behind Jack. He had a Galil in his right hand and an oversize pistol in his left. Even in shock and at this distance, Jack recognized the pistol as a Desert Eagle, a .50 caliber semiautomatic reputed to be the most powerful handgun in the world. The barrel included a muzzle brake, which not only made the weapon look more foreboding but lessened its recoil.

Jack, still dazed, went down on his knee but drew back his hand as the prone man's chest heaved. Doc didn't hesitate—he slid down on the other side and grabbed the man's sidearm, another Desert Eagle. He hit the man's forehead with the butt end, then stuffed the gun into his belt.

The man had a radio in his tac vest but its headpiece had been ripped off when the car hit him. Doc grabbed the small brick and tossed it as far as he could. Then he undid the man's tac vest and tossed it to Jack.

"In the car, go, go!" said Doc.

Jack nodded, fumbling with the gear and looking up as his heart pounded. While they fought, the other two guards had loaded a bomb-shaped crate onto the plane, and the aircraft was starting its takeoff run.

Doc was saying something as he moved to engage the two remaining guards, but the words didn't connect to any rational thought. Things were moving too fast. Jack knew from experience that he had to dampen down his adrenaline, and in effect slow the world around him down. Take each piece of action on its own, slowly, and he would win. Life is like a clock, Jack heard his father say. Everything fits together.

"Jack, duck!" yelled Doc.

Jack pushed himself toward the door as the windshield

shattered. The sheet of broken safety glass flew into the front, punctured by bullets from a gunman thirty feet ahead.

Jimmy, somehow unaffected by the bullets or debris, aimed to fishtail the rear end of the car into him, but the sand and his speed made him lose control. As he tried to brake, the car went into a three hundred and sixty spin. It whipped around, and then that smacked broadside into the man who'd been firing to stop them.

The guard went under the car as it continued to spin, getting pulverized by the wheels. No matter how loud the car and plane were, they still didn't manage to drown out the sickening sound of bone, muscle, and flesh being blended.

Dizzy, Jack grabbed for the door latch as Doc yelled at him. He ignored his friend, stumbled, then found his footing, and started running toward the plane.

"Get down, get down!" shouted Doc behind him.

Jack either fell, or threw himself, to the ground. Bullets hit the dirt nearby, kicking up mini-explosions of grit and sand. Doc maneuvered behind him, trying to get an angle on the final guard. Jack saw a flash of light on his left, down in the sand. It was one of the fallen rifles.

Jack leaped on it like a drowning man on a life preserver. He squirreled around to get it into position and put his eye near the scope to see. Meanwhile, the white flashes in front of him rose, and the mini-explosions came closer. Jack put his finger on the trigger and the rifle roared, a dozen bullets spitting out before he could stop it.

There were no more flashes, and no more gunfire. Jack looked behind him but couldn't see Doc, Jimmy, or the car. He rose to his knees, searching, then heard the plane's engines whine.

Gotta stop the plane! he thought.

He was a good twenty feet from the edge of the runway, and the plane was at the far end, another thousand or so beyond. He'd never run that distance fast enough to stop the aircraft from taking off.

Then the car was beside him, Jimmy's maniacal smile filling his addled vision. Jack all but clutched at it, his arms somehow wrapping around the section between the passenger side windows. There was no longer any glass to prevent his bear hug. The windshield glass was draped across the wheel and the passenger seat. The engine screeched, and then he was yanked off the ground as the car hurtled toward the taxiing plane.

Jack dug at the glass, trying to reach the door handle. The wheels spun but caught enough solid ground to lurch the vehicle forward again, making his fingers scramble across the door. Jack held on for dear life as the battered car skidded and veered across the concrete.

The plane was moving down the runway. There was gunfire to Jack's right, and flashes down near the building. Something burst through the side window behind him.

"Stop the plane!" he howled. *Because I'm dead anyway*, he thought.

There were no other ideas in his head, no great philosophies, no justifications, or moral arguments about good and evil. He was utterly focused on the car and the runway and plane. The desert wind bit at his face. He smelled the blood of the men they'd hit and the fumes of the car. He felt the bruises that covered his body. He heard the car and airplane thundering toward each other.

A light flashed on and the EV-55's turbines whined, the plane's pilot finally realizing the car was coming for him. The two vehicles roared at each other, racing together like a pair of mad dervishes. The plane started to move left; Jack felt the rear wheels slide out of control. White light flashed in his face and the earth seemed to fall below him; there was a roar so loud his eardrums felt as if they broke.

"Jimmy!" he screamed, as he fell. "Jump!"

Then a tornado of dirt, fire, fuel, and oil spun him around, pummeling his head until he shot into a black hole of pain.

40

Unconsciousness was a purgatory of pain and confusion—a dizzy swirl where the world made no sense. Jack's mind churned at a level below dreams and sensation. He was at the bottom of a deep ocean, able to breathe only through some accidental miracle. Finally, something prodded Jack to rise. It was a feeling of light, color, and shape that pushed slowly upward. Only gravity was holding him back. His head was heavy. More lights, colors, and shapes began to drift out of the blackness before him. He began rising more quickly. His chest hurt. His legs were bent at odd angles. His ribs screamed with pain.

His heart pounded. He wondered, *Am I going to die? Am I dead already?*

But then he saw the desert sky above him, and felt the desert sand beneath him, as well as the desert heat all around him. Finally, he was conscious, looking up at a familiar face he couldn't quite recognize.

"D-Doc?" Jack finally sputtered.

The old soldier nodded. "Good boy. Stay awake. Upsy daisy."

"W-what?"

"Come to papa, Jack." Doc pushed his arm under him and lifted, scooping him to his feet. Still dizzy, Jack began sliding in the direction of Doc's tugs. "You're just in time," Doc said gravely. "He's been asking for you."

"W-who? What is going on?" Jack shook his head, trying to clear his eyes and his mind. "The plane . . . !"

"Yeah," Doc said, slowly lowering him back to the ground. "The plane."

Jack found himself sitting amid a circle of bent metal and broken glass. He vaguely recognized some of it—a wheel here, a wing there. It was the twisted remnants of the car and the plane.

It wasn't like in the movies. The crash hadn't resulted in fireballs and explosions. Just two man-made machines torn apart by velocity and contact. A strange elation tore into Jack's head, but it only brought more stabbing pain. Even so, through the haze, he thought: *We had done it. We stopped the plane.* But then there was another, unwanted, thought. *At what cost?*

The cost came into view a moment later. Jack was sitting next to a small, prone, body. He saw Doc hunch down on the other side of the horizontal form swathed in white. Then, shining through, came the smile. Weaker, but still there.

"Mr. Jack," said Jimmy weakly.

Jack's vision cleared some more. He saw the man laying there amid the wreckage, battered and bloody. As if not to see it, Jack raised his gaze, but then he saw Doc's solemn face. Just before Jack looked back down, Doc shook his head slightly. No.

"Jimmy," Jack breathed. "You didn't have to. . . . Why did you do it?"

"It okay," Jimmy mumbled. "Wanted to tell you before . . . wanted to thank you . . ."

"Thank me?" Jack blurted incredulously. He had brought the poor man to death's door. "Why?"

"Waiting," said Jimmy, his voice getting softer as Jack listened. "Waiting to join family. Just . . . wanted to find right time . . . right reason . . . didn't want to just throw life away . . . !"

Jack was rendered mute by the man's mourning, pain, and sacrifice. He stared, head spinning, as Jimmy attempted one last smile.

"I did good, yes? Save many people . . . ?"

"Yes, Jimmy, yes," Jack said. "Maybe millions."

He thought Jimmy was going to cry. But, to his astonishment, he saw the brave man trembling . . . and silently laughing.

"Jimmy," Jack said hoarsely. "Why are you . . . how can you . . . ?"

Jimmy feebly shook his head, his mouth still twisted in a happy smile, his words getting weaker with each syllable. "It's okay, Mr. Jack. I laugh because I know something they don't know. . . ."

"What, Jimmy?" Jack asked, his eyes wet even in this heat. "What is it?"

Jack saw the man mouth the words, and even though he didn't hear them, they were as plain as day. "We win."

With that, Jimmy's eyes shut for the last time.

Jack took a deep breath, then closed and opened his own eyes several times, trying to get them refocused. He took another breath, this one slow and deliberate. He started to rise to his feet, but the dizziness intensified. He sat back down.

He could no longer see where he was. He leaned over, putting his left hand out as a prop, then his right. He began to crawl slowly away. He didn't know where he was going. He just wanted to go away. But he didn't get far. Jack lay on the ground, on his face, and closed his wet eyes.

Either a few seconds, or a few lifetimes later, Jack's eyes and ears, opened again. "I'm amazed he lasted that long, considering his injuries," was the first thing Jack heard. "I guess he was holding out for you."

Jack found himself looking over at Doc, who was crouching beside him. "And he thinks we gave *him* something."

"That's the way true heroes think," Doc said. He made a point of changing the subject. "You ready to go on?"

"More now than ever," Jack breathed. "Though I have to tell you—I feel like I've got the worst hangover of my life."

Doc snorted. "That's a good sign. At least you're feeling something. Wasn't it the writer George Sand who said something like 'It's better to feel something, even if it's teeth.'"

"When did you read her?" Jack asked, buying a few more moments to collect his wits.

"Those e-book readers are great and, man, I take a lot of long flights. You finished stalling now?"

"I guess so," Jack admitted, now that he'd been busted. "My head is pounding. My stomach feels like a collection of cramps, but my legs are fine."

"And there, ladies and gentlemen, is Jack Hatfield in a nutshell. The man who once told a nation it's all right to have different views now tells his body the same. At least you can string sensible words together now."

"Compared to five minutes ago—or when I was on the air?" Jack asked, delaying one second more.

Doc grinned but did not answer. Jack focused his eyes on a flame in the distance. As it came into focus, Jack could see more pockets of flame here and there. Then the whole image came into sharp relief. His back was against the wall of the main building. There were fallen bodies here and there, but Jimmy was gone.

"Back in the real world, huh?" asked Doc, walking away from him, in the direction of the runway.

"If any of this is real," said Jack. He started to get up.

"Hey, all kidding aside—why don't you just stay sitting for a while," suggested Doc, returning to reinforce his suggestion with a hand on Jack's shoulder that kept him from rising. "You might have a concussion."

"I don't think so."

"Yeah, like you'd know. How many fingers am I holding up?"

Jack stayed where he was, feeling relief at the decision, and looked up at his tall friend. "One, wise guy. I see it rising proudly from the others."

"Okay. What about short-term memory."

"What about it?" Jack asked.

"What's the last thing you remembered?"

Jack thought. "Stop the plane," he said, letting his mind slide backward. "I was yelling, 'Stop the plane.'"

"Nothing after that?"

"Not really, no," Jack said. "What happened?"

Judging Jack was finally aware enough, Doc told him. "You jumped, or fell off, before Jimmy crashed the car into the back of the plane. I can't tell whether he was trying to flick you off before he hit, or he was just turning the car to catch the back of the plane's tail. Either way, you rolled out of harm's way, and then both vehicles started to spin. You can see the result."

He could indeed. By the marks on the runway, Jack could guess that the car skidded at the same time the plane did. Then the plane rolled right on top of the car, crushing its middle. Then both vehicles started to tear apart.

"You call this 'out of harm's way'?" he groaned. But then he realized: the bomb was on board. Why weren't they all dead, and the area turned into glass? He rejected that thought. Although this place sure wasn't heaven, it wasn't miserable enough for purgatory, or hot enough for hell.

"The others?" Jack asked, his mind getting faster.

"All dead," Doc informed him. "The ones Jimmy didn't run over or you shot, I took care of. Guess what? All Russians."

"What? How do you know?"

"I found their passports and documents," Doc said. "They were in a burn bag—you pull the tab down and the whole thing's supposed to go up in flames."

"Obviously they didn't," Jack added. Doc made a face that said, *With me pulling the tab? Hardly.* "Maybe they're forgeries."

"Doubtful," said Doc. "They already had one set of forgeries—Jordanian passports were in there as well. This was well planned . . . if not for us flies in their ointment. . . ." Doc stood and looked around at the so-called Saudi Air Force Base. "This whole place was wired for self-destruction. Explosive devices everywhere. They must have planned to leave nothing behind when they left."

Jack, with some effort, all but crawled up the wall to his feet. He looked around, feeling frustrated and empty at all the foolish waste. "So what now?"

"We go back," Doc told him. "Don't you have some interviews to do?"

Jack looked at his friend as if he were insane. Then he looked at the destroyed plane and car. "How?" he wondered. "Take the transport truck? Even if it had enough gas, we'd never get there in time!"

"Transport truck?" Doc echoed. "We don't need no transport

truck!" He checked his watch. When Jack opened his mouth to complain, Doc held up a long, bony forefinger. "Wait for it—"

Jack was about to snarl at him, forefinger or no forefinger, when he heard a sound. It was a high-speed swooshing noise coming from the east. He turned to look at the distant hill just in time to see the tiny shape of a Gulfstream G650 appear.

Doc pointed at it. "Boom," he said. Jack looked at him with recrimination and amazement. "What do you think I've been doing while you were busy 'resting'?" Doc said with faux incredulity while holding up his military-grade smartphone for Jack to see.

"Reading a botanical book?" Jack hazarded.

"So happens I may have, you illiterate oaf. And *Gray's Anatomy*. It's always good to know what the enemy eats and looks like inside. But that's not how I spent *this* past hour."

Jack stared. The plane, designed to land on short runways, touched down easily, debris or no debris. Then the pilots, both ex-military and old friends of Doc's, made quick work of it. One helped Jack on board while the other hauled on some items with Doc. Then they quickly turned the plane and took off again. It couldn't have taken more than five minutes.

They had only been in the air a few more minutes when Jack heard a *whomp* and saw a growing fireball out the window. He snapped his head over to Doc for corroboration, there seeing a small device in the man's hand. It had a red button and an antenna. Jack looked out the jet's window again to see the base disappear in fire and smoke. He looked back at his friend in wonderment.

Doc shrugged. "Place was covered in AN-M14 TH3 incendiary devices," he said. Jack knew that they contained a thermate mixture that burned extremely hot. He could practically smell stinking slag iron all the way up here.

"I thought it best that the local constabulary not have any reason to charge us with espionage or murder," Doc concluded.

Jack saw the cold-blooded logic in that, but there was more on his mind. "Jimmy?" Doc's expression grew sad. He remembered placing the telescope in Jimmy's crossed hands in the hole Doc had dug before shoveling dirt and sand back on him. "He's with his family."

"But the evidence . . . ?"

Doc shook his head. "We didn't leave any evidence behind."

Jack's eyes widened. "You have the bomb?"

Doc looked at him evenly. "Yes. I have the device they were flying out." Without another word, Doc got up, grabbed a long duffel bag, and slid it over to lay between Jack's feet.

"Why didn't it go off?" Jack blurted. "How did you . . . ?"

Doc held up his forefinger again while unzipping the duffel. Jack looked down to see what he both recognized and dreaded. It was almost a textbook example of a homemade nuke—a capped silver pipe with a wide joint in the center, attached to what looked like a silver flask, as well as an exposed on-off switch.

"Oh, my Lord," Jack breathed. "How do we—I mean, what the hell should we do with it?"

Doc shook his head again. "No need to do anything, Jack. Look." He reached down, and, as easily as opening a safety seal from a jar of peanut butter, Doc removed a section of the bomb's surface.

For a second, Jack thought he had gone crazy, or he actually was dead back on that desert runway. For the "bomb" was hollow. It was just an empty shell.

41

San Francisco, California

"It's a double blind," Sammy said as he jabbed his finger at the screen.

"What is a 'double blind'?" Ana asked, looking apologetically at Boaz who—joined now by Sol—made a small semicircle behind them.

"It's a fake-out," Sammy said. "A distraction. A diversion."

"But that makes no sense," Sol murmured, almost to himself. "Why would they do that?"

"I don't think they are doing that," said a sixth voice—a strong, certain, female voice.

Dover Griffith stepped up from where she had been standing in the shadows.

"Who let you in?" Sol asked. "And why?"

"I admitted myself," Dover replied, smiling. "Jack took the liberty of sending me the code in case I needed to see you all off-the-grid."

"The FBI in my lap," Sol made a face. "That's what I get for trusting a love-sick *shmendrick*."

"Most men would not mind this FBI in their lap," Ana observed.

"Actually, you've got the resources of the FBI in your lap, not it's eyes and ears . . . or anything else," Dover said.

"That answers the 'how' of your being here, not the 'why,'" Sol said.

Dover ignored the question. She pointed a short, well-manicured fingernail at Ric's screen. "This e-mail evidence from General Morton's private hard drive clearly suggests that the conspirators were targeting Mecca and Jerusalem. Either at the same time or one after the other. Look—it's right there."

"But that's from last year," Sammy stressed. "That may have been the original plan. Since then, Morton has been bogged down in details and cover-ups."

"That's part of the picture," Dover agreed.

"What's the rest?" Sol asked.

Dover smiled lightly. She saw at once what Sol was doing: the way he made his demand let her know that her being here was provisional, that this was no quid pro quo situation. Either she put up or she would be put out.

Sammy missed all of that as he pointed at his screen.

"This account—Morton hasn't been using this platform for months. But it's still in use. Someone took it over and was making parallel, even alternate, plans."

"You get all that from 'Firebird alt feint'?" Dover asked him. But her eyes were still on Sol. There was more to him than he let on.

"Not just that," Sammy responded. He nodded at Ric, who slipped back into his own chair beside Sammy. Ric's thick fingers flew across his own keyboard, bringing up previously secret correspondence. "Look," Sammy continued, pointing at Ric's screen. "Samson doesn't want to blow up Jerusalem. But Pegasus says it's a go." Sammy read from the conversation: "Thor decided a year ago."

Dover continued to look at Sol. "Interesting, don't you think?"

"What is?" Sol asked.

"The Bible, Greek mythology, Norse mythology."

"What's so interesting about that?"

"At the Bureau we call that 'covering your fingerprints,'" she said. "People tend to use passwords or code words that reflect something in their lives. Partly vanity, partly an easy way to remember. That jumble of cultures makes it difficult to follow."

"Unless we're dealing with a Jew, a Greek, and a Viking," Sol pointed out.

"That would be dumb," Dover said. "A person's heritage is easy to trace."

"Morton," Ana said thoughtfully. "I think Morton said something about talking to Thor one of the times I was with him."

"Thor was a call sign General Brooks used when he was younger," said Sammy. "He's Thor Actual in that division history I read. That's army slang. Let me find it."

Before anyone could stop him, Sammy started typing furiously on his own keyboard, bringing the file of links he'd gathered on General Brooks. The division history was actually a webpage recounting the exploits of several companies during the First Gulf War and Panama. Brooks had been the commander of an ad hoc strike team known as Thor Company. Thor Actual would have been the call sign of the commander—Brooks.

"It sounds like an argument to me," said Dover, "not a diversion."

"Wait, wait, wait," Sammy implored, his fingers still flying, returning the original information to his screen. "All that was from the past year. The 'Firebird alt feint' is from the past weeks. None of the original conspirators were involved, or even privy, to these newer communications."

"Then who were?" Dover asked

Sammy pursed his lips, staring at the screen. "I don't know . . . yet."

Dover stepped up and put her hands on Sammy's shoulders, eliciting a sharp glance from Ana that the FBI agent didn't notice. She kept one hand on one shoulder and slapped his other shoulder with the other. "I don't know," she said regretfully. "It's all a little tentative."

Sammy squirmed a little, but not for the reasons that made Ana react. Dover removed her hand—also not because of Ana.

"My brother used to do that," Sammy said under his breath. "Doubted me."

"I'm not doubting you," Dover insisted quietly so the others couldn't hear. "Merely suggesting—"

"No," he insisted, loudly. "This adds up."

"But why?" Sol thought out loud. "What could anyone possibly gain by creating a false bomb plot? If I didn't know better, I'd think this was our doing—a way to trap the conspirators." He looked at Boaz, who looked back with arms raised in a "We had nothing to do with it posture."

"I'm guessing the 'why' will become clearer when we know who the parallel conspirators are," Sammy told them. "That's why I called you," he said directly at Dover with a sidelong glance at Sol.

Their host did not look pleased. Sammy didn't care. The mission was what mattered, not making sure that this thug liked him. That in itself was a big step for Jack's half brother.

"What I really need is information on these IP addresses that were used to access the web building sites. They don't come up in a regular search, and even if they did, I couldn't coordinate them to actual users. But the IPs have records that can. They'll know who was using the computer, or at least they'll have an account and address that can be traced. Can you do that for me?"

Dover thought about it for only a moment. Then she tapped Sammy on the upper arm. "Move over," she said in a clipped, professional tone. In a moment, she was seated and her fingers did their own keyboard flying. Screens popped up and vanished on the monitor.

Sol and Ric exchanged quietly delighted looks. Boaz was studying the woman's every move. Even if she erased the trail when she was done, the Israelis now had a safe way into what they assumed would be the FBI's computer network.

In less than three minutes Dover said "Go," and Sammy was indeed tied into the FBI system. She returned his seat to him. It was as if a brand-new universe had suddenly opened for him.

"Oh, and gentlemen?" Dover said to Sol and his minions. "Once those keystrokes are used, the computer resets. That was my way in for today only."

"*Mazel tov*," Sol said. "You don't think I have my own resources?"

"I'm sure you do," she said, replicating the glance he shared with Ric. "You just don't have mine."

As Sammy tapped away, looking like a kid on Christmas, Ana was at his side. Ric went to walk Eddie while Miwa prepared the dog's food. Boaz drifted downstairs to see if Ritu needed any help, knowing that she didn't, but also knowing that she didn't mind him checking. Dover, meanwhile, drifted away with Sol at her side.

"Can we call a truce?" she asked.

"Who was at war?" Sol asked innocently.

"We were," she replied. "We *are*." She dipped her head toward Ana. "You like women you can control."

"I won't deny that," he said.

"Good. At least you're honest."

"Most mobsters are," he said. "Otherwise, deals couldn't be made by handshakes. You only need written contracts when people are crooks."

"Fair enough," she said. "So: where are they now?"

"On their way back to Riyadh," Sol informed her. He crooked his head toward Sammy. "What he's saying checks out with what Jack and Doc found."

"I know," Dover said. "Why do you think I connected him with our system so readily?" She exhaled slowly, thinking furiously. "As monstrous as a strike on Israel and then Saudi Arabia is to start with, why make a *fake* weapon of mass destruction? Is Brooks now so twisted that he would create a perverted game like this just to keep Jack jumping?"

"At the cost of more than a dozen innocent men's lives?" Sol asked. "I don't think so. Anything is possible, but on the basis of all our research, Brooks is still sane." Sol shrugged.

"But if he is the man behind this, and if he pulls it off, millions will be killed, so who knows? Maybe he just doesn't care about human life anymore, his, or anyone else's." Dover nodded. "Yes, all our research also said that Brooks, and Morton, for that matter, seemed to think they were doing the right thing. But at this point I don't think I'd be surprised if we found out they had been replaced by aliens or terrorists who had plastic surgery."

Sol snorted. "And your superiors are still not on board?"

Dover snorted in return. "What do you think, Sol? They're sane and consider imaginations a detriment to the job. All I can do—all

I've been doing—is to point out web chatter and say, 'That looks interesting.'"

"Got something!" Sammy interrupted.

The others came back to the computer consoles, Sol and Dover in the lead. Boaz had returned and joined them.

"I tracked down the Internet providers that had accessed the Firebird's websites," Sammy told them. "One was a large provider in Tel Aviv. The other was a very small company in Haifa that not only recorded every single access made by its customers, but had a data exchange policy with the American FBI, thanks to an ongoing money laundering case Israel and the United States were trying to crack. The user who had accessed the Firebird site had also spent considerable time in a secure chat room located in Estonia where participants communicated via encrypted messages."

"I can get a subpoena," said Dover. "And we can look at their logs."

"We don't need a subpoena," said Sammy. He signed out of the FBI system—causing Boaz to start visibly and Dover to grin; the tech ace would probably have loved to try and backtrack—then put his computer skills to use on his brother's back-up laptop so the penetration would be harder to track. "I started by testing the system's front end. The security was excellent—unless you had the credentials of an administrator, in which case, you had full access to everything on its servers. So how do I convince it I'm an administrator?"

They watched him type in a nonsense series of numbers and letters, then tap return. Access denied. They watched as he did it two more times. Access denied, access denied. "Sammy . . ." Sol started. But it was Ric, back from doggy duty, who held up a finger and smiled.

Sammy did it a fourth time, and then another message popped up on screen. "Forget Your Password?"

"Why, yes, I did," he told the machine, clicking the yes box with a big smile.

A temporary password dropped into the still-open e-mail account a few seconds later and they were off and running. For the next thirty minutes, Sammy, Dover, and Ric scanned the log books, while Boaz and Sol looked on, and the other women started preparing a meal for everyone.

When the trio finally left the computers, they didn't feel like eating. Still, they sat with the others and conferred in miserable tones.

"Convinced?" Sammy asked Dover.

"That another group created a fake bomb as a diversion? Yes. But only because your brother found out that it already happened. Although we know the alternate conspirators' screen names and locations, the damage is already done and they're probably long gone by now."

Sammy looked crestfallen. Ana put her hand reassuringly on his shoulder before Dover continued.

"But," she said, "I am also convinced that a group of seemingly sane men were, or are, still plotting to detonate a device in or over Mecca. Whether or not they have, or will, accomplish their goal, I'm not sure."

"You understand that we have to proceed as if they have," Sol maintained. "If Brooks wants a war with the Muslims by destroying Mecca, it's our necks next."

"Of course," said Dover.

"All they're going to do is piss Islam off so bad they'll fight to the death," Boaz added.

"It's like the Japanese bombing Pearl Harbor."

"Except in this case, Brooks wants that fight," Sammy emphasized. "He wants a fight to their death. That's what this is all about."

"What if we just tell the Saudis?" Dover considered.

"You think they'll believe you?" Sol asked pointedly. "And if you're wrong . . ." He looked around the table. "If we're all wrong, kiss your career, and my cover, good-bye." After that, they all sat, literally and figuratively, chewing on it. Finally, Ana could stand it no longer.

"So what can we do?" she cried.

Dover straightened, brought her head up, and pushed back from the table. "I don't know about you, but I'm going back to my office to start barking orders and taking names." Sol's eyebrows raised. He had said the same thing seemingly a lifetime ago, and realized he had not done so since. He stood with her, then Sammy joined them.

"In Jack I trust," Dover said, heading for the safe house's door. "He found the fake bomb. Maybe now he'll find the real one."

42

Riyadh, Saudi Arabia

It was not the same Jack Hatfield who deplaned the private jet at the airport as the one who had gotten on it less than a day before. And the change was more than just the fact that he had showered, rested, and changed into a new suit and tie on board. His expression was different—more experienced, more knowledgeable, and far more angry. He carried his notepad as if it were a cleaver.

Jack felt a pang when he didn't see the smiling face of Jimmy waiting by the car—just a sunglassed, blank-faced chauffeur from the prince's office—but then his fleeting lock of loss and regret passed, and his eyes became cold and determined.

Doc's eyebrows lifted admiringly at the sight of the car. It was a 1996 Bentley Rapier, specially modified to be a stretch limousine, with far more back-seat room than originally designed. Considering that the original car was priced at more than four million dollars, Doc couldn't imagine how much this one cost.

The world could be coming to an end and material things still grab our attention, he thought with a touch of self-reproach. *Then again,* he asked himself, *what is life if not a succession of little joys in the midst of trials and turmoil?*

The blank-faced driver's head only turned as Doc, also freshly suited, was about to get in after Jack. "I was told there would be an interpreter with you," he said in perfect English, albeit with a thin Arabian accent.

Doc stopped, straightened, and looked down on the man. He considered saying *"He's buried with work,"* but, in deference to his honored, fallen comrade, he didn't take the occasion to make a quip. "He's indisposed," Doc said simply. "But do we really need an interpreter? I hear the prince's English is perfect."

The chauffeur thought about it. "That is true," he agreed. "Very well."

Doc got in after Jack, now regretting that he hadn't made the Bond-ish comment. He realized Jimmy would have liked it. He settled into the plush, luxurious passenger section of the Bentley beside Jack, who waited until the chauffeur had closed the one-way privacy partition.

"Do you think they have listening devices installed back here?" he asked.

"Of course," Doc replied. *"Salaam alaikum,* Prince Riad al-Saud. All our best to you, and thank you for your hospitality."

"You're kidding?" Jack asked.

"I most certainly am not," Doc replied. "Don't say anything in here you wouldn't say to his face," he advised. Then his expression became concerned and solicitous. "How are you holding up?"

Jack thought about using the most general and clichéd of terms, but decided honesty was the best policy. "I've interviewed my share of important people, but I've never interviewed a Saudi prince," he admitted.

"Sends a thrill up my leg, I know," Doc said.

Jack shot him a look. "I've certainly never interviewed an individual where the stakes were so high."

"I'll give you that," Doc said as he glanced at the smoky glass partition, imagining the driver both listening and watching through either a mirror or closed-circuit screen, then grinned.

"I mean, we're not just talking about the weather," Jack replied. "This is about world peace."

Doc chuckled mirthlessly. "The jokes on me, though," he said. "How do you mean?"

"If I keep winning battles like this, I'm out of business."

Jack smiled at that. It was true. A professional soldier fighting for peace; just showed what a stand-up guy Doc truly was.

Having had their say, the two leaned back and enjoyed the ride to the prince's compound, marveling at what oil billions can buy in the way of architecture. *Apparently*, Jack thought, *Vegas with an overactive thyroid and delusions of grandeur.* Jack stared at the excess with its arguable taste, but, strangely, found himself not thinking of the looming interview, but of the clocks he wanted to work on next. He thought of Eddie. He thought of Dover. He felt her hand sliding down his neck. He closed his eyes and let himself imagine the warmth of her fingers as they sat out on the concrete deck of his apartment, the electricity of her touch as her hand slid down his arm, across his chest, and back toward his hip. Her fingers lingered over his thigh—

"Hey."

Jack snapped out of his brief, happy memory. "What?" he asked, trying to sound innocent.

"We're here," Doc informed him.

Jack blinked. Prince Riad al-Saud headed the Ministry of Minerals and Resources. While the ministry's main office was on Airport Road near the Riyadh airport, the prince's personal office was in the Al Faisaliyah Center in the business district. This was in keeping with his position within the royal family, and a nod to his status as a powerful, up-and-coming young man.

The building was a monumental, four-sided pyramid, more rocket than skyscraper, with a glinting globe supporting the peak. The globe held a three-story restaurant; a world-class hotel took up several floors. At nearly nine hundred feet, it topped the Transamerica Pyramid by twenty feet, and would have dazzled anyone anywhere in the world.

Deposited right outside the door, they were met on the sidewalk by a man in a white suit. Addressing Jack as "The Honored Mr. Hatfield," he led them across the wide plaza to a door at the side of the main lobby, ushering them past a red velvet rope and the watchful eyes of two private security guards whose crisply tailored suits didn't quite hide the pistols strapped to their chests. The greeter deposited them in an elevator; the doors closed as he stepped back, bowing his head slightly in good-bye.

There was no panel on the elevator to indicate where it was going. The only control was a single button with lettering in Arabic and the word HELP in English. Jack tried to find a joke in that but there wasn't time. The elevator whisked them to their assigned floor within seconds of the doors closing. The car opened on a marble hallway bathed in light from the nearby windows. Three men in robes and headdresses were waiting for them.

"Mr. Hatfield, a pleasure to meet you," said the man in the middle of the delegation sent to escort them. He wore a sport coat over his robe, and his headdress was tied with a braided robe. "We are extremely honored by your presence."

"I am the one who is honored," said Jack, falling right into the niceties. It was like a sporting event or a rumble between gangs. The combatants or rivals were extremely polite to each other, even though they clutched razor sharp knives behind their backs.

"We have some brief necessities," said the greeter, gesturing behind them. "I am so sorry to inconvenience you."

"It's not an inconvenience at all," said Jack, knowing he was referring to a security check.

The corridor they walked along bordered the glass wall of the tower. It was impossible not to stare at the city and the rising haze of the desert heat in the distance. The sun shimmered the landscape before them. Though they were barely halfway up in the tower, Jack felt as if he were standing on the top of the world. He wondered if having an office here might not make the prince think the same.

Their escort led them to a large, empty room just around the next corner of the building. Two men with submachine guns were standing at the doorway. Inside, six guards, all with identical weapons, flanked a millimeter-wave scanning machine similar to those used in airports—only far more advanced and fashionably styled. The guards were dressed in Saudi full dress military uniforms. All had a significant number of ribbons on their chests. A short Asian man with a nervous look on his face darted out from behind them. He was the machine's operator.

"Pulling out all the stops," murmured Doc. "Those are MP5 submachine guns, by the way. A little old-school, but you can't argue with the choice. Battle-proven."

"This model or these particular weapons, I wonder," Jack said.

"From the wear on the grips, I'd say both."

Jack had done a show on the dangers of backscatter X-ray devices, once in common use by the TSA. These were different, more effective machines, working with low-powered radio waves. Supposedly, they posed no health hazard, though Jack was somewhat suspicious of those assertions. The real problem with the machines came from their false alarms—they were said to give false positives about twenty-five percent of the time. He motioned for Doc to go first. Doc nodded, smiled at the guards, then casually pulled the Glock automatic from a shoulder holster under his jacket, and politely handed it to the nearest security officer. Jack raised his eyebrows, but no one else was fazed.

"Please treat it well," Doc said to the security man holding it between two fingers. "It has great sentimental value." Indeed. Jack knew it had been used on at least one Russian.

"Of course, sir," said the escort, who was apparently nonplussed by the incident. His English had a very proper British accent to it, something very likely picked up at Cambridge or Oxford, if not earlier at prep school. "Mr. Hatfield, do you have a similar declaration?"

"No, I'm fine."

"I assume your associate has a permit."

"Of course, sir," Jack echoed in kind.

The man smiled. The digicam and Jack's notepad was carefully hand-checked. "Very good, very good," he said. "Gentlemen please, this way."

He swept them back out into the hall, leading them to another elevator around the corner, where two men dressed in robes and jackets stood in front of the elevator. The men had MP5 submachine guns slung in front of their chests and were dressed in long robes.

Like executioners, Jack thought, thinking back to images he had seen of public beheadings.

Their guide led them to the elevator door, which he opened

with a key. Once they were inside, he took a step out. "Gentle-men, a pleasure. You may collect your things on the way out."

"A lot of security for a guy who watches the weather," Doc com-mented after the elevator started up.

"That is least of his portfolio," Jack replied just as diffidently. "Control the weather and you control the world." He smiled thinly at the concave mirror in the corner of the elevator ceiling.

"Control the woman who controls that man and you've really got a lock on it," Doc observed.

More men in robes with submachine guns were waiting when the door opened. Their stares were aggressive and menacing, but they were silent, and when Jack stepped forward, they parted.

The floor was completely open, unobstructed by interior walls or even pillars. It wasn't the top, but must have been very close. The view was even more stunning than the one Jack had seen be-low. The glass windows had electrochromic devices that reduced the glare, so that it was possible to look directly at the sun—now about a quarter of the way up in the sky, shining directly into the eastern windows.

The floors were covered with silk Persian rugs so that only a few strips of the sleek marble beneath them were visible. A pair of settees had been placed in the middle of the room; they were the only pieces of furniture.

Prince Riad al-Saud was sitting on one. Jack had already briefed himself on the prince's background, but he was surprised to find the man looked at least ten years younger than his resume indi-cated. There was no question that it was he—he had the same dim-ple in his chin, his eyes flashed with life, and there was even the slight touch of gray at the temples and in his beard. But the photos hadn't done justice to the man's vibrant energy.

He rose as Jack approached. The prince may not have heard what Jack said as he went, since he hardly moved his lips, but Doc did as he brought the digicam up.

"We're live."

43

Jack extended his hand to meet the fair, small hand of the prince. "Your Excellency."

"Mr. Hatfield, a pleasure to have you with us." The prince placed Jack's hand between both of his. His eyes held Jack's, and he smiled broadly. "You are hungry, I hope."

"We are," admitted Jack, "but I never eat on duty. I hope you understand."

"Ah, well, perhaps we will tempt you with something besides." The prince raised his hand.

Jack expected him to click his fingers, but he did nothing so gauche; he quickly lowered his hand. Moments later, two men entered from a door next to the elevator carrying two trays of pastries. A third trailed a few steps behind with coffee and tea. The prince was playing a game Jack knew very well. It was difficult to be hard-hitting with a croissant hanging out of your mouth. Jack passed on the pastries, even though they looked and smelled as if they had just come from the kitchen of a master baker. The prince, however, chose a few while complimenting Jack on his cable show.

"I was particularly taken with the one on the effects of depleted uranium," he said, "which included stock footage of the war to liberate Kuwait." He snuggled back in his seat like Jack had seen

Eddie do on the boat. "It's an issue not many people face, yet you addressed it in a comprehensive manner."

"Thank you," Jack said, concentrating on appearing just as easygoing as the prince. He wanted the man to feel that he had the upper hand, to be comfortable, but he reminded himself that was just what Riad was—a man. They were boxing—more than boxing, really. An interview like this was an elaborate dance.

"You have been to Riyadh before?" asked the prince.

"Briefly," said Jack. "I'm afraid I've never been here long enough to really enjoy the city."

"But I did not know this." The prince looked as if he were surprised. "I should have had a guide meet you at the airport, and given you a tour."

"That would have been wonderful," Jack answered honestly. "But I'm here on business and my schedule is tight. As I'm sure yours is as well."

"Of course, of course." The prince reached over and took a pineapple tart from the tray. Jack noted that the delicacies even included the sugar-free, low-fat, no-dairy baked goods that he favored. Hardly a coincidence, he was sure. The prince must've had a research team that put Jack's to shame—even at the height of his success on *Truth Tellers*.

"I want to say, before we begin, that I appreciate that you took this time for me," said Jack. "You've been so generous."

It was a nod to propriety that he begin with a compliment. The prince acknowledged this with a slight, grateful nod. But Jack was not finished. He wanted to know how seriously this guy took himself.

"Though I have not seen much of your country," he went on, "I cannot imagine anything more splendid than this residence. The building itself is a treasure."

The prince appeared to be suddenly, very slightly on guard. Two compliments when one would have sufficed? His smile belied any suspicion he might have as to Jack's motives.

"Yes, it is quite majestic." The prince leaned forward conspiratorially. "Much nicer than the ministry offices." The prince smiled. He seemed to be mocking himself—*a tactic*, Jack thought, to make him appear more humble and therefore likable. *So he's suspicious of suck-ups*, Jack thought. He might not be as easy to manipulate as Jack had hoped.

Doc knew what Jack was doing and his mouth twisted as if to say, "You're wasting time." The prince put down his tea, signaling it was go time.

"So, you are here to talk about nuclear weapons in the Middle East.

"Weapons of mass destruction," Jack clarified.

"Ah," said the prince. "I assume that you are against them."

"I'm neither for nor against, to be honest."

The prince leaned back with an expression of mild surprise that quickly shaded to appreciation.

"You are indeed an honest and very unique man," he commented. "Certainly unique among Americans. What I have found is that those whose countries have weapons of mass destruction do not want them for others, and vice versa."

Jack thought back to the days-ago discussion with Sol Minsky. "Power is not to be feared in the hands of one with integrity."

The prince raised his hands as if in prayer. "You speak the truth."

"Which brings me to this, Prince," Jack went on. "Nuclear weapons are still a big deal around the world, yet nuclear power has lost favor in my country and many others. Nonetheless the Kingdom plans to build sixteen new nuclear reactors. Why is that?"

Prince Riad al-Saud smiled. "We have great, and growing, electrical needs—eight percent more each year. And there are some notable difficulties imposed by climate on other forms of power."

"And what about nuclear weapons themselves? Are you, like Iran, publicly opposed and privately for their development?"

"The question has no relevance, since the reactors cannot produce material that creates weapons," answered the prince.

"They could be adapted."

"Not easily, as Tehran has learned at great cost. In our case, there are safeguards we have insisted upon, overseen by international inspectors."

"So apart from the difficulty, there's no interest in developing a bomb or weapons of mass destruction?" asked Jack.

"None."

"Even if Iran managed to build one?"

"Iran will not," said the prince.

"But let's assume, for the sake of this discussion, that Iran did build a device of some kind. Would Saudi Arabia feel threatened?"

"No one really frightens us," said the prince mildly. "We are not the West, Mr. Hatfield. I know what is going on in my realm. Do I look like a man who has fears?"

He was relaxed, and Jack knew that the Saudis had secret police, the Al-Mabahith, second to none.

"Of course," the prince went on, "circumstances can change. If they do, we have an adequate military to deal with problems."

"With American help."

"If America is willing. Who can tell if you will always be willing?"

Touché, thought Jack. "How do you feel about Pakistan's repeated attempts to develop their own weapons?"

"Will you be running through each nation, Mr. Hatfield?"

"Sir, with your indulgence, Pakistan is a unique case," Jack said. "There were loans from your Kingdom," he said carefully. "It's said in some places that Saudi Arabia paid for the entire development of the weapons."

The prince took a knowing sip of tea. "It is true."

Jack seemed surprised. "You're admitting, Prince, that you funded Pakistan's program?"

The prince smiled. "Mr. Hatfield, I was merely referring to your comment, 'It is said.' Nothing more."

Jack smiled inwardly at the prince's theatrical timing. "If I may, it's also said that if there were a crisis, the Pakistanis would be obligated to give some of their weapons to the Saudis."

"Our brothers in Islamabad may be generous," the prince said mildly, reaching for another pineapple tart, "but I doubt that generous."

"And so," Jack quickly summarized, "if you'll forgive my pressing the matter, there does appear to be a need for Saudi Arabia to develop its own WMDs. Because of Iran, and the unreliability of allies. Including the United States."

"There are many moving parts in your conclusion," the prince said. "But I would agree that some people might believe that."

"At the risk of pressing you on an issue you seem reluctant to discuss, are you one of them who believes that Saudi Arabia should have a bomb?"

"Candidly, Mr. Hatfield, I believe that Saudi Arabia should have at its disposal any means necessary to protect itself, just as every civilized nation should."

"Sir, is there a Saudi program to develop a bomb?"

The prince was unfazed. Jack wasn't surprised. The question did not exactly come from left field.

"You Americans have no idea of the threat we face," he said. His tone remained calm. He looked straight into the camera. "You see our country, you think sand and oil. Two things. We are faced with a Shia empire across our northern border, from Iran to the Mediterranean. You invaded Iraq. What is it now? A satellite of Iran. A new Persia. As you feared in one of your books written during Bush's mistake. And Syria—you start a war, the Iranians finish it. Now *they* seek a bomb. And what should we do? Sit here without defenses?"

Jack let the statements lay in the air for a few silent seconds. The prince wasn't the only one with a sense of theatrical timing. "So that's a yes."

"No." The prince remained calm and seemingly forthright. "We do not have any program to develop a nuclear weapon or any device of similar capabilities. We have signed the international treaties saying that we won't. That is on record."

"You have nothing near Yanbu?"

"The port? No."

"Can I inspect any place I want?"

Prince Riad al-Saud gave him a quizzical look. "Are you a one-man United Nations?"

"Two-man," Jack said, indicating Doc.

The prince smiled at that. "I see. You will forgive the affront," he said to Doc.

Doc nodded.

"If you have nothing to hide, then surely I can go anywhere I want," said Jack. "You don't mind that."

"Permission to travel anywhere in the country is not mine to give," said the prince. "Other ministries are in charge of security."

His first major deflection, Jack thought. "So how can I ascertain that, as you imply, there is no secret facility in the mountains north of Yanbu."

The prince's gaze shifted from the digicam's lens to Jack's eyes. "I have just told you there is no such facility."

"Nothing near Yanbu, in the hills."

"There is nothing." The prince's face was outwardly calm, but his eyes seemed suspicious. He was either the finest actor Jack had ever seen, or honestly taken aback. Jack didn't know which, nor did he care.

"I'm afraid there is."

Silence fell. Silence stayed. The prince looked at Jack. Jack looked at the prince. Doc continued to video, silently. Jack waited, wondering if the prince would leave, or call his guards, or even throw the remainder of his tea in Jack's face.

Finally the prince spoke quietly. "Where did you get such information?"

"I was there myself, earlier today." More silence.

The prince's gaze shifted briefly to the camera.

"Already loaded everything on a cloud storage site," Jack said.

"I assumed as much," the prince said. "But that is not what I was thinking."

"Oh?"

"I would very much appreciate if you would show me this evidence," Riad al-Saud said. The prince was back in command. It was not a request. It was an order.

Jack motioned for Doc to show him what they had. Doc was smart enough to only show him the non-battle footage. He showed him only the video he had took when they were watching from the top of the hill.

When Doc thumbed off the playback, the prince did not sound shaken or angry. But he did seem very serious. He didn't even bother to try pretending that the location on the video could have been anywhere in the Middle East. The mountain positioning didn't lie.

"What will you do with this footage?" he asked flatly. "You know your so-called media will not care."

"Our so-called government might," Jack countered.

"My government might as well!' Riad exclaimed in a rare moment of total candor, surprising everyone—perhaps even himself. "I can assure you, Mr. Hatfield, I have no knowledge of this so-called base, but I can also assure you that will not be true much longer."

He stood smoothly, strongly, his hands shaking as if he were keeping them from balling into fists with only a great show of will-power. Jack and Doc watched him silhouetted against the sunset filling the windows. "I truly thank you for bringing it to my attention, but now I believe you have another interview to conduct, do you not?"

Jack could see that the prince was holding himself back from running out of the room, booming for his staff. "I do indeed," he agreed sharply, deciding to end their encounter as the master of understatement. "Thank you, your Excellency."

"No," the prince said, already withdrawing. "Thank you."

And with that, he was gone like a sirocco across the Sahara.

44

"Thing is, I believe him." Doc said as he took one of the bottles of water from the limo fridge "I don't think they have a program."

"What?" Jack snorted, sprawled on the backseat.

"Look at the video," prompted Doc. "Tell me he's not surprised when you mention Yanbu."

The prince was either kind enough to let them use the Bentley, driver and all, for the ride to Brooks's hotel. Or the original instructions had been to let them use the vehicle all day. It made no difference either way. The two men were back in the limousine and they were going to talk freely, bugs or no bugs.

"Whose site could it possibly be, if not the government's?" Jack wondered. "Maybe it's a different branch? A shadow organization in the Saudi hierarchy?"

"That's not the way these guys work," Doc maintained, then almost emptied the water bottle with one long pull.

Jack snorted again. "Well, I think at least Prince Riad doesn't work that way. Which is why I had you show him the video in the first place. Considering what we're up against, I realized we needed all the support we could get—and not just from half a world away. What do you think they'll do once they swarm over the site?"

"Make the same conclusions we did," Doc rumbled, taking another swig of much appreciated water. "Foreign intrigue on Saudi soil. They will not be happy, but I doubt they'll blame the messengers. We're the ones who brought it to their attention. Don't you think they would have kept us there if he really did know about the site?"

Jack frowned, and then slowly nodded. He looked down at the video playback in his hand. The prince said there was a threat; the prince denied that they had a program; the prince maintained he knew nothing about the secret facility. Jack raised his eyes to the limo's ceiling and sighed, feeling more conflicted than he ever had in his entire life.

The city outside the Bentley's windows was glittering like it had rained diamonds, but the glitz of Riyadh held no pleasure for Jack Hatfield. Even though he was about to have dinner with a true American hero, he couldn't help feeling that, appearances aside, he was truly heading into the heart of darkness.

The Four Seasons was another luxury hotel in an all-star building—the "bottle opener" as Jimmy had called it when they first arrived in Riyadh. There was security, but nothing like what they'd encountered with the prince. One of the general's aides met them in the lobby and took them to a private dining area. Doc had left his weapon in the limo this time, but wasn't searched.

"Figures," he grumbled, the video camera in his hands as they walked through the corridors.

General Thomas Brooks sat in a private room, at a small, white-table-clothed set-up for two, with a broad, friendly, welcoming smile on his face. He was in full uniform, with every pin, star, ribbon, and badge imaginable gilding his shoulders and chest like armor.

"Ah!" he said as if seeing a Warhol at a flea market. "Jack. So good to see you!" No "Mr. Hatfield" for Brooks. He behaved as if they were already the best of friends. He took Jack's proffered hand in both of his, looked him straight in the eye, then enthusiastically motioned for Jack to sit down. As he sat himself, he looked up to Doc. "Can we get you a seat as well, Mr. Matson?"

"That's okay," Doc demurred. "I'm good."

"On the basis of what we could find of your record, Mr. Matson," the general replied, "I'd say you are indeed. Jack must be proud to have you as a colleague."

Doc and Jack shared a quick glance. They shouldn't have been surprised that Brooks had done his homework, but it was rarely stated so baldly. Going for that "we're all just bosom buddies here" vibe, Doc realized.

"I'm just his cameraman today, General," Doc said. "Don't mind me."

"Very well," Brooks said. "But anytime you need anything, just say it."

"Will do."

And with that, Brooks brought his full attention, and full force of his personality, back on Jack. He was charming during the meal, regaling Jack with stories of his early days in the army, and then a rambling history of corruption and culture in the Middle East and the world. He ate and drank lustily, almost as if it were his last meal. That, alone, made Jack a little queasy. He ate little and avoided the coffee completely. His stomach was sour enough as it was.

"Twenty years ago," Brooks lectured, "Shia and Sunni coexisted more or less peacefully. Now the two branches of Islam are at each other's throats, regularly blowing each other up in Iraq, Syria, Egypt. It was tempting for us in the Western powers to take a hands-off approach: let the two sides destroy each other. Certainly, in the short term, that seemed like a wise move: if the main branches of Islam were busy killing each other, they would leave the West alone."

Brooks took a moment to eat some more, then returned to his subject, waving a fork for emphasis. "But this strategy missed the deeper current: Islam in general was becoming more and more radicalized along tenets of the religion that demanded absolute purity of belief, and preached intolerance toward anyone who did not share that belief. To put it simply and bluntly: if a coreligionist should be killed, what was the fate of someone who did not share even the outward trappings of that religion?" He only paused for a nanosecond, then answered his own question. "Annihilation."

They started in on dessert before Brooks carried on. "It was commonly, but mistakenly, thought that internecine war left the victor fatally weakened. But history has shown that was incorrect in the majority of cases. Countless historical examples—France under Napoleon is an easy one for Westerners to grasp—showed that, on the contrary, victors were extremely dangerous to outsiders. Whether Sunnis conquered or Shia dominated, once victory was assured, the triumphant forces will turn their eyes, and their weapons, to the West."

Brooks lowered, and shook, his head. "In the meantime, the West was hollowing itself out. I will admit. I am alarmed by the cheapening of Western values—the parallel to Roman decadence is so overwhelming as to now be a cliché. The absurd morals of Hollywood have permeated America and Europe; they were now working their way through Asia at a rapid pace."

Brooks leaned back, finishing the dessert and raising his coffee cup. He became almost wistful. "You know," he mused. "In some ways, I don't blame the Muslims for wanting to stamp out the pestilence. Licentiousness and depravity undermines all human societies equally." Then the general seemed to notice Doc and Jack, as if for the first time as individuals rather than a generic audience. He strove to find a happy ending to his tale. "Slowly, things started to change," he said. "A few of us, a small core, worked very hard to get the service in the right direction. And from that acorn, a mighty oak . . ." He smiled, then glanced at his watch. "But you know all this. No matter. Shall we get started?"

"Absolutely." Jack glanced at Doc, who'd been filming everything. "We can shoot right here."

Brooks didn't seem to hear Jack's interjection. His face grew serious, as if his body had sprouted an instant mask, and he leaned in. "The greatest threat the West faces today is Islam." He looked intently at the camera. "No doubt about it. There will be a war. Someone will use big, messy weapons first. Who? Iran maybe, or Al Qaeda." He turned his eyes to bore into Jack's. "The who isn't important. The problem is what comes afterward. We need to have the will to see the battle through to the end. We need to stamp out Islam. It's the only option, really."

Jack had been prepared for a fire-eating speech, but this took him by surprise. "What do you mean by 'the only option'?"

"You know what I mean," Brooks maintained. "You, especially.

We have to go balls to the wall. This is a fight to the end. They aren't going to give quarter, and neither should we. That's what the lefties and liberals don't get. Sympathy won't work. Understanding won't work. Negotiation? They'll laugh at us behind our backs as they *stab* us in the back!"

"General—" Jack started, but there's was no staunching the flow now.

"The corrosion has already started. We let them multiply and fester and grow until they get strong enough. Look at Great Britain. The Muslims are reproducing in such numbers that, within a generation, they won't need a war to institute Sharia Law. They will simply vote it in. And that population will spread across Europe, across America. And somewhere along the way they will attack Israel. Israel will be first. That's my prediction. Maybe Israel will retaliate, maybe they will opt to strike first—weather the international censure to ensure their survival. Of course, in private, virtually every nation except a few in the Middle East will sleep a whole lot better.

"*If* they survive retaliation," Brooks continued. "How much longer until Iran represents mutual assured destruction? Do you really think that the Syrians have turned over all their chemical weapons?"

Jack broke in. "Speaking of which," he said, returning to the interview and intel he still wanted to acquire, "what about the Saudis?"

"What about them?" Brooks replied. He seemed startled to have been pulled from the soapbox where he was clearly very, very comfortable.

"Do you think they have WMDs?" Jack asked.

"I doubt it," said Brooks dismissively. "The Saudis feel insulated by their oil. No one wants radiation or botulism in their gas tanks. The Saudis have been corrupted by their wealth and inbreeding. The ruling family has, not the rabble. They are as poor as ever. And, more dangerously, they are turning from secular cash to religious propaganda for solace and deliverance. Whatever happens," he stressed, "whenever the masses revolt, we won't be strong enough to defeat them." Then the general stopped, thought for a moment, smiled, and leaned back. "You see Jack," he continued, seemingly the very voice of reason, "if we don't finish it quickly, it will continue for years, decades. Them wounding, maiming, and even crippling us. And every month, every week, every day, it will get worse. Killing us with a thousand small slashes—the ancient Arab way. And the longer we wait, the worse it will get because our enemy will become more powerful. The war has to happen now. Don't you see? The sooner the better, radical Islam has to be eliminated. You've said so yourself."

Jack almost sucked in a breath. Suddenly Brooks had thrust the ball into his hands. "Eliminated," he echoed, "yes. But the right way. The American way."

"By trial? In the courts? Give me a break—"

"No," Jack replied. "On main street, at high noon, one-on-one. The ordinary man, the small town sheriff, the big city cop—he or she has to show these lunatics that we're not afraid to face them. And when we stand up to them, who do you think will cave? Us?"

"I admire your confidence in the American spirit," Brooks said. "But this is the twenty-first century and we've got to fight fire with fire. I've heard what you've said. I've read what you've written. You, of all people, know the truth of what I'm saying. You've advocated it." He wagged a scolding finger at Jack, moving to the edge of his chair. "Don't you go weak on me now. Not you! You got weak once, and let them throw you off the air! The greatest voice of reason in the entire country and they throw you off the air."

Jack got very cold and became very still. "They threw me off the air because I asked one question—"

"Yes!" the general all but exalted. "And you were one hundred percent right in asking that question. Because, make no mistake, the Islamic terrorist will get their hands on a weapon of mass destruction and they will not hesitate to use it on us. That is why we have to stop them before they can." Brooks pointed at the camera. "You know that, I know that, and now we have to tell the world! We have to be strong and smart enough finish it, finish them! Once and for all." Brooks leaned back, smiling and certain. He positively beamed with righteous fervor.

"Yes," said Jack quietly. "But what about starting it?"

Brooks blinked. "I beg your pardon?"

"On *Truth Tellers*, I asked one simple question. 'How would you feel if Muslim extremists got hold of a nuclear weapon?'"

"Yes, yes," said the general nodding, leaning forward. "That's what we have to stop."

"But how? The heroic way or the way of the desert jackal?" Jack asked, leaning forward himself so their faces were no more than six inches away from each other.

"Stop comparing us to them—"

"Why? General, what would you do if you had a nuclear weapon or some other WMD?"

It was as if Jack had just told him he had won a million dollars. General Thomas Brooks leaned back, lay his crossed fingers onto his stomach, and smiled like he had just had the best meal ever.

"There's no 'if,'" he said point-blank. "I do have a weapon of mass destruction, one the world has never seen, and I am going to use it to start a war that will end the Muslim extremist threat forever."

In his four decades of life, Jack had been face-to-face with hundreds of people advocating hundreds of beliefs, expressing veiled and unveiled threats, proposing violence and aggression. He had battled fanatics with words and deeds. He had even defused a pair of weapons of mass destruction.

Most of the people he encountered in his life and career were sane, just extremely, often blindly, passionate. A few CEOs had lost their moral compass due to greed and yes-men. A few politicians had been radicalized by vocal constituents, or by colleagues who vigorously espoused opposing viewpoints, or both. A few big-mouth professors held positions inside ivory towers where the lack of strong contrary voices or the easy submission of students made them feel intellectually invincible.

Yet no one in Jack Hatfield's experience was as coolly, obliviously off-his-rocker as the man who sat before him.

Not that there hadn't been mad or homicidal generals in American history. William T. Sherman threw men, ordnance, and flame at the South in hellish, impersonal numbers to crush Lee. No one would accuse George A. Custer of letting reason cloud ambition . . . and patience. Truman was afraid to give Douglas Mac-

Arthur access to nuclear weapons for fear he would use them prematurely and with enthusiasm. During the Vietnam War, General Curtis LeMay was vilified for advocating carpet bombing the North back to the Stone Age, even if the collateral damage included Soviet and Chinese citizens whose death would draw those nations openly into the conflict.

Right or wrong, none of those men had the devious mind and steel resolve of General Thomas Brooks. He was ready to fall on his sword, to go outside the checks and balances of the Constitution, to work his will. Even at the height of his hubris, the current President of the United States—a tyrant at heart who did end runs around American law—had never risked anything so despotic.

The general was advocating a war many times more destructive than World War II, with a free exchange of weapons of mass destruction. He was proposing—no, promising—to start a war with all of Islam. A war to exterminate all extremists, but also, unavoidably, everyone like Jimmy including countless other good, decent, peaceful human beings in America as well as the Middle East. It was a war destined to touch every corner of the planet. Once the fight was started, no one would be allowed to be neutral.

Jack stared at the man's power-infused expression—which, more than anything else, inspired his next words. "So," he finally said softly, "it's as I've been saying all along. You're no different than a Muslim extremist now."

"You, a radical, ostracized by his colleagues—you *dare* throw stones at me?" Brooks's face lost all superiority, replaced with shocked affront.

"What do you think cost me the friendship of my colleagues?" Jack shot back. "I'm a Truth Teller."

"You're a poseur," the general said. "What gives you the standing to say such a thing? When did you lose whatever vision you had?"

"Insulting me doesn't make you any closer to being right," Jack said. "Those lunatic terrorists of the Islamic State of Iraq and Syria, otherwise known as ISIS, have threatened the same thing," Jack stressed. "The question that threw me off the air was about the danger of allowing Muslim extremists to get the bomb. Because they're the bad guys. We're the good guys. We don't set off bombs that can wipe out entire populations."

"We're the only ones who had the courage enough to!" Brooks barked back. "We're the only ones who *did*!"

"Only when it became obvious that the World War II Japanese government would sacrifice themselves and every individual citizen, one by one, rather than surrender their evil cause."

"It's the same!" Brooks maintained. "Don't you see? It's exactly the same, only no one will admit it. This war is not of my making. The Fort Sumter of this conflagration was the 1993 parking garage bombing at the World Trade Center. There's a straight line from that event to the attack on the USS *Cole* in Yemen in 2000, to the attacks of September 11, to the London rail bombings in 2005—with a bus thrown in solely to provide a visual image to horrify people—and on and on."

"No one denies that there are radical elements who want to tear down the West—but they are relatively few in number," Jack said, trying to stay in the rational center of this debate, hoping he could draw the general in from the fringe.

"They may be few in number but they are being hidden by the many," Brooks said.

"That's sheer speculation."

"No, Mr. Hatfield. That is fact. Law enforcement watches mosques and what happens? The so-called moderates say we're profiling. If they were helping us find the terrorists, our guys could be off fighting drug dealers or human traffickers. Look at what happened to the stop-and-frisk program in New York City. The police in high crime areas, which happened to be heavily populated by black youths, invariably stopped a high percentage of black youths to frisk them for guns. Sure, a couple of innocents were stopped and say they were embarrassed. But illegal weapons were confiscated in record numbers and countless lives were saved. As soon as that program was stopped by the courts, homicides went up. It's the same here."

"Then fight for strategic, surgical operations in civilian areas," Jack suggested. "Use your platform for programs that don't involve genocide."

"We are past 'programs,'" Brooks said dismissively. "In the Muslim mind, it's been 'us' or 'them' since the Crusades. They've been biding their time for centuries, lashing out when they could to keep the flame of hate alive. That is their doing, Mr. Hatfield, not ours! They've just been waiting for a time like this when they could finally acquire weapons of mass destruction. Well, sir, I would be derelict as a patriot, as a man, as someone sworn to protect America if I did not eliminate that threat. I thought you of all people would understand that!"

"General, if we were on my old TV show right now I'd probably go to commercial so you could cool down," Jack said. "I'd like to recommend that: take a time-out. Let's talk. You said it yourself—who else but me is going to listen to what you said and not judge you, just point out the shortcomings in your scheme. Let's find a better way."

"There is no better, more certain way," the general shot back.

"There *is*," Jack insisted. "Let me put your voice out there. I have the means and I still have an audience."

"Talk and diplomacy?" Brooks said dismissively. "Isn't there enough of that? An idiot president tried that with Iran and what did it get the world? An Islamic theocracy steps closer to having nuclear weapons." Brooks leaned forward now. "And for every voice like mine, ten bleeding hearts, ten ACLU boosters, ten peaceful-sounding Muslim clerics, ten *thousand* entitled college kids, will pile on for the other side. You don't have a megaphone big enough so I can be heard over that." He sat back. "I do. And it goes 'boom.' It's no different than colonial patriots, fed up with talk, throwing British tea into the Boston Harbor. There comes a time, Mr. Hatfield, to leave the table and push the button. That time is now. And, dammit, you *know* it! By bombing Mecca during the Hajj we wipe out millions of the world's most radical Muslims."

"All I know is that the other way has kept a relative peace for most of the world," Jack said. "Your way will involve that world in a conflagration of unprecedented destruction."

"It's coming whether we want it or not," Brooks said. "We might as well land the first blows."

"Like Pearl Harbor?" Jack asked.

Brooks was silent.

"General, you can't blow up Mecca. You'd be as guilty as the

Japanese, and we all know how that ended. All those moderates you accuse of secret complicity—your action will radicalize them."

"Good," Brooks said. "Then we'll know who to shoot, burn, and bomb. Which, may I remind you, is how we beat Japan."

"The world is different now," Jack said, grasping for intellectual straws.

"How? Didn't we round up Japanese in America and put them in camps, just to be sure?"

"Yes, though we didn't round up Italian-Americans," Jack said. "Many fought heroically against their ancestral land."

"Show me one Muslim who will take up arms against the Quran, Mr. Hatfield. I'm not talking about hollow words of pacifism. I mean, when the shooting starts what Muslim will take out an imam? These cowards take our money in Egypt, enjoy the bounty and opportunities of America, sell us oil—yet politically they hang to the rear in case things go south for us. Then all of them will suddenly shout '*Allahu akbar.*'"

Jack considered what Brooks said. As the general spoke, Jack had been sifting through the rage and rhetoric to find something he could hang on to, a wedge to get through to the man. He regarded the general, who was still chillingly calm for a man who had proposed genocide.

"Abraham argued with God that Sodom should be spared if there was one righteous man in the city," Jack said. "Genesis 18. You believe in the Bible, don't you?"

"I have said before that I believe in Bible, fist, and gun, in that order," Brooks replied. "And I put it to you that no man who believes in the Quran *can* be righteous. Believing in the Bible, I can be devout and American. My enemy? He can only be Muslim. I am not in contradiction with Abraham or God. They are a cancer that must be eliminated, and sometimes healthy tissue goes with that. *You* know that, Mr. Hatfield. I know you do. Your whole career has been predicated on speaking the truth, not softening and subverting it." Brooks looked profoundly disappointed, and waved his arm as if in dismissal. "Who are you? You're not the Jack Hatfield I know and respect."

Jack gripped the edge of the table and rose halfway to his feet. "I'm the Jack Hatfield who knows the difference between good and evil. I'm the Jack Hatfield who knows if you strike first, without warning, it will not turn out well. It never does. It never will."

For the first time Brooks looked over at Doc. Jack had been so focused on his *Truth Tellers* tack, ignoring the camera operator, that he had forgotten Doc was there.

"You're military, Mr. Matson," Brooks said. "What do you think of this man's position?"

Doc was unfazed, and the camera lens steady. "He stared down a dirty bomb and saved our city," he rumbled. "And some pretty toxic stuff after that."

"No one is questioning his courage, Mr. Matson. Only his judgment."

"That's what I'm getting to," Doc replied. "What would you have done in his position?"

"The same thing, of course."

"Since I wouldn't impugn your courage by disagreeing, let's assume you would've," Doc said. He smiled lightly. "Or would you have?"

"What the hell do you mean?"

"I mean if a Muslim radical had destroyed the Golden Gate Bridge and half of San Francisco, wouldn't that have solidified 'our' cause? Mightn't that have won many of those moderate Muslims to 'our' side. Wouldn't that have isolated and eventually quarantined the extremists the way the attacks of 2001 started to? Until we went to war with Iraq," he said. "We tried to slip that in under a kind of 'Remember the Alamo' clause but it didn't fly. All the credibility we had went out the window when we became what we beheld, when we attacked the way we had been attacked."

Jack smiled proudly. Brooks grinned humorously. "I appreciate your loyalty to your friend, Mr. Matson. And your points are not without merit—intellectually. You know as well as I that in the real world, boots on the ground, you hit a hive of wasps before they can sting you."

"Mecca isn't just a hive," Doc pointed out. "That's like comparing a den of Irish gunrunners to the Vatican. You don't take out St. Peters to make peace in Ireland. I think you'll find that would have had the opposite effect."

Brooks bowed in the first concession of the exchange. He turned back to Jack. "Your friend makes a valid point—about Catholics. But they are rational. Muslims are not." He looked from one man to another, and stood. He placed his fists on the table.

"Gentleman, tomorrow, there will be a nuclear strike on Jerusalem, followed, almost immediately, by a bigger attack on Mecca, the likes of which the world has never seen and won't soon forget. The plan is too far along to stop now. So your choice, your only choice, is to get with the program or get run over by my tank treads."

He looked at Jack with an infuriating "all-is-forgiven-come-home-to-papa" expression on his face. "If you make the right choice, I want you to be the good fight's spokesman in all media. I want you to take your rightful place as the only man with the balls and brains to lead our people to the right side. This is your destiny, Jack. This is what you were born for. You know it, I know it, now let the rest of the world know it."

If Brooks expected Jack to run into his arms he was sorely disappointed. He was, however, somehow taken aback by Jack's suspicious expression.

"Sure," he said drily, "and how do I know you won't pull the same scam on me that you did here in Riyadh?"

Brooks blinked again, his fists coming off the table. "What do you mean? What are you talking about?"

"Please—don't give me that innocent routine," Jack chided. "You know very well what I'm talking about. The whole song and dance about having me track the copy machine switches to a fake Yanbu base with an empty bomb. Schoenberg, the eleven workers, our interpreter Jimmy. How many people did you have killed just to keep me busy?"

Doc saw it first. Jack's words were hitting the previously assured general like a flurry of little, rock-hard, fists. Brooks's eyes narrowed, then widened. He even took a step back, his mouth opening.

"You've lost all perspective, General," Jack pressed on, still not really seeing what effect he was having. "With this terrible plan, you lost all your humanity!"

Finally Jack stemmed his own flow of words. He stared at Brooks, his own eyes widening. He wanted to swear, but couldn't find the profanity amid the roar in his own brain. "You . . . didn't . . . know?" he finally breathed.

Brooks stood stock still, but his eyes were ratcheting in their sockets like pinballs.

"Doc," Jack said as calmly as he could. "Show him."

Then Doc, as calmly as he could—which was very calm indeed—walked over, turned the digicam so the general could see the playback screen, and showed him the base, the aftermath of the battle, and the revelation of the bomb's empty innards.

Jack watched Brooks's face as the video played. By the end he seemed as ashen and empty as the bomb itself.

The general stepped back again, as did Doc, who also returned the digicam back to its RECORD setting, calmly placing it on the level of Brooks's face. The general looked as if he wanted to hold up a cross toward the digicam, to ward off its blood-sucking truth.

The man who spoke again was not the same man they had seen when they entered the room. His body language and face was the polar opposite of the prince's. The prince had been galvanized. General Thomas Brooks had been gutted.

"I'm afraid that's all I have time for, Mr. Hatfield," he said quietly, beginning to turn.

Jack was taken by surprise. "Wait a minute! How does this affect your plan? Will you stop now? In God's name, will you stop?"

"Will *you* stop?" Brooks shouted over his shoulder as he quickened his pace.

"Never—General!"

But all Brooks did was continue to move away. All he said was, "I'm sorry, Mr. Hatfield, I have many appointments to keep."

Brooks then turned and almost ran toward the door at the far end of the room. Jack jumped up to follow him. Doc shifted out of the way, but kept the digicam aimed at Brooks.

"General, you must know this compromises your plan. There's no way the results you want can be achieved now. Where's the other bomb? Will you stop the other bomb?" A sudden realization slowed Jack down. "Can you?!"

Brooks flat out ran. He slipped through the far door and slammed it in Jack's face. They all heard the lock snap into place.

When Jack turned to Doc, the old soldier was already thumbing the SEND feature on the digicam to e-mail addresses at the safe house and an FBI office in San Francisco. Even so, he never stopped moving in the opposite direction. He slipped the digicam into a jacket pocket and kept moving. When Jack didn't automatically follow, too overwhelmed to think straight, Doc only said one urgent word.

"Run."

45

The next three minutes were a period of remarkable, single-minded focus for Jack. He was reminded of a time, in a journalists' charity football game, when he caught the kickoff and ran downfield. All he saw ahead of him were a clutch of knee-jerk liberal administration apologists between him and the goal. There was no way he would let them stop him.

And they didn't.

To the people in the hotel hallways and lobby, this was not a sporting event. They saw two men running haphazardly, as if they'd knocked off a bank and didn't have an escape strategy; and two uniformed guards from General Brooks's security staff in pursuit, their sidearms in their hands, their legs churning hard with practiced stride.

"Stop those men!" one kept bellowing, but most of the people they were shouting at didn't know English. And the ones who did simply froze, confused or frightened, or both.

Jack hazarded a glance at a window as he ran, saw the reflection of the military police coming after them. Would they shoot? Would they go so far as to fire in a crowded lobby—something to which local authorities would not take kindly.

Jack didn't think so. Moreover, Brooks couldn't have barked

more than a few words at them. What was the order? Stop them? Wound them? Shoot to kill?

Not that it mattered what the orders were, Jack decided. In the heat of the moment, anything could happen. Survival was measured in seconds, as he imagined the moments of life were treasured by someone who was about to be hanged.

All that counted was that he had not been shot when Doc burst out the hotel door and all but leaped to the side of the prince's limo. Jack saw the chauffeur stagger back as Doc lunged into the Bentley's rear section, and all but bounced back out, his Glock raised in his hand.

Jack sped, then slid toward them, but froze, his hands up when he heard a booming "Stop!" just behind him.

He turned slowly to the side and saw the two security men in their well-trained positions: heads tucked, both arms straight, guns aimed at his head and chest.

For an endless second it was a stand-off: the men ready to drop Jack, and Doc standing beside him, his gun also ready.

Then the second was over, and, as if a moving picture had entered a still photo, the prince's chauffeur wandered between the two sets of weapons, his hands out to both sides.

"I shall speak English because I assume you do not speak Arabic," he said to the security men. "Correct?"

They didn't answer, but their eyes started to waver between Jack, Doc, and the chauffeur. "Correct?!" the chauffeur snapped more sharply.

The lead security man nodded.

"These men," the chauffeur said, motioning to Jack and Doc, "are under the personal protection of Prince Riad al-Saud of the Royal Family of the Kingdom of Saudi Arabia. As such, if they are harmed in any way, the people who are responsible for harming them will be subject to the regulations of the Islamic Sharia derived from the Quran and the Sunnah. Do you understand?"

The eyes of the military men wavered even more, but they didn't change their stances. "We have orders pertaining to these two men," the lead officer finally said, despite knowing the severity of the Saudi legal system.

"I am sure you do," the chauffeur replied amiably. "But since these men are under the personal protection of the prince, and are not members of the military, your orders have no bearing here. *You* have no authority here. You are already in jeopardy under our strict weapons regulations, rules that I will not hesitate to invoke if you do not immediately withdraw."

The question of which was more severe, Saudi law or the wrath of General Brooks, clearly weighed on the men.

"I have no information regarding the military status of these individuals," one of the men said, reaching for straws and also trying to buy time to think. "The general believes otherwise," he added, ultimately passing the buck.

The chauffeur looked questioningly at Jack and Doc as if asking, "Are you, in fact, civilians?" Doc nodded in such a way as to communicate that Jack and he were, indeed, no longer members of any military.

"Your general is incorrect," the chauffeur said.

"With respect, sir, we have orders," the lead man repeated stubbornly, almost desperately.

The chauffeur sighed. "Well then, if I may ask, what were your orders?"

The lead man thought for a moment, then answered. "To stop these men."

The chauffeur put out his hands. "Excellent. As you can see, they have stopped."

The lead man was flummoxed. "Sir—" he sputtered, then stopped.

"No further discussion is required," the chauffeur suggested. "Congratulations on a job well done. Please go back and tell your general that the orders have been carried out and if he has any further orders concerning these gentlemen, he should take them up with Prince Riad al-Saud. Thank you for your attention, good work, and I would put away your firearms and withdraw before the local authorities arrive—which should be momentarily," he added, listening as the sound of sirens rose from down the street.

The chauffeur clapped his hands and then all but shooed the security men away. The staff and bystanders let out a sigh of relief and continued on. Just to be on the safe side, the chauffeur took Jack's arm and brought him beside Doc, then stood calmly between them and the security men, who were lowering their weapons and looking at each other with indecision.

"You enjoyed that, didn't you?" Doc whispered at him.

The chauffeur shrugged.

"You're not just a chauffeur, are you?"

"You're not just a cameraman, are you?" the driver said quietly.

Doc grinned, but the grin disappeared when he looked down at his camera. There was a red light flashing. He opened the viewing screen where a message waited. It was a red cross in a red circle with the red letters UNDELIVERED.

Doc looked up at the building. Something, or someone, had blocked his video e-mails.

46

The man who had blocked the signal stared down at Doc and Jack from the one-way window of the general's suite. When the general burst into the room, he saw Peter Andrews there, casually holding an XM2010 enhanced sniper's rifle.

"Are you mad?" the general snapped, yanking the sleek and deadly looking weapon from his event coordinator's hand.

"I was about to ask you the same thing," Andrews replied casually, seemingly unperturbed by the gun's removal from his grip. "You're behaving like a drunken seaman, brawling in public."

Brooks stared at his aide as if seeing him for the first time. They were alone in the luxurious, almost cavernous, suite, with all of Riyadh stretched out around and below them. Brooks's face went from amazed recrimination to angry steel in the wink of an eye. He threw the rifle onto a sofa and planted his feet.

"Explain yourself."

Andrews reacted like a spoiled brat who could ignore his parents order to "clean up your room!" Andrews snorted through his nose. "Americans are such imbeciles," he said quietly. "And your security is laughable." He looked back out the window. "Look at those fools. Stymied by a driver, of all people."

"Never mind that," Brooks growled, his hands curling into white fists. "What about the Yanbu device?"

Andrews glanced over his shoulder. "What about it?"

"They showed me video of the container! It was empty, an empty shell!"

Andrews laughed. "Of course it was, General. Do you think I'd let them take the real bomb?"

Brooks winced as though he had been hit in the face by a fierce Arctic wind. "What? Then you mean—?"

"Of course, General," Andrews repeated reassuringly. "I also blocked any e-mails they might have sent. The same way I blocked any e-mails anyone might have tried to send on the Rossiya airplane."

The mention of the downed plane and all its innocent passengers so cavalierly murdered—not to make a point but to satisfy someone's bloodlust—assaulted Brooks's mood again. He felt a pang in his stomach, an actual physical reaction. It passed when he reflected on the greater good that would come from dealing with the devil.

"So," Brooks started, his shoulders dropping. "All is going according to schedule?"

"Of course," the event coordinator said a third time. "Don't worry. By the time those meddlers can do anything, it will all be over, and you can get on with the rest of your good work, making the world safe for democracy."

Brooks almost seemed to deflate with relief. He was so relieved that he hadn't picked up on the sarcasm of Andrews's comments. Instead, he patted Andrews reassuringly on the shoulder, then started to move slowly toward his desk. "Thank you, thank you," he muttered.

"*Pazhalooysta*," he replied in Russian.

Brooks appeared not to have noticed. "You've become very valuable to me, Pyotr. You and your people. I'll be counting on you in the future."

Andrews grinned thinly—both at the general thinking it right to use his actual name, and at the mention of his people. "I am glad to hear it."

"The future will be terrible," Brooks continued, almost to

himself. "Difficult. I assume you've gathered that, from everything you've been involved in. You're not a stupid man, not a simple one."

"The two do not mean the same thing," he said.

"I'm sorry?"

"A simple man may have strong but limited guidelines that serve him well through life," Andrews said. "A stupid man is one who has no guidelines."

"I see," Brooks said. "Yes." The general wavered at his desk, and then finally found his attention distracted by the amply stocked bar in the corner of the room. He started to wander over to it. "So, back to the matter at hand. We have a little problem that needs to be contended with. It's my fault, really," he said. "I thought I could control him, use him. He's a journalist. It's ironic." Brooks paused as he searched for a bottle of bourbon. He found it, poured a shot into a glass. "Most journalists—I'd say just about all—are so easy to read, easy to deal with, easy to control. They want access to newsmakers. Their careers are built on that, not on the merits of the news itself. In exchange for that, they will print any pablum they are handed."

"We are the only ones left with any integrity, it would seem." Andrews had intended that, too, to be ironic.

"That is very true," Brooks said. But he was in a pensive mood and still talking—mostly to himself, like a man taking stock of his life. "A lot of those reporters hate me. Hate the military. I would imagine you don't have quite the same problem in Russia. The media all work for the state."

"Yes, but that forces them to be clever," Andrews disagreed. "Their readers are not educated but they are astute and literate. They read a great deal, unlike Americans. Russians have learned to say things subvocally—in their inflection, not in their words— or to select language in print that communicates ideas a fast-reading bureaucrat will miss."

"I suppose that's all true," said Brooks absently, hardly hearing what Andrews was saying. "But it's worse than being merely illiterate or incurious. In my country, they hate patriotism in general. And religion. It's all lumped together as some kind of radicalism. The hyphenates rule—the African-American, the Asian-American, the Gay-American. I am an American. Period. And these reporters—" he snickered—"they pander. Everything is softened with euphemisms. 'The N-word.' 'The F-bomb.' People know what they're saying—why not say it? The way Jack Hatfield did."

Brooks seemed almost sad when he mentioned the man's name.

"Hatfield," he said as if Jack were an estranged son. "I thought you would understand. I thought you would see."

Brooks's voice trailed off, his train of thought hopelessly mired in disappointment. He took his drink and sat heavily on the sofa. He looked up to see his event coordinator approaching, a beneficent smile on his face.

"Put that aside, General," he said. "I understand your disappointment. It was a noble effort."

"I thought I had him, dammit," he said quietly.

"You want this Hatfield taken care of, yes?"

Brooks tried to think it through. That which he could not win over must be punished. It must be destroyed.

"Yes," he said, the sibilants at the end of the word stretching out. "But he's not stupid, and he has help. He must be dealt with aggressively. Can you do it?"

"Of course."

"Good, good."

Brooks took another slug from his glass. He felt his mind seemingly cycling back toward the desperation he felt trying to convince Hatfield. The drive was contagious, spilling over its boundaries, infusing everything. He wanted to win. He intended to win. He looked down into his glass as if he couldn't recognize something so simple. He felt a pain in his stomach again, only this time it also radiated into his head.

"Would you like another drink?" he heard. He looked up, almost in surprise, to see Andrews leaning over him.

"Yes, yes," he said, struggling for normalcy. "But only if you're having one."

Andrews took the general's glass and walked to the bar. "It is against my religion to drink alcohol," he said.

Brooks shook his head. What was that about religion? He looked up again as Andrews chuckled, and approached, holding out the glass.

"I know, I know," Andrews soothed. "You are getting close to the moment you have always dreamed of, but you don't know how to deal with that."

Was that it? Had he piled all his drive on conquering Hatfield, now that the end of the race was here, victory in sight. *Old soldiers never die, they just look for a new war*, he thought. But what if there wasn't one?

Andrews looked off to the windows and the doors, making sure all was in readiness. "I saw this sort of thing in Chechnya once, when a commander I respected was about to lead an attack on a Russian police station. The commander had planned and planned and planned. Yet as the time got closer, he became so excited that he couldn't actually get dressed to carry out the assault."

Andrews made sure the general had a firm grip on the glass before he finished his story. "So I shot him in the head. It was an act of mercy. I pray to Allah, the one true God and creator of all things, that I will not be like that when my cherished moment comes."

Brooks frowned. Andrews's words had finally trickled through his own self-absorption.

"Wait—w-what are you saying?" stammered Brooks. He thought back to the comment about drinking. He looked up with an uneasy blend of confusion and concern. "You're—Muslim?"

Andrews's reply was a slow, proud nod.

"But you're Russian," insisted Brooks. "You come from Moscow."

Andrews stepped to the side of the couch. He slipped his left hand inside his sport coat and ran his finger along the lining, finding the handle of the syringe.

"You are *Russian*," repeated Brooks. The reality dawned an instant before Andrews spoke it.

"Actually, I am from Chechnya," said Pyotr Ansky. He saw his moment but waited. He wanted to enjoy this.

"No."

"Enjoy your drink, General." Pyotr slipped his finger into the lining, breaking the loose thread and taking the hypodermic in his hand. The needle was made of carbon, but was as sharp as the

finest surgical steel. "I imagine it's going a long way toward settling your stomach."

"But I checked you and your people out." Brooks squinted, as
if trying to visualize whatever piece of paper or computer screen
he had seen declaring the rebel mercenary group Pyotr headed as
bona fide and anti-Muslim.

"It's really funny to hear you say that," Pyotr said.

"I don't understand."

"I believe that, which is tragic," the Russian said. "You, who
have relied so much on your gut, so much on instinct, bet everything on *data*. That which is so easily, so commonly falsified, is
what you rested the entirety of your undertaking on. Did your
heart say nothing about me?"

"It warned me," he admitted.

"Not just your ordinary caution, no?"

Brooks shook his head. His mind was racing now, trying to
figure out his next move. "No. You were—too violent."

"Not violent," Pyotr said, his mood darkening. "Thorough.
Unsentimental."

Brooks started to rise and Pyotr swung his fist into the general's
face, catching him off balance and sending him backward over the
couch. This was inconvenient; not only did it make noise but it
put the general out of easy reach. But Pyotr was too focused on
his mission to worry about any danger, or even to pause. He moved
over quickly and plunged the hypodermic into Brooks's neck.

Then he reached down and pulled the general back around to
the couch. Just under eight milligrams of Tetrodotoxin were now
finding its way into Brooks's bloodstream, added to the sedative
he had laced the coffee with.

"Yes, Hatfield's a journalist," Pyotr hissed, checking Brooks's
eyes. "And who thought an American journalist wouldn't want
coffee? I thought all Americans were hooked on caffeine!"

Brooks looked wonderingly at the man he had depended upon,
the man who had killed whoever he had ordered him to, and tried
to comprehend his mistake. His eyes widened and his mouth
gaped.

"No matter," Pyotr decided. "I was hoping you'd all be unconscious by now, but no matter. It's too late." He watched

Brooks closely. "You seem to be having trouble, General," said Pyotr. He slipped the now empty syringe back into his jacket. "Don't you care to continue our conversation?"

"Somma bitch," slurred the general.

"Interesting. I've never seen the mouth react so fast. The neurotoxin I placed in your system, synthesized in this case from an octopus, is an extremely potent neuro-poison that acts on the voltage-gated sodium channels, blocking the muscles and not allowing them to contract. This has numerous effects very quickly, the first of which was paralysis of the voluntary muscles—those in the legs and arms, but also the diaphragm and those needed for breathing."

All General Thomas Brooks could do was stare, bug-eyed.

"Little wonder," said Pyotr. "The dosage is, in fact, some sixteen times what is needed to kill a human. I have done that for two reasons." He held up his fingers. "One, because I thought I might have to pour it into a drink, in which case the poison would not be as effective, and, two, the volume necessary was so small."

When he was sure the general was all but paralyzed, Pyotr put his hands on the back of the couch and shoved his face into Brooks's. "So General, the great war you're looking for? It's already begun. It's been going on now for forty years. It will take several more. But you know what the outcome will be. Despite your ludicrous behavior, you are not a stupid man."

Pyotr smiled at the irony. "As for your Mr. Hatfield, yes, he found our diversion. But it wasn't for him. It was for you. And yes, he killed my men there, but I can always get more." Pyotr sneered directly in Brooks's face. "There's never a shortage of people who love to kill Americans."

Brooks began to gasp. The poison could take up to twenty minutes to actually kill a man, though as a rule victims were comatose much sooner. Pyotr actually would have preferred waiting around to see him die—he never grew tired of admiring his artistic work—but there were many things to do. But there was no doubt that he would die: the poison had no known cure.

"Do you have any last words, General?" Pyotr hissed in his ear. "No? Then I have some for you. Some you can take with you to whatever hell will have you. You'll be pleased to know that your one and only bomb will still be put to good use . . . just not in the place you were planning. No, it will be used in the place you should have wanted all along. . . ." Pyotr stepped back as the general's hands moved sloppily to his throat. He would be in cardiac arrest in another minute. Pyotr took a look around the room, then went to the door and opened it.

"I think the general is having a heart attack!" he shouted.

As the others rushed in to help, Pyotr took a tentative step into the hall, the sort of step one might take when he didn't know what to do or where to go. He took another, glancing at the security man at the far end of the hall. The man was eyeing him. Pyotr threw out his hands in an expression of confusion, and coaxed him forward.

The man ran forward. Pyotr thought of knocking him across the back of his head, but he had so much to do today, and that would potentially be counterproductive.

"A heart attack! Get a doctor!"

The man rushed into the suite. Pyotr took a step back, then, after making sure he was out of eyesight of the suite interior, he turned and headed quickly for the elevator.

"Hey, wait a minute!" yelled someone.

The elevator door closed as two of the security people ran out of the suite, guns drawn. Pyotr pressed the lobby button, then threw himself to the floor as a precaution, but there were no gunshots.

A lucky break. He could not count on another one. But he wouldn't need one. He punched the button for floor 11. As the elevator slowed, he hit every other button on the panel.

The doors opened. Moving quickly, Pyotr walked down the corridor to the emergency stairs. He trotted down to the landing on the tenth floor, and walked to the door. He opened it, saw the hallway was clear, then stepped across and grabbed the fire extinguisher. Back in the stairwell, he began to descend quickly, opening the extinguisher as he went.

The extinguisher had been emptied of its fire-killing contents; it was now a mankiller. Instead of powder, an MPG-84 submachine gun sat inside. A descendant of the famous MAC-10, the submachine gun was used by a number of forces, most notably the Peruvian military, often in security details. Its main value to Pyotr was its size and easy breakdown, which had made it possible for it to be hidden and quick to reassemble.

He had it together by the time he reached the fifth floor. Now free to concentrate on where he was going, Pyotr took the steps two at a time, his right hand against the wall and his left holding the gun. He went out on the third floor, which was just above the two-story lobby and main reception desk. Pyotr held the gun down at his side—if you walked quickly enough, he had learned years ago, most people didn't notice. Few of those who did would attempt to stop you.

He'd reached the escalator and was already eyeing the door when two black-suited members of the general's security detail crossed toward the main entrance below him. They'd obviously been stationed downstairs. Unsure of how many others there might be, Pyotr hesitated for a moment, but only a moment. He raised the gun and quickly put a half-dozen 9mm bullets apiece into the men's bodies.

The magazine boxes Pyotr had for the gun contained thirty-two rounds. Pyotr disliked carrying guns that were only half-full, and so he emptied the rest of the box, spraying indiscriminately across the large hall. With glass falling and women shrieking, he dashed for the door, reloading as he went.

A hotel security guard made the mistake of stepping out from his post at the side. The man was reaching for his gun when Pyotr shot him in the face with three bullets, a quick squeeze of the trigger. He was out of practice with the weapon. There was a time when he could have controlled it so carefully that he would have used only one.

Pyotr swung around, back to the door, and scanned to make sure no one else had gotten a clean view of him or was following him. Sure that everyone had taken cover, he pushed outside, then trotted to the white Toyota approaching from the far end of the street.

"Move quickly," he told the driver as he got in. "Our schedule today is tight."

Pyotr frowned at the phone's screen. It was inconvenient, but he had to answer. "Yes," he snapped, holding it to his ear.

"The men are en route," said Stefan in Russian. Stefan was reliable in many ways, but he suffered from deafness, a result of a car bomb that exploded prematurely in the Balkans some years before, and so he spoke far too loudly. At times Pyotr thought he didn't need a phone at all.

"Good."

"You realize they will be there and—"

"That's none of your business," said Pyotr curtly. "Everything else is arranged."

"I thought you needed the heads-up."

"Yes. Good job."

He hung up and turned to the driver. "How long will it take us?"

"Two hours to get there, an hour to load it." The driver shrugged. "We'll move as quickly as possible."

"We'd better," said Pyotr. "We have a bomb to deliver."

47

The chauffeur drove relentlessly back to the prince's office. "It is imperative we get there," he said. "There we will find a powerful Wi-Fi source that is less likely to be compromised."

Jack nodded, knowing that no air-based communication system was hijack-proof. But both he and Doc were in agreement that the need for haste was absolute. The sooner they get Brooks's confession to Dover, the better. They sat on the edges of the limo seats. The men were so tense, in fact, that they had been sparring from the moment they sat down.

"I can't even imagine the devastation an attack on Mecca would wreak," Jack was saying.

"Best not to try," Doc advised.

"I can't be that complacent."

"It isn't complacency," Doc protested. "It's insulating the mind from overload."

Jack shot him an angry glance. "How can anyone insulate his mind from *this*?" he said accusingly.

"By not thinking about it," Doc said.

"No," Jack said. "That's not possible. Or maybe it's just the difference between a soldier and a journalist."

"What the hell does *that* mean?" Doc said. "To me, the difference is that your heart bleeds in empathy while my heart bleeds for real!"

"Come on, Doc. You know me better than that," Jack said.

"And you know me better," Doc shot back. "It's like the first responders in 9/11. We can't afford to let the magnitude of this in or we won't be able to move."

"It's more than that," Jack said. "It's been that way since we started this—'documentary,'" he said, in deference to the Arab driving the car. "You conquer by force, I attack with reason. I believe in fighting ideas with better ideas, not with bullets."

"Balls," Doc disagreed. "I always give someone a chance to talk before I shoot 'em."

"Yeah," Jack said. "'Raise your hands or I'll put a slug in you.'"

"I'm still alive, aren't I?"

"Yes," Jack agreed. "But I've carried a weapon in the field, too, Doc. I know the military drill. I like my way better."

"Right. Don't you see, though—you're doing exactly what I'm warning against. You're letting the scope of this thing get to you and it's clouding your reaction. The 'drill' as you called it is no different than if you're running to stop a bus or disco from being bombed. Focus on the steps, not the outcome."

Doc had a point. That's how Jack was able to get through the last two crises he faced. Not knowing the potential horror that would be unleashed if he failed, he was able to stay keyed on the target.

"Words," Doc muttered. "Weren't those the weapons your guests used against you when you posited something like this scenario on the air? Didn't they beat you down with ideas? Sorry, brother. My way is better. Shoot first—an object lesson—and persuade the survivors. That's the price of going to war."

Jack didn't see the point of continuing the discussion. They were not just splitting hairs they were grinding them to powder. They were on the same team. That was all that mattered.

"All of which is beside the point," Jack said. "What's the game plan going forward?"

"I don't know," Doc said. "I'd say it's fluid."

Jack thought aloud. "Mecca holds a population of roughly two million people, though it routinely holds as many times that number of religious pilgrims. Every Muslim is, at least in theory, expected to visit the city at least once in his life. But no non-Muslim is ever permitted to go there. Christians, including you and me, would be shot on sight if we dared enter."

"Even to warn of the bombing?"

"Even to warn of the bombing."

"That's nuts," Doc decided. "With that kind of stupidity, maybe they deserve to get their clocks cleaned."

"Doc—don't," he said, flashing his eyes toward the driver. "Not now."

Doc shut up. Jack exhaled to stay calm.

"Gentlemen, if I may be permitted?" the chauffeur said. He did not wait for permission to speak. "The city is the holiest of all Muslim centers because it holds the Kaaba, the sacred granite cube that every Muslim faces when he prays. According to the Quran, the Kaaba was built by Ibrahim—Abraham to the other people of the book—and was the first house where Allah was praised. Before the time of Muhammad, the Kaaba and the surrounding area were designated as a place of peace and sanctuary; no one could fight within the area."

"Well, this will change that!" Doc exclaimed, his knee shaking up and down.

"But it was Muhammad who declared the site sacred only to Allah," the chauffeur continued, "evicting the other gods and their worshippers who had gathered in the city. Mecca, an important trading center even before becoming enshrined as the first city of Islam, expanded until it was one of the largest urban centers in the Muslim world."

"Yes," said Jack. "Though history was its essence, it has spread and modernized itself over the centuries, pushing up against the valley it's located in. That same valley would concentrate the effect of a blast. The shock waves would surely devastate the city center. They might also help to contain the lethal agent."

"That's a double-edged sword," Doc mused. "It might lessen damage outside the city, but it will make any cleanup a bitch and a half."

"What did your countryman hope the effects on Islam be, I wonder?" the chauffeur said.

"First, I want to be clear about this," Jack said. "We're countrymen like you and Osama bin Laden were countrymen. I don't approve of his methods. At all."

"Thank you for that, Mr. Hatfield."

"What Brooks hopes is that it will bring on an all-out war," Jack explained. "In his opinion, that can be the only way Islam will be contained."

"The Kaaba has been damaged before," the chauffeur informed them, "but those were accidents. A deliberate act against our religion's holiest site would be catastrophic not for Islam but for the world."

Jack, desperate to get his mind off their helplessness, grabbed on to the only hope he could conceive at that moment. "Maybe it would bring war," he said. "Or maybe the act would be so heinous, so incomprehensible, that it would bring people to their senses. Maybe they would see that extremism meant death, and death is not the answer."

"You sound like Abe when you talk like that," said Doc, referring to their liberal friend who had been murdered years before. "A wild-eyed, bleeding-heart, new-age hippie."

Jack turned on him. "It comes down to what you believe about people," said Jack. "If you think people are basically good—"

"I think it was Cervantes who called the world a dungheap and everything on it a maggot," Doc said. "If you think people are basically good, you're insane. The extremists will go all carpe diem on our asses and take this situation over, Jack. That's human nature."

"There's good in the world," countered Jack.

"Not in my experience," Doc said. "You know what Islamist radicals are like. They blow themselves up to kill children. What does that say?"

"Not every Muslim is like that," the driver pointed out.

"Enough are," Doc replied. He turned to his old friend. "Frankly, I'm surprised at you, Jack. You used to be a realist."

"I *am* a realist, dammit. I'm just not hopeless. I can't be."

Doc grinned. "Well, you're in love. Maybe Dover is responsible for this."

Jack softened a little. Thinking about the young woman made him smile inside. Doc could have a point.

"Anyway," Jack said, "just because we're up against evil, that doesn't mean we have to be evil as well."

"Okay," Doc said. "Tell me one Muslim who would have tried to stop someone from nuking the Vatican in Rome."

"I bet Jimmy would have."

"All right—maybe," admitted Doc.

"I would," came a voice from the front seat.

Doc looked at the back of the chauffeur's head, remembering what he had already done for them. He sat back. "Touché to you both. I'll shut up now."

"Don't shut up, Doc," Jack said, softening. "Just help me. We've got to figure out a way to stop this."

"I'm stymied," Doc admitted. "For the first time in my life, I don't know who to shoot at. And I don't like it."

"We're here," said the chauffeur.

The heat of the discussion instantly dissipated as all three men barreled from the limo and charged into the lobby. Despite the hour of the evening, the place was as active as it had been at noon. The chauffeur was first at the information desk and spoke in rapid Arabic. Doc raised his eyebrows at Jack when they saw the deference the men at the desk paid him in body language, expression, and action. He was certainly not just a chauffeur. A desk man raced to prepare the way as if his hair was on fire as the chauffeur motioned for Jack and Doc to follow him.

"This way," he said. He led them quickly to the building's security office, which looked to Jack like a set out of a James Bond movie. Glittering lights were everywhere and a row of desks were outfitted with the most sleek, costly, and futuristic machinery oil money could buy. Huge, flat, wide-screen monitors encircled the room, showing every inch of the building and surrounding grounds.

"Here, here, here," said the chauffeur, striding over, and pointing, to a desk on the right side wall. Jack grabbed the phone while Doc tried to resend the video. The general's confession was already flying across the world, seemingly before the digicam even registered SEND.

Jack checked his watch. San Francisco was ten hours behind

Riyadh, so it was midmorning for Dover. Perfect. "Do I have to dial anything to get out?" he asked the chauffeur, who had sat down at the computer.

"No," he said, his fingers dancing on the keyboard.

Jack dialed "their number" and waited anxiously, his toe tapping nervously. As soon as the connection went through, Jack's energy welled up and he started talking.

"Dover, listen," he barked. "Doc's just sent you a video where Brooks admitted it. He's planning to bomb Jerusalem and Mecca. Get it to Carl Forsyth, Kevin Dangerfield, everyone! They're planning to do it tomorrow."

"Christ, Jack—"

"But be careful," Jack cautioned. "There may be people even higher than Brooks involved in this. Maybe the administration has set Brooks up—maybe they were the ones who thought we'd all benefit from Armageddon. Regardless, we've got to stop it, any way we can!"

"Jack, are you—"

"I'm fine!" he shouted. "Go! Please!"

Jack took a breath and listened to the sound of rampant activity going on behind her. It was too busy to be in the safe house. It had to be the offices of the FBI.

"Jack, we got it!" she said after a few long, tense moments. "The video came in from Sol minutes ago."

"From Sol?" Jack asked.

Then he realized what Doc had done. Although he would have gotten an UNDELIVERED message for Dover's line, Sol's more powerful safe house system must have pulled it in.

"Good, good," Jack said. "What can I—what *should* I do?"

"Jack," Dover said urgently, as if she hadn't heard him, "listen to me."

"Yes, what?"

"General Brooks is dead."

"Are you sure?" he asked, stunned.

"Fresh from the Pentagon," she replied. "Jack, talk to you later. We've got to find out who's really running this show."

48

Pyotr Ansky walked quickly through the maze of narrow, refuse-strewn, potholed paths that made up the district of Al-Suwaidi in the southwestern corner of Riyadh. He ignored the notorious places where prostitutes of both sexes secreted themselves, despite contentions that they didn't exist or had been wiped out by the dens of criminals, terrorists, and strict ultraconservatives who infested the place. It was a closed market on depravity in any form. No one entered the district at night unless they were looking for death. Pyotr Ansky entered the place after dark, and quickly ducked into a seemingly benign, peaceful café, filled with the smell of potent coffee and clouds of hookah smoke. As always, Pyotr's eyes had taken in everyone even before he stepped completely inside, but then he moved quickly to a table in the back, where a small, wizened, man sat. Although he wore a dirty robe and upraised hood, Pytor could see his face—both the color and texture of a shelled walnut.

"Teacher," Pyotr bowed his head as he sat down.

"Here, we are as one," the imam said, his voice just above a whisper. "We wear the enemy's costume. Something to drink?"

Pyotr sensed it was a test. He had not lived a blameless life. There had been long periods of dissolution—not just in Russia but

Chechnya itself. For long intervals vodka had been a great solace, providing both courage and forgetfulness—qualities much to be valued. But he had put those needs behind him even before meeting the imam and coming to understand the true nature of his calling. The smell of the café brought the evil of his vices back. His stomach turned bitter, and he tasted the first pangs of vomit in his mouth.

"A bit of tea, if it is convenient," he said.

The imam smiled, and signaled a waiter. Moments later, a fresh cup had been poured. Pyotr, still uncomfortable, remained silent, and didn't sip until the imam nodded to him.

"What news?" the imam asked. He spoke in Russian to make it difficult for eavesdroppers to understand. This was a surprise; Pyotr had not thought the imam could speak Russian so well. He should have known. After all, he knew Pyotr so well.

"The weapon will be in place within twelve hours," Pyotr replied, also in Russian. "I have the fusing device. It will be a simple matter of attaching it and flying to the proper altitude."

"You will do this yourself?"

"Yes."

"You are using the general's own transport?"

"It was there, it was best," said Pyotr. "My man is there. I have nothing to fear."

"You are sure?"

"I am absolutely positive."

The imam stared at him and Pyotr felt a single bead of sweat begin to emerge from his scalp. "You have failed before," the imam said without judgment—simply as a statement of fact.

That was true. A year before, Pyotr and his men had stolen a bomb from a Russian storage depot at great cost. But it had a core of uranium refined to only seventy-six percent quality for the weapons-grade material. It was too weak to explode properly. The original intention was to refine it further, but that proved beyond the imam's means.

"I learned a great deal from that failure," Pyotr stated. It was a failure that had led directly to the present plot, where Pyotr had pretended to cooperate with the American general.

That seemed to satisfy his imam. He nodded approvingly. He

had been working on both plans—and perhaps a dozen more—for years and years. Pyotr wondered what else he contemplated.

"Others attempted to take your weapon," said the imam. "They were not content with what you gave them."

"As I anticipated," Pyotr responded. "So I created a distraction for them."

The imam nodded again. "Then you alone will make the final attack."

Pyotr nodded. It was a decision borne partly of determination not to fail, and partly of selfishness—he didn't want anyone else sharing his glory. "My target remains true?" he asked.

The imam nodded once.

"We cannot change it back to Jerusalem?"

"No. The result would not be as desirable," said the imam calmly. He could have been speaking of a soccer strategy. "There would have been no stopping the Israelis, and they are the ones we must fear. The Jews are the ones who will be ruthless, because they have already tasted so much blood. The Americans will remain weak for quite some time."

Pyotr nodded. "They are weak, but they can be tenacious."

The imam shook his head sagely. "Not they. He."

"The reporter?"

"More than likely he is with the CIA and only claims to be a reporter."

Pyotr did not contradict the imam, though he knew this wasn't true. He had learned a great deal about Jack Hatfield in the past few days.

"This will be an attack ten times greater than the one on the Twin Towers and the Pentagon," said the imam. "A practical, as well as a symbolic strike. The heart of the American evil will be torn out. The filth it purveys to the world will be shut off at the source."

"The target is well chosen," said Pyotr. He had heard this speech many times over the past several years.

"The devil's songs will cease, and it will be easier for us to lead our people," said the imam. "But you will be in Paradise, enjoying your bounties, thanks to the Prophet's largess, blessed be his name."

Pyotr bowed his head. He needed no more encouragement—he understood that his entire life had led him to this moment. His name would be enshrined at the head of the list of martyrs; he would be better known than them all.

And he would savor the moment of death. It would come at exactly 18,500 feet, in exactly thirteen and a half hours.

"I must go now, imam, if I am to catch my plane," Pytor said abruptly, rising.

"Eternal peace be with you, brother," said the imam, without a trace of irony. "May Allah's will be done."

"It shall be," said Pyotr firmly before striding from the café to find a taxi.

49

San Francisco, California

"You're kidding, right?" Dover said, gripping the coffee mug so tightly Carl Forsyth thought it would shatter in her hand.

"Dover, we've only known each other a short time," her boss said, "but I have to believe that you wouldn't think I'm a kidder. Yes? Certainly not about something like this."

She nodded.

"The whole thing has to be a hoax," he went on. "There's nothing there. Believe me, I've talked to a lot of people in Washington who know . . . or *would* know if something were going on."

"Isn't that the whole point of covert operations?" she asked. "Secrecy?"

"In the field, yes. In D.C.? No. Everything gets found out, usually sooner rather than later. This one? You'd need a lot of moving parts."

"Or a bunch of tight-lipped, loyal fanatics like on 9/11."

"Again, you don't find that in Washington, at the Pentagon, Dover. That's why authors write about it. It's fiction."

"Until one day it isn't," Dover said. "Until one day someone depends on exactly that mind-set." She felt as though her head would explode. "Carl, it was right there," she continued, trying to keep from gesticulating wildly. There were too many windows in his office and too many eyes were on them. "General Brooks said so right into the camera. He said, in effect, 'I . . . am . . . going . . . to blow up Mecca!'"

"Agent Griffith," Forsyth said patiently, and not without some sympathy. "Think like an agent for just a second."

"I am thinking like an agent," she seethed. "An agent who wants to prevent a catastrophic attack before it's too late!"

Forsyth just shook his head sadly. "No, you're thinking like a—a *friend* of Jack Hatfield's."

Dover's mouth snapped shut and her lips grew very thin. He was going to say "girlfriend." Dover knew it. And her narrowed gaze told Forsyth that she knew it. But he had checked himself in deference to her previous good work.

She knew why her superior thought that. Jack was in trouble, and she obviously, seriously hated the fact that she wasn't able to help him. She believed, even if Forsyth didn't, that he'd stumbled onto something even bigger and more deadly than the Chinese plot that had spawned their relationship, and hated the fact that she didn't have all of the information on it.

Most of all, she hated the fact that she wasn't with him.

"Come on, Dover," Forsyth went on. "Ask yourself: why on God's green earth would Brooks admit that in public, let alone directly to a camera? Especially when there was time to stop it? Not a lot of time, I grant you, but still time."

Dover thought about it. Yes, it did seem reckless at the very least.

"His immediate superior—" Forsyth checked his notes "—Army Chief of Staff Ortiz, said Brooks was borderline certifiable. A man, and I quote—" Forsyth checked the report again, "'—whose entire life was dedicated to the army, and a man who would do anything to remain relevant on the eve of his retirement.'" Forsyth tossed the report back onto the high stack of papers on his desk. "What does that say to you?"

"I don't know," she said numbly, struggling to focus on this—trivia.

"Does it mean that we're dealing with someone who posed a

credible threat? Or a desperate, sad, lonely man who just wanted to force people to take his life's work seriously?"

"But the missing container . . . the plane c-crash?" she stammered.

"Now, as before, they happened," Forsyth agreed. "But that doesn't mean they're connected."

"And the Schoenberg murder?"

"What about it?"

"If it wasn't part of this conspiracy—"

"See, there's the word that always sets off alarms," Forsyth said. "Conspiracy."

Dover could practically see a satisfied grin on Forsyth's face.

"Schoenberg apparently had a lover back in Germany who was thrown over," the FBI officer told her. "That's what that is about."

"That's absurd."

"Really? You don't think a woman is capable of murder?"

"That's not what I mean, Carl, and you know it." *Especially not now*, she thought, growing increasingly frustrated with her boss.

Forsyth held up his hands in supplication. "Okay, but this German girl was a crack shot, and she just committed suicide. There's even a suicide note."

"Anything about killing Schoenberg?"

"No, but that's not for us to muck about in. The murder is a local case, Dover. It is being credibly handled by our friend Jeffreys. In any event, it's not my case, not our case, and we really can't afford to waste time with it."

Dover found that her teeth were biting hard enough to threaten her fillings. She unclenched her jaw, and her fist, and tried to control herself.

Forsyth saw and appreciated it. He sighed. And crossed the line he had hesitated to cross before. "Look, Dover, I understand you have feelings for the guy. And frankly I like him. Usually. I owe him something for letting me take all the credit for the Chinese affair. Believe me, I understand. But this—this is a lot of confetti flying around with no pattern, no sense but what he's struggling to make of it. Hell, that's what journalists do!" He leaned closer. "Brooks wanted to feel important one last time in his life. He wanted to alert the world of the threat he felt Islam posed. Maybe he knew he was dying. He wanted one last bit of footage that would outlive him."

"By threatening to destroy the world?" Dover asked incredulously.

"What better?" Forsyth countered. "In this age of YouTube getting millions of hits for a drunk TV star eating a hamburger? The second-highest-ranking officer in the U.S. Strategic Command swearing he's going to blow up Israel and Mecca? If this footage ever got out, hawks and doves would use it against each other for decades."

"So that's it?" Dover said tightly. "That's really why you think he did it?"

"If I had to bet money? Yeah," he said. Forsyth shook his head. "Believe me, Dover, I ran with it. The CIA nearly laughed me out of their office."

"They didn't take it seriously?" Dover exclaimed.

"Oh, they took it seriously, all right. For about an hour. And when nothing, and I mean *nothing* that they found backed it up, they saw it for what it is. A sad man's last gasp." Forsyth stood and took Dover by the arms. "Face it, Agent Griffith. The threat was a sham. And the threat died with Brooks."

Dover was silent. She rose, excused herself quietly, and stood down the hall, out of view of Forsyth. She tried to find a way to agree with him, but her compass needle kept swinging back to Jack. And not because of their relationship. His boots were on the ground, he had been through this from the start. Whose gut should she believe? His or the armchair director a dozen yards away?

Within minutes of leaving her superior's office, Dover made a call and then shared Forsyth's estimation with Jack. He put the call on speaker so Doc and the chauffeur could hear.

"They don't believe us," she said.

All three men appeared stunned. Only Jack said, "What?"

"They think it's all a figment of your, and Brooks's, overactive imaginations."

"Imaginations?" Jack said.

"My imagination is limited to women and handgun concealment," Doc said. "What kind of psychos do they think we are?"

"This can't be happening," Jack said. He was still processing what she'd told him.

"They're stubborn," she admitted.

"But how—we've got evidence—"

"Circumstantial, they say."

"Dover, they can't be that blind," Jack said.

"Whatever their reason, that's their position."

Jack looked at the chauffeur. They were in a security office half a world away, near the epicenter of the plot. Yet he never felt so disconnected. He addressed the driver. "What's happening at Yanbu?"

"The investigators are there now," the driver reported. "It is as you said. But, as you also said, there is no sign of real radioactivity or actual bomb making. Except for the corpses, it looks like an elaborate hoax for reasons we cannot yet fathom."

"But the dead bodies *are* there!" Jack said. He got back on the phone. "Dover, you have to go back to Forsyth. They can't be this blasé about it! Too many pieces fit, and fit in a way that doesn't allow another interpretation!"

"I know, I know," Dover said. "But they'll come up with reasons for the corpses and I'm betting they won't involve Brooks. Christ, I could come up with other explanations—"

"You, too, Dover?" Jack didn't like the fact that he was suddenly echoing a dying Julius Caesar.

"No!" she protested. "I believe you. Awful as it is, your interpretation is the only one that embraces all the facts. I just don't think their minds can process what you're telling them."

Jack looked over at Doc and apologized with a twist of his mouth. Doc accepted with a little nod.

"The thing is, they want Brooks to have died a hero," Dover said. "They don't want the military to look bad."

"Or nuts," Doc muttered. It made perfect sense to him. They found an empty bomb. That's how the authorities were now thinking of Brooks. An empty bomb equals an empty threat.

"But there was supposedly enough material for two bombs," Jack told Dover. "And there were several switches and other items, so there may be other bombs, or one other bomb. I don't know. But we should make sure that your boss knows that."

"I did," she assured him. "I have. But for him and all the others, the operative word is 'supposedly.'"

"And the operative phrase," Doc added sourly, "is 'I don't know.'"

Jack swore under his breath and looked around the room for any straw he could grab onto.

"So what do we do now?" he asked plaintively.

"I can't be seen still working on it," Dover said quietly. "But Sol, Ric, and Sammy still are. And you know they won't give up. I just spoke with them before calling you. They'll do everything they can, and one of us will let you know as soon as we find anything more."

"But will it be too late by then?" Jack asked, mostly to himself. But he found that Dover had already disconnected her side of the call.

Jack looked helplessly down at Doc, who, having seen so much death and destruction in his decades of service, just looked philosophical and shrugged.

"I guess we'll find out for sure tomorrow," he said.

50

Riyadh, Saudi Arabia

The traffic was so heavy that Pyotr told the taxi driver to go directly to the hotel. By the time he stepped into its impressive confines, he had made the transition from Pyotr Ansky back into Peter Andrews. He grinned wickedly, thinking that the power he felt at this moment was greater than he would feel when he performed his last, great act.

I know something all of you do not, he thought proudly. *I know that the world is about to change.* Would these people feel awe or terror knowing that he was the chosen one? Probably both.

If the activity in the lobby was any evidence, nothing was out of the ordinary. It wasn't until he reached the floor of the general's suite, however, that things changed noticeably. The place was crawling with military police, medical personnel, American consulate officials, even high-ranking members of the ambassador's staff. Someone he didn't know checked his credentials at the elevator door. The guard couldn't find his name on the approved list for a few moments, which allowed Pyotr to fantasize killing the man with his bare hands.

Just before the guard was going to check with higher-ups, they both heard "Peter!" They looked over to see Colonel Tristan Ashlock walking toward them, concern etched on his face.

"Peter, where have you been?" A guard sought to block Pyotr. Ashlock looked at the guard dismissively, and waved him back with an assured, "He's okay."

Andrews opened his mouth to answer the question but Ashlock shushed him while pulling him out of the reach of prying ears.

"You know what happened, then?" Ashlock asked as they moved through the worried staff.

"Know?" Andrews retorted. "I was there when it happened. I reported it!"

"Good Lord!" Ashlock exclaimed. "Then where did you go? All I could get out of the security men was that you ran like a man possessed."

"Yes," said Andrews. He leaned in conspiratorially and spoke in a stage whisper. "The general had privately charged me with making sure certain details were taken care of in case of his death . . . if you know what I mean." Andrews looked both ways to make sure the right people were listening in.

"Ah," said Ashlock knowingly. They began walking in the direction Ashlock indicated.

Andrews smiled inwardly. Say something like that to any American and he will fill in his own blanks, depending on whatever their personal vices happened to be.

"Then I heard the gunfire in the back areas," Andrews continued, his voice returned to its regular volume. "What was that all about?"

"Damned if we know," said Ashlock. "The surveillance cameras showed nothing." It was Ashlock's turn to lower his voice and look around. "I saw to that." By then they had reached the military police officer in charge. "This man witnessed the general's—event, Captain. He can tell you what you may be missing."

The captain studied Andrews a moment then nodded, taking him by the arm. "Sorry about this," he said. "But the general ordered that all security cameras and listening devices be removed prior to his checking in."

"Yes, I know," said Andrews. "The general is—" Andrews caught himself, trying not to grin, "*was* a very important, very private man."

"So any information you can provide will be of enormous value," the captain added.

The questioning was routine. Andrews, a trusted member of the general's staff, detailed what he "saw"—using the classic signs of a heart attack within his description. That aligned with what the captain wanted to believe, on the basis of his instructions, so Andrews was free to go about his business within the half hour.

His business, as he and Ashlock made clear, was to accompany Brooks's body to the airport and a waiting plane.

"Military high command wasted no time getting a transport to Riyadh," Ashlock informed him as they adjourned to the hotel's loading dock, where an unmarked ambulance was waiting. "They want Thom swept under the rug as fast as possible." Ashlock looked at the body swathed in sheets in the back of the van. "They treated him like an old age pensioner. The hotel deals with retirees passing on all the time. They even have a freezer for the bodies."

"Remarkably efficient," Pyotr said.

The ride across town was uneventful as they prepped the coffin. Ashlock and Andrews even avoided looking at each other, lest they be tempted to say something they'd have to kill the ambulance driver for. They arrived at the designated airport hangar in time to see a subtly marked C-17 taxiing in. They hopped out of the military medical vehicle as a female guard with a clipboard and earpiece approached.

"Personal effects detail?"

Ashlock nodded.

"Good," the young guard said. "We've got a little bit of ceremony to go through, proper handling of the body and all. Then he's yours. You need help?"

"We can handle it," Andrews replied, taking a respectful step backward. It was easy now. All he had to do was wait.

The big cargo aircraft slowed as it approached. A black hearse drove out from the other side of the hangar. Two black SUVs with flashing blue lights overtook it, passing at the side. Another group of soldiers arrived in a troop truck; they scrambled out and augmented the honor guard already standing at full attention.

The cargo plane stopped, its lights blinking. Andrews, always a man to appreciate irony, thought of how fitting it was that he was here—after all, the general had made it all possible.

The honor guard snapped to attention as the plane's ramp was lowered. The casket, now covered with an American flag, was slowly wheeled up the ramp. That struck Andrews as wrong—a flag-rank officer ought to be carried out, with a band accompanying the solemn parade. But this honor was perfunctory. If Brooks's superiors had their way, the general would have been dropped off a pier somewhere.

Andrews waited. Only after the hearse, the honor guard, and the SUVs had left did Colonel Ashlock return to his side. He'd been supervising what the loadmaster called "the disposition of the body." They stood there for a moment, looking at all the activity of a modern city airport. Even so, they were alone in the crowd.

"Are you ready?" he asked Andrews.

"Of course."

"All right. Come with me."

Ashlock turned abruptly. Andrews followed him into the belly of the jet.

"It's there," said Ashlock, pointing at a large metal crate after glancing to make sure even the pilots were absent. "No one has touched it. You can see by the seals."

"Excellent."

"You'll need a forklift," said Ashlock. "I'll get the loadmaster to help you. Is everything else ready?"

"Impeccably so," Andrews replied.

Ashlock grimaced. "It's taken a long time."

"Yes," Andrews agreed. "And much planning." He looked directly at the colonel. "You will handle the others?"

"Naturally," Ashlock muttered. "As far as they're concerned, everything is on schedule. When Jerusalem and Mecca are not destroyed, I will be as surprised as they." Ashlock waved a forefinger in the air with mock severity. "I will get to the bottom of this if it's the last thing I do," he mimicked his upcoming performance. "Heads will roll."

Andrews sniffed, sneering.

Ashlock nodded, then took a final look at General Thomas Brooks's remains. His expression was unfathomable. "You fly out tomorrow morning," he informed Andrews.

Andrews seemed a little disappointed. "Nothing sooner?"

Ashlock shrugged. "Although there's nothing better the army would like than to have him skulked out under cover of darkness, they thought it best to send him home at sunrise. Symbolism of sneaking him out in the dead of night—someone at the DoD might grouse about that."

Andrews nodded, happy to have the time to go over the plan yet again. The two looked at one another, and then Ashlock started toward the exit.

Andrews had known him for a while, and felt a certain nostalgia at their parting. It wasn't really an emotion, he thought, just an acknowledgment of shared experiences. They had both been trained by the Russian military at first, although Ashlock had continued in the sleeper spy services. In fact, he was one of their most successful double agents. Andrews could understand why. Ashlock, as a triple agent—even quadruple, if you count his plotting with Brooks and company—had played his role extremely well, fooling everyone—even his Russian masters.

"Colonel?" Andrews called back.

Ashlock turned around. "Yes?"

"You have our eternal gratitude."

Ashlock smiled broadly. "My pleasure," he said with a wave. "*Ashokrulillah. Alhamdulillah. Subhanallah.*"

Thanks to Allah, praise to Allah, glory to Allah.

51

Jack never thought he'd sleep. He never thought he would be *able* to sleep until after Brooks's deadlines for the attacks. But after the prince returned late that night to report that there was no evidence of an actual atomic device having been made—*and he would know, right?* Jack thought. Jack plopped down into a security office chair . . . just to rest for a bit, he told himself.

But as he absently watched the prince return upstairs, and he watched Doc confer with the chauffeur, Jack felt the last two days catching up with him. It reminded him of a colonoscopy, of all things. The doctor assured him that he could watch the procedure on a video screen, and he was actually looking forward to it, but once the anesthesiologist gave him a light sedative and had him count back from ten, he was out until long after it was done.

Doc glanced over when he first heard Jack's light snoring. He saw his friend all but collapsed in the chair. Doc smiled grimly. Given Brooks's declaration and Jack's rapid eye movements under his lids, the old soldier couldn't imagine what the reporter might be dreaming.

Jack was dreaming that he was walking up to the door of the federal office building. There was a big sign on the door that read, CLOSED BECAUSE OF FUNDING DISPUTE. Even so, the door swung open. Jack hesitated, then pushed it all the way open and walked in. He was in the middle of what looked like a bank lobby, with marble walls and fancy tile work on the floor. The place was completely empty.

There was a safe at the far end. Open. Jack went to it and saw stacks and stacks of thousand-dollar bills. He resisted the temptation to take some, and instead tried closing the massive door. But the door was so heavy it wouldn't budge. Finally he gave up and went outside.

The streets were deserted. He heard the sound of an airplane flying above, and watched as it crashed into the Transamerica Tower. A man in a black burka ran up the street, carrying a Kalashnikov. A dozen others followed. Jack watched them pass. He began trailing the last one, moving toward city hall.

Dozens and then hundreds of men in similar clothes, faces obscured by scarves, appeared and joined them. They seemed not to notice Jack, or at least not to care that he was there. When they got to city hall, Jack saw that television screens had been set up on the sidewalk. They were playing a news program.

AMERICA UNDER ATTACK! shouted the graphic. A pretty female news anchor sat at the desk, blindfolded; a man held a gun to her head. To Jack's eyes, she looked like Dover. Jack's eyes caught the scroll at the bottom of the screen: CONGRESSMEN ARRESTED AS TRAITORS. When he looked back at the anchor and her captor, he saw that the man's gun had been replaced with a long, thick sword. He started to scream, to warn her, just as her head exploded at the same moment it was chopped from her neck—

Jack woke with a start. For a moment he thought he was still in the dream, since he was staring at a computer screen that had a BBC international news feed playing. The male anchor, unencumbered by a gun- or sword-wielding captor, was talking about the possibility of another government shutdown in the United States.

A clever time for an attack, Jack found himself thinking, realizing the report had seeded his dream. Terrorists could time their strike as the military and security forces were throttled back by furloughs and cuts. Essential forces were not supposed to be affected, but Jack knew from talking to federal workers the last time around that they were hit in hundreds of little ways. Beyond that, morale always suffered. The response to the attack would be slow; vulnerability would be at its height.

"Hey, you okay?" he heard. Jack looked over to see Doc approaching, while the chauffeur was moving in the opposite direction. "You were quivering like a kitten dreaming of a pit bull."

"That's kind of how I feel," Jack grumbled, then groaned as he tried to sit up. The awkward position had given him a crick in his neck. "It wasn't a pit bull," he muttered. "It was worse. It was Brooks's worst fear."

"Islam taking over America?" Doc suggested, planting his haunch on the side of the desk.

Jack looked up at his friend, impressed. "Good guess."

"You just started all those anti-Commie films they used to show us in school playing in my head," Doc said. "Hey, if the threat from Islam is any indication, maybe we all had more to fear from the Reds than we realized."

"Yeah," Jack said. "But the joke's on us. Who could've known we'd end up with a president who would slip us a Pinko Mickey under the guise of social reform."

"We're back to agreeing with one another," Doc grinned. "But given it was your maze-like brain at work, I doubt your dream left it at that."

"Right again," Jack said, digging the heels of his palms into his eyes. "I think my subconscious was warning me that, if Mecca doesn't go, the real danger was a U.S. government shutdown being used as a pretext for a takeover."

"By?"

"Sleepers, strategically placed around the seats of power."

"Wow," Doc began to disparage the idea, but then his lips and eyes narrowed.

"I dreamed of arrests of congressmen for doing their jobs," Jack mused. "The appeals to patriotism in the face of a manufactured crisis. . . . I've seen all this before. A debt ceiling battle would lead to the imposition of emergency powers by the president. Take over the purse strings completely, and there would no longer be a check on the presidency." He looked up at Doc. "They called Nixon's administration the Imperial Presidency, but that would be child's play compared to this."

Doc slowly nodded, but instead of supporting Jack's new theory, he said, "You're adding more trees, Jack. We don't need more trees. We got plenty of trees already."

Jack considered that. "Are we missing the forest?"

Doc jutted out his chin. "Yeah. They're being blocked by a German industrialist, a fake base in the desert, and a pit of dead bodies."

Jack stood and shook his head just to jar his thinking. "Some people see what they want to see, some people see what they need to see, and too many people in authority explain away what they see."

Doc pondered that. Doc remembered the time he was hunting in the back forests of northern California and became hopelessly lost. Because he tried to rely only on his instincts, not on his instruments like a simple compass. He remembered following a stream down a mountain. Until it ran into a slightly bigger stream. He was sure this would eventually lead him to an open clearing and back to where he wanted to go. Instead he recalled how his heart dropped when the last stream led him not to a clearing but to a wide raging river, too deep and too fast to cross. The feeling of absolute terror and hopelessness. The understanding in a flash through his bowels that his instincts had led him to a fatal miscalculation.

"If there isn't another explanation for what we've seen and heard, what is the answer?" Doc asked.

"Who was it who said that once you eliminate the impossible, whatever remains, no matter how improbable, has to be the truth?"

"I think it was Sherlock Holmes," Doc said. "Eliminating the impossible is not going to be that easy after our interview with Brooks." Doc shook his own head now, seemingly overwhelmed by the possibilities.

"An empty bomb . . . maybe a missing bomb," Jack mused.

Doc stood up beside the desk. "I've been proceeding on the basis that another bomb might be in play," he told Jack. "So is the prince. So while he's thanked us for our service, he's given us the go-ahead to leave the country. While you were busy having your nightmare, I was having the jet fueled and prepared for takeoff at dawn."

Jack snapped from his reverie at the mention of sunrise. "What time is it?" he asked, looking for any clock.

"Five A.M.," Doc informed him. "Whatever the truth is, we should get to the airport and into the air." Doc lowered his head regretfully. "If Brooks wasn't lying, it'll be quite a view out our aircraft windows! Funny . . ." he said, his voice trailing off.

Jack knew that reflective tone of voice. He turned his head toward his friend. "Funny? What's funny?"

"Flying out at dawn," Doc replied. "Coincidentally and ironically, that's the same time the military is planning to send General Brooks home."

Jack's eyebrows shot upward. "Not tonight?"

"No," Doc said. "With a high-profile passing like this, that would smell like there's something to hide—like they want to keep it from a day's news cycle. Still, tomorrow A.M. is a pretty quick turnaround. They want him out of town and under a rug ASAP."

Suddenly Jack was no longer playing catchup. Doc recognized *his* expression, saw that his old friend was chewing on something . . . hard.

"What is it?" Doc asked.

"We got everything?" Jack asked sharply.

"In the limo," Doc reported.

"Then let's go," Jack said strongly. He called the chauffeur who had gone into an adjoining room. "Can you get me close to Brooks's plane?"

"I can get you as close as possible without running people over," he replied.

"As close as possible will do it," Jack assured him. He looked at Doc. "Don't talk. I've got to think."

Doc raised his hands in surrender as he followed Jack and the driver out.

The prince's chauffeur proved as capable as ever, getting the two onto the tarmac just as the first sliver of dawn was cracking the horizon. The G650 pilots helped load the plane with the pair's few bags, but Jack only had eyes for the C-17 making its own final preparations for takeoff across the field.

Jack and Doc got out of the car.

"Doc," Jack called. "You got the digicam ready?"

Doc didn't bother answering. He simply walked over and held it out on Jack's eye level. The chauffeur emerged and joined the two.

"Zoom in on the man directing the others," Jack instructed.

The fellow in the suit was just an insect-size stick figure from that distance, but Doc started to get a close up on him. The driver was trying to figure out what the pair was focused on.

"The man in the black Brooks Brothers," Jack said.

"Oh, yes," he said. "Peter Andrews, the general's event coordinator. Quite the *wald dhroot*."

"What's that?" Jack asked.

"Son of broken wind," the chauffeur translated.

Jack looked at him. "Who'd he burn and how?"

"Everyone," the chauffeur said. "Nothing anyone did was good enough for him."

But both men were alerted by Doc's sudden stiffening. Jack looked over quickly, thinking his friend may have been struck, or even shot, but Doc was just ramrod straight, staring into the camera eyepiece viewfinder.

"What is it, Doc?" he asked. "What's up?"

But as he was asking, Doc was already fiddling with the digicam's playback. "Look," he instructed Jack, holding up the playback screen so it was next to the view of the event coordinator directing his aircraft's crew.

What was playing on the screen was Doc's video from the morning Schoenberg had been killed. It was near the end, when Doc had raced for the tower that the assassin was escaping from. He freeze-framed at the moment when he got his clearest, distant view.

Jack looked from the screen to the distant man, and back again. Same height, same weight, same build. And, on the evidence of a single lock of hair emerging from the assassin's hoodie, same color mane.

"Have we gone completely nuts?" Doc asked incredulously.

"No," said Jack with certainty. "I think we just went totally sane." He looked at Doc and the chauffeur. "We've got to get into the air."

"Why?" Doc asked.

"I don't understand," said the chauffeur. "If there's a problem, why do you not just tell someone what you suspect?" The chauffer's question was as innocent as it was direct.

"Did you ever hear the story of the Boy Who Cried Wolf?" Jack asked.

The man shook his head.

"The authorities back home didn't believe me before," Jack said. "Do you think they'd believe anything I say now?" He stabbed his finger at the C-17 in general and at Peter Andrews in particular. "We've got to beat that plane back to America!"

52

San Francisco, California

Anastasia was worried. Israel and Mecca still stood, but Ana was still worried. Sammy had not eaten and not slept. While the others would eat, shower, rest, and even allow themselves to be comforted by their friends, Sammy would only begrudgingly accept coffee, and then only take time to relieve himself of it in the bathroom. Then, quickly as possible, he was back in front of the computer screen.

Ana had stopped trying to convince him to rest even his eyes. Even after Brooks's deadline had come and gone, and the world had not been plunged into war, Sammy drove himself relentlessly. Finally she walked up to him and hopelessly said, "Sammy . . . dear . . . you don't have to prove yourself to anyone."

"I'm not trying to prove myself to you!" he snapped, then realized who he was talking to. Finally he turned from the screen and attempted a weak smile. "I'm sorry," he confessed. "Here, come here, sit down." He put out his hands, she placed hers in his, and he brought her into Ric's seat beside him. "Maybe I'm trying to prove something to myself." He dropped her hands and turned back to the keyboard and the screen. "Jack's in the air, racing

Brooks's plane back here, and now we know this Peter Andrews guy might be involved." He started back to work, his eyes ever closer to the screen. "I agree with him, Ana. Finally, after all these years, I agree with my brother. I think there's danger. Great danger, and I'm going to do everything possible to help find out what it is."

"What can I do?" Ana asked.

"Hear me out," he said, pointing at the screen. "I've got to talk this through. There's nothing about the bomb or the plot. I spent hours going through defense alerts, security blogs, and message boards, trying to see if there were even any rumors. Nothing. Then I began cataloging everything we knew so far. One: there had been a conspiracy to bomb Mecca. This was what the code word Firebird referred to. Two: it involved Brooks and some foreigners—maybe from Russia and Israel. Three: it had been responsible for moving sensitive bomb parts to Saudi Arabia, where we think the device had been assembled. It was also responsible—or maybe it had only received—the bomb material stolen from Russia, which involved a plane crash. All that could only mean that the conspirators were not just highly capable and well-placed, but also extremely brave, or maybe ridiculously foolhardy."

"But Mecca has not been bombed," Ana said, equally as quiet. "And your brother said that the material for the bomb was missing when he got there." It was eerie the way the two seemed to exist only in the light of the computer screens, their voices hushed.

"Yes, yes," Sammy agreed tightly. "What are we missing? What am I overlooking?" He looked at Ana, but only seemed to see her face as another screen. "I went back to the chat room that had the info about attacking Israel. It no longer existed. Everything there was gone."

Ana looked lost. "What does that mean?"

"That even though Brooks is dead, someone else is still active in the plot."

"The event coordinator?"

"I think so. But there's absolutely no information on a Peter Andrews that I can find. At least not about a Peter Andrews attached to General Brooks's staff, and/or a Peter Andrews who advertises services as an event coordinator."

"No, no," said Dover. "Worse. Much worse."

Both women looked up and over as they heard someone else speak. Montgomery Morton was standing in the open door to the backyard.

"What are you doing in my house?" he snapped at Dover. "How dare you. You have no right!"

But Dover's presence had the effect she had wanted on Cynthia Morton. Like a hostage suddenly set free, Mrs. Morton's head rose and her voice, when it came, had an accusatory strength even Dover wasn't expecting.

"What does she mean, Monty?" She all but swung at her husband. "What have you done?"

"Cynthia, we'll talk about this in private." He stepped forward, his hand out imploringly, but his wife was having none of it.

"No!" she exploded, swatting his hand away. "We'll talk about it now. I will no longer just stand here—a captive in my own home—as you eat away at yourself from the inside."

"Cynthia, please, you wouldn't understand."

Dover kept a grimace from her face with great willpower. It was the worst thing he could have said to her.

"Oh, I understand plenty!" she exclaimed. "I've understood so much from the moment you started working with Brooks. I've understood more than you!'" She whirled back to Dover. "What has he done? What has my husband and Brooks done?"

"General Brooks is dead," Dover reported somberly. She was surprised by Morton's aghast reaction. "You didn't know?"

"No," he said. "I've heard nothing of his trip to the Middle East."

Dover saw a world of distress in his denial. He had to know by now that the plan he had helped nurture was lost.

"He's been walking around this place like a zombie ever since General Brooks left," Mrs. Morton told Dover. "Something's eating away at him."

"How did he die?" Morton suddenly blurted.

"We're not sure," Dover admitted. "It appeared to be a heart attack, but—"

"But what?" The vehemence of his interjection took even Dover aback.

"The man who was with him at the time disappeared for several hours, so anything is possible."

"Who was this man?" Morton snapped, becoming more and more sure of himself.

"His aide, Peter Andrews."

The name had a telling effect on his expression. "Andrews killed him," Morton said flatly. "I knew there was something wrong with that bastard."

"Are you sure?" Dover asked.

Morton nodded once.

"He's accompanying Brooks's body back to the States," Dover informed him. This time his expression fluctuated between deep concern and sudden panic.

"General Morton," Dover said. "I know everything you've done was out of a patriotic love for this country. But I know, and I think you know, that now it is this very country that is in danger."

Morton's eyes were hollow when he searched Dover's face with them. "What do you want of me?"

Dover thought carefully about her next words. If she revealed that her superiors still wanted to believe that the threat had died with Brooks, Morton might think that he could get away with all his collaboration if he just stayed silent. "Come with me now," she said. "Help us stop Andrews."

Morton took one step back. Dover silently cursed the luck. "N-no," he stammered. "I-I've got to think . . . !"

"What is she talking about, Monty?" Cynthia demanded. "What are you not telling me?"

He answered by backing away, waving his hands in a futile effort to wipe out the last year. "Just leave me alone!" He staggered back into his study, and slammed the door. Dover immediately pressed her business card into Cynthia's hand. "I'm sorry, but I've got to go. If I'm right, we're all in terrible danger, and I've got to try to stop it." She pressed her hands on Cynthia Morton's shoulders and looked deeply into her frightened, shaken eyes.

"Go to your husband, Mrs. Morton. Make sure he doesn't kill himself."

54

Baja, California

Pyotr never ceased to be disgusted at the casual wealth of America, and how it was expressed in so many thoughtless ways. It was a sign of extreme decadence, a complete loss of values. But it was also an opportunity for him, and in using it he was surely fulfilling the intentions of Allah that decadence seeds its own destruction.

He could depend on Americans for three things: a pathetic appreciation of sob stories, a begrudging following of orders, and their worship of the all-mighty dollar. So getting the pilots to make an unscheduled landing had not been as difficult as anyone else might have supposed.

After all, he told them, he was not a military man, nor a member of Brooks's family. Let them claim his body without him, an interloper, nearby. Besides, Colonel Ashlock needed him to disembark with their ordnance at a completely different airport.

The pilots had checked their schedule, and, after pocketing the hundred-dollar bills the event coordinator had slipped them, found the stop workable. Peter Andrews smiled at their cooperation while thinking, *The Americans are sleepwalking toward their destiny*. But that had been true from the very start. Even Brooks, who, in some ways, was the only person Pyotr encountered fully aware of Allah's intentions, was blind to the threats within his conspiracy.

So, hours later, he stood on the tarmac of the private airport with one of Ashlock's sleeper agents dressed in overalls. "Is the fact that the average American is completely blind to the battle that was being waged another sign of their decadence?" the agent asked.

"Were they so drunk on their evil diversions, their sex and their drugs, their movies and music, that they did not understand that the world was at war with them?" Pyotr replied. He laughed. "So many of them bought the ridiculous claims about Islam being a religion of peace—what is a religion of peace? How could such a religion exist? War is a necessary part of human existence; a religion that does not get involved in it would surely be wiped out and cease to exist."

The two climbed back into the cab of the truck after having secured their payload—the one the pilots had been so kind to help them unload—in the back. As they started forward on the access road, Pyotr began to consider why he was feeling so contemplative this evening. It was as if the imam was talking to him from inside his brain.

These grave questions of righteousness and fate—these were things the imam spoke of, not things that Pyotr contemplated. He was a man of action, one whose lust for blood—he could admit that now, in his final hours—had been used by the one true God for greater purposes. He was not a man who thought idly, but practically. He was not a teacher, and certainly not a prophet. He was a doer.

Perhaps at the end, everyone became a prophet. Perhaps that was the final preparation for Paradise.

He stopped ruminating and leaned forward as the new plane

came into sight from around a corner. It was a thing of beauty: a single-engined Cessna Super Cargomaster EX. Some forty-one-and-a-half feet long, powered by a single Pratt & Whitney PT6A-140 turboprop, the aircraft could carry a maximum payload of 3,665 pounds and cruise at roughly a 185 knots; it had a maximum altitude of 25,000 feet, and most importantly for this mission, could take off in roughly two thousand feet, depending on its weight.

"Is it ready?" he asked the truck's driver.

"Prepared. A dream to fly. Brand-new."

Pyotr hopped out of the truck as it rolled to a stop. He inspected the aircraft while the others took the weapon from the truck.

"There is one difficulty. The runway is too short," said Ashlock's agent as Pyotr entered the cockpit. "It is only fifteen hundred feet, not the two thousand we were expecting."

"How was this mistake made?"

The agent shook his head grimly. "The macadam was broken up for some sort of project and then not repaired. We cannot take the plane over it. We have to lighten the load to get in the air. The fuel is the only variable. So we will have to alter the course to make a direct line to the target."

"No," said Pyotr. "That is not acceptable. The flight plan has been well established. It is imperative."

"Flying over the ocean and making the approach—"

"The Americans can be very suspicious of last-minute deviations. The route has been established to avoid any questions," said Pyotr. "We will lighten the load."

"Commander, the fuel has already been lightened. That is my point."

"And use one pilot if necessary."

The agent tightened his lips. It was to have been the two of them in the plane, and he already guessed that Pyotr would not give up his place. "We will recompute it and see." Pyotr allowed it. He knew what the result would be. He, alone would fly the plane into history, as he had always supposed. He wanted to do this himself. It was his final act, and he didn't want to share the glory with anyone else.

The imam would not have approved, but that was no longer a

concern. Pyotr no longer had any concerns, except for staying exactly on his course. It would be a glorious feeling, to be alone in a plane, flying toward Destiny. *The Muslim Charles Lindbergh*, he thought, with a smirk. It was an intoxicating feeling to think about all the people who would die the next time he crossed the altitude threshold to set the bomb off.

He would push down and there would lightning, tremendous lightning. The hand of God would smite a million people in one blow. Millions of others would die over the next several weeks. The hundreds of thousands of those initially infected would linger for weeks, suffering from internal bleeding and diarrhea. Without sufficient quarantine they would spread the disease and cause the health care system to collapse . . . dragging the rest of the state and municipal infrastructures with it as people failed to report for work. Los Angeles would die quickly; the rest of America would follow with shocking alacrity.

Pyotr's only regret was that he would not see each and every death. But perhaps that boon would be given to him in Paradise.

"I will take off in an hour," said Pyotr. "I will fly the original path, and I will succeed. There is no other possibility."

55

San Francisco, California

If the situation hadn't been so dire, the gathering at the airport would look like a reunion.

Jack all but bounded off the private jet as Dover and Carl Forsyth approached him across the tarmac. The sight of Dover's superior confused him, but not as much as the sight of the C-17, which was at rest some three hundred yards away.

"What, they landed already?" he complained.

If Jack looked confused, Doc looked positively perplexed. "But, how . . . ?" he started, then turned to Jack. "Our Gulfstream is a hundred miles per hour faster and has three times the range." Both he and Jack were frustrated enough that they had to refuel twice during the eight-thousand-mile flight from Riyadh to America as it was.

"Did they screw around with the scheduling to throw us off again?" Jack wondered. He smiled in relief at Dover, but his smile disappeared when he saw her grave expression. "What? Did you get him? Has Peter Andrews been detained?"

"That's a decoy, Jack," she said, stabbing her head angrily toward the C-17. "We were all over it as soon as it landed. It has Brooks's coffin, but nothing else."

"Where is the rest?" Doc growled, his eyes narrowing, his memory of that gnawing fear returning.

"We checked every landing and departure for a thousand miles around," Forsyth stressed to Jack. "Doubts be damned, I had the whole office working on it within minutes."

"And?"

"And they made an unscheduled stop, Jack," Dover told him with concern. "Andrews deplaned at a small suburban airport and took a large crate with him."

"Small?" Doc echoed. "For a C-17?"

"Just large enough," Forsyth shot back.

Jack stared at her, and then her boss, in disbelief. "We have no time for quibbling! I gave you new information," he said accusingly. "Sammy found a target in America. And when the attack might take place." He checked his watch. "Soon!"

"No way an American general would target Hollywood," Forsyth contended. "No way."

"Not Brooks," Jack yelled at him. "This Andrews guy."

"How do you know for sure?" Forsyth countered.

"Check the e-mail accounts yourself," Jack told him. "If my brother could get in, so can you."

"We will," said the FBI special agent.

"Do it now."

"We need a warrant," said Forsyth. "There's a process."

"Don't you have some sort of emergency exclusion or something?" asked Jack. "While you're fooling around getting a subpoena, Andrews may be on his way to blow Hollywood up!"

"I want to, Jack," said Forsyth. "That's why I'm here. But I need proof that will stand up in court."

"The hell with court," raged Jack. "You're arguing about some law school garbage when people are trying to destroy America."

Forsyth stared at him. "Your word isn't enough! Maybe there is a threat, and maybe there isn't. You've cobbled together information from sources that may or may not be sources at all. There's simply not enough here for probable cause."

"You're talking like a lawyer, Carl," Jack pleaded. "Come on!"

"I am a lawyer, Jack. I got my law degree before I joined the Bureau."

Frustrated, Jack turned and started to storm back to the plane. Dover reached to stop him, but he kept going. This was insanity. But he had to do something.

"Jack, wait," said Dover, running after him. "What are you going to do? Where are you going?"

"L.A. If that's what Andrews is targeting."

"His name isn't Andrews," came another voice. Jack looked over, and saw, emerging from the FBI SUV, Montgomery Morton.

Jack's jaw fell as he looked from Morton to Dover to Forsyth. So that's why they had all come to meet him.

"He's a Russian mercenary named Pyotr Ansky," Morton said heavily, coming to stand between Jack and Forsyth. Dover hadn't even gotten to her car outside the Morton residence when she saw the general emerging wearily from his front door. It had been a choice between suicide and coming clean . . . and his wife was not going to let him try suicide again.

"Ansky was hired by Brooks to obtain the Russian bio-agent that you were tracking. He was very good at his job. Ruthless. The general came to depend on him far more than me. I—I still had a conscience."

"Did he kill Schoenberg?" Jack asked.

"I honestly don't know. But I would guess yes, probably. It has his signature—efficient, no trace. He had sniper training. By then the general was depending upon Ansky exclusively." Morton looked down to the black tarmac. "I thought he was going to kill me as well."

"He's told us everything, Jack," Dover said. "How they were planning to smuggle the bomb into Mecca in a crate of books for needy children, and how they were going to have their fellow conspirator, Andrew 'Bull's-eye' Taylor, fire a flaming arrow from a helicopter into the crate to detonate the bomb."

Jack looked aghast at Morton, who avoided his gaze, but then concentrated his fury on Forsyth. "So you have a confession. Not just from him—" Jack pointed at Morton "—but Taylor, too." He stopped when Forsyth didn't meet his eyes. "You *have* got Taylor, haven't you?"

"He's disappeared, Jack," Dover said softly. "We've got APBs out for him everywhere."

"But you've got Morton!" Jack stressed. "Isn't that enough for you to open all the stops for this attack on American soil?"

"Dover has been working with your brother to locate all the foreign conspirators," Forsyth told him, "and you wouldn't believe the international activity that's going on right now to track them down and arrest them, but that was for Brooks's conspiracy. We've got nothing tangible on a second, real, bomb, or an attack on L.A."

"I was right about Jerusalem and Mecca," Jack exclaimed, "and I'm right about this, too!" He turned on Morton. "Do you have any idea why Andrews—I mean, Ansky would want to bomb Hollywood?"

"I don't know," Morton said miserably. "I'm not sure."

"But you heard Brooks yourself, Jack," Dover reminded him. "All that stuff about Hollywood poisoning American minds. It was in your interview with him."

Jack was dumbstruck. Could Ansky be completing Brooks's desires with the one bomb they had left? "It doesn't matter why," he said aloud. "We can figure out 'why' later. Now we just have to stop it!"

"We have proof that there was an attack planned for the Middle East," Forsyth told him, "but we don't have proof that the attack didn't die with Brooks. My hands are tied, Jack. There's nothing I can do."

Jack stared at the man for a moment. He had stressed the words "my" and "I" in his last two sentences. He had come all the way down to the airport just to confront him personally.

"Doc!" Jack called. His old friend popped his head out of the private jet. Jack had been so intent on Dover, Forsyth, and Morton that he hadn't noticed the smartphone seemingly glued to Doc's ear, or that the jet was just about to finish refueling. "I need to talk with Sammy and Sol ASAP," he said, all but trotting to the jet's steps.

"Already established a connection," Doc said as he stepped back to make way for Jack to reboard. "They're on two separate computer screens. The safe house isn't the only place with good Wi-Fi."

Jack saw Sol's face on one computer screen and Sammy's face on the other, with Ana and Ric behind him. Jack was about to start barking orders when he realized that someone was standing beside him as well. Someone shorter, warmer, and shapelier. He glanced over to see Dover on board. She was making sure her sidearm was tight in its holster. Jack hadn't noticed Forsyth motion with his head for her to join them.

Jack couldn't help but smile despite the death sentence that was hanging above them. "Sol," he called. "Have Boaz get Professor Peters."

"Boaz is on special assignment," Sol informed him. "I'll get him myself."

Before Jack could ask about what possible special assignment could take precedence over this, Sol was out the door. Jack immediately shrugged it off. "Sammy?"

"Yeah, bro?"

"Even if someone wants to drop a bomb on Hollywood, they need a registered flight plan or they'd be shot down before they got close. Dover?" He turned toward her. "Tell Sammy where the C-17's unscheduled stop was. Sammy, check flight plans for every airport, open field, and dirt road in a ten-mile radius."

"On it, brother."

"Jack?" Doc called from the cockpit door. "Speaking of flight plans, where to?"

"Where do you think?" Jack retorted. "We're going to Hollywood."

56

Jack had no idea Doc had become so tech-savvy.

"It's a whole new world out there, Jack," Doc grumbled as he made the connections allowing everyone to hear each other. "Stay current or get washed away."

They all kept in constant touch even as the Gulfstream was taking off down the runway.

"How fast can we get to L.A.?" Jack asked.

"It's about three hundred and eighty miles," Doc replied. "Our top speed is about six hundred miles an hour, so about forty minutes."

"We got that much time to find out where this bastard might be taking off from," Jack told Sammy.

"We'll find him," said Sammy.

"Sol," Jack called. "What's your twenty?" He used the adapted law enforcement phrase for his location and/or status. "Can you find Professor Peters quickly?"

From the low-angle position of the video camera in Sol's smartphone, Jack and Doc could see he was in one of his many cars—from the sleek looks, and the throbbing sound of it, his fastest and most powerful. From the glimpses of the foliage out the window, Jack could tell Sol was heading for Peters's wildlife preserve cabin.

"Yes," Sol replied, adding, "between you and me, Jack, I've been monitoring him since your first meeting."

Jack was surprised, and even a little impressed. "So the prof was right. He was being watched."

"And not just by me," Sol informed them. "But that's not all I've been doing. Speaking of that, got to go. I'll log back on when Professor Peters is secured."

Jack and Doc shared a look as Sol's screen winked out. *What could he be doing?* they wondered. But they didn't have time to dwell on it, since Sol's screen came winking back on almost immediately—just in time to see Professor Peters's legs come bundling into the passenger seat of the car.

"Wow, that was fast," Jack commented. "How did you get him into the car so quickly?"

"Told him Jack needs you," Sol answered. Peters, for his part, was looking every which way to try to locate where Jack's voice was coming from.

"Down here, Professor," Jack said. "Sol's smartphone." He waited as Peters bent and all but stuck his face into the screen.

"Ah, there you are, Jack. Have you cracked the conspiracy?"

"Yes, Professor. They've brought the bomb back here. They're going to try destroying Los Angeles."

"That's ridiculous!" Peters exclaimed. "Even if they secure the bomb in a van, sure, they'd kill many people, but they wouldn't even come close to destroying all of L.A." Then he thought for a moment. "Unless . . . do they have a plane?"

"Yes, we think so. We're trying to trace any possible flight plans now."

"Damn it. Altitude, Jack, altitude."

"Altitude how, Professor?" Jack asked.

"When an aircraft bomb is armed, it is set to go off at a certain altitude. This occurs when it is dropped. If it is dropped from thirty thousand feet, as it passes through the proper altitude— let's say five thousand feet—the bomb is armed and explodes. This is a very simple type of fuse. But effective."

"What does that mean for us?" interrupted Jack.

"For maximum effect," Peters continued, "the explosion should be an air burst, so that the weapon explodes above the target at a carefully calculated altitude. Then the destruction of life will be . . ."

"Do you know what altitude?"

"One thousand, five hundred meters above sea level. But this is the interesting thing—the fuse will not set itself until the aircraft is above that altitude. If it then descends, it will explode."

"So once they're over five thousand feet . . ."

"Four thousand, nine hundred, twenty-one point twenty-six to be precise," said Peters.

"Once they're over that, they can't come down?"

"Well, of course they can, but only to blow up. That is the type of fuse they have chosen. At least on the basis of the materials they have smuggled in."

"You're sure?"

Peters didn't even pay attention to the question. "The damage with an air burst at that altitude is well calculated and the most effective. If I were trying to destroy or contaminate the population of an entire city, that is what I'd do."

Jack's jaw set. "Thanks, Professor. Let me know if you can think of anything else that might help us."

"I have an immediate suggestion," Professor Peters offered.

"Yes?"

"Don't let that plane take off."

Jack turned to Dover. "Tell the air force that if there's a plane with a bomb, it can't go under five thousand feet or it'll explode."

"Jack, under five thousand feet? How do you think planes land?"

"They should shut down the air space around L.A. Send everything out through the desert."

"That's not going to happen, Jack."

"It has to. At least until we get this figured out."

Dover shook her head, but grabbed her phone to call Forsyth and tell him the latest. Jack leaned back in his seat, gazing at the landscape below.

"Jack," Doc said quietly. "Say we find him in time. Do you have any idea what we're going to do when we get there?"

"I don't," he admitted. "This jet doesn't have air-to-ground missiles, does it?"

Doc smiled grimly and shook his head regretfully. "Just in case it comes in handy, maybe you should take this. Jimmy would have wanted you to have it." He handed Jack the other Glock, the one that had been in the possession of their late friend.

As he gratefully accepted the weapon, Dover tapped him on the arm.

"Forsyth's pushing all the buttons he can," she said. "He's got a search warrant for everything in Morton's home. He has also managed to convince the Army's Criminal Investigation Division to begin an investigation of Morton and Brooks's work computers. They won't be able to seize the computers until morning."

Jack bit his lower lip, sticking Jimmy's Glock in his pocket. Dover looked apologetic.

"Tell the CID liaison to get in touch with Kevin Dangerfield from the CIA," Jack told Dover. "Tell him everything we know."

"Already done, Jack. Dangerfield is hitting a brick wall, too. No one wants to believe that they were so asleep at the wheel. They are telling themselves the L.A. attack is impossible."

Jack wanted to rail against the stupidity and injustice of it, but he was distracted by what was happening on Sammy's computer screen. Ana had leaned forward and was listening intently to what Sammy was saying as he pointed at something Jack couldn't see.

"There's a lot of information to untangle," Sammy was telling Ana. "I'm looking at a dump of data that's left over from five different conversations, parts of which have been erased."

"It's all numbers," said Anastasia.

"Mostly, yeah, it's an encryption of some sort of picture. You can tell by this pattern here. It's a file header."

"It has words in it," she said, pointing to a line close to the very bottom. "Bayward Park."

Jack looked at Doc and Dover, with hope in his expression.

"Really?" Sammy looked at the screen. Anastasia was right. He scrolled up. There were other words as well. "It's an image of a map," he realized. "It's not encrypted—it's just what the bytes look like when they're not assembled by the program."

"What does that mean?" asked Anastasia.

"It means that if I can find the right program to read this data, we can see what the picture says." He hit the keys to scroll up, then back down. "It's not a typical image file. It comes from some sort of program that I've never seen."

"Sammy!" Jack shouted. "We don't need to know where he plans to go. If he gets high enough into the air, we're done for. I just need to know where he plans to take off from."

"Right," Sammy agreed, his fingers already back at work.

"We're about ten minutes out of L.A.," Doc told Jack. "Where do you want to go?"

"Can you take us over Hollywood?"

Doc nodded. Jack sighed, almost as if in defeat. "You might as well take some video, too," he suggested. "One way or another, the world must know what happened here."

Dover rested her hand encouragingly on Jack's shoulder and they all watched as the jet approached the city from the east, flying over Glendale toward the center of Hollywood. The city glowed gold in the distance, and the glitter only increased as they came near. Staring at the vast expanse of the city, Jack felt how small he was in comparison, how hopeless, how improbable this all seemed. But he refused to let his confidence melt. Not now.

"Jack, it's Sammy," said Dover, pointing insistently at the computer screen.

"I'm looking at a flight simulator program," Sammy said. "It's Russian. I think it's the pattern that the plane is going to fly. The FAA and the FBI hasn't found anyone else who has filed a similar profile. It's a Cessna that supposedly comes in from Baja every couple of days."

"Baja, California?"

"Yes, except that the plane didn't take off from Baja today. It flew up yesterday, on a lease. It was due back today but didn't show. I talked to the manager. The flight was canceled. But get this—first of all, yesterday's flight? No flight plan was filed. And second of all, today's? There's a flight plan out of Baja. And there's a plane with that call sign who filed roughly that course, about twenty minutes out of L.A."

"Amazing, Sammy. You're a lifesaver. What's the planned altitude?"

There was the briefest pause as Jack's words filled Sammy with warmth. But there was a bomb to stop so he said, almost instantly, "Eight thousand feet, and descending on a gradual slope."

Jack was on his feet. "The location of takeoff!" he shouted. "Give us the exact location of takeoff!"

Doc relayed the information to the pilots. If the coordinates were correct, the private airplane was about fifty miles away. At their speed, they would arrive at the location in about five minutes. They all prayed it wasn't too late.

"What do we do if he's already in the air?" Doc asked.

"If the air force won't bring him down, we'll have to."

Doc did not ask how. The word "kamikaze" was the only method that applied.

Dover went immediately to her phone. As she spoke urgently to Forsyth, Sammy stared at his screen, trying to figure out something, anything, to get his mind off the possible tragic outcomes.

"Why is he planning to come in from the west?"

"Less chance of being told to drop his altitude," said Doc. "You don't have as much traffic and there's more room to maneuver. The Baja plane has flown this pattern for weeks. You said so. So he's much more likely to be ignored."

"Exactly," Jack agreed, hopping up and going to the cockpit door. "He wants to attract as little attention as possible. Most times it's not going to be a big deal, but if a few minutes of confusion are going to make a difference, that's the edge he wants."

The door opened on his first knock and the pilots let him scan the horizon through the jet's windshield.

"Jack," Sammy called.

"Yes?"

"We have a Google Map picture of the takeoff point. It's an abandoned airfield in the hills. According to social media, kids were using it for radio controlled planes and some sandlot sports until it was padlocked up about a year ago."

Jack was momentarily distracted by the sound of Sol's car engine almost screaming into his smartphone. Doc almost chortled at the panicked look on Peters's face, but instantly remembered why they were all here.

Jack turned his head toward Sammy's screen for a moment. "That long?" he blurted. "Pyotr was planning this that far back?"

"Of course," said Dover. "According to Morton's information, that's when he started working with Brooks directly."

"Jesus," Jack breathed. "Did Brooks create the international conspiracy just to get the money and power to collect the bomb parts? Was he planning to blow up L.A. all along?"

"No," Dover said, echoing her boss. "Not an American general. No way."

"Maybe that's why he was relying on Pyotr more and more," Jack stressed. "Because he knew the others would never go along with it."

"Jack!" came Sol's booming voice. "Since you passed on Morton's positive identification of Ansky, Boaz has tracked him. Yes, he's a Russian mercenary—but one who converted to Islam twenty years ago!"

The people inside the plane were thunderstruck. "How do you know that?" Jack blurted.

"It was before he went to work as a merc," Sol said. "He was converted in prison, by an imam we have been watching for decades. An imam who's been preaching the evils of Hollywood for about that long."

All the intrigue, all the death, all the tension, all the racing from one place to the next . . . they combined in Jack's mind like the pieces of a high yield-to-weight bomb, and just exploded. "Of course!" he exclaimed. "Had to be! I knew it all along . . . even Brooks somehow knew! He was infected by the same evil that wants to corrupt and destroy America. Islamic terrorism was behind this all along . . . !"

"Jack," interrupted the urgent voice of the pilot.

Jack turned to see him pointing. In the distance, at the top of a hill, was the no-longer-abandoned airfield.

"It's still on the ground!" Jack all but bellowed. "The Cessna's still on the ground!"

"Not for long," growled Doc, who was standing beside Jack in an instant. "It's warming its engines."

"Get the FAA to make him change course," Doc told the copilot.

"I'll try," he said, already working the radio. "But I don't think that's going to work."

Jack spun to Dover. "Air Force? National Guard?"

Dover looked up from her phone long enough to say. "Not enough time!"

Jack looked back to the Cessna despairingly. "The only way to stop him is to run right into him," he realized.

"That would not be advisable," the professor said. "If you can keep him from taking off, the bomb will not detonate. If you engulf him in a double ball of flame, that may not be so."

"Better to minimize the damage out here then let him get to L.A.!" Jack countered.

"Can you keep him from taking off?" Doc asked the pilot.

The pilot looked doubtful and challenged at the same time. "It would take incredible timing and maneuvering to buzz him, keep him grounded," he said even as he was starting to prepare for it.

"How much time might that buy us?" Jack asked the copilot, whose face had gone white.

"A couple minutes, maybe ten, tops. We have to come in at such a speed and angle that he can see us as he's taxiing and realizes that he has no room for takeoff. But he might just play chicken with us, certain that we'll veer at the last second."

"Don't play chicken," Sol said. "Just disrupt the airflow on his trajectory, try to rattle him."

The pilot was smiling like a wolf. "Great idea. We just have to cut across his runway as he's taxiing. This baby's speed will screw up the air currents enough to keep him grounded."

"How long can we do that?" Jack asked.

The pilot pursed his lips. "Till we run out of gas or he gets pissed enough to try and bully past us."

"Go for it," Jack said, then turned back to Dover. "Get an ETA for the Air Force."

Dover nodded then went back to the phone. Jack turned just in time to hear a call come in on the jet's communication equipment.

"Gulfstream G650, this is Colonel James Wright. I am seventy-five nautical miles north of your location. A no-fly zone has been established around Los Angeles. I have orders to engage and shoot down any aircraft that violates it. And I will follow those orders, sir."

"Yes," sputtered Jack. "The Cessna—you have to get it."

"You are ordered to change course immediately," said the Air Force pilot, not even bothering to acknowledge Jack's response. "Go north."

"Where are you?" Jack asked. "How long to get here?"

"Zero ten—respond to my orders immediately or you will be shot down."

"Ten minutes isn't going to cut it," Doc said. "You better hit the afterburner. We'll keep him here until you arrive."

"Negative . . . negative . . . !" Wright started, but the copilot cut the audio with Doc's one short motion of his thumb across his throat.

"He's taking off!" the pilot yelled suddenly. "Christ, he must have heard the AF pilot. He's taking off no matter what we do!"

"Stand off! Stand off!" warned the air force pilot. His voice was so strident, the copilot had felt impelled to turn the volume up again.

"Colonel, you *must* shoot the Cessna down!" insisted Jack.

"For the last time, I am warning you—turn north or you will be shot down!"

"Dammit, the Cessna is your target!" yelled Dover from the back. "Get your orders straight!"

"Crash into him," Jack said to the pilot with deadly certainty. "It's all we can do."

"Jack!" came Sol's booming voice. "Don't do anything stupid! Leave that to me!"

Jack's eyes snapped open and saw what Doc was pointing at through the windshield. Everyone saw as an armored SUV none of them had ever seen before came crashing through the abandoned airfield's gate and barreled directly at, and then into, the side of the Cessna.

57

The result of the collision was all they could have hoped for.

The Cessna skidded to the side, a wheel collapsed, and the entire aircraft spun in three-and-a-half dusty, ground-spitting circles until it came to rest against the far fence. The armored SUV's face was crumpled, but it had been designed for the impact. All twelve airbags had deployed, but the vehicle's occupants were well prepared. Six flak-jacketed men emerged, carrying Uzis and Glock 9mm automatics.

Even from this distance, Jack could see that they were being led by Boaz. Jack spoke his name in surprise.

"As soon as Sammy figured out the target, I immediately sent Boaz to the area," Sol's voice filtered into the cockpit. "I assigned him to prepare a team and a vehicle. I've been feeding him the information the same time it came into the safe house. They've been racing to that hillside airport from their L.A. base camp from the moment Sammy found the address."

Good driving, Jack thought, then watched, dumbstruck, as Boaz and his flak-jacketed men ran toward the Cessna, its dust and dirt cloud just settling around it as if from a particularly disastrous magic trick. He felt a rush of hope as he saw the Cessna's door open and Pyotr stagger out. The hope sank when he saw that the terrorist was holding a wired, yellow-tubed, black based, red button thumb switch.

"Get down there," Doc growled at the pilot.

The pilot reacted wordlessly. They had plenty of room now, and the Gulfstream came to a stop where the Cessna had begun. One of Boaz's men was waiting as the jet door opened.

"He's calling for Jack Hatfield," the man reported.

Boaz stood with his hands up, fifty feet away from Pyotr. The terrorist was injured—he had one arm wrapped around a plane prop just to remain upright and blood was coating his face—but he held the thumb switch tightly in his other hand.

Boaz exchanged a look at Jack, then concentrated his attention on Pyotr. "Okay, he's here," Boaz shouted to the terrorist.

"Good," Pyotr almost laughed. "Come forward Jack Hatfield. It goes without saying that none of you could kill me before I set off the device. Not at this range, not with those weapons."

Jack didn't require coaxing. Dover almost put her hand out toward him, but resisted. She knew he mustn't weaken—or let Pyotr see that they had a connection. Jack walked slowly forward. When he was about ten feet away, the terrorist told him to stop.

This time Pyotr did laugh.

"You people," he muttered through is grin. "You are so easily distracted . . . you never learn. The World Trade Center was bombed in 1993. Eight years later, it was hit again . . . destroyed. How did you allow that to happen? You had deadly cases of Ebola in 2014. Your president and his ineffective Ebola czar had every opportunity to safeguard the public. Did they? No. There was infighting, finger-pointing. I wonder," he chuckled, "who will take the fall for this?"

Jack wanted to rush him. Time was running out and zero progress was being made.

"What exactly is 'this'?" Doc asked. It was as if he'd read Jack's mind and was trying to distract Pytor, give his friend a chance to make his move.

"Surely you know by now," he said. "A genetically engineered form of Ebola that is inert until exposed to tritium. Then it becomes a respiratory killer, carried far and wide by the wind. It won't die, you see, when outside the body. Not for days. By then it will have spread from west to east, infecting and killing millions . . . perhaps tens of millions."

"To what end?" Doc asked.

"To your end!" Pyotr cried. "So the world can descend further into chaos where men like me can lead, prosper, conquer!"

"You'll be dead," Jack pointed out. He thought about going for Jimmy's gun but he knew he could never be fast or accurate enough.

"If I cannot deliver death to the wretched scum who poisons the world with its lies, then I shall go to Paradise looking into the eyes of the man who stopped me . . . as he, and all his beloved friends, boil in the hellfire I will rain upon them."

Jack had no option. He went for the gun—

Then watched as Pyotr's right thumb, the one over the red button, exploded off his hand in a splash of red, followed by his arm being jerked back hard. Pyotr screamed in surprise and overwhelming pain, then spun to land, face-first, against the Cessna's fuselage. Jack raced forward, diving, sliding, and rolling until his hands grabbed unerringly on the fallen thumb switch.

Although splashed with blood, the button was untouched.

When Jack stood, he saw that the others had also charged, and were now standing around Pyotr's fallen body. A wave of relief swept over him. But that wave turned to ice when he heard Pyotr laughing.

He ran over to the site, glancing at Doc. His old friend motioned his head at the terrorist's crumpled body. Jack looked down at Pyotr. The bastard was holding his ruined hand, but he was also chortling insanely.

"Good shot," he babbled. "Amazing shot. Like none I've ever seen. Who did it? Which one of you did it?"

The men, and one woman, just silently stared at him.

"No matter," Pyotr half-gagged, half-chuckled. "No matter . . ." The terrorist's face seemed to freeze in a twisted grin, but then he turned away.

Doc's eyes shifted from Pyotr's quaking body to Jack. "Well I'll be," he muttered, beginning to walk away. "What's he doing, crying?"

Jack just stared down at the man who almost killed millions. "No," he realized quietly. "He's not crying." He suddenly grabbed Doc's arm. "He's *laughing*. Doc, why is he laughing?"

The two men took only a moment to lock eyes before Jack was diving into the crippled Cessna, Doc right behind him.

"Three triggers!" Doc realized. "One for altitude, one for the thumb switch, and one for—"

"Time!" Jack shouted. "It's a time bomb now!" He scrambled up to the device anchored down to the Cessna's floor, and saw that there was a digital clock on its side, counting down. It was at four minutes and thirty-seven seconds. . . .

"Professor!" he wailed. "Get me the professor!"

Doc was clambering in beside him, holding out his smartphone. On the view screen was the interior of Sol's car. The professor's face was filling the image as if he were examining a particularly interesting insect.

"Show me, show me!" he demanded, and Jack slowly waved the smartphone's front screen all around the bomb's surface as if it were an X-ray machine. "Good, good," the professor said. Jack exhaled. That meant Peters knew what they were dealing with. "Okay, Doc, unscrew the main panel. Be quick about it."

When Doc was done, the clock was at 3:57.

"All right," said Peters. "Try disconnecting the wire from the battery to the detonator." Doc pointed at the mentioned parts. Jack grabbed the blue and red wires.

"Wires?" he echoed, already pulling.

"No, no, no, no!" Peters yelled. Jack froze. "Not wires, plural, wire, singular!"

"There are two," Jack moaned.

"Then it's booby-trapped," Peters stressed. "You'll have to re-move the trigger instead."

Doc was on one end of the bomb, while Jack was at the other end.

"What's the difference between the trigger and the bloody det-onator?" Jack yelled.

"The detonator triggers the bomb," Peters replied. "The trig-ger opens the lead container filled with tritium."

"Okay . . . what should we look for?" Jack asked calmly. "What does the trigger look like?"

The clock read 1:42.

"It looks like . . . a trigger," Peters said helplessly. "Like a thermostat with a lead container attached. It will be wired to whatever contains the inert toxin, probably a test tube with a hinged cap, something that will open after the tritium is released."

Jack's eyes searched frantically through the mass of hardware. He saw solid blocks, microprocessors, more wires underneath, a test tube like Peters had described, and then—

"I *see* it," Jack replied, but there was exasperation in his voice. "It's under every damn thing else, including the booby trap."

"Then never mind the trigger!" Peters shouted back. "Too late now. There's only one thing we can do. Remove the con—"

That was when the smartphone lost its connection.

58

Jack actually screamed in frustration. The cell reception at Peters's cabin was always spotty, but this was ridiculous! "Get him back!" Jack bellowed. "Everybody, try to get him back!"

Everyone tried. Dover even started running for the jet, hoping the computer connection was still intact. But both she and Jack knew it was an act of desperation. She'd never get there in time.

The clock read 1:13.

"What did he mean?" Jack asked everyone. "Remove the con? Remove the coil? Remove the convex lens?!" He looked helplessly on as the clock continued to count down. It was at 0:48 now. He started to scramble across the device, looking for anything removable that didn't have two wires.

"Convection?" he babbled. "Contraction? Convent—?"

Doc shot up straight at the mention of the last word. He had been scouring the other side of the device all along.

"Convent!" he repeated. "Conventional!"

He reached down, pinched his fingertips around a thumbnail-sized mass of what appeared to be putty, and ripped it from the device, sending several very small, fine silver wires flying. He hurled the putty away, out through the broken passenger side window, where it landed on the grass. He dropped to his knees, spent.

"Conventional explosive," he said to Jack, both tiredly and triumphantly " 'Remove the conventional explosive.' If the device wasn't going to be set off by altitude, or a button, then he needed something like a timed blasting cap to pop the tritium container and the Ebola test tube simultaneously. Oh, and all those wires—the little plastique would've set off larger explosives to send the bad stuff this way and that into the atmosphere."

"A nickel-sized explosive," Jack said weakly. "That was what you threw?"

"That was what I threw," Doc replied. "Military IHE—Insensitive High Explosive." Which meant without the timer and detonator it wouldn't go off no matter how far or how hard Doc had thrown it. As they watched, two of Boaz's men were already collecting it.

Jack looked at the countdown clock. It read 0:03.

When Doc and Jack finally stumbled out of the wrecked Cessna, Dover and Jack grabbed each other, while Doc noticed that Pyotr was missing. The old soldier anchored his eyes on Boaz.

"I was hoping to tell the man what I thought of him," he said.

"Me, too," Boaz replied. "But he's probably dead by now. And, if he isn't, I'd much prefer the Mossad to have a chat with him, rather than anyone who might just want him out of the way. Wouldn't you?"

"I'll get back to you on that," Doc grunted, then looked over when another armored vehicle appeared from around the corner and through the destroyed gate. Doc glanced back at Jack, but he and Dover were still too involved in their "debriefing" to really notice.

As the other flak-jacketed men secured the location, Boaz and Doc approached the newer, undamaged vehicle just as its side door opened. Inside were three more men Doc recognized from the auto switch they had done in San Francisco all those days ago after Levi Plaza and the Filbert Steps.

But there was a fourth man Doc recognized, sitting behind them, holding a now-empty Cheyenne Tactical M200 Intervention sniper's rifle. Doc knew the weapon well. A special bullet was made just for it—one that would lose no altitude, power, or accuracy from as far away as two miles.

"Colonel Taylor, I presume," Doc sighed. "Seen the error of your ways, I gather?"

Andrew "Bull's-eye" Taylor's jaw was jutted in defiance. "What I did I did for this country," he seethed. "No way I was going to let it be attacked."

"Nice shot," Doc commented.

Taylor sniffed. "I was the only one who could've done it," he said, vain visions of immunity dancing in his head.

Doc looked over at Boaz, whose face was the very model of innocence. "Another present personally hand-wrapped by Sol?"

Boaz looked as if he were thinking seriously about it. "Well, maybe not 'personally.'"

Doc looked over to where Dover and Jack were still clutching each other as if they would never let go. He wondered if Dover would be happy to know that she was the link between Morton and Minsky that allowed the Mossad mobsters to steal Taylor out from under the FBI's noses.

Doc considered informing her of that fact. He even took a step toward her. But then he reconsidered.

Doc Matson headed back to the Gulfstream to let everyone know that disaster was averted as the area began to fill with American military planes, U.S. intelligence helicopters, bomb squad vehicles, and even Lawrence Livermore Lab radiation containment vans.

Dover Griffith and Jack Hatfield didn't seem to care.